PRAISE FOR
THE BOY FROM COUNTY HELL

"Thomas Pluck's *The Boy From County Hell* is raucous and rollicking, just like The Pogues song it adapts its name from. There are echoes of James Lee Burke, Barry Gifford, and Joe R. Lansdale, but Pluck's book burns hot and bright with its own indomitable punk spirit. Joyous, wild, dark fun."
—William Boyle, author of *City of Margins,*
A Friend Is a Gift You Give Yourself,
The Lonely Witness, and *Gravesend*

"Blistering, violent, and written with Technicolor flourishes that are Pluck's unmistakable signature. *The Boy from County Hell* is a hell of a book."
—Laird Barron, author of *Swift to Chase*

"Pluck has crafted a hard-charging thriller that stomps the pedal from page one and never lets up. Crackling with exciting characters and language that pops off the page, *The Boy From County Hell* is a mad tale of rage, retribution, and no small helping of heart and soul. I loved it."
—Bill Loehfelm, author of the Maureen Coughlin series

"Wow. *The Boy from County Hell* by Thomas Pluck is as wild as a night in a cage with an amorous monkey. So smart and tense and relentless. Pluck decides on his premise, and stays true to it until the rowdy end, but the real star here is his control of style, both hardboiled and poetic at the same time. Impressed."

—Joe R. Lansdale

"*The Boy from County Hell* is a harrowing and at times deeply philosophical journey through the heart of rage. Thomas Pluck is our trustworthy tour guide through that undiscovered country. With deft prose and an eye towards redemption and revelation Pluck accomplishes an amazing feat. We find ourselves feeling sympathy for the boy from county Hell"

—SA Cosby, *New York Times* bestselling author of *Razorblade Tears*

THE BOY FROM COUNTY HELL

BOOKS BY THOMAS PLUCK

Blade of Dishonor
Bad Boy Boogie
Life During Wartime

THOMAS PLUCK

THE BOY FROM COUNTY HELL

Copyright © 2021 by Thomas Pluck

All rights reserved. No part of the book may be reproduced in any form or by any electronic or mechanical means, including information storage and retrieval systems, without permission in writing from the publisher, except by a reviewer who may quote brief passages in a review.

Down & Out Books
3959 Van Dyke Road, Suite 265
Lutz, FL 33558
DownAndOutBooks.com

The characters and events in this book are fictitious. Any similarity to real persons, living or dead, is coincidental and not intended by the author.

Cover design by Zach McCain

ISBN: 1-64396-234-5
ISBN-13: 978-1-64396-234-4

*Dedicated to Sarah Bennett Pluck
and all my Louisiana friends & fam.*

*On the first day of March it was raining,
it was raining worse than anything that I had ever seen.*
—The Pogues, "The Boys From County Hell"

Sidney Barton Bennett Jr.
In Memoriam

PART 1: FORTUNATE SON

But in the course of time the laws of the land were corrupted;
Might took the place of right, and the weak were oppressed,
and the mighty
Ruled with an iron rod.
—Henry Wadsworth Longfellow, *Evangeline*

1: OPENING RIFF

June 11, 1985

When Evangeline pulled back the hammer on her Colt revolver, the blond armored truck guard stopped looking at her tits. He drew a breath as she dropped the swaddled baby, and his face fell as the doll warbled "Mama," rolled to its back, and mocked him with its flat blue eyes.

Evangeline unsnapped his holster and winged his sidearm over the canebrake into the bayou. She put two fingers in her mouth and whistled.

Andre popped from behind the raised hood of their wood-paneled AMC wagon with his M16 and high-stepped toward the armored truck as if the narrow gravel road were a rice paddy.

The bank truck lurched around the station wagon. The driver chanced getting stuck in the ditch. The windshield snowflaked, and the report of an enormous rifle crackled across the water. The truck shuddered to a stop.

Blondie hit the dirt at Evie's cowboy-booted feet.

Shooter Boudreaux was perched somewhere out in the bayou with his personally customized .50-cal, and had punched a hole clean through the truck's armored glass and the passenger seat headrest. He might've been in the abandoned eagle's nest, or on the rusted-out oil derrick further back. You never knew with Shooter. He earned his name.

The driver held up his hands, hunched beneath the dashboard for cover. Andre tapped the door with the M16's muzzle. When the driver crept out, Andre directed him to fall prone next to his partner.

Evie wiggled a finger in her ear to stop the ringing, then bent to smack her hostage on the ass. "Boys, unbuckle your pants and get 'em down to your ankles."

The driver obeyed, wriggling like a worm.

Blondie blushed. "Darlin', I ain't wearin' nothing underneath."

She tugged his Dickies down, the muzzle of her Colt by his ear. He did not lie.

"You like to live adventurous, don't you?" She yanked his trousers down to his patent leather boots, then took his handcuffs and tossed them by his face. He knew what to do.

She backed up to cover him while Andre cuffed the driver. The rear gate of the station wagon creaked open and Pitou and Ti' Boy crawled from beneath a blanket wearing matching guard uniforms, their long hair netted beneath badged caps, their faces shaved fresh and clean. Ti' Boy's shirt stretched over his massive frame. He rolled his pumpkin-sized head on his shoulders to get out a crick.

Pitou flipped a Randall hunting knife from his sleeve and snipped the guard's belt loops. He buckled the thick leather belt over his pants, checking the radio, turning up the volume.

Ti' Boy's gun belt would never fit. He pitched the radio into the water and noosed the leather tight around both guards' ankles. They yelped as the Cajun giant dragged them to the edge of the ditch like a stringer of catfish.

Andre stepped back, sharp-eyeing the road over his weapon's iron sights. He about-faced and did the same up the road. He held up a fist and opened his palm. Shooter covered them from afar while Andre dropped the hood of the wagon, turned the engine, and pulled over so the truck could pass.

Pitou climbed into the driver's side of the truck and held a slender brown thumb high. Ti' Boy stepped on the running board and slapped hundred-mile-an-hour tape over the windshield damage. Pitou nosed the truck around the wagon while his giant partner squeezed in, pulling the door shut on the third try.

The armored truck held the cash receipts from the Angola Prison Rodeo, the Wildest Show in the South. The pride of Warden Burl Calvineau, who had announced his retirement after turning the most violent prison in the country into a profitable, self-sustaining enterprise.

Evie lowered the hammer on her Colt Diamondback and tucked it in the back of her Daisy Dukes.

"Please don't make me go in the water, Miz Calvineau." Blondie said, squinting up at her.

Her punch-drunk smile faded. "My name's Desmarteaux now. You tell my daddy that, when he puts the screws to you." She took two hundred-dollar bills from the tiny pocket of her shorts and tucked them into his boot. "One's for your partner. Now get off the road. Don't want some doodle-bugger running y'all over."

"What if there's snakes?"

Her smile returned. "I wouldn't worry." She nudged his tight butt with her boot. "Just whack it with your big ol' thing."

Andre had the wagon rolling before she had the door closed. She tossed the baby doll prop into the back seat. They followed the armored truck. Five miles ahead, Kung Fu Bill waited in a ten-wheeler with ramps to roll the armored truck in the back. Then it was forty miles to the Mississippi border, to an abandoned tire plant where they had welding equipment and explosives to crack the egg and see if the haul was all their inside man said it was.

"The scam worked better with the boy," Andre said. Evie squeezed his hand and held it to her heart. They had promised not to talk about the boy until the job was done. They had to stay focused.

She put his hand on her thigh, and he gave it a quick double squeeze. "We're going back for him."

Their boy would be moved from juvie to the state pen in

Rahway in six weeks. They had a friend inside to watch over him, and the cash from this job would finance a hit on the prison transport and bring their boy home. Evangeline's heart jumped, caught in the dream.

They hadn't planned to raise the boy outlaw. He chose that path on his own. Evangeline had decided never to bring a child into this world, but the boy had been a gift. Not from God, but the Devil herself. From whose claws they'd snatched the child and raised him as their own.

They had the will. They had the guns. And now they had the money. Their boy would live free. Andre's platoon leader had a good gig across the border, down with the volcanos and pyramids in the jungle, and had invited them to join him.

They'd be a family again.

The seat rest beside Andre's neck exploded, the windshield spider-webbed, and Evangeline's world went red. Andre shoved her under the dash and cut the wheel hard as a second shot punched through the radio. The wagon crashed through the canebrake and the engine sputtered dead as it sucked water.

Evangeline howled in pain. She tried to wipe the blood from her eye and gashed her finger.

Andre rolled out the door with his rifle, his shirt red and smoking between shoulder and neck. He fired short bursts and sidestepped through the cane. "Get out, Evie! He's firing tracers!"

Rounds thunked into the wagon's sheet metal. Evie hit the water and heat roasted her back as the gas tank went up. She swam under and went for the far side. When jobs went to hell, you meet up later.

The boom of Shooter's .50 and the tinny cracks of Andre's M16 still traded fire when her head cleared the surface. Evangeline spat water spiked with oil and salt and pulled herself behind a cypress knee.

Sirens whooped in the distance.

Across the water, two cruisers came down the road from opposite directions. A tall sheriff exited one cruiser and his deputies cuffed Andre and shoved him into the back. The parish sheriff was Kane LeFer, a Calvineau family flunky sent to bring her home.

Shooter shinnied down a tree with his rifle slung across his back.

Evangeline gritted her teeth and pulled a shard of glass from her ruined eye. Her scream howled over the bayou.

Sheriff LeFer jabbed a finger toward her hiding spot, and his deputies ran for their cruiser.

She tied a bandanna over her eye and jogged toward a camp road. It would take the pigs twenty minutes to race their way to this side of the feeder canal.

A wizened Cajun in a bent-frame Chevy stopped for her thumb. She stuck her gun in his crotch, huddled beneath the dash, and made him drop her at the first honky tonk they found. There she wired another truck and drove to the tire plant after dark.

The hideout was empty and showed no signs of her crew.

Her betrayers were elsewhere, divvying up the take while her man rotted in Sheriff LeFer's parish jail. Surely dangled like bait to bring her back to her evil family.

She uncapped a hip flask she found in the glove box of the stolen truck, took a slug, then poured the raw moonshine into the wreck of her eye. Her screams echoed off the walls of the abandoned factory and sent pigeons flapping from the rafters.

Evangeline Calvineau spun the open cylinder of her Colt as hate blew out her heart like an offshore rig unleashing hellfire, and she swore revenge on the men who jailed her man and stole her blue-eyed boy's last chance at freedom.

Six brass irises stared back at her one steely eye.

One bullet for each son of a bitch who needed killing.

2: BONNIE AND CLYDE

Jay Desmarteaux parked the Challenger in front of a bullet-pocked stone monolith, a shrine to ancient slaughter.

His work boots crunched gravel as he exited the ticking road beast, its purple flake paint scarred and speckled with the corpses of a thousand love bugs. He approached the stone memorial with reverence.

THIS SITE MAY 23, 1934
CLYDE BARROW
AND
BONNIE PARKER
WERE KILLED BY
LAW ENFORCEMENT OFFICERS

The corners and edges had been chipped off by souvenir hunters. Ghouls had shot the names of the dead thieves and nearly wiped them clean.

Jay touched the cold stone and thought of his mentor.

Leroy "Okie" Kincaid was seven years old when lawmen massacred the lovebird outlaws, and he saw their bloody bodies and ventilated Ford V8 coupe paraded through town on the back of a flatbed truck. The civilized folk displayed the corpses in the local pharmacy alongside a soda jerk selling phosphates, as a warning to all who might take arms against the banks who had bled the people dry.

Men dipped their handkerchiefs in the blood, and women dabbed their scarves. Little Okie sneaked between their legs to stick his finger in a bullet hole in the pretty dead lady's side like she was Jesus on the cross.

That was the day I went outlaw, kid. When I saw what my fancy-ass neighbors who smiled in church really were. You remind a square that everything they own can be taken away by a richer man with a pen, and they'll lap up your blood while it runs down the gutter.

Jay had met their wrath himself, when he defied the natural order and took a hatchet to a boy who had hunted him and his friends as his rightful prey.

He extracted his Papa Andre's war tomahawk from its hideaway beneath the Challenger's rear seat and slipped it in the hammer loop of his jeans. Then he counted his steps down a ragged path into the woods behind the stone marker until he found an ancient black walnut tree. Scores of initials had been carved into the bark.

On the far side he dug under the roots with the tomahawk until he hit a large smooth stone the tree had swallowed. He chopped through a tendril and rooted beneath the stone with the hawk's spike until metal scraped metal. He clawed with his hands, scaring pill bugs and angering a black thousand-legger, then heaved the melon-sized chunk of granite aside.

The rusted handle of an ammo can poked through the black earth. He cleared the edges, but the roots held its prize dearly. He popped open the lid and got a whiff of old air.

His folks smiled up at him from the depths of the ammo can.

A cracked Polaroid glimmered atop a stack of twenty-dollar bills.

A young outlaw couple posed on the fender of a '69 Ford Galaxie wagon with fake wood sides next to a man with a devil-red beard over his pocked and scarred face, fading hair tied back with a bandanna. Tall and rangy, Jay remembered the sting of

Okie's fists in the prison boxing ring.

His partners were practically teenagers. The man had eyes too old for his face, which was shaved clean. Jay hunched like he'd taken an uppercut to the heart.

Papa Andre was gone, died while Jay was in prison, Mama Evangeline said. The loss hurt worse than the chunk of his liver the bullet had carved out.

Jay had never seen Papa Andre without his beard. Black hair in a long ponytail, his hatchet in one hand, the other around the young woman's waist. Skinny and joyful, blonde hair glowing, shorts cut so high the pockets showed, shirt tied snug under her chest. Mama Evangeline had her arm looped around Okie's neck, a black Colt dangling from her hand, and her leg kicked over Andre's lap. Okie's sparse beard couldn't hide his grin. His big left hand, always snappy with a jab, was cupped tenderly under her heavy right breast. The copperhead tattoo that wound around Okie's forearm resembled the asp biting Cleopatra. His other hand held a bank sack.

Jay stared, taking it all in.

He'd known them as loving parents and patient mentors. Not sex-crazed outlaws. He turned over the photo. *April 29, 1974*, in faded blue ink.

Jay had been three years old. He might have been taking a nap in the back seat of that Ford.

Okie had told him the location of several grubstake caches while they marked time together in Rahway prison, but this was the only one Jay could remember how to find.

He gathered the twenties and found a bed of oilcloth. Something heavy inside.

The old wound in Jay's gut ached at the thought of holding a gun. He couldn't shoot worth a damn anyway.

He unwrapped a slender boot knife with a hilt of rose gold.

The handle was lignam vitae, a wood brown as earth and hard as stone. Swirled with patterns like human hair, the name Evangeline carved into the grain. With a tug, he bared the greased blade from its darkened leather scabbard. The slim hunting blade looked fit for sliding between a man's ribs to the heart. The top was sharp half its length, like a dagger. Jay ran the edge along his thumbnail and it sang, leaving a deep notch.

His mother's blade.

Above the hilt in block letters, the blade was signed PITOU.

He wiped off the grease with the cloth, slapped it into its sheath, and tucked it through his belt. He left a few twenties wrapped in the oilcloth and buried the ammo can as best he could. In Okie's pantheon of outlaw folklore, it was bad luck to leave a grubstake dry. He put the photo into his work shirt pocket.

He carved his initials into the tree with the knife's sharp point. Later, he filled his belly at a soul food buffet and found a cheap room outside Shreveport near the Indian casino where he sat in bed and stared at the photograph all night. Papa Andre was dead, and Mama Evangeline had been on the run for twenty-five years. Her family name would keep the law's hands off her, but they'd tip off her family, so she was always moving.

After Jay got out of prison, he'd managed to track her to Bay St. Louis. Before he could find her, he had raised hell with people who wanted him dead and spent a month in the hospital before he could pick up her trail. Now she could be anywhere.

Anywhere except the parish with her cursed family name.

Jay wondered if he would recognize her.

And if he had ever really known the woman named Evangeline.

3: ONE-EYED EVIE

The last place Jay wanted to go was a church. There was a lot of Jesus this and Allah that in the joint, and he'd had none of it.

He nursed a fury for the Higher Power since he was five years old, when he'd been torn from Papa Andre and Mama Evangeline and returned to his birth mother, a track-marked night hag who pimped him to pay the man who killed her pain.

It took months to learn the Witch's tells, what would flip her from angel to devil. Others thanked the Good Lord and said "get behind me Satan," but Jay knew whatever ruled this world was a singular, two-faced entity that could never be trusted.

The Witch had crouched down and looked at him like he was a mirror, as he clenched his little fists in defiance.

If you think I'm a bad mother, I wish you had mine. She'll wrap you in barbed wire and feed you to the beast.

Instead, his birth mother tied his ankle to the sofa leg like she always did after the Gator Man came to use him and paid her with a spike in her arm. But that morning, little Jay had hidden the carrot peeler between the cushions, and took out his rage on her sleeping face.

He spent five days leashed beside to her rotting body, parched with thirst, before he woke to the face of Mama Evangeline. The face became that of his one true God.

And She was a jealous God.

One whose golden rules were to do unto others *before* they

did unto you, and to keep your damn mouth shut.

Like the gods of old, his true mother had many names. Up north, she was Angeline Desmarteaux. There, Jay had found a birth certificate that read Evangeline Antoinette Calvineau.

But in Bay St. Louis, they knew her as One-Eyed Evie.

When Jay had rolled in, everybody in the small Gulf town was in the church parking lot for a cochon du lait to help feed folks put out by the flooding of the Amite River.

Jay found a priest in collar and jeans ladling out jambalaya. It was his nature to balk at authority, especially the heavenly variety, but this church had taken in needy families, and he wouldn't sneer at faith expressed through deeds.

The preacher-man walked the walk, and the jambalaya was righteous.

The priest nodded at her name and pointed to a couple old-timers watching couples dance the two-step in the fais do-do. Jay left a ten-spot in their donation jar, then wandered their way, tapping a foot to the music, shoveling rice and andouille into his mouth with a plastic spoon.

"One-Eyed Evie, we miss that gal. Hot damn she a pretty one." An old Cajun smiled and stroked his sun-spotted skull. "Wish I had hair for her to cut, she!" His puffy-cheeked compatriot jiggled with laughter, his face hidden by a walrus mustache and a red trucker cap pulled down low.

"Said she was lookin' for a big ol' man," the walrus said, shaking his head with the memory. "Told her I right here. She kiss my cheek then slap it."

That sounded like Mama, all right.

"How long she been gone?"

"Few month now."

"Six weeks, no more."

He let them argue it out while he cleaned his plate.

"Tol' her I heard a man up in Henderson run a swamp tour boat, he real big. call 'em Ti' Boy, like they do."

Short for petite. People liked calling giants "Tiny." Daring them.

"Him crack a six-foot gator's mouth open like a crab shell, leave it to die. Mean sumbitch, that Ti' Boy Garriss."

Jay spent the night in a church outbuilding on a cot with the flooded-out folks, and in the morning he tuned their generators and central air system. Mama Evangeline's trail was cold anyway, and it felt good to work for good people.

He left with a freezer bag of boudin balls that he ate like candy on the ride west.

Henderson was Bayou country. Near the fishing camp in Catahoula where Mama Evangeline and Papa Andre had raised him. His hands tingled on the steering wheel.

He was going home.

4: SWINGING DICK

Avoiding New Orleans made the trip longer, but that was a mob city and they had a price on him for the hell he'd raised in New Jersey. His route took him through Iberia parish into the beauty of the Atchafalaya Basin.

The road atlas had an ad for a joint called Margaux's, so he gunned it up the gravel road over the levee to the bayou side, where a red slat building nested among trees shaggy with Spanish moss, jutting out on pilings over the shining waters of the swamp.

He parked with the nose facing the exit and left Papa Andre's war hatchet in the hideaway beneath the rear seats. Pitou knife's hilt dug against his belly, but his work shirt concealed it well. He rubbed the wood handle like worry beads. A talisman that would bring him to his mother.

Shiny trucks and minivans crowded the lot, parked haphazard. A pontoon boat full of tourists pulled away from the dock with a well-tanned man at the tiller, talking through a megaphone. His rich Cajun patois echoed off the water as the outboards gurgled. Inside, a young hostess led Jay to a seat by the window overlooking the bayou.

His liver clenched like a bruised purple fist at the smell of liquor, but a cold beer always hit the spot when your ride's climate control consisted of cranking down the windows. He ordered a schooner of Canebrake Ale and a plate of gator bites.

He sipped on his translucent ruby red cup of ice water and

studied the gator skins and heads decorating the rafters as he waited for his meal. The waitresses were warming up for the lunch crowd that would flood in when the swamp tour returned. Most, like the hostess, had their hair tied back and probably cut it themselves in the mirror, or knew someone who cut hair in her home. An older woman had big blonde curls that didn't match her eyebrows. She'd know hairdressers.

She wasn't his server but came over when he gestured.

"What can I get you, darlin'?"

"Ma'am, if you don't mind me asking, I'm looking for family. My Aunt Evie used to cut hair, real pretty like yours. Know where I could find a hairdresser who might know her?"

"Evie," she said. "I get mine done at Billy Hermann's, but there's no Evie there. Those girls all know each other. Billy's is down on Jefferson."

His waitress brought him the beer and battered chunks of gator leg and tail. He dusted them liberally with the green can of Creole seasoning on the table.

"Thank you, ma'am." Jay watched the bayou and listened to zydeco and country on the speakers while he ate his gator and let half his beer go warm. He'd forgotten how his home state made battering and frying everything on this green earth into an art form. Even a prehistoric lizard became delicious in their hands.

The head waitress stood by the kitchen. He left cash on the table and approached her on the way out.

"Thanks for your help. Aunt Evie used to know this big fella they call Ti' Boy. He live around here?"

Her expression turned as severe as a prison matron's. She jabbed his chest with a finger. "She sure as hell won't be with him if she got any brains in her head. Had my way, I'd skin him like one of his gators and nail his head to the wall."

"She ain't *with* him. And I'm no friend of his." He palmed her a twenty.

"The boat tour fellas deal with him. We don't let him in here no more." She tucked the bill in her brassiere. She caught him looking and gripped his biceps with an appreciative wink. "You be careful, now. Ti' Boy eats bigger than you."

At the docks, men readied a pontoon boat for the next tour. Camo pants and caps to keep the sun off their lined faces. Hands horned with callus. Jay changed his gait to pure Jersey strut, like he had an iron sash weight swinging between his legs. Money wouldn't work here. It would only disrespect them and make them silent to him forever.

It was a job for a swinging dick.

"Y'all seen Ti' Boy?"

No greeting, no sign of respect. In this country, only muscle for the goombahs or the Dixie Mafia would have the stones to treat a man that way. And that's what he wanted them to think.

They shook their heads.

"Where he at?"

They puffed a little to keep their pride. "Down the levee road, all the way to the end."

He nodded and walked to the Challenger. They laughed under their breath and joked about getting to get a truck to pull that fancy car out of the mud ruts on the back roads.

5: TI' BOY

The fishing camp roads were too small to be found on Jay's atlas and could only be approached from one direction, so there would be no chance for surprise, nor a speedy exit if things went sour.

He reversed and palmed the wheel, backed down a path overgrown with weeds, marked with a rusted oil company sign. Leaves shrouded the car. He dropped Andre's war hatchet into the hammer loop in his jeans, slipped the knife in his boot for backup, and walked up the road along the canebrake. In summer, he remembered that these trees would smell like a fresh shot of jizzum as they spread their pollen, and the thought brought memories that he pushed away.

He heard no boats on the water, only bird calls and the whine of insects. The path to the camp house was overgrown, and a rusted truck sagged in the ruts. The bed was dark with old bloodstains, and flies buzzed, sucking out its last sustenance.

There was no porch or front door so he followed to the back, eyeing the windows for the mountain of a man.

The butcher shop scent of blood hung in the air. He hefted the hatchet and peered around the sagging corner of the house. A swollen old gator tugged even larger prey toward the water.

Ti' Boy must've cleared four hundred pounds, even with one leg gone. A black hole of flies where his face had been.

Mama Evangeline had been there and gone.

Jay sensed her wake. Her fury burned hot, and her adopted boy was attuned to it. Why she'd killed her old partner, he did not know.

He pulled the back door open with the hatchet's spike. Inside, the place stank of rotten food and unwashed sheets. A single room centered around a wood stove. In one corner was a bed built for a giant.

The wood was spalted maple, and Jay recognized the joints and finials. The headboard was carved with the face of a wild man, his hair and beard flowing out like sun rays. Papa Andre had built it. Jay ran his hand along the greasy, scarred wood. He pressed a catch on the right side, and a cubby opened. His father's trademark.

In his own bed, Papa Andre had hidden his war hatchet there. In this one sat a stack of Polaroids. Jay carefully dragged them with the hatchet's head, and they spilled onto the floor.

What they depicted made his insides churn.

Back in the Challenger, he listened to the insects and birdsong on the bayou's edge and thought of his next step. He had left the pictures of bruised and degraded Black girls on the dirty floor for the police to find and started a fire in the busted truck to bring them. Smoke rose in a cloud behind him.

Shooter Boudreaux stared from the postcard in the ashtray, his aviator sunglasses like the eyes of a green bottle fly. The card had been on the kitchen table under a dirty plate.

It read: *Shooter Boudreaux's Annual Second Amendment Expo.*

On it, a tight-faced white man wearing a rebel flag trucker cap held a black, heavily accessorized rifle in each hand. *Celebrate your birthright. Tactical Gear and Training.*

Jay knew the name. A Marine sniper attached to Andre's company in the war. They told stories about him that verged on the supernatural. He could disappear like a chameleon and pick off targets with iron sights that others could barely see with a scope. He'd built his own rifle from a Ma Deuce, and the .50-caliber rounds cut through the jungle like heart-seeking missiles.

The expo was next month in New Orleans at the Superdome. The card had an address for Shooter's Palace, his firearm depot in Baton Rouge. Jay put it in the glove box and eased out the rutted road back the way he came.

He had no idea if Shooter was friendly, but he was the only lead. He had let thoughts cloud his head and nearly missed the black Tahoe following him six cars back, changing lanes, hugging the shoulder, trying to get an eye on his rear plate.

The U.S. Marshals had a price on him, too.

Jay signaled a right turn with the blinker. The truck pulled under a Waffle House sign. Nothing showed through the window tint. When the light changed, Jay smoked the tires and hopped the divider into oncoming traffic. Horns blared as he squealed up the onramp and shot off like a purple demon that had dunked its ass in holy water.

The truck bounced after him then met a wall of traffic. Everyone paused until the shock and smoke faded. Jay put the pedal down and raced over the two-lane bridge toward Baton Rouge.

6: SHOOTER'S PALACE

Jay picked up a pair of cheap sunglasses and a roll of bright yellow tape at a truck plaza and ran racing stripes down the purple Challenger's road shark body from nose to tail. Louisiana State Tigers' colors. Even in Ragin' Cajuns country, big state purple and gold would serve as camouflage.

He swapped his North Carolina plate for one off a late-model Challenger in a Walmart lot. He knew he should ditch the car, but whenever he tried, it pulled at him. They'd been through hell. Sentimentality was his weakness.

Shooter Boudreaux had a TV show on cable where he built custom firearms for collectors and trophy hunters, and a store on Airline Highway with a sign you could likely see from space. His face was on the sign but his ass was nowhere to be found.

Jay parked in a strip mall adjacent to the gun superstore and walked over. The store was a tactical Disneyland, full of paramilitary gear for wannabes and plastered with photos of the man himself posing with politicians and leathery old celebrities from action movies Jay remembered watching on stolen cable while his parents slept late.

A display case enshrined a battered Remington M40 bolt-action rifle and a bronze plaque which listed seventy-one confirmed kills in the Vietnam War and mentioned a two-mile kill shot using a 20mm recoilless rifle that was "unverified, but unbroken." A stack of books with Boudreaux on the cover aiming a .50-caliber Barrett at the camera, titled *Evil in the Crosshairs*, was for sale, signed, at forty bucks a pop.

The thump and rattle of gunplay beat behind the soundproof glass separating the sales area from the pistol and rifle range. Men with sidearms holstered at their belts worked the counters. All you needed was a Louisiana driver's license to buy, and sales were brisk.

Jay studied Shooter's personal firearms museum mounted on the walls. The infamous .50-caliber rifle hand-built from an M2 machine gun, a bullpup AK-47 engraved with a Crusader's Cross, a 12-gauge sawed-off shotgun that held three in the pipe and one in the chamber and could fit in a front jeans pocket. The Shooter Shorty, nine hundred dollars with a federal tax stamp, available in 10 gauge, .410 for youths and women, and custom anodized colors, including rose pink for the ladies.

Jay smelled cop on two customers and at least one man behind the counter. Okie had always said some police could sniff outlaw, so he kept quiet and cool and let the customers do his asking for him.

"Does the man himself ever stop in?" Father and son, buying matching camouflaged AR carbines.

According to the staff, Shooter personally trained all the on-site gunsmiths and signed off on all firearms bearing his name. He did, on occasion, attend special events, such as the upcoming fundraiser to reelect Sheriff Kane LeFer Junior in Calvineau Parish.

That name perked Jay's ears.

He pretended to admire a tricked-out Smith & Wesson .44 revolver until a salesman spun his spiel about its timing and accuracy, and how Shooter himself won several championships with that exact model.

The seller took the wheelgun from the case, cleared the cylinder, and handed it to him.

"Feel the balance. It's not half as heavy as it looks."

Jay clicked the cylinder home and sighted on a zombie target hanging behind the counter.

Mama Evangeline taught him to shoot her Colt Diamondback. *Cross your thumbs over the backstrap. Don't close an eye. Just focus one until the sights fade into what you want to hit. And don't you ever point your gun at anything you don't mean to kill.*

He hadn't been much of a shot. Couldn't catch a ball worth a damn, either. Doc said he had a wandering eye. Papa Andre played catch with him until they trained it out, but Jay's eye still wandered when it felt like it. At the moment it turned his attention to a flyer on the wall.

The Wildest Show in the South!

The Angola Prison Rodeo. Every Sunday in April.

Bronco Busting! Convict Poker! Crafts!

The center photo depicted a mad bull plowing through a table of inmates holding playing cards. The photographer had captured a Black inmate suspended in midair above the two-ton beast's horns.

Jay's eye settled lower.

Under Crafts, a man with thick arms stood proudly beside a carved wooden rocking horse, glowing with varnish, alive with detail. The man's gray-shot hair was tied back in a ponytail, and a dusting of beard covered his face.

The heavy revolver hit the glass hard. The salesman lurched to catch it before the expensive hunk of metal hit the floor. A customer who'd set Jay's outlaw-sense tingling beelined for him.

Jay tore the flyer off the wall and hit the door like the Devil was on his tail.

He lost the cop in the parking lot and doubled back to the Challenger, sank down in the seat, and studied the craftsman's face. He was so sure the man was his Papa Andre, he'd bet his life on it.

PART 2: THE MIDNIGHT SPECIAL

Let the midnight special, shine the light on me;
Let the midnight special, shine the ever-loving light on me.
—Traditional Southern prisoner folksong

7: HELL UP IN HENDERSON

Like most towns that subsisted off the Atchafalaya Basin's natural bounty, there wasn't much to do in Henderson except fish, hunt, eat, drink, and fuck.

Thibaut "Ti' Boy" Garriss heartily enjoyed all those endeavors. His bed stank and his truck had a busted axle, so the fucking had been sparse. But a Cajun boy with a fishing pole and a gun won't ever starve, and his hulking frame was evidence of that natural fact. The older boys joked that he must've split open his mama at birth, at least until he mashed one of their faces to hamburger on the pavement. That was the first time he felt the deep joy in letting loose his anger, and the reward of using his size to get what he wanted.

Back then, boys liked to scrap. They'd come at him three or four at a time, so they could say they took on Ti' Boy.

It became a pastime at Breaux Bridge High School, a hazing for the junior footballers. Three of y'all go jump Ti'Boy, bring us his cap. His boots. His underwear.

The senior quarterback sent his front four and came to watch. Ti' Boy clubbed them all down with his meat hooks, then pulled the college-bound star out of his Ford Flareside and wrenched his leg around like he was winding a jack-in-the-box.

No more LSU for that boy.

The coach and a dozen fathers came for Ti' Boy with ax handles and gave him his pretty face that night, and busted his leg so badly that he wore a special boot with a four-inch-thick sole to make up for the stunted growth.

You grow up on the side of the levee? Sheriff Kane LeFer would ask, every time he saw him.

Ti' Boy pulled on his Frankenstein boot and a Tigers cap with the strap extended with duct tape for his oversized melon, then took the thirty-aught-six rifle Shooter Boudreaux had given him back when they were tight. Now the slick city sumbitch was too big to help old friends. He tucked his last three shells into his flannel shirt pocket and a plastic hip flask of whiskey into his shorts and headed out of his tin roof camp house, crunching pecan shells as he headed for the water where his flat boat was tied to a mangrove knee.

He pull-started the motor and it sputtered. The little Evinrude was a finicky bitch.

The gators were small this year. Margaux's Landing bought them for meat, selling gator bites and shellacked heads to the tourists, leaving him the hides to sell to the tanner. He'd save some leg meat if his hooks had any gator today. Leg meat was tastiest, like thighs on a chicken, or a woman.

There was something about a very big man, even one with a crooked jaw and a belly the size of a grown hog, that fascinated some girls. They giggled when he picked them up like children. They liked how their hands disappeared in his. The heat that came off him like a wood stove, how his heart pounded against his chest, the fur on his arms like the beast from the Disney movie. One they thought they could tame.

Then the sadness behind the fear in their face, when they realized the fairy stories lied about monsters being good inside.

He pulled the cord again, then set the rifle down and pulled it a third and fourth time, finessing the engine how it liked, but it did not fire. He unscrewed the gas cap.

He flinched as something sharp bounced off his face. A spark plug landed at his feet.

"It's half full, but you ain't going anywhere, you overgrown sack of shit."

He reached for the rifle and heard the bone-crunch click of a revolver being cocked.

"Turn your big ass around slow."

He knew that voice. He obeyed.

She was a tanned, rangy blonde, her hair shot with gray. An eye patch covered her left peeper, and the right one burned like the pilot light in a crematorium. She held arms thrust out in front of her, gripping a black revolver, steady as a statue.

Recognition bloomed on his face.

"Don't say a damn thing."

He didn't.

"What you gonna say? It's been thirty years? That only makes it worse."

Ti' Boy hadn't known or cared about the machinations of the betrayal. He'd tuned out while Shooter explained it to him and Pitou, thinking only of the money. Back then he had a coke-hungry girl who rode him like a Brahma bull, and all he thought about was how to stay on that biscuit-wheeled gravy train.

"That was all Shooter," he said, rolling his ankle. It cracked in his boot. "Me and Pitou didn't know nothing till the split."

She lowered the gun a notch. "He always was a slimy son of a bitch. You didn't cry none when it came time to count though, did you?"

He raised his hands slowly. She was closer than she ought to be. Even with his Frankenstein leg, she had seen Ti' Boy rhino his way through a honky tonk and knock a whole gang of bikers on their asses before they cleared leather.

"You'd have done the same."

She would have. She would never have worked with Shooter again, but that was how it would play out.

"And I'd know to watch my back for the rest of my days. You forgot that part."

Thinking ahead of his next meal usually made him want to hurt somebody. But he didn't want to die, not as long as the world had pussy for chasing. He knew how to make her flinch.

"I'm sorry about the boy."

Evangeline's good eye twitched and the long barrel of the revolver dipped an inch.

He made his rhino charge.

The Colt Diamondback cracked and his shoulder burned and he struck her low. She hit the dirt gasping and he wrestled for the gun with the arm that still worked. He kicked at the dirt to walrus his way on top of her. Crush her. Mash her smirking face to jam.

She had never looked at him like he was a man. She never called him names, but her smiles salted the wounds he carried since childhood. Why was he thinking of that? He could have her now, if he wanted.

His face tingled like he slept on it wrong. Her bullet had cut deep. Shooter had ported and tuned her damn magnum. The .357 round had gone clear through his beef slab shoulder. He wrapped his hand around the gun and squeezed, thumb over the cylinder.

Evangeline screamed as her fingers crunched against the checkered grips. She jerked her hand and the revolver kicked.

Ti' Boy's thumb flew off and skipped into the water. He howled and stared at his four-fingered hand. The skin was blown clear off his palm. He killed a black bear once with his daddy. When they skinned it, the carcass looked just like a man. They ate it anyway.

Meat was meat.

Evangeline kicked out from under him, heaving breaths. She aimed, two-handed, thumbs crossed over the backstrap like Andre taught her.

"Shooter told us Andre was dead." He started to pant like a dying dog.

"He might as well be. While shit like you's walking around enjoying life." She cocked back the hammer.

The black hole of the barrel drew Ti' Boy's eyes like a lure.

"Why you wait thirty years to kill me, Evie?"

"So it hurts," she said, and put four rounds into his massive skull.

8: THE FARM

"You gonna have that chifforobe done in time for my anniversary, aren't you?"

Andre Desmarteaux looked up from the wooden tombstone cross he was sanding and basked in the enormity of Warden Kane LeFer. He'd been lost in his work and hadn't sensed the spectacled bear of a man walking up until he had tapped him with the cane of purple heart wood that Andre had carved for him.

Born with gridiron size but none of the discipline, Kane LeFer had followed in the footsteps of his forefathers, who had served as lawmen, and before that slave catchers for the Calvineaus. After he broke up the gang of armed robbers that their wayward daughter Evangeline had used to terrorize banks, armored cars, and jewelry stores across her family's namesake parish, Kane had been rewarded with an appointment as warden of the state penitentiary, better known for the name of the plantation it was built upon:

Angola.

The plantation in turn had taken its name for the country that the majority of its enslaved captives were taken from, and after emancipation, the Calvineaus and LeFers filled its cells with newly freed Black men, unless they sharecropped for their former enslavers. Working men to death and enriching the soil with their sweat and blood.

A snake pit from its creation, the Farm's ignominy peaked in

1957 when thirty-one inmates called attention to its hellishness by slicing their Achilles tendons in protest of the abysmal conditions.

They were christened the Heel String Gang in the newspapers, and little changed.

Twenty years later, Angola become infamous for its tacit acceptance of sexual slavery of weak inmates by the strong, until a federal court demanded action. In came reformer Warden Maggio, who inmates called The Gangster because of his Italian heritage and strict enforcement of the new rules: inmates would work the Farm to feed other prisoners across the state, they would learn skills and crafts no matter whether they would ever walk free again or not, and they would pray to the Lord for mercy on their souls.

Some became servants in the governor's mansion, to prove how much trust was held in their rehabilitation. Others, accused of murdering a guard, would serve the longest stretches of solitary confinement since Dumas wrote *The Count of Monte Cristo*. Still more would entertain crowds twice a year in the Wildest Show in the South: the prison rodeo.

In prison stripes they would ride bucking broncos for their eight seconds of glory. They would prove their mettle by sitting at a card table while rodeo clowns lured a tormented bull to charge through them like bowling pins. And those braver still could fill their commissary fund by snatching a poker chip from between the horns of a Brahma bull after it busted out the gate.

The inmate with the highest score in all events would be crowned the All-Around Cowboy and wear a handmade belt and silver buckle naming him so for the next year.

Of the six thousand inmates in Angola's walls, a full forty-eight hundred had no hope of ever walking free. Hospice care became the new craft to learn, as ailing men were confined to bunks so that they might die in prison.

Andre Desmarteaux walked into Angola in 1989 to serve fifty years for armed robbery. He had once dreamt of making it to eighty-seven years of age and walking out those gates of his own volition. Now he ignored the ache behind his lowest left rib, and the tumor which mocked his dreams.

Where Warden LeFer now prodded him with the cane Andre'd made him with his own two hands. "You done lollygagging?" He stroked Andre's flank like a horse groom inspecting his stock.

Andre winced. The prison docs didn't have much equipment, and blood tests took weeks to return. His had come back marked *lymphoma*. Outside you had a fifty-fifty chance with it, if you could afford the chemo and radiation. Inside, you were in the Lord's hands.

And Warden LeFer was the Lord.

"I'll be done in time for your anniversary, sir," Andre said. "Just finishing up a cross. Funeral's Sunday." For a fee, inmates could be buried in a church cemetery instead of Point Lookout, the hill of crosses on Angola grounds that served as a potter's field. When they knew that death was coming, some inmates worked like dogs to avoid that fate, to fill their commissary and buy a plot at Redemption Row at the Calvineau Parish Church. Family was more likely to visit you there than make the trip to the prison grounds.

LeFer grunted. "See you entered in the woodworker's contest at the rodeo. How many times you won that now? Give someone else a chance."

The rodeo was the only time Andre got to see real people. His Evangeline couldn't visit on family day. They'd lock her up until her family got her. The last thing in the world she wanted.

But every year, she had managed to sneak by his spot in the crafts show. So many people came to the rodeo, they couldn't watch them all. The trusted cons stood there in their denims and work boots and got to feel human, selling tooled belts or jewelry or furniture they had built with their hands, for real cash money.

"Maybe you ought to go for Guts and Glory. Grab that poker chip. You do that, we'll get that lump under your tit looked at."

Andre couldn't tell if LeFer was serious or playing with him. Both were equally dangerous. When he was first inside, Andre had rode bulls, sat in the chair for convict poker, and tried to grab that poker chip from between a mad bull's horns. He was no champ, but he'd grabbed it once, and the Cajuns in the crowd had gone wild to see one of their own do good.

LeFer nudged Andre in the ribs with the head of his cane, probing the tumor bulging there. The head was carved with the LeFer family crest, a fist gripping an iron key. "I know that's how your woman gets to you. Read it in in her letters. The ones you flush down the toilet. I had Louie the sewer man fish one out of the trap. Dried it out in the oven."

Behind his steel-framed spectacles, LeFer's eyes were unreadable. Large, but not warm. To Andre, they looked like the eyes on his boy's teddy bear, perfectly round and shaped to look friendly, but made of something hard and unnatural that would outlast his bones.

"Your girl's family wants her home. Old Sam Calvineau wants to see her before he staggers off to his reward. So, no craft show this year. You gonna ride in the rodeo and have a tearful little reunion. I'll give y'all some time together. Conjugal, in one of the visitor bungalows. Like you're free, not that high school fooling 'round you been doing in the craft yard crapper. Think I didn't know?" He shook his head. "Long as she goes back to Whiterose, she can visit you whenever she likes. You got to tell her to put this vendetta to rest and come home."

Andre looked down at his work. He was more likely to sprout wings and fly up out of the prison yard like a whooping crane than convince her to do that.

LeFer patted Andre's flank and closed his mitt over the lump. "You put Evangeline back with her family, and we'll take you to Our Lady of the Lake three times a week. Get you through this. You hear?"

Andre nodded.

LeFer squeezed the tumor like he was checking a persimmon

for ripeness. Andre broke into a sweat, frozen in place. "Yes, sir."

"You don't, you can live out your days in Camp-J with the worst."

A rivulet of sweat broke out from Andre's receded hairline and ran down his cheek. Guards quit or called in sick to avoid work in Camp-J. The disciplinary wing. And inmates sent there for punishment came back changed.

"Now put away these crafts and get to work on my chifforobe."

LeFer smiled, his large teeth gray around the edges. He turned and left the wood shop, patting inmates on the shoulder or the back, holding up the purple heart walking stick like a scepter.

9: CHOPPER TEWLISS

The man called Chopper exited his black Chevy Tahoe and ducked under boughs of the heaven-trees, moving quietly for his size. The air was tinged with black tire smoke. The fire truck had come and gone, and a breeze off the bayou brought the scent of blood from Ti' Boy's camp house. He would hunt deer out of season and gut it where everyone could see, knowing the law wouldn't come down here unless he'd kidnapped a nun.

But today Ti' Boy's land was full of law.

Sheriff Junior LeFer stood with his hands on his hips, and his deputy wore a face like he'd stepped in fresh shit. Junior's daddy was the warden at Angola, but the son was a veteran and mostly all right, Chopper thought, for a Marine. They had served in different desert wars but respected one another. The deputy was a dumbass Calvineau cousin who couldn't be trusted with a cap gun, much less the Shooter Boudreaux tactical hand cannon at his hip, so Chopper announced himself loud and early.

"Friendly coming," he hollered, and approached with his arms held out like the silvery image of Jesus on the cross in his mother's kitchen. Chopper was a shade darker than Jesus in the painting and kept his hair in a close fade instead of a halo of Afro. He dangled a cut-down pump shotty from his right index finger.

"Tewliss, someday you're gonna get your head blown off sneaking up like that." Junior LeFer waved him over.

Chopper holstered the Shorty pump gun. It was a Shooter Boudreaux special he'd taken off a biker with swastikas tattooed on both cheeks, who had fled trial in Arkansas. The fool had tried to bribe him with it, and now it was his favorite piece.

He stood next to Junior, watching two well-tanned Cajun fishermen pull an enormous corpse without a face onto a tarp.

"Guess I won't be talking to Ti' Boy."

"This time, gator got him," one of the Cajuns said, nodding to the gaping wound at the right hip. The death roll had popped the giant's thigh off like a drumstick.

"You here 'cause he liked dark meat." The deputy grinned.

Junior leaned on his good leg. "Enough of that, or you'll get an ass full of titanium."

"This skip tracer gets more respect from you than your own lawmen. He isn't even a real cop. Not anymore."

"Realer than you are." Chopper'd been New Orleans PD as long as he could take the corruption and hypocrisy.

The deputy spat into the pecan shells. "Chopper Tewliss. Not even a real name."

Chopper's street name always made him grin. He'd inherited two things from his daddy: a knack with computers and a fondness for jokes cornier than an Iowa septic tank. When the pimps who lost fingers to his cane knife dubbed him Chopper, pairing that with the Irish maiden name of his great-grandmother—who claimed native Tchoupitoulas blood—was irresistible. His partner Suzane worked gris-gris, and told him never to use his real name on the street. Real names have power.

"Who you like for it?" Junior LeFer was clean-shaven, tan and lean, ruddy-cheeked and fit. The wind printed his slacks against the titanium left leg, the meat and bone lost in Anbar Province.

Chopper stepped closer. The dead man's face was big and doughy as an apple pie. Someone had punched five holes in it, like Little Jack Horner sticking his thumb through the crust. Close range with a small, fast round.

Ti' Boy had five decades of hurt under his belt, which meant plenty of enemies. A killer with a money beef wouldn't waste more than a cartridge or two. And if he'd had anything worth stealing, thieves would have waited until he was out on the water.

"Someone who hated him. Talk to the women who work where he sells his gators."

Junior LeFer snorted. "Shells in his pocket, but no gun. And what brings you here to the scene of the crime, Tewliss?"

Calvineau Parish was the most corrupt and segregated out of the sixty-four in Louisiana. Carved from Bayou Vipère to split off from Baton Rouge after integration, it housed Angola prison, a stretch of interstate known for speed traps, and a parish jail kept full by selective enforcement of laws against the Black and poor.

Only missing Black children would bring Chopper here willingly.

"I saw the smoke," he said.

"You want some titanium, Tewliss?" Junior LeFer didn't take kindly to Chopper and Suzane investigating in his parish. The sheriff's office was overworked and understaffed, but he had his pride.

"The family of Keshawn Wallace." The fourteen-year-old had disappeared after school. Never showed at his job.

"Damn shame. But you know. A kid gets a taste of freedom, makes his first money, and he runs." Case closed, as far as Calvineau Parish was concerned.

There had been several missing children cases surrounding the parish over the years, all good students, all gone.

"Mind if I look in the house?"

"Hell yes, I mind," Sheriff LeFer said. "We searched it already. Nothing worth mention."

"Ti' Boy had a Shooter Boudreaux sniper special," the deputy said. "He never shut up about how Shooter gave it to him, and how he was gonna sell it and retire. Someone finally killed him for it."

Junior LeFer scratched his tight belly, which bubbled with annoyance at his underling's big mouth.

"I know Shooter will put up money, but we're gonna keep that quiet a few days, Chop. Word travels faster than shit through a goose around here. See who pawns a thirty-aught, or brags about taking down Goliath. Got it?"

"Aye-firmative," Chopper said.

The men dragging the body made a ramp with a slab of plywood on the back of their truck. They struggled with the load and looked his way for help.

Chopper hawked up a mouthful and spat it on Ti' Boy's stained white T-shirt.

"Ain't you got respect for dead people?" the deputy sneered.

"That ain't people." Chopper walked back to his truck.

He parked at the Waffle House where he'd chased the purple Challenger he'd spotted leaving Garriss's road, and ordered hash browns all the way. He called in the license plate to a friendly trooper while he waited on his meal. The North Carolina tags were registered to a 2017 model, not a classic.

Interesting.

He opened his laptop on the yellow table.

A search on 1971 Challengers returned none on the stolen list, but a BOLO bulletin from the U.S. Marshals service mentioned one as the vehicle of a fugitive wanted for questioning in involvement with several murders in New Jersey.

No bond, but the family of a slain mayor had put up twenty thousand dollars in reward for his capture. Usually those came with the caveat of "leading to conviction," and the skinflints never paid. This reward had no such language.

Chopper committed the details to his iron memory.

The name of the suspect in question was Jay Desmarteaux.

10: VENGEANCE TRIP

Jay parked behind the library under a live oak.
Andre's as good as dead.
That's what Mama Evangeline told him when he'd asked for Papa.
She knew he'd haul ass down here to see his Papa Andre, when there were men up north she wanted dead in the ground.
But being a lifer in Angola was as good as dead.
No one escaped the Farm for long. Okie had said it was tucked in an oxbow of the Mississippi River surrounded by ten miles of swamp and forest. The guards bred hybrid wolf-dogs to hunt anyone foolish enough to try that route.
No, that hadn't been exactly what he'd said.
Angola's the nipple on a big round tit of land hugged by the Big Muddy, nothing but shithole swamp where you're up to your ass in alligators and trigger-happy peckerwoods for ten miles around.
Jay studied the photo of Okie and his adopted parents. He couldn't break out Andre, but maybe he could see him. He would have no way to get on the visitor list without writing a letter, and who knows how long that would take. Whoever was in that black truck—mob or cop—would find him again eventually.

* * *

The library had copies of the prison newspaper, *The Angolite*, on microfiche, and after the librarian showed him how to use the machine, Jay whizzed through it looking for photos of the inmates selling their work at the rodeo. Almost every year, the old man from the flyer was photographed with a trophy. Jay followed him back through time, until his hair grew black and the beard vanished.

He reached up and touched the screen, choking back a shaky breath.

In the newest issue, he found photos of members of the Calvineau Parish First Evangelical Church praying with inmates in the Angola chapel, after leading them in a performance of Jesus's parables.

He looked up the church. Just over the border from Baton Rouge.

In his family's parish. The one Mama Evangeline said to never set foot in.

The one even his evil birth mother called Hell.

He thumbed the handle of the knife for comfort.

Mama's blue-eyed boy was sick of killing. Like the burn of whiskey, killing didn't quench the thirst, it only distracted you with pain. The dead he saw in his sleep had become a tapestry, a Last Supper of bloody faces calling him Judas. The thought of adding to their army made the wound in his gut clench and send acid into his throat.

He swallowed spit until it went away.

The church had a website, even online services for shut-ins. And a help wanted section.

They needed a handyman to keep the grounds and to maintain equipment. Jay had certified on two-stroke and four-stroke small engines while he rotted in Rahway prison.

Okie didn't believe in fate, but said, *When the world speaks to you, you listen.*

Jay sat back and wondered if he could say his prayers without burning his tongue.

11: CHURCH

The Calvineau Parish First Evangelical Church was a red brick turret tucked in a quiet neighborhood full of old but modest, well-kept homes, two-story Cajun cottages and ranch houses, and even an old dogtrot with a breezeway through the middle, painted to match the lavender wisteria vines draping over it.

Next to the church were a ball field and a small cemetery with white stones jumbled up like bad teeth in the back, then rows of neat monuments dwarfed by a central mausoleum topped with an equestrian statue of a Confederate officer with his cavalry saber raised high, facing north. The name CALVINEAU was chiseled at the horse's feet.

Girls ran soccer in the field and the boys played shirts and skins, pink as piglets under the sun. After-school activities.

A tall handsome man in a *Geaux Tigers!* polyester polo shirt coached them, tanned arms folded over his trim chest. His steely eyes flicked Jay's way as he walked into the cemetery to run his hand over the names on the family mausoleum.

No Evangeline.

The newest was Joyce Anne Calvineau, *b.1951 d.1976. Dear daughter.*

Sweat broke across his brow.

The maggot-ridden face of the woman who'd birthed and scarred him leered through the ages. He banished her with a shudder and thought of Mama Evangeline. Her sister, his savior.

This was her family's church. His family's.

Cold claws gripped his entrails at the thought.

He wiped his brow on his sleeve and walked to the church.

Inside it was cool. He found a printed sheet asking for a handyman and groundskeeper on the bulletin board and tore it off its thumb tack. He knocked on a locked office door in the back.

No answer.

Behind the church was a wooden barracks-style building decorated with garlands and a sign announcing that the children's performances of *Bye Bye Birdie* would begin next month. Sounds of rehearsal came through the windows. The door was unlocked, and he entered quietly.

Teenagers stood on a raised stage, acting out a scene. More lingered on the floor, looking at scripts, poking through a rack of '50s-era costume clothing donated by parishioners. A slender woman with strong shoulders watched the actors. Her black ponytail twitched like a fox's brush. She wore a loose, long-sleeve shirt tucked into faded, paint-flecked mom jeans, one worn tennis shoe tapping as she observed her charges.

"Try that again, Alex," she called. "A little more eager."

Jay crinkled the paper as he approached her.

She gave him a quick appraisal, and kept her chin raised in guard. "How may I help you?"

He held up the sheet. "Sorry to interrupt, ma'am. Here about the job."

"Ten-minute break," she called up to the stage. "Don't wander off."

She led him backstage. The building had been retrofitted with old Klieg lights and a stereo, wires running along the rafters. "I know it says mowing lawns, but we need a carpenter and an electrician, too. I wanted to bring in a friend from the stagehands' union, but they don't pay well enough for a family man."

Jay held up his left hand, wiggled the empty, tanned ring finger. She saw a lot. He'd have to keep on his toes. "I can swing a hammer, and I know engines. Gas and electric. Wiring, I know enough not to mess around with it."

She took him outside to the field. "Our old handyman had an accident. Drove his truck into Bayou Vipère. You like a drink?"

"I'd love a cold water."

"I meant, are you a drinking man?"

"I like to keep in shape. Drinking's counterproductive." He shrugged to flex. She'd been eyeing the way his shirt stretched across his chest. She stopped.

"Most of the equipment's donated. There's a riding mower, but we can't get it to start."

The coach held his hands behind his back. Four of the older girls had a good game going, one shouldered another aside and drove past her toward two orange cones that served as goalposts.

"Pastor Eagleton," she said. "This man's here about the handyman job?"

He didn't look away from the field. "Thank you, Molina. You can get back to the show."

After she walked away, the pastor took Jay's measure.

"You are?"

"Jason, sir."

"What's your family name."

"Demonde," Jay said, giving it the Cajun pronunciation. He had papers to match.

The pastor smiled wide. "Healer of the world," he said. "We need a man who can fix things. Our grounds need to be kept tidy, the facilities maintained. We don't pay much, but there's a room in back of the theater. No drinking, no women, no music. It's the house of the Lord."

"Not a problem, sir."

He gripped Jay's forearm with surprising strength, bore into his eyes. "I catch you spitting on this consecrated ground, I'll kick you to the curb myself." He looked like he could try. Gym body, a basketball player who'd taken to running once he'd aged out. "Understand me, Jason?"

"Yessir." Jay flinched. That was what the man wanted.

"You dependable?"

"If I say I'm gonna do something, it gets done."

He ground Jay's hand bones and held his gaze, then broke into a sudden smile, teeth large as tombstones. "Then welcome to our flock. Go see Miss Ardith in the church office." He laughed and shoved Jay's shoulder toward the church. "Knock hard, she's deaf as a post."

12: THE ROUGAROU

Chopper searched the name Desmarteaux in his truck, Black Sabbath and the air conditioning blasting. He found a lot of reading.

The suspect had been in prison since he was a juvenile. He hacked another kid to death with a hatchet. It was before Chopper's time, from the '80s Satanic Panic era that his uncle talked about when he'd introduced him to Sabbath and Slayer.

The killer had come home to roost. And possibly graduated from hatchets to firearms.

A kid killer. Many of the Calvineau Parish disappearances occurred while Desmarteaux was still in prison, but that didn't mean he wasn't involved. Garriss had been a suspect, but he liked older, full-bodied girls and women. But turds of a feather flocked together.

Suzane called the missing children the Rougarou murders. The two of them theorized they could be a Nazi gang initiation. Chopper filed that away.

He poked around on his laptop, sitting in the back seat of his truck shaded by the limo tint, until he identified the hot rod as a 1971 Hemi Challenger. There were fewer than a hundred made that year. Any still rolling would have been snapped up by rich collectors for restoration. This one looked like it had been in a bad wreck and hastily repaired.

If the driver was smart, he'd sell it and buy a damn Honda.

If people did the smart thing, Chopper would have a much more difficult job. He was a hunter, and patience was a hunter's weapon. People were animals, they liked the familiar, it made them feel safe. Apply any sort of pressure and they fled to the same old dens and holes they knew they'd be caught in.

Shooter Boudreaux would pay for information on whoever who hit his old pal Ti' Boy. Chopper hadn't dealt with him since he was NOPD, when he had returned a truck full of stolen full-auto firearms to Boudreaux without alerting the media. Shooter paid well for the courtesy.

His phone rang. Suzane. He turned down the stereo.

"Sweetness."

"I'm in Jeannetta," she said. Her voice shared a weariness. All business. "With Keshawn's family."

Most of the kids who'd gone missing were from Baton Rouge. Keshawn was an outlier.

"Don't think it, Wesley," she said. "This is Rougarou's road."

Just like a witch to use your true name against you. Only she and his folks called him Wesley.

They named their predator after the boogeyman of bayou country who came for naughty children, the werewolf known as the Rougarou. Except this one didn't discriminate.

Boys and girls. Some stars of their class. Others known for acting out.

They had not found a pattern except Black, young, and poor.

Under Suzane's shirt, the green ink of a pentacle protected her heart, flanked by two opposite-facing crescents. She inherited witch blood from her grandmama, and had to walk the good path. Chopper didn't believe in much, but he had seen things he couldn't explain. Either her witch sense was true, or she was a trickster who should be onstage in Vegas instead of flipping tarot cards in the Quarter.

"I'll come down and see what I can find." She worked the families, and he worked the streets. They were a good pair that way.

The killer she called Rougarou seemed immune to both of their magics.

Chopper didn't believe in the rules of magic or the law but thought the illusion of rules was the load-bearing beams of civilization that kept us safe when storms raged all around us. It was impossible to hunt those who thrived on misery without feeling tempted to flout man's law and resort to shoveling human shit. A chop to the neck on a bayou's edge was all it required. The gators did the rest.

Which they both feared was the cheap magic the Rougarou practiced.

Suzane had warned Chopper that if he walked that bloody path for vengeance, she would know, and he would walk it alone.

That's how Chopper knew that magic, like the law, was an invention of humans, and as fallible.

13: GONE SHOOTIN'

Evangeline sighted the sniper rifle at the buoy bobbing out in the water. A pelican balanced on the top, eyeing the waves. A Winston burned between her fingers.

She took a round from a box of ammunition and slapped the bolt home. She couldn't shoot her pistol worth a damn at anything past twenty feet after Shooter took her eye, but a rifle didn't matter so much. The sight traced a tiny figure eight as she braced her elbow on the roof of the Dodge wagon. She slowed her breath and timed between heartbeats, then eased the trigger.

The pelican flapped away as the report rippled across the waves.

She pulled the bolt and collected her brass in a styrofoam coffee cup with three butts in it.

It was time to start killing.

She wanted Andre to have the honors, but five years was a long time on the Farm even when you didn't have a tumor the size of a golf ball poking through your ribs. He was lucky if he lasted a year.

The Angola Rodeo was coming, and the thought that she might see her man for the last time turned her blood to ice. She fired again.

The bullet clanged off the metal buoy, turning it left. She'd winged it. She ejected and reloaded, stubbed out her Winston and lighted another.

And she'd lost touch with the boy.

That had been three months ago, and she'd been mobile since. No-tell motels, flops, or the back of the Dodge Magnum wagon. It reminded her of the sleeper getaway cars Okie had favored, and with the full limo tint it kept her hidden in plain sight. As long as she stayed out of Calvineau Parish, she was safe. In the other sixty-three, her name made her untouchable. She'd shown that she would kill to keep her freedom. And if they so much as wrenched her shoulder putting her in cuffs, they knew they would find themselves fed to the gators of Bayou Vipère, badge or not.

You couldn't escape the Calvineau clan in Louisiana, and until Andre was out of prison, that was where she stayed. She considered driving out to Whiterose and shooting her mother's silhouette in the plantation window. Burning it to the ground.

But that wouldn't set her Andre free.

When Evangeline learned why her big sister took heroin and fled home, she pledged her life to the god of vengeance, throwing poison spears at her mother's heart. She took the boy north, when her mother wanted nothing more than a grandchild to raise in hate. She loved Andre, even though he would never walk free.

That gave Mother Hesper Calvineau the death of a thousand cuts, salted with spite.

She shot through two boxes of thirty-aught until the buoy rang like a church bell. Then she drove toward Shooter Boudreaux's mansion on the lakeshore of Louisiana State University in Baton Rouge and watched the swans skate atop the golden mirror of the water, while citizens sat down for supper.

14: SUNLIGHT EYES

Andre lay on the high bunk watching a baby cockroach navigate a crack in the ceiling. Made him remember a dumb joke he'd first heard in a tonk the year he came back from Vietnam.

He had come home after his fourth tour to find his father's woodworking business shuttered and the man buried in a potter's field. They lived downwind of the Dow chemical plant, and by the time he was a senior in the class of '68, his father had taken to coughing into a red bandanna to hide the blood.

When Andre's draft card came up, his old man told him to burn it, as the country burned around them. *They ain't bombed Pearl Harbor. This is Korea all over again.* His papa lost his brother Nicholas there, and cried for him some nights in his cups. The mob had blown the president's head off five years prior, and his father was convinced the world would end in nuclear war. Then they killed Dr. King and the president's brother, and Andre saw his father's predictions of the world's fiery end coming true.

Which prepared him for the green hell of Vietnam.

He counted the days like everyone else, but re-upped when he got the letter that his father was gone. As his squad was winnowed down by bouncing betties, heroin, and the freedom bird, he found himself taking chances on point. Wanting that first bullet to have his name on it.

He took his ticket home and begged the bank to let him buy his father's workshop with his cash-out money, but it had been foreclosed and left to turn moss green as the swamp reclaimed it, with the tools rusted inside.

"You'd have to pay three times what it's worth," the bank lawyer told him. "Watch the newspapers for the auction. That way you can start fresh."

He blew his money on a Boss 351 Mustang and joined a construction crew doing molding and detail work, preferring to work alone because every man felt he had to make excuses about flat feet, heel spurs, or boils on their asses that kept them home during the war. Andre didn't give a damn and wished he had burned his draft card like his daddy had told him.

Then by luck, when he was fixing a rotted porte-cochère on a Bayou Vipère plantation, the lady of the house showed him an antique credenza that had been ruined by the floods after Hurricane Edith. He wrapped it in an old blanket, stuck it in his Mustang's trunk, and broke into his daddy's workshop to do the repairs. She told her friends, and soon he had more side work than he could handle. Andre told his ball-busting foreman to go fuck a duck and struck out on his own.

His old high school friend Pitou lent him a truck to haul off his daddy's tools and start his own shop. Leonce Pitou was an ironworker, repairing wrought fences and balconies as far as New Orleans, and as a side hustle, made fighting knives for families to send off with their boys to war.

Andre spent the summer shaping knife handles for Pitou and lathing new legs for rotten antebellum tables and chairs.

That's how he met the girl with the cold steel eyes.

The Calvineau estate was a former sugar plantation named Whiterose, a sick flower nestled among live oaks and willows. The lanky king of the castle sat beneath a willow tree in a white suit, fanned by his servant, drinking sweet tea he spiked with a flask from his coat. The queen, a short woman with tightly pressed lips, made Andre remove his boots before coming inside to see the master bedroom set she wanted him to mimic. It was large and ostentatious, much like the house itself. She said she needed it by next June, and to talk to her husband about the money.

The money was good.

They shook on the deal, the man's long fingers cold and limp, just as a new silver Corvette convertible rolled to a stop on the pecan shells littering the car path.

The driver smiled like Andre would have if the girl in the passenger seat was with him. There was light behind her eyes that had nowhere to go. She kept it behind a tight smile, but a glimmer escaped when she saw Andre, his work sleeves rolled up, his shirt salted with dried sweat.

The men spoke as if Andre had become a piece of his own furniture, but she offered her hand, and he took it. She asked what he was doing there and he told her he was making her father a new bedroom set. Her eye-light dimmed.

"Daddy, he could build me the loveliest little jewelry box!" She held out her hand to show a diamond solitaire. "Roy gave me this big old thing and I've nowhere to put it."

Andre liked that she never asked questions. She said what should be. While the master bed and chifforobe cured, he carved her a jewelry box with room for more. He didn't know how much gold she expected to get, but the Corvette boy looked like he could fill several jewelry boxes on a whim. Pitou made a silver mirror to mount inside.

Business had picked up. People stayed home, fearful of the news on the television, and wanted beautiful things to distract them. Andre couldn't stop thinking about the girl, and drove his Boss 351 to the plantation to deliver the jewelry box and let her parents know the bedroom set wedding gift would be done ahead of schedule.

The drive to Calvineau Parish took him over the Bayou

Vipère bridge and down a road flanked by rows of live oaks linking arms overhead, then the levee road with the canebrake keeping the waters at bay.

He swerved right, branches drumming his fenders as the silver Corvette blew past, coming the other way. Made him wish for a claymore mine to stick under the boy's driver's seat, blow his ass through his brainpan. Workers or fisherman walking the road would have to jump into the canebrake to get out of his way.

Up the road he found Evangeline walking barefoot, holding her high heels over her shoulder. He rolled alongside.

"Can I take you home?"

"I can walk just fine, thank you." She winced as she stepped on a sharp stone. "Just feeling stupid. Ella warned me about taking rides with that bastard."

She must've thought that only happened to the help.

"I made your jewel box. See if you like it."

"I'm sure it's beautiful. My father will pay you for it, but I won't be needing it anymore." She held out her unjeweled fingers. Her arm had been manhandled, and there was blood on her knuckle. "I threw that trash out the window. Roy tried to put my hand on his tool." She huffed a laugh, her lipstick mussed.

Andre lurched the car ahead of her, stopped, then reached across and opened the door. Took his war hatchet from under the seat. "You want to teach him a lesson, I can catch that sonofabitch before he makes the bridge."

The light she hid behind gray-pearl eyes flared like the sun behind clouds.

Andre opened up the engine and she hooted, waving the hatchet out the window as he buried the needle. The Corvette was parked in the middle of the road while the driver kicked through the brush, looking for his diamond.

Andre held her shoulder as he pumped the brakes and they fishtailed to a stop. She laughed and fixed her lipstick in the rear mirror. "I didn't know boys could play seat belt without getting a handful of titty. You're pretty slick, Mr. Desmarteaux."

He wanted to show her why his name meant Of the Hammers, after a trapper in his ancestry who claimed to have knocked out a bear, but she demanded that all he do was hold the rich boy flat on the ground while she danced around his precious Corvette, laughing and splintering the fiberglass with the tomahawk.

They left her former beau howling in the trunk and spiked all four tires.

15: SHOOTER

The mist over the lakes flickered electric blue and red, revealing the swans as they huddled by the shore. Sosthène Boudreaux slowed his rig.

"What do you think it is this time?" Laulie Boudreaux folded her arms and knocked her head back into the leather seats of the Ford F-350 Platinum. She called it his fashion truck. It had a dual rear, a crew cab, an eight-foot bed, and a plush leather interior with all the accoutrements, as befitting the ride of Shooter Boudreaux. He had a gun shop employee take it mudding once a week to keep it looking like he was out hunting jihadi training camps in the bayou. "Some fan waiting with a rifle he wants signed? Or maybe one of your old friends escaped from jail and needs a place to stay?"

He and Laulie had long ago filtered each other's words out as white noise. They had been married thirty years and raised two children who went to LSU and left the state for California. San Francisco of all places, a city Shooter had vowed never to visit again. He'd been stationed briefly at the Presidio between tours in Vietnam, which most considered a plum assignment, if you liked hippie chicks with armpit hair and draft-dodging pussies with hair longer than the girls.

He and two doggies had gone off base to see what they could see, and the seamen said they should roll some queers. They got lit in a port bar where the Korea veteran bartender let them drink their fill for five bucks, then wandered the Tenderloin until they found a bar with no women in it, where a big blond bohunk drank whiskey and eyed them like a dog outside a butcher shop window. He bought them doubles, and they matched him shot for shot until he asked if they liked blow jobs. They followed him as he staggered out back to the brick alley.

One of the doggies unzipped and the bohunk fell to his knees like he'd seen Jesus. Shooter and the other doggie each took a big old slab of wood and held them like baseball bats while that bohunk took hold of that sea dog's pecker like it was full of mother's milk. They waited until his lips were nearly wrapped around their buddy's meat whistle before they drew back and cold-cocked the bohunk across the shoulders with all they had.

They had each done a tour and experienced the exhilaration and belly sickness of killing and thought themselves bad men. Then the bohunk looked up with big sad eyes and said, "Now why'd you boys have to go and do that?" Like they had tickled him with boa feathers instead of cracking him with two-by-fours. They both just about shit ice cubes.

The bohunk swung their buddy by his pecker into the wall then tackled them into a trash pile. He kicked Shooter up the ass so hard that he puked all over his shirt. He curled up in his sick and played dead while the sea dogs caught their beatings, lost their wallets, and they all watched the big bohunk sumbitch stagger back in the back door of the gay bar like it was just another Saturday night.

When Shooter's children showed him photos of their five-thousand-dollar-a-month apartment on top of Telegraph Hill and the parrots that perched on their balcony, and tried to explain to him exactly what they did at work with their expensive degrees, all he could think of was how that kick in the ass felt like he'd been skewered by savages to be roasted on a spit, and how no Christian white man should ever walk the streets of this country unarmed.

He rumbled up the driveway and squinted at the police lights flashing around his million-dollar ranch home like lightning inside thunderheads. "The hell?"

"Best put your TV face on, your mouth's gonna catch flies." Laulie rolled her eyes and looked out the passenger window at the swans. They mated for life, people said. Not all of them, she bet. Some of them wised up.

Shooter steeled his eyes into the thousand-yard stare.

A Baton Rouge officer waved them over. Shooter tapped the button that lowered the window. He supplied the force with their duty weapons and trained their armorers.

"Everything's all right, sir. No sign of entry."

"Start from the beginning. Tell me everything." People liked to feel important. Fill that need and they'll do anything for you, he'd learned.

"Sir, a neighbor across the lake reported gunshots a half an hour ago. We searched their land and found one of your rifles, so we came right over here to make sure you and Mrs. Boudreaux were all right. Then we saw your front door."

Shooter lowered the running boards and stepped out. Uniformed police searched his grounds in pairs. The officer followed his long strides, shining a small tactical flashlight ahead of them. When they reached the porte-cochère, he aimed the light at the oak front door.

It had been splintered by eight rounds from a high-powered rifle. The grouping was shaky. The shooter had fired too quickly for their skill level. But they hadn't missed once.

His phone vibrated in his pocket. The alarm company. He made the officer wait while he gave them the password.

"Show me the rifle."

It was in a long clear evidence bag in the back of a cruiser. One of his early models, worth a small fortune these days to the right collector. He had bought surplus M1903 Springfield rifles and tightened the headspace, smoothed the triggers, expanded the integral magazine. Made them the equal of the more popular M1, for a lower price. This one he recognized from the beanstalk crudely carved into the stock, a joke between him and the owner.

Thibault Garriss.

Shooter had gone legit thirty years ago. When the TV money rolled in, he settled all his old beefs.

All except one.

The Calvineau family wouldn't take blood money for their daughter Evangeline's lost eye. They shackled him into the fold instead. He called them business partners, but they owned him just as they'd enslaved their workforce on the plantations and prisons. Got him the contract to arm every lawman in the state and bought nearly as many weapons themselves. The Calvineaus believed a racial holy war would harken the coming of the Lord, and decided flooding the streets with guns and electing right-minded politicians would hasten His return.

Evangeline always said her family blood was poisoned by their deeds.

And the crazy one-eyed bitch would know.

Shooter looked at his door and asked himself how she could make that grouping from five hundred yards at night with iron sights.

With veins full of pure hate.

16: GONNA WRITE ME A LETTER

Jay's room in the back of the theater overlooked the cemetery, and the tombstones glowed in the moonlight like white pebbles on the beach of night's ocean. He stared at the Angola Rodeo poster, studying Andre's face.

Jay woke with the sun and made work for himself before one of the church people made it for him. He replaced lightbulbs high in the rafters, hosed down the front steps, and kept the grass edged and mowed between every tombstone.

Andre said he'd prayed in the jungle and heard no answer. *We heard the voice of God, boy. The beat of the air cav choppers coming in low.* If Jay could get into Angola with the church group, he could see him regular. All it would take was a letter to suggest Andre get with the Lord, coded in a way only he would understand.

Jay would have to act the role of a saved man. He'd worn one mask or another most of his life, so crafting one more was not much of a challenge. He was sorry for what he'd done, just not for the reason people wanted to hear. He was sorry he was on the run, and sorry that he had a .45 slug cut out of his liver, but not for what he'd done to get there.

He wore his penitent face when he spoke to Miss Ardith, the hefty old woman who managed the church office.

"I taught history, you know. Until they started the busing," she said, punctuating with a wistful giggle like a bird call.

"Then I retired to serve the church."

The congregation was whiter than a box of rice, but Jay's school in New Jersey had only a handful of Black children, and they all lived on two blocks in the redlined town: one for workers, one for professionals. When his Yankee friends went on about the South, he wondered how many took a good look at their own house first.

Ardith rested a cold hand on his arm. "When integration came, the Calvineaus led the drive to secede. We were so grateful, we named the parish after them. They have a long history here, so it's only right. They saved us all. Just look at Baton Rouge!" She shuddered.

He gave the conspiratorial nod those people liked.

"Then you know what we dodged."

"My uncle, he got in trouble in Baton Rouge. Got in a fight with some of them boys, one got killed. Now he's in Angola."

She peered at him through her narrow lenses. "You know, we bury those sinners right here on our grounds? In a special section, of course. We call it Redemption Row." She spread her face in a self-satisfied smile.

Jay looked down. "He was good to me when I was just a boy. I visit when I can, but I'd really like to help him get with God."

She touched his arm. "Ooh, he must need the Lord in the worst way, caged with the animals. I'll let the pastor know you want to join the prison outreach. I think he'll be tickled pink."

Jay thanked her, and said he had to get back to his work. He rubbed the cold spot on his arm where she'd touched him.

The brick markers of Redemption Row were lined against the back fence, away from the rest. The grass had nearly overgrown them. Jay took the weed trimmer from the garage and bared the bricks. Some were covered in dirt, which he cleared with a trowel, and ran his fingers over the names.

***

Molina's day job sent her all over the region in her blue Subaru. She met with youth group for practice after suppertime. When Jay finished his work, he pulled the tarp off the Challenger and gave the engine its legs.

He took the interstate against the thick Baton Rouge traffic, the hot September air like a hair dryer against his face.

Shooter Boudreaux was the only connection he had to Mama. He dropped his book at the library and borrowed an ink pen and paper to write Boudreaux a message.

I am the son of Evangeline and Andre Desmarteaux. I am looking for them. I heard them mention your name when I was a boy. If you can help reunite me with my family, I will be forever grateful.

He wrote the number of a pay-go phone he bought at a gas station.

The front of the shop was full of cars and the slap of bullets hitting backstops pattered through the walls of the range. He parked far away, walked in behind two men laden with hard-shell gun cases, and pretended to gawk at the photo of Shooter golfing with the president until the employees were busy, then flicked the envelope onto the floor behind the register.

17: JEANNETTA

Chopper rolled toward Jeannetta to follow up on the missing boy.

Suzane told fortunes and worked roots in a skinny storefront in Tremé not far from Marie Laveau's Tomb. The money funded a sanctuary for women and street kids, which is how they met. When he took enslaved children from pimps—and an extremity, thus his street name—he knew from experience that dumping them into the system was no kindness.

Sex workers who had learned that his word was bond told him about Suzane.

He earned her respect by trusting the children and women who did not want to return home.

Home could be hell.

He worked in the force as long as he could, but when the violence and apathy surpassed everything he had seen fighting an insurgency on foreign soil, he quit and went private. Most of the time he could pay the bills and sleep at night. This month, things were tight.

Like his eight years being a New Orleans street cop, and his six months in Anbar prior, life as a bounty hunter and private investigator meant walking a gray path. Part of the job meant being a piece of shit to people who'd been done dirty by a corrupt system.

A system he was still part of, as Suzane constantly reminded him. And he reminded her that she needed someone in the system.

He was her sin-eater.

He tried to avoid hurting people who didn't deserve it. But it was unavoidable, and there was no washing away those sins. You couldn't drink them away or tip the scales by doing good. They stayed with you like an army of ghosts.

He told the Bluetooth to call Rosie Ardoin Bail Bonds.

"Chop Tewliss. Thought you didn't work with bloodsuckers."

Suzane said bail was a holdover from slave-catching days and should be abolished. "Only you, Rose. I know you only suck cause there ain't nothing else you good at."

"How your mom and pop?"

"They're good," he said, flat. "Got any scumbag skips 'round Jeannetta?"

Rosie clucked his tongue against his bridge. He'd lost a chunk of his upper jaw to cancer and wore a prosthesis with teeth too bright to match the coffee-stained originals. "You wanna see your folks, I got the boat. I'll go with you, you want."

Chopper's folks lived off-grid. When the levees broke, they went to help, and got caged by the National Guard as looters. Now they lived in the swamp with like-minded folks, waiting for the world to end.

"Thanks, Rose. Just need a skip, now. A bad man."

"All right." Tapping of keys. Rosie knew Chopper's requirements. Pimps, rape-os, Nazis and their ilk.

"Ralph Ora. He stuck me for a hundred thousand. A couple of Banshee MC regulars vouched for him, now he's ghosting me and his trial's in two weeks. Their warlord says he ditched them for the Heimdall Brotherhood, and they got a safe house in Jeannetta."

The HB were a prison gang turned Outlaw Motorcycle Club. Named after the whitest of the Norse gods. Chopper bet they hated that a brother played Heimdall in the Thor movies.

"What he do?"

"Tattoo artist, gave a bunch of his customers herpes, dirty needles. One of them got physical, and he put three bullets in him."

"No self-defense?"

"Not for a felon. Ora did ten in Nasty-Toe-Cheese for stat rape. Traded ink for young pussy." Nasty-Toe-Cheese was what they called Natchitoches prison. Chopper added Ora to his mental Freak File. His mother taught him to read before he was three and he had a mind like a safe.

"Thanks, Rose."

"You know I don't leech off our people. No matter what your woman say."

"I ain't got unlimited minutes."

"All I get in here are sob stories and buckra who done fucked up so bad their own won't give 'em bond. You got your head in the clouds, but at least it ain't up your ass."

"Get a dog. Or a plant. They say plants like when you talk to them." He hung up before Rosie caught traction.

Jeannetta was one of many Cajun country towns near Bayou Vipère with antebellum mansions a few streets away from tilting shotgun shacks.

Chopper found the family's old but well-kept single-floor house and worked from there. Suzane had talked to them and left him the neighbors. Like the boy selling on the corner who kept his stash behind a shingle.

He pulled up like he wanted to buy and the boy approached his window.

For ten bucks he told him he didn't see nothing of Keshawn. "His head's in outer space. You hear him coming, it sound like Star Wars, pew pew pew. Makes his own sound effects."

Suzane had said he was a nerdy boy with few friends and middling grades. Possibly on the spectrum, they said now. A hard way to grow up, Chopper remembered.

He found the drive-in and traded his leather coat for a suit jacket, flashed the manager his investigator's card, told him he was working for the family. "I already told all this to the police." The man had mousy hair and eyes too close together, like the headlights on a Jeep. "He was a real good worker, once you got his attention."

Chopper tilted his head.

"I mean, you know how they uh, teenagers are. I don't mean anything by it. They run off all the time. I can hardly keep this place staffed."

"I'm sorry for your loss." Chopper gave the man his back.

He walked the path to Keshawn's neighborhood, his suit jacket open, a large frozen Coke to keep cool.

Back at the family's house, he knocked and got no answer. The mother worked, the younger sister was in school. He explored the yard. He'd been a short child and fascinated by small things. Worm castings in the dirt, the raw sugar cotton-candy of a praying mantis egg sac hidden on a twig.

He studied the windowsills for smudges, the hard-packed dirt for footprints. The yard needed a mow and the corner held an overgrown garden, tomatoes and okra plants dried out to vines. It would hide a peeping tom from the street. He stood in its shadow and looked in the window of the children's shared room. Then he bent in half and pored over the grass and dirt. No worm tracks, but a dust of ashes grayed the yellow blades of dead grass. He poked through them but found no cigarette butts or ends.

The smoker had been wise enough to collect them.

He creased his brow at the dirt, shaded it with his hand and let the sun reveal silvery patterns that glistened like slug trails, but weren't. Dried out dollops of a slimy creature's leavings.

Chopper knocked on doors and spoke to old ladies and men who said they'd heard what happened, it was a shame, but they hadn't seen anyone who looked like they might do such a thing.

Their Hunter knew better than to drive down streets where homebodies would see him follow his prey, but there was always the chance it was a local. He found a woman named Charlene who liked to talk about everybody in her neighborhood. He ate her stale biscuits and smiled when she laughed at her own jokes and touched his forearm.

"He just keeps to himself, never bothers no one," she said. "Except that one time. That was when he was a boy."

He gave her a long hug goodbye, then walked back to his truck to plug in his internet hotspot and run the name on his laptop.

In 1997 Timothy Lee Baines had been a fat freckled lump of dough who'd been arrested for multiple counts of trespassing and served two years plus mandatory counseling.

A tough sentence for a white boy. A little digging through the parish paper's archives and he found an article about a girl who woke up to find a man in a mask performing a lewd act in her bedroom, and a warning for folks to close their windows in the stifling July heat.

He changed out of his suit coat, pulled on a hoodie, and got his kit together.

Two blocks down and around a corner, the sunbaked Baines house had a view of the frontage road where school children walked home every day. Or it would, if the windows weren't yellowed from generations of cigarette smoke. The grass had gone shaggy and wild, growing around the bumpers of a rusted blue truck. A single furrow through the weeds led in back.

One a motorcycle would make.

That would be enough for him to boot in the door and say he heard Ralph Ora was holed up here.

It wasn't tampering, if there was no investigation in place.

He came at the Baines house from the angle with the fewest windows. Knocking was no guarantee of intention not to trespass, and a boy like Baines would likely fetishize weapons. And with only a misdemeanor on his record, he could legally own as many as he liked.

When Chopper was in grade school, a Japanese exchange student looking for a Halloween party had been shot to death for knocking on the wrong door. The shooter claimed he felt threatened and walked free.

If a jury considered a Japanese teenager dressed as John Travolta from *Saturday Night Fever* a viable threat, Chopper knew a six-foot Black man could be shot at a hundred yards with his hands up, and his killer's case would be dismissed. Cop or civilian.

So he might as well kick the damn back door in like he planned to all along.

18: SIGNED, SEALED, DELIVERED

Shooter Boudreaux held the letter between two fingers like a stinking diaper. "No one saw this gold-digging sack of shit?"

The store manager looked at his boots, gray mustache bent into a frown. "He knew where our cameras are. He's a white boy, that's all we got."

Of course he was a white boy. He was *the boy*, the one crazy Evangeline and Andre took on jobs as a decoy. Now a killer with a quarter century of prison under his belt.

Prison up north. Maybe he drove that purple Challenger seen leaving Ti' Boy's place.

And maybe he'd sent eight rounds of thirty-aught through Shooter's front door.

Shooter couldn't tell if the letter was a trap or in earnest. No matter what it was, it would lead to the crazy one-eyed bitch Evangeline. Over the years, she had burned down his billboards and busted his shop windows until he built the current cinder block building with no glass.

Why did she kill Ti' Boy now, when he'd been farting up his couch for twenty years? No one waited that long for revenge. Something had lit a fire under her ass. And now someone claiming to be her boy wanted a meet.

He remembered the baby. He didn't fuss and was good camouflage. Evie hid her Diamondback in the brat's swaddling clothes or his stroller. They lost the runt after a stretch in parish jails, then went north. And when they came back eight years later, hungry for work—like they hadn't left their crew high and dry—the boy was gone and never spoken of.

The boy had Calvineau blood. Untouchable.

Shooter's alliance with the family had made his fortune. LeFer had caught him balls deep in a whorehouse and put a Smith & Wesson at the base of his skull, told him how it was. Time to stop robbing The Man, and work for him.

In court, Shooter pled for mercy to a Calvineau judge, and the papers lauded the war hero who'd gone wrong, and then turned on his fellow thieves because they planned to use the loot from the armored truck heist to fund a terrorist attack on a Yankee prison detail and release a notorious child murderer.

The boy. The infamous Jay Desmarteaux, who'd briefly made national news as The Nutley Ax Killer.

Robbin' banks is one thing, but letting mad dogs loose? I can't truck with that.

That became his catch phrase in the local access TV commercials for his gun shop. *Brady Bill? I don't truck with that. Even California Ronnie Reagan don't want that bleeding heart foolishness, and he's the one got shot.*

Shooter, the bad boy turned lawman's friend. He sold in bulk to whoever LeFer told him to, whether it was Desire Projects bangers or the Heimdall Brotherhood. He had made more money than he'd ever dreamed of stealing.

And now Evangeline and her killer kid Desmarteaux were gunning for him.

Like running recon in the jungle, sometimes you avoided the ambush and other times you called in napalm.

Shooter took a Colt Python from the trophy case. Accurate as hell but a bitch to fix when the timing went out. This one had been Andre Desmarteaux's. He kept it to remind himself he could be bought, and that he would pay for his sins.

"That's a fine-looking gun," a customer said. "A classic."

Shooter looked past his face. Men liked his thousand-yard

stare, like he was working out how to kill everyone in the room.

Shooter thought most people, including himself, were assholes. Looking at them made his stomach turn. He understood the gunmen who went off and shot up churches and schools and concerts.

Laurie shook her head at the near-daily news of mass shootings. *Why'd they go and do that? Don't they know it's a beautiful world, if you let it?* He loved her as much as he could love anyone, but she would never comprehend what the world demanded from a man, how it kept him caged, and how *good* it felt to go wild.

It wouldn't be a bad way to go, seeing how many he could take with him. Maybe get on top of the scoreboard in Tiger stadium. It held ninety thousand fans and it was packed, most games. Smuggle a couple of Shooter Stoner rifles fitted with full-auto sears and hundred-round snail drum magazines, and his tally would be tough to beat. He'd top that Vegas shitbird in no time flat.

"Have you fired that one, Mr. Boudreaux? I'd like to buy it. It would be an honor."

"She ain't for sale," he said, aiming at the Angola Rodeo poster they'd replaced on the wall. He thumbed the hammer and sighted on Andre Desmarteaux's face. "This one's a custom order."

He dry fired, and several customers flinched and stared. Shooter quick-holstered the Python cross-draw style in his belt, left with a curt nod, and locked the armory door behind him.

He picked up the desk phone and held it between his ear and shoulder as he punched the speed dial. He thumbed the hammer of the Python and listened to its timing as he waited for his master to pick up.

19: HANDY MAN

It took Jay the better part of a day to repair the lawnmower. Pastor Eagleton was delighted and told him sunset was the best time to mow the grounds, being cooler and all.

Molina held youth group at night. Some kids shot hoops outside and some worked on the show, running lines or making props while music played over the speakers. Jay took a cold shower in his room and pulled on a pair of jeans.

He crashed on the lumpy single bed and thought how to send Papa Andre a cryptic message, when someone knocked on the door.

Unused to privacy, he waited for them to barge in like prison COs.

"Hello? Mister Jason?"

He put on a clean T-shirt and opened the door. It was Molina in a baseball shirt, sleeves past her elbows.

"We're not too loud, are we?"

"You don't bother me at all."

"We're putting some sets together. We could use another set of hands, and we get pizza after."

Jay smiled. "You get one with pepperoni, you're on."

She had experience with carpentry, so he followed her directions. The kids wanted to help and she knew how to delegate. Some of them could be trusted with a hammer or saw, and others would find a way to hurt themselves while sponge painting.

The teenagers were boisterous and full of nervous energy, but they had a calming effect on Jay's mind. He swung the hammer and nails squeaked into the fresh wood.

He'd been their age when he'd brought his hatchet down on the skull of Joey Bello.

Death had been too kind for that boy. He'd earned death with the rape and torment of his victims, and Jay spent little time mourning the decision that defined his life. Until Okie had shown him there were other choices, besides killing and letting evil run free.

Okie had no taste for killing. He was a heist man, and said if you spilled no blood, there was always some other crew with blood-lusty freaks that the law would rather take down than you. The lesson he'd learned from sticking his finger into the leg of Bonnie Parker was that she and her beau were not role models but good bad examples.

You could've busted that boy's hands for him.

It took years of boxing for Jay to get the killing beaten out of him. He relished the physicality, punishment for his sins of impulsiveness and vengefulness. Swinging a hammer felt good, whether you hit nails or a skull. Molina settled next to him, tacking boards up after he framed.

"I hear you teach inmates in Angola how to put on plays, too."

"We do."

"If you need someone to help build sets there, just ask." *The Angolite* said they usually put on a show or two before the rodeo. Vignettes, Bible scenes.

"You work fast," Molina said. She had a sheen of perspiration on her forehead and worked in a good rhythm. "But it takes a calm demeanor. There's a lot of rules, and it can be frustrating."

Jay smiled and bent a nail on his next swing.

"Mother," he said, and yanked the nail out.

A girl snorted and covered her mouth. The room hushed.

"Sorry." Jay held his hands up. He felt like he'd mooned a nun.

"Put a quarter in the jar," Molina said. "At least you didn't say the other half."

The kids snickered. One boy on a ladder laughed so hard his paintbrush went flying. He lunged for it and toppled. Jay dodged the brush and leapt like a cat, his boots skidding on the polished wood stage. He caught the boy by the belt before his face hit the floor.

"Whoa."

They stared at Jay like he was a tiger that escaped his cage.

He lowered the kid onto all fours. "Next time let it drop. It's only paint."

Later, they sat on the floor and ate pizzas from the box and drank Cokes.

"My daddy says he can tell Baton Rouge Coke from other Cokes," a thin girl with corn silk hair said. "We have the best water in the country."

Jay wasn't sure it tasted any different from the Cokes he'd had on his way to Louisiana from New Jersey. The pizzas were heavy on the toppings and weak in the crust.

The kids talked about school and parents and friends who tempted them with trouble, and Molina listened and gave advice obliquely, letting her teenage charges think they had figured it all out by themselves. Jay listened, arms folded, arching an eyebrow or nodding. He had a thousand of these talks in Rahway prison. Anger management. Impulse control. Seeing the other person's side.

That had been the tough one. *Everyone's got a different perspective.*

Well yeah, but they're wrong had been the usual answer from his fellow inmates. Okie was a master at putting on another man's shoes, which made him a great thief and a better chess player. He'd only been caught when he had to put together a new crew. One of them double-crossed him, stole the take, and left him with a star-shaped bullet scar in his face.

Jay stared at the newly painted set walls, his folded pizza slice dripping grease on his blue jeans. Why had Okie needed a new crew? Because Papa Andre and Mama Evangeline had left for Jersey with their boy.

He took a slug of Coke from the can to dilute the guilt brewing in his belly.

"What about you, Mister Jason?"

Jay grunted and set his slice on a plate. "Sorry, I was off somewhere."

Molina said, "Alex was saying he has trouble with forgiveness. Go on, Alex."

The boy looked down. "I know we're supposed to forgive, but sometimes you just know they're gonna sin again. Then it's like, fool me twice, shame on you. I mean, you know. Fool me twice, shame on me."

Jay had no argument. He'd done some Bible reading inside, to get in good with the preacher. He dug around in his head.

Molina said, "The Lord says, judge not, lest ye be judged. We can protect ourselves, but we shouldn't treat someone like they've already sinned against us. Do you agree, Jason?"

Jay nodded. "Vengeance is mine, saith the Lord."

He knew most of all, that following that precept was easier said than done.

20: HOSPICE

The mess bell rang and Andre hopped down from his top bunk, hiding his wince from his dorm mates. Pulled on his clothes and ate a glop of grits and white toast and dry scrambled eggs splashed with hot sauce, then shuffled to the workshop to put time in on Warden LeFer's chifforobe.

He was a big stripe, one of the near five thousand inmates who had no expectation of leaving Angola alive or dead. Andre had seen enough hell in life that he couldn't believe it waited for him after death. Maybe he didn't deserve heaven, but when did *deserve* come into it? He and Angie had saved her nephew from evil. All they'd wanted was to raise him.

Her parents refused. They wanted the boy for their own.

They sent Sheriff LeFer to track them down. With no cash, they'd gone desperate.

They had fun for a while. Shooter Boudreaux sniping, Okie planning and driving, Angie and the boy as decoys. Then Angie found the trail of the boy's father and learned how he'd abandoned him with her sister after giving her a taste for cocaine.

They followed the boy's father north, used his illegitimate child as leverage to get Andre a job, and live as citizens again. They became good neighbors. Andre fixed rotten porch steps for an elderly Italian woman who made them lasagna in exchange, helped old men in yellowed undershirts with the trellises for their grapevines.

Their boy made friends with misfits, which was only fair, because misfits was what their little family was. Then it all went to hell. It had been a fool's dream.

The knot behind his ribs had begun squeezing on his lung and his breaths felt cramped. He still jogged in the yard and hit the weight pile, but knew he was far from the man he'd been when he won All-Around Cowboy. The rodeo was a young man's game.

The oldest winner had been Woody the Fox.

Woody was a lifer, in on a juvenile bank robbery that had gone sour. He'd rehabilitated himself and become editor of *The Angolite* prison magazine, making appeals that went nowhere, even after the Supreme Court deemed giving juveniles life without parole was cruel and unusual punishment. He'd survived decades in solitary and kept fit, looking better at seventy than Andre had at forty when he walked in the gates.

The Fox had become LeFer's worst enemy, exposing his redemption shuck for what it was, cover for selling prison labor to enrich the Calvineau and LeFer families. If Andre was to survive the rodeo, he'd need the Fox on his side.

He had no line to the man.

A friend who did was Murray Lo. A big stripe, in for life, living in hospice. Andre put his tools in a locker and walked down to the death ward in Cypress Two.

Lo was a Hmong fisherman turned jailhouse lawyer who wrote a column in *The Angolite*. He perfected his English pleading his own appeals and writing them for others. Short and thick-set, his waist had no taper and his head was square, like he'd been built out of bricks. He had fought the Viet Cong and fled with his family after Saigon fell, made a living in the Gulf, and stabbed a man who tried to steal his boat.

Andre had met him when the vets brought the Traveling Vietnam War Memorial Wall to Angola. He knew there were a lot of vets on the Farm, but he'd been shocked how many came to touch the replica inscribed with the names of the fallen. Andre traced names and his tears came unbidden. The names of Murray Lo's people weren't on the wall, but he knelt and prayed anyway.

On a hospice bed breathing oxygen, Murray drank from a little bottle of chocolate gunk. He and Andre slapped hands.

"Come to see what you'll look like in a year, Desmarteaux?" He looked cored out, his skin loose.

"Think it's that shit they sprayed in the jungle?"

"Don't matter if it's Agent Orange or a voodoo spell, it hurts all the time now. When you carve my cross, you say I'm a veteran. 1954 to 1975."

Andre put a hand to his heart.

"Sorry those appeals never took."

"Wasn't your fault," Andre said. LeFer wanted him here. Knew if he was loose, Shooter Boudreaux would be gator shit in a week. "Got a favor."

He told him what he wanted, gave him pen and paper from inside his shirt.

"You want to mortgage your ass to the Fox, that's your business."

"Warden means to kill me with an audience, to hurt my girl. Make her come home to her shit-ass family."

Murray knew the story. "At least you ain't got a baby-raper cleaning shit out your ass." He nodded across the room, where Philo Salva emptied a Black skeleton's bed pan.

Balding and muscular, an oil rigger's arms and a rough drinker's face mottled with rosacea. His hospice work did not absolve him in Andre's eyes, but he wasn't going to risk death or a life sentence to shank the scumbag.

It was a citizen fantasy that inmates meted out justice to rapists. The strong lorded it over the weak, and Salva would not die easy. He sported the Tyr rune of the Heimdall Brothers, but wiped asses of every color in the death ward. It gave him access to syringes and drugs that his HB masters sold. Even the race gangs held green supreme over all colors.

"This cancer's got a sweet tooth," Murray said. "Bring me twenty Zagnuts from the commissary. Something with nuts in it, if they're out. None of them Three Musketeers or Milky Way, they remind me of baby shit."

He squeezed Andre's hand, shivering with the effort.

21: HONOR

Evangeline wiped her eyes at the dinner table.

"That doesn't sound like your cousin Roy," her father said, his Adam's apple bobbing as he spoke.

"He's a perfect gentleman," her mother said. "Practically a saint, with his patience for you."

Hesper Joy Calvineau weaved her long fingers. Years of contempt had carved the alabaster of her face with severity. "I don't want to hear another thing about this."

Ella, their maid, stood stiff by the table as they ate supper.

"Sheriff Kane said he saw you out riding with that coon-ass we hired to make your bedroom set," her father said. "I told him to give him a talking to."

"I won't be hiring that beast again." Her mother pinched her lips. "Roy said he tried to defend your honor, and he vandalized his car for his trouble."

The food soured in Evangeline's throat. They had gone for ice cream after, nothing more.

"I'm not feeling well," Evangeline said, and left the table without excusing herself. She cried in bed a while, then remembered how good it felt to swing that hatchet at Roy's Corvette.

Her older sister had fled home two years before, and sometimes sent letters that Ella intercepted and gave to her before her parents could burn them. She had a job as an oil doodlebugger's receptionist. Said he was going to marry her as soon as his divorce up north was final, as his wife couldn't bear children. Then she would send Evie money so she could leave home.

Not soon enough.

While her mother listened to seventy-eight RPM records of chamber music and her father held court at the Pelicans Lodge, she packed her favorite clothes, then crept downstairs to take the banknotes kept in her father's office desk and use the phone to call Desmarteaux's Son Wood Shop.

"I'm sorry for all the trouble," she said.

"Just people being people," Andre said. "Ain't no trouble." He lived in a set of garages in town that he rented as a workshop, surrounded by his daddy's tools. He had rolled a fat joint for the evening, and liked to smoke with the doors open and listen to the night sounds, away from people.

"My sister's out in St. Charles. I could use a ride to the bus depot. I'll catch the first bus in the morning."

He heard the hiss of tires up the road. They were coming.

"Too late for that, firecracker. You sit tight for now." He hung up and took a surplus M14 out of a C-bag, smelled the cosmoline. He waited with his war hatchet at his right hand and the rifle aimed toward the street.

Soon enough, a shiny red-and-white Chevy C/K truck squealed on a turn and bounced over the curb. Four crew cuts with ax handles hopped out the back and went to town on his Mustang with them. Busted the rear glass, ran up and down the sides denting the sheet metal.

Andre took a deep toke and balanced the joint between the teeth of the circular saw blade.

Roy stepped out the passenger side, dressed in clean jeans and cowboy boots, holding a Coke bottle with a rag stuck in the top.

The ax handle boys flanked him as he approached.

"Maybe you're new around here, coon-ass. But no one fucks with a Calvineau."

Andre exhaled out his nostrils, then stood and shouldered the rifle. He liked the old 14s when he didn't have to lug them through the jungle. Steady and true. He shot the top off the Coke bottle and sprayed Roy with its contents.

His buddies froze or stumbled. An ax handle clattered to the concrete. Roy put up his hands and his jabbered, eyes aflicker.

Andre couldn't hear a word over the ringing in his ears. He sighted on Roy's chest until his knocker-squad set down their weapons.

Sheriff Kane LeFer's black-and-white squad car rocked to a stop and blocked in the Mustang. Built like a footballer, his silver-and-gold battle flag belt buckle nearly reached his cruiser's roofline.

Roy's blabber about what he was in for began to trickle through the ringing in Andre's ears.

"Desmarteaux, put that damn rifle down," LeFer shouted.

Andre held it port arms. One of Roy's crew-cut boys reached for his ax handle, and Kane booted him in the ass. "Desmarteaux, why don't you set that rifle *all* the way down, and we'll talk this out."

"See my car, Sheriff sir? I'd say we're even. I got no beef with these boys. You get them off my property, we got nothing more to talk about."

"He drew first blood, LeFer." Roy held out his hand. The Coke bottle had cut a jag across his palm.

"Best go get that looked at, Master Calvineau." LeFer nodded toward the truck.

The boys left their ax handles and piled in. Roy wrapped a white handkerchief around his hand. "This isn't over."

He stared at Andre as they drove away.

LeFer walked over slow. "You offended that boy's honor in front of his fiancée. You know his kind."

"Rich shitbird's still a shitbird." Andre held out the joint, and the Sheriff took it.

He took a deep drag and kept the joint. "Tastes better than

the shit we smoked behind the schoolhouse. Why the hell you pick a fight with the Calvineaus? They own every damn thing."

"They don't own you, do they?"

He socked Andre on the arm, hard. "They can rent me, but nobody owns Kane LeFer."

Andre rubbed his arm for show. Kane puffed the joint and passed.

"You still got a chip on your shoulder bigger than my dick for rich boys. That Evangeline is magazine-cover pretty like her sister, but they're both six kinds of crazy."

Andre took a deep hit, eyeing the damage to the Boss 351. First car he'd owned that he wasn't picking parts for out of salvage every week to keep running.

"That girl's got your nose open, and you ain't even dipped your wick. You should've joined me in the police. They like the uniform, and their dry-balls husbands can't do shit about it." He snagged the joint for a long drag, then ground the roach under his boot. "You gotta spend the night. Her folks'll break my balls if you don't."

Andre smiled to say, *I ain't gotta do shit.*

Kane's hand drifted toward his revolver, then he winked. "I won't close the cell door."

He followed Sheriff LeFer to the station and got a clean cell next to a drunk who moaned all night and sweated grain alcohol. When they released Andre in the morning he paid his fine in cash and drove back to find Pitou staring at the smoldering ashes of their livelihood.

The fire truck had been and gone, and a rainbow glimmered in the morning haze over the ruins of the wood shop.

22: TOMBSTONE SHADOW

Jay was edging the brick-like grave markers in Redemption Row, dragging the raven's-beaked tool through the dirt, bearing the names of the impoverished Angola dead, when a shadow blotted out the sun. He looked up, grateful for the shade, and wiped his forearm on the red bandanna tied around his forehead.

Pastor Eagleton stood in pleated chinos and a white polo. He didn't even glisten at the hairline or the throat in the heat. "Come with me, De-monde." He broke the name in two, exaggerating the French.

Jay stood. He blinked to hide how his eyes scanned for police cars. "What can I do for—"

"You can zip it and follow me."

He walked toward the tool shed.

Jay followed. He tucked the edging tool into his back pocket.

The Challenger was parked behind the shed, covered in a tarp. Pastor Eagleton's tassel loafers crunched on the pecan husks. He stopped and looked back. "Don't walk three steps behind me like a geisha."

Jay caught up. He stepped to the pastor's left, so he could swing his right arm if need be.

The pastor sidestepped onto the grass to keep Jay on his right. Most citizens weren't so aware. It put Jay on edge.

"That's what I like about you, *Demonde*. Always looking for what needs to be done. You've only been here a week, and

Ardith tells me you've almost run out of things to do."

"Thank you, sir. There's plenty left that needs fixing."

They rounded the shed. The Challenger was still covered, not surrounded by police. The pastor spun on one foot, walked backward three paces, and leaned on the trunk of the car. He pulled up the tarp, revealing the temporary tag Jay had pinched outside Shooter's Palace.

"You should get permanent tags if you plan on staying a while."

"I will, sir. Come payday."

Pastor Eagleton took out a slim wallet and held out two crisp fifties. "We want you to stick around, Jason."

Jay waited a beat, to not seem desperate. "Thank you, sir."

He drew the bills back. As expected.

"This is an advance on your pay. Ardith will give you an envelope on Sunday, after services. You are expected to attend." He tucked the bills into Jay's shirt pocket.

"Yessir."

The tall pastor sat on the trunk lid and slapped the metal. "Come here, De-monde. Set a spell."

Jay leaned against the trunk. The rear leaf springs creaked under their weight.

"Miss Molina tells me you want to join our prison outreach. That's very admirable, but we don't put their souls in the hands of just anyone. Saving souls isn't the same as refurbishing a carburetor. What makes you think you're worthy?"

"Not worthy, sir. Helpful. I was in a little trouble myself, when I was younger. It was touch and go for a while, then a chaplain name of Sidney set me right. He told me to pay it forward. That's all I want to do."

"Molina wouldn't have anything to do with it?" An elbow nudged his ribs.

"She seems a good woman. But my momma told me not to uh, mess where you eat."

His steely eyes turned stormy. Then the clouds broke into a

belly laugh, in three harsh chops. "That's wisdom right there. Wise words we should all follow. Tell me more about this female font of wisdom."

"My Mama was a Calvineau," he blurted, like a kid with a secret. "That's what daddy always said. She died when I was real little, so I don't know that side." He'd practiced the lines in his room, talking to the mirror.

"You should be proud." His eyes glinted with a fire Jay had only seen in zombie movies. "You're part of a fine, old family. What was her name?"

He named a cousin that Mama said had run off with a man and never came back.

"And your daddy?"

"Leroy Demonde."

"The king! Father of the healer," the pastor said, with a broad smile. His sermon voice had a touch of Robert Mitchum. "Where's Mister Leroy these days?"

Jay blinked his eyes slick. "He was a rigger." He raised a fist, then opened it, like a platform disappearing in a flower of flame.

"I'm sorry, Jason. To lose one parent is misfortune, but to lose both, that looks like carelessness."

Jay pinched his eyes and rubbed his nose, the second play of the cry-pantomime, which hid his confusion. He couldn't tell if the pastor was fucking with him, or simply that callous. He stared out at the trees.

The pastor broke the silence with a laugh. "Forgive me, Jason. Trying to inject a little levity. You say you're a Calvineau, and you didn't use it to get the job. That's a first."

"Didn't feel right."

"A man of integrity in our midst! They are so difficult to come by. Maybe I *shall* let you tend to our prison flock."

"I wouldn't let you down, sir."

"You'd best not, unless you wish to court eternal damnation," the pastor said, then punched his shoulder. "You tell Molina you're in the van next week. I don't know what you do with your nights, but I best see you practicing theater with her and our children. And sitting in youth group."

"I will continue to do so, sir. I enjoy it. You've got good children here."

"The convicts up there make our kids look like Einsteins. But don't let your guard down. Their kind are born with animal cunning." He slapped a manicured hand on Jay's grapefruit of a shoulder and kneaded it, juicing it up. "Wait until I tell the elders. They'll want you for dinner at the plantation. A Calvineau boy! Oh, they'll eat you right up."

Jay kept his sad, confused eyes on. Okie taught that when in doubt, play stupid. When they're stronger or smarter, it's best they underestimate you.

"Don't fret, son. When you're a Calvineau, blood is everything."

He slapped Jay hard on the back, then brushed off his pants. Jay watched him saunter back to his Escalade, whistling "Bringing in the Sheaves" over the birds' afternoon chatter.

The sun began to melt into the treetops like a dollop of rainbow sherbet in a punchbowl. Jay slipped his mama's knife from his boot and carefully picked the dirt from his fingernails.

Knowing he would walk through prison gates sent ice down his spine.

23: WORM CASTINGS

Chopper didn't literally kick the door in. He wedged his peepaw's cane knife, a rust-red steel cleaver with a worn wooden handle and a hook for cutting sugar, between the door and the frame and popped the cheap lock.

The cane knife went back to the sheath at his hip, and he held the Shooter Shorty close to his side, one hand on the front grip, sweeping the foul-smelling front room.

The Baines house was a packrat's den of magazines stacked to the ceilings, buttressing the walls, the floor littered with wads of tissue and piles of unopened mail. Mouse droppings peppered the envelopes and crunched under his shoes. He heard no response to his entry, so he closed the door and tied a bandanna around his mouth. He'd read about people getting the plague from breathing in rodent shit.

He peered at the shorter magazine stacks covering the couch. One cover depicted a woman hog-tied, a red ball gag in her mouth, her breasts pinched between two crossed straps, while a masked man wearing a Santa hat held a cat o' nine tails over her bare rump. Another pile was *Tactical Handgunner*, a third a motorcycle rag.

He made his way slowly toward the kitchen, where the magazines gave way to yellowed boxes of kitchen gadgets and cheap plastic crap that Chopper remembered from growing up in the nineties. The kind you got delivered from TV shopping networks. He navigated the maze and peered into the kitchen.

Mason jars of pocket change covered the counter, organized into pennies, nickels, and dimes. The round table was stacked with papers except for a tiny crevice where a plastic bowl of curdled pink milk sat next to a spoon and an open box of Lucky Charms cereal. The floor creaked under his feet, and roaches skittered out of the box and disappeared into the mail.

The hallway carpet was sticky. He squeezed past display cabinets swarming with glass animals and souvenir mugs. The bathroom door was pinned open by a bucket full of rusted batteries. There he found the source of the bad smell.

Under the sink sat a blue trashcan overflowing with wads of stained toilet paper. The toilet ran, the sound muffled by the maze of magazines. The shower stall was open and several mops leaned in a corner. He moved on, and a cough came from low behind him.

He spun with the Shorty aimed at the floor.

A brown dachshund limped from behind the trash can, a wad of shit paper in its mouth. It hunched and hacked the paper to the floor, then gave a weak shake and a whimper.

Poor thing needed water. But it would have to wait until he cleared the rest of the house. He turned back to the bedrooms.

The first room was a child's, or had been. It looked frozen in time. The sheets on the twin bed were from some cartoon where the people had animal heads, and the walls were postered with Japanese animation and video game posters of big-eyed girls with cat ears and tails. They centered around a hand-drawn picture of a white-furred wolfman wearing an SS officer's coat, with one paw stroking his slick pink dog dick and the other firing a Schmeisser sub machine gun as he shot his wad.

What the fuck? Chopper mouthed. He'd seen a lot of bad shit, even dragged in a serial horse fucker who'd jumped bail for beating his wife, but this was just fucking weird.

The windows were blacked with paint and the ceiling stickered with stars, the kind that glowed in the dark. There was a computer on a desk of recent vintage, a yellowed beige monitor and keyboard, and a Mötley Crüe record album lined and stained from someone cutting lines on it. A cut-down red Sonic straw sat next to a ceramic purple paring knife.

The next door was closed. The dog butted against his calf, whimpering. A weak, muffled moan answered.

Chopper kicked the door open.

He saw a flash of pasty white, a doughy man with close-set eyes in stained white briefs tied much like the woman on the cover of the titty magazine. The man looked up, and spit bubbled past his ball gag. The door slammed into a tower of flat white boxes. The boxes avalanched across the bed. The hog-tied man whimpered as they buried him.

The dog yipped and tried to jump on the bed but couldn't leap in its weakened state. Chopper kicked the boxes away until the man's face emerged, blinking in terror. He had marinated in his own juices in the heat for some time. Chopper was glad for the bandanna around his own nose and mouth.

"Timmy Lee?"

The man nodded and sputtered behind the ball gag. It was made from two bungee cords and an eight ball from a pool table. The dog yelped frantically.

Chopper picked up the pup and set it by the man's face. It licked his slobber. He holstered the Shorty and took out the cane knife. The man's cheeks ballooned.

"You been jerking off outside people's windows, Timmy?"

The man shook his head, butting the dog. It didn't care. His face might have been made from steak, the way the pup went on licking.

"Tell me about Keshawn."

Timmy Lee stared.

Chopper ran the edge of cane knife against the cord. It sang like a straight razor. "This can go two ways. Your little doggy's hungry. I saw a bag of kibble in there swimming with mice. I never had no pets, but I hear when you die, they don't fuss about eating on you. How we gonna feed your pup?"

"Muh," Timmy Lee said.

"You scream and I'll crack your head."

He hooked the bungee cord. It was thick and the hook wasn't very sharp. He tugged at it and Timmy Lee's face contorted.

The fart-splatter of a motorcycle with straight pipes rumbled alongside the house and around the back. Timmy Lee wriggled like a fat white worm on a hook. Terrified.

As his eyes adjusted, Chopper saw the boxes were printed with firearm company logos. Stacked to the ceiling. Long arms and pistols. He sheathed the cane knife and took out the Shorty.

"Nod once if that's a biker by the name of Ralph Ora."

One.

"Twice if he's strapped."

Two.

Chopper clicked off the safety. "You wanna live, here's what we got to do."

24: CAWFEE

At youth group, talk ran late and the kids were spared cleaning up as parents came to take them home. Jay helped Molina gather up pizza boxes and put away tools.

"Thank you for sharing tonight," she said, tired but still bright. "Just between us, I've been arrested, myself."

"You don't look like the kind that gets shot." Another Black teenager murdered by police was in the news, and the kids repeated what their parents said, that he was "no angel." Jay had cut them off by saying he'd been arrested and served his time.

"This parish has a history. I went to a magnet school in Baton Rouge. We were like the United Nations. This place, though? When they get nostalgic about the fifties, they mean the 1850s."

"When my family moved up north, there were four Black kids in my whole school. It's bad all over."

"But you're from down here, aren't you? You have an accent I can't place."

"Catahoula," Jay said. Andre had a camp there, where they had hid out when he was a kid. "You want to talk, we could get a drink."

"I don't drink," she said, but stepped closer. "You like tea or coffee?"

"Coffee." He winced as he said it. He'd kept much of his Louisiana twang as he could up north out of pride, but buying a cup of *cawfee* showed his Jersey years.

"Sure you're not from New Yawk? You wanna *wawk* my *dawg*?" She laughed and swatted his butt with a cleaning rag.

Jay grinned. "You got me. I went to school in New Jersey with a kid they called Tony Baloney. That kinda rubbed off."

"What else are you hiding, Mr. Jason?" Playful admonishment, but her glance had an edge of seriousness. "I don't go for *cawfee* with just anyone."

Jay held up his hands. "I did some time for some foolishness. But that was a long time ago."

Molina gathered scripts, looking away from him. She stacked them on a table.

"Don't tell Pastor Eagleton, okay? I don't want him holding anything over my head."

She went rigid. The scripts slid from the table and she lurched for them, stretching her arms out of her baseball sleeves. The insides of her elbows were scarred with deep pocks.

Jay flinched. The Witch in Sulphur had tracks like shotgun patterns on her arms.

Molina yanked her sleeves down. "Shit!" The script pages spread across the floor. She folded her arms. "Don't go telling the pastor. He already knows."

"I ain't a snitch."

"But you're judging me. I see it in your eyes. You think you know all about me."

"No. Your tracks just made me think about a good friend who I helped kick. She's gone." His cellmate Raina had wailed in his arms all night in withdrawal after her source dried up. She called herself Rene then, and killed the pain of her family's rejection with heroin smuggled in by the guards.

Molina pointed her fox nose away from him. "I'm sorry. I was judging you, too."

He needed her, to get in the prison. For that he needed trust. A bond.

"One secret deserves another." He stepped closer and peeled up his shirt. "I got shot robbing a liquor store."

It was a lie. The bullet scar came from a man who'd wanted him dead.

Her eyes lingered on the white centipede across his muscled belly, where the doctors had taken out half of his liver. "We all got scars," he said, and pulled off his shirt. He wasn't young or pretty, but he knew he looked good to women, a roughly carved Greek statue. He flashed a boyish smile that filed off the edges.

"Put your shirt on, Mister Desmond." Her hand went to the Stanley knife clipped in her pocket.

He turned to show the burn scars across his back, like molten candle wax, from when the Witch hurled a pot of hot roux.

"My God."

Molina touched the thickly puckered skin. Jay couldn't feel her gentle touch through the scar tissue.

"I need to see my uncle in Angola, Miss Molina. He saved me from the one who done this to me, when I was a little boy. Andre and my *tante* were thieves, but they saved my life. So I won't ever rat you out to nobody, much less a shitbird like Pastor Eagleton. Whatever he's got on you, I'll help get you from under."

She punched his shoulder. "Put your shirt on, Jason. Make a pot of *cawfee*, and let's talk."

He set the pot to brew while she took the trash out and scanned for the pastor's truck. They sat cross-legged on the floor with the coffee pot and two paper cups between them.

"I've been clean five years. In the mornings I go to a meeting in Baton Rouge. I was heading back to Ville Platte and took a shortcut through this parish because traffic was backed up on the highway bridge and got pulled over because my tags were expired. The judge violated my probation. I'm doing community service here for the time being."

"Beats jail," Jay said.

She didn't respond.

"Or does it?"

"The pastor can be a hard-ass. As you've learned." She took a long sip of coffee. "Last thing I need is him seeing me stay late with you. Tell me about your *nonc*, Andre."

She used the Cajun for uncle.

"I been away longer than all those kids been alive. Back in high school this boy raped my friend. We killed him, and I went away for it. This all went down in New Jersey, 1985. You can look it up. Know all about me."

"Vengeance is mine." She rolled her head back. "Oh, my Lord."

"I lost everyone. My daddy's in Angola, my mama's on the run somewhere. I just want to see my daddy and find my mama. She's a Calvineau. That's what brought me here."

"This is a lot to take in."

"Eagleton thought I was trying to get in the prison outreach group to get in your jeans," Jay said, blowing on his cup. "You fill them out just fine, but that's not my reason."

"That sounds like something he'd say. What's your reason?"

"With my record, I can't get on Papa Andre's visitor list."

"Why don't you write him?"

Because two weeks ago Jay thought he was dead. And he thought they could trace the letter somehow and get him, put him back inside. The fear was that bad. His stomach in knots at night, knowing he'd have to walk through the prison gates with bullshit papers to see his papa. Going in with a church girl, he might have some cover.

"I'm no good at that." He let the fear show a little.

"I can help."

She took a yellow pad from the script pile and a pen from her carpenter jeans pocket. "You're in the van. That's less than two weeks. I'll get you a church envelope, that'll get priority."

Jay's handwriting was gnarled and the letters ran off the page, sinking off the lines as if drawn down by gravity. She wrote for him as he hunkered over her shoulder, slowly reciting the words, watching her penmanship the same way she had marveled at how quickly he fixed a busted shop vac.

"I pass the post office on the way home." She folded the paper and stuck it in a pre-stamped church envelope she retrieved from her car. "Don't tell Ardith, or we'll both be in trouble. Sometimes this feels like prison."

"This ain't nothing like being inside. It's different in there," he said. "Everyone treats us like they think God expects us to suffer, and they're doing his will."

"That's not His will."

"Okay then, maybe they're the Devil's administration. He reports to the Almighty." Jay chuckled. "How come if he rebelled against God, he's in charge of punishment? Don't make a lick of sense."

"Maybe we can bring that up at the next circle." She got up and slapped the envelope against her thigh. "I've got to get home."

"Go on, I'll close up." Jay winced as he stood.

She put a hand on his ropey forearm. "Are you all right?"

"I'm fine." He tapped his side through his shirt. Smiled with crinkled eyes, like a dog with a limp that's thrilled to see you. "Still hurts sometimes."

"Take care of yourself." Molina turned her head and gave him a chaste side hug. "See you tomorrow."

25: BAD AURA

Beneath Ralph Ora's feet, the house creaked like an old fishing pier. Footsteps crunched over the mouse-turd-flecked junk mail bedding of the human gerbil cage. He knew he should leave, but the HB wouldn't take kindly to him abandoning a house full of guns to thieves or skip tracers without at least trying to defend it.

"Timmy Lee!"

Timmy shuddered but remained silent. He wanted to cry out and tell Ralph where the big Black bastard was hiding, but he was afraid of him. Even though he'd petted his pup Scarlett, while Ralph kicked her every time she got in range.

Scarlett whimpered and wriggled into his armpit. Maybe if they killed the Black bastard, Timmy would get initiated into the Heimdall Brothers. He stored their guns and let them hide out here. Once they'd brought him a skinny white girl who kept sucking snot into the back of her throat. She wore the white wolf ears and tail he'd bought online, but Timmy couldn't get it up. She couldn't compare to the Nazi wolf girls in his imagination.

So one biker fucked her, and the others made Timmy suck them off while he watched. He closed his eyes and pretended he was a Nazi wolf girl servicing her SS masters and stroked his dead grandma's ratty old silver fox stole against his crotch.

Some of them came by when they didn't have a pickup or a delivery. They said his titties were bigger than the meth head girls. They called him Wolfette and branded the Tyr rune of the

Brotherhood on his left tit just like the featherwoods.

Now some big Black buck wanted to take it all away. They ruined everything, just like the HB said.

Ralph didn't call out again. From the creaks, he was in the hallway, breathing heavy. He'd just checked the computer room and would be passing the bathroom soon.

When Ralph had shoved the pool ball in Timmy's mouth, Timmy thought he'd hit gold. Then Ralph left him here in the heat all day, until he couldn't hold it any longer and let out half a turd. Now he was half buried in weapons for the racial holy war. And his collectible cat-girl anime figurines.

The thought of them being damaged curdled Timmy's fear into rage. He didn't care how scary the Black boy was. Ralphie was tough and would kill him. Then they'd celebrate.

He had to die. Breaking into his grandma's house.

But even with the wet turd in his undies, Timmy had gotten a chubby when the big Black bastard had hefted him by his bonds. He clenched his eyes shut against the fantasy of that big Black cock in his face. It disturbed him so much he cried out in warning.

Across the hall, Ralph nearly fired a round into a stack of mops in the shower. The cry came from the bedroom where he'd left the fat weirdo. The door was ajar. He couldn't see the bed where he'd left Timmy tied up. The creep had liked it, thought he was gonna get some cock. Ralph had met his kind in Nasty-Toe-Cheese prison. They liked pussy, but when cock was all that was around, they ate it up like gator sausage.

Ralph kicked the door and it bounced back at him. The fuckers were behind the door. He fired two rounds waist level through the paneling, then the house shook with an impact that set the stacks of boxes collapsing like an imploded building made of guns and dildos and titty magazines.

Ralph fired blindly. Then the world exploded white.

He was on fire and screaming.

* * *

Chopper had squeezed into the bathroom, which was narrower than he was tall. He walked up the walls and rested his shoulder atop a sagging stack of cardboard boxes, leaving one arm free with the Shooter Shorty. When Ora started blasting, he dropped from his perch and fired his opening salvo, a magnesium flashbang round. It blinded the biker and set his clothes on fire.

Chop racked the slide fast and pumped two police rubber riot rounds into the beefy biker's back. They were labeled "less than lethal," but only if compared to a 12-gauge slug or double-aught buckshot.

Ralph Ora forgot to stop, drop, and roll. It was understandable, as his jeans, jacket, and hair were on fire. Little orange meteorites sizzled in his scalp and burned pinholes through his denim jacket. A box stack toppled against Chopper and the shotgun fell. He shoved through the boxes and brought his cane knife down on Ora's gun hand. The dull side. The wrist cracked and the Ruger flopped out and he kicked it away. Ora screamed and rolled onto his back like a dog wriggling in a pile of shit. Chopper stomped him in the crotch and zip tied his wrists together.

Chopper shoulder slammed the bedroom door. He found Timmy Lee Baines with a chunk missing from his forehead. The dog licked frantically at his twitching face.

Things were fucked.

Junior LeFer owed him a few favors, but he couldn't chance it. A Black man with a dead white boy in Calvineau Parish, bounty hunter or not, were not odds he cared to play.

"Burns!" Ora screamed, hunched over his crushed nuts.

Chopper grabbed from a pile of dirty laundry and shoved something moist and stained in Ora's pie hole. He kicked him in the ass until he started crawling through the packrat labyrinth toward the door. The little dog wriggled against Timmy's ruined face, desperate to wake him.

Chopper sucked teeth and scooped the wiener dog into his hoodie.

26: MASKS

The sun made diamonds of the raindrops on Jay's windshield. He ran his thumbprint over the edge of the knife, feeling it yearn to draw blood as he watched Pastor Eagleton from his parking spot on the other side of the gravestones. The pastor stood outside his truck, looking over the grounds. Looking for Jay, so he could tell him to wash it.

He'd washed that truck every day this week. A wipe down after a sun shower wasn't good enough.

"We got the acid rain. Eats through the paint. Why don't you drive down to the store and get some wax, put a few coats on? Just because you're a Calvineau doesn't mean you can succumb to sloth."

Jay had cleaned up two months of leaves and debris in a week. Fixed and tuned every piece of equipment in the shed and the church, down to the gas generator.

Know what the reward for hard work is? Okie had asked. *More work.*

Jay looked down at the blade. Easier to carry than the hatchet, and a similar link to his lost parents. He slipped it into its sheath.

Molina's Subaru sat by the theater. Jay climbed the rusted fleur-de-lis iron fence and slipped in without the pastor seeing him.

Molina was alone. On a ladder, wiring lights.

"Hey."

"Hand me that staple gun, would you?"

He did and braced the ladder. He wanted to climb up behind her, encircle her with his arms. Hold her like a rock, ride out the storm in his chest that desired to thrash him toward a whirlpool of blood.

You don't gotta kill every shitbird that needs killing.

The ladder creaked in his grip. Molina tacked the wire to a beam. He stepped out of her way as she climbed down. She gave a glance to the door.

"I read up on you." She looked in his eyes.

Okie would kill her. Snap her neck, hang her over the top of the ladder and kick it over. They'd find her record, and the church wouldn't want parents knowing they had employed both a junkie and a convicted murderer.

She placed her hand on his heart. "I'm so sorry."

Something broke in his chest at her words. His jaw trembled, his hands fell to his sides. He was no outlaw. Just a scared child wearing a bandit mask.

He slumped as if exorcised. The devil he wished he could be exited him in a ragged breath.

"Inmates try to play us a lot," she said. "You can be yourself, around me. Like you were with the kids that night. You didn't know it, but you looked like you were fifteen years old."

He blinked a few times, breathed deep. Let the masks fall away. He had a wardrobe full.

The dumb worker mask.

The not-so-dumb worker who'll do what you say 'cause you're the boss.

The don't tread on me mask.

The grinning bad boy. The remorseful "I learned my lesson this time" mask.

The emotionless killer, haunted only later by what he'd done.

His natural expression had a touch of weariness from wearing them all.

She hugged him around his arms. "It's all right. You're

forgiven." She squeezed the trembling out of him, and the tears came.

Molina touched the Stanley knife clipped to her pocket. She knew nothing more dangerous than a child with a man's strength. The prison outreach leader had told them that. Their charges were often emotionally stunted and could go from joy to lashing out in anger in a heartbeat. She had seen it in advanced meetings, when someone had a "breakthrough" and a chair sailed across the room, launched by a poltergeist of pent-up rage bottled in them like a ghost trap since childhood.

Jay buried his face in her shoulder and kept his hands at his sides, whispering "thank you" over and over. He thought of her neck broken, tangled in the ladder, how easy that possibility had been. He sank to his knees and looked up to her.

Like the statue of the weary Roman fighter with haunted eyes, she thought. She touched his head. "You're not that boy anymore, Jason. From what I've seen, you're a good man."

He tried to be a good man, like Papa Andre. But he would always be the blue-eyed boy who followed Mister Death.

Molina held her hand palm up. Jay took it, and let her help him to his feet. She pulled a bandanna from her pocket and gave it to him to dry his eyes.

27: WOODY THE FOX

Prison life was one of routine. Andre compared it to marking time between missions. It could drive you bugshit if you didn't spend it wisely. You jingled coins in your pocket, but you never knew when you'd come up empty when Death came to settle your tab. Most soldiers died off base, not in the jungle. You either acclimated to walking alongside Death, or you joined her minions.

Andre had first thought of Death as a man, the reaper, cold and eyeless. Now he saw her as a lady welcoming him to rest his weary head on the lattice of her chest bones, encircled in the shackles of her bony arms.

He saw Death on his last tour. She called him from the steam rising off a rice paddy littered with mines, luring him off the safe path to join her. She had the face of his mother, who died in a wreck when he was a boy.

Little Andre was in the back seat of the Ford on the long ride home from grand-mère's. Mama was tired and she told Andre to sing along to the radio to keep her awake. Tuned to WTIX, they sang to Fats and Little Richard and Big Joe Turner until Lady Death cradled them to her cold bosom to sleep. The Ford crumpled on a bridge abutment, and the policeman who pulled Andre alive from the wreck cried that it was a miracle.

Andre only knew he'd failed his mama and let her die. He had a busted arm to remind him of his failure whenever the weather turned cold.

He was nearly done with the warden's chifforobe, giving him a few weeks to make pieces to sell. The sun had been on his mind, and he'd collected scraps of tiger maple all year. He sketched out a sunburst. Death had become a woman who would welcome him home, but the sun had always been the searing eye of God. As the knot behind his ribs grew, his past misdeeds played in his mind, warring with the kindness and virtue.

He knew which side would win.

Andre went to work. Pierced ivy doors, jigsawed by hand. He took his set of rasps from a locker and sat filing in details by a window, soaking up heat from the cloud-smothered sun. The rain had blown away but the chill remained in the stone walls and floor. Before he could get into a good pace, a tall dark man with natural hair clipped in a manner forty years out of style blocked his light.

Andre looked up. "Good morning, Fox."

Wilbert "Woody" Foxton had survived over fifty years of incarceration and twice dodged the lightning in the now-retired Louisiana electric chair. He was far from the oldest inmate, but had earned the mantle of prison elder, peacemaker, and Pulitzer-prize-winning writer over the decades. The warden despised him but could not hurt him directly without damaging his cover as a hard but fair man who only wanted to mete out justice while respecting the taxpayer's dollar.

Fox smiled but his face carried the weariness of his life in the cage. "I'm told He of the Hammers wants to grab that poker chip one more time."

"I was told that too," Andre said, setting down his tools and standing in respect.

"The Fox will have your back. It will stick in LeFer's craw. And we just might survive. But I don't deal in flesh."

"Loyalty ain't flesh."

"Is when it's bought."

Puzzlement pinched Andre's deep-set eyes tighter. "I'm no do-gooder like you, I'm just an old coon-ass who wasn't raised to respect man's law."

"Helping you hurts LeFer," the Fox said. He held out a soft hand, only the fingertips calloused from hitting typewriter keys. "And you're a thorn in the side to the Calvineaus. I'm tired of them bleeding my people to fuel their hate."

Andre nodded. Evangeline had told him her family history. It wasn't his fight, but the knob of gristle behind his rib tightened like a fist in solidarity. How long did he have before it put him in Point Lookout? You needed something to live for, if you were gonna beat the big C.

Like one last act of rebellion against the biggest sons of bitches in the Pelican State.

Andre gripped the Fox's hand.

28: GONE MAMA GONE

Evangeline roared the Dodge across the Pontchartrain Causeway toward Bogue Chitto. As she cut around a slow-moving double semi, lightning flickered through a wall of thunderheads looming off in the Gulf, threatening to stampede. She fingered the checkered grips of her Colt Diamondback in the cup holder.

Pitou had closed his fancy knife shop in the Quarter. The sign read *On Vacation* but she knew he'd been warned. He forged his blades in a workshop north of the city that he thought was secret.

She wished she'd kept Ti' Boy's rifle. Pitou had once thrown a Randall knife twenty yards and stuck it clean through a mirliton squash as tiny as a politician's heart.

Paying the bridge toll put a bad taste in her mouth. Like the instant grits she'd been served up north, at one of their cute chrome railroad car diners, unseasoned and gummy as library paste. But the causeway cut an hour off the trip.

Once she and Andre went outlaw, they lived in places she never knew existed, on the edge of the bayous where she met the descendants of the enslaved people whose blood and sweat enriched the Calvineau family. They told of their memaws with backs striped with scars, and how they were made to dig a hole in the dirt for their swollen belly to lie in and protect their baby from the whip. Not because they held a precious child, but because of the child's worth at the slave market in New Orleans.

The lies she'd been raised on came crashing down.

Her mother taught her that the North was jealous of the South's fruitful harvests and superior trade routes and wanted to poison their land with industry and their uncouth ways. Growing up in clover, Evangeline thought she'd earned it somehow, by being her daddy's pretty youngest girl.

The shame of how stupid she'd been still stung.

She remembered a gentle groundskeeper named Mamou. Flashes of skinning her knee as a toddler and being cradled in big tender hands and brought to her mama. She had asked Ella about him. She said he left to live with his family.

Drusilla, one of the old women who lived on Bayou Vipère, told her the truth. Evangeline's older sister had taken too much of a liking to him. A silly young girl crush had been enough to seal Mamou's fate.

Samuel Calvineau and four other men came to Mamou's shack with ax handles and shotguns, not even bothering to hide their faces. They broke his arms and legs in front of his wailing family, bound him in barbed wire, and tossed him in the trunk of her daddy's long black Cadillac. They drove him out to the bayou and dumped him in a gator hole. They laughed and drank whiskey while Mamou tore himself bloody as he struggled to stay afloat, and pairs of gleaming orange eyes and maws of white teeth came to fight over his bobbing, screaming body and rend him apart limb by limb.

Calvineau gift wrap, they called it.

When Okie brought them in on their first heists, Evangeline demanded they hit Calvineau family interests. Juke joints that played Johnny Rebel records, which her family financed. Businesses who paid to use chain gang labor. Payroll trucks that came from the Calvineau Parish bank. Jewelry shops all over the state, even when under mob protection. Their victims didn't dare fight back, knowing she was part of the crew. So much as bruise her fair skin, and they'd join Mamou in the gator hole.

Despite the evils of present and past, she only felt at home in

Louisiana. She'd returned north only once, when the Yankee warden who'd killed Okie retired to the Jersey Shore.

His boat was named the *Something Stupid* and he headed out early for stripers and fluke in the summer. She watched him for two days, then it rained for a week straight, so she holed up in a fleabag shore motel until the weather broke, letting her hatred smolder.

Then as the former warden of Rahway prison slow-motored out into the sunrise off Lanoka Harbor as the mist burned off the bay, she crawled out of the cabin of his Sundancer 260 and shot him in the knee. She took the billy club he used to subdue bluefish and worked him over as she imagined her father had done to Mamou, and the warden's men had done to Okie with their batons. Then she rolled him over the transom and christened him with a bucket of chum.

There were no sharks or big blues running to end his gurgles and wails. She smoked three Winstons before he went under for the last time.

It didn't bring Okie back, but it felt good.

Just not as good as Okie had.

Andre had understood. He exuded a calm manliness that shielded his big heart, and together they'd forged bonds no hammer could break. There was something about that grinning red devil Okie Kincaid that set her off. It was plain Satanic. His raw bravado, and the copperhead tattoo coiled around his left arm. Like Eve and the snake, she wanted what he was selling.

It wasn't something she expected anyone else to understand. Andre knew her heart like his own. She would die to set him free. Every rodeo, she passed a wad of cash to the old biddy running the bursar's window at the craft show so she'd look the other way while she and Andre slipped into the ladies' room for a bunny fuck.

Now Andre had the cancer. The kind you don't always survive when you're a rich man, much less a poor Cajun boy with five more years before he could max out of Angola.

The low rumble of a truck's engine braking rose above the distant thunder. She pulled into the shoulder to pass and flicked the flashers on. Red and blue flashed far ahead. The police knew her plates. Unless she had a dead white child stuck in the grille, they were unlikely to pull her over.

At the head of the jam was a roadblock. She took her Calvineau license from the console and touched the button to lower the driver's side window. A police Explorer backed up to cut off the shoulder. She stomped the brake pedal barefoot and skidded to a stop, scattering road debris.

A cruiser squeezed through traffic to block her retreat. She shifted into reverse. The Dodge Hemi had enough torque to push it clear back to New Orleans.

"Get the fuck out my way if you want to see your families tonight."

"Miss Evangeline!" A man's silhouette filled her side mirror. The lawman patted the roof of the car with a gloved hand, like he was calming a horse. "Don't think my daddy the warden would like me come home missing more parts." The handsome, clean-shaven face of Sheriff Junior LeFer smiled down. "Let's be civil."

"I ain't going to that evil house, Junior. You know that."

"And I'm not asking you to. It's the boy they want."

She knew the boy was in state. Gallivanting around like a fool in that purple car. She'd raised him smarter than that, but he had a reckless heart, like Okie.

"You think I'm gonna let them poison my son like they did my sister, you're dumber than a box of cocks."

"You know Andre doesn't have much time. Spend it with him. All you have to do is bring the boy home and get him to stay. They got a pocket judge ready to commute Andre's sentence and a bed waiting at Our Lady of the Lake."

Her boy Jay was fresh blood. A breeding stud to rekindle the dead family line.

"Look me in the eye so I can see you're not lying."

He leaned down to look into her fierce steely eye.

"I would never intentionally—"

She gripped him by the testicles and shifted into drive.

"If I goose the accelerator, I might not get away, but you'll be keeping your balls warm in your ankle socks for the rest of your life."

He closed his gloved hand around her wrist. "Easy, Miss Evangeline," he said through gritted teeth. "I've always been fair to you."

"That's why I ain't ripped these off yet." She eased off the brake pedal and the car began to roll forward.

Junior LeFer tiptoed along like a toddler taking his first steps, bracing himself against the roof. "You know I have no choice."

She gave his crotch an appreciative squeeze. "Everyone's got a choice, Junior. When's enough money enough?"

He gritted his teeth. "I've seen junkies go clean and sing in choirs. Once a man's rich, though…"

She twisted his nuts like a rusty doorknob. "Clear the bridge, or I'm gonna hang these like fuzzy dice from my rearview mirror."

"Wilson! Move that damn vehicle!"

The Explorer's window slid down. "You said she was a dangerous fugitive."

"I am," Evangeline called, shifting to neutral and revving. "And I'm about to stretch the Sheriff's scrote as big as a bedsheet, if all y'all don't scooch your asses outta my way."

29: BLOOD IS EVERYTHING

The pastor treated Jay differently once he knew he had Calvineau blood. Less like a thoroughbred he owned, and more like a rival lion. But an animal, all the same.

He didn't like Jay mowing the lawn while he gave the afternoon service to the old white ladies who came every day before supper. So Jay pruned the tree branches hanging low over the convict graves, out of sight. He watched the well-dressed women file to their Buicks and Lincolns, and they watched him back.

He headed to his room to clean up.

Pastor Eagleton stood at the back door, smoking a cigarette. He usually wasn't around after services unless he was directing choir. He snapped his fingers. "Where do you think you're going?"

Jay didn't answer. Taking orders had begun to grate on him, in a parish that bore his name.

"Ardith says the ladies' room is filthy."

"I'll clean it." Jay reached for the doorknob.

Eagleton gripped his shoulder. The man's fingernails were manicured, the hands soft but strong. "Did you notice how the old jezebels looked at you? You inflame their carnal desires." His teeth had a translucent glow. "I ought to have you polish the pews during services and see how many die of the vapors."

"You want, I can scrub down the whole church."

"We've got the old Black gals for that. No one cleans like

they can. It's in their blood. Just clean up that filthy mess, then come to the office when you're done." He took another drag.

Jay left him there.

A tampon wrapped in toilet paper graced the trashcan, and someone had baptized the toilet seat with a tinkle. Jay mopped the bathroom floor and wiped down the porcelain in case the pastor decided to come in with a white glove.

Molina's car was in front of the theater when he returned. He found her opening the makeshift theater.

"Hey, Jason. We're not having a circle tonight. Just rehearsing."

"That's fine." Jay broke out a chipped-tooth smile. "I was gonna ask you on a date."

"We're not in high school." She raised a shield of coolness in her eyes.

"I'm just tired of eating alone. And you're good to talk to."

"It's not a good idea. The pastor wouldn't approve."

"Don't you need to tell me about the prison outreach?"

She thought on it a while. "Meet me by Mike the Tiger, tonight at nine. If he likes you, maybe we'll go to the Chimes."

In the office, Pastor Eagleton rubbed Miss Ardith's shoulders while she stretched out her arms and wiggled her fingers as if playing an invisible piano. He had his thumbs deep into her dowager's hump. "Oh, that's better. I can feel my pinkies again."

"The ladies' room is clean," Jay said. He waited to be dismissed, out of habit.

"Wash up, De-monde. You've been invited to supper with the Calvineaus."

Ardith sighed. "You are blessed."

"Not blessed," the pastor said. "Chosen."

"Whiterose is simply a gorgeous plantation," Ardith waxed. "Mrs. Hesper's roses are world champions. Whenever I visit for

Plantation Days, I'm a little girl again. Reminds me of when times were good."

Good for her kind, at least. "I'm honored. Thank you, sir."

"Don't thank me yet." He smiled and sat on the corner of Ardith's desk. "Put on your best clean shirt and scrub the dirt out of your boots."

"I have a pair of clean shoes. What's the address?"

The pastor chuckled. "I'll drive, Jason. We need to talk about your future. Wait by my truck."

He took Ardith's hands in his, thumbs stroking the veins. "Let's pray, darlin'."

Jay closed the door.

As he showered, ice hit his belly. *They'll wrap you in barbed wire and feed you to the beast.*

30: CHOPPED

Chopper knew his hearing had come back when he heard Ralph Ora moan through the plexiglass barrier in the back of his truck. He turned up the stereo. The bluesy rock of Clutch's "From Beale Street to Oblivion" drowned out the biker's complaints.

His bounty was chained in the K-9 cage in the back of his Tahoe, hidden by limo tint. Leg chains ran through an eyelet on the floor, and his cuffed hands hung from a D-ring bolted through the roof. Ora had two purple welts the size of tennis balls on his bare back. His jacket smoldered in the back seat, and smelled like meat that had gone off, sizzling on the grill.

Chopper let him moan. He shot Timmy Baines, and now Chopper was stuck with the dead boy's wiener dog.

It burrowed into a pair of its owner's sweat shorts on the passenger seat.

"Come on, man. I gotta piss. You hit my kidney."

The cage had a Weather-Tek liner deep enough to hold four inches of fluid. Chopper kept a bottle of bleach for cleanup.

"There's a hundred grand worth of guns in that house. You turn back, cut me loose, we split it. Why should the pigs get it?"

Chopper veered into the shoulder to flatten a dead armadillo. The rear axle bounced, and Ora's arms yanked against the cuffs.

"Fuck! You broke my wrist. It hurts!"

He pulled off the highway and followed an oil company road near Bayou Vipère, where every Christmas, families built tall bonfires atop the levees to guide Santa Claus to bayou country. The levees were bare, the driveways empty. Parents at work, kids at school. He took a road to a dump site where locals burned trash.

He killed the engine and let Ora stew in the heat. The windows began to fog immediately. He checked the chamber of the compact nine he kept inside his belt, then stepped out to survey the polluted beauty of the marshlands.

Chop looked out into the bayou over the burned-out fifty-five-gallon drums and smashed television sets pocked with bullet holes. The refinery tang was a comforting smell from childhood.

His folks were out there somewhere.

They had worked all their lives and their retirement had been stolen by the double whammy of Katrina and the recession. They had paid off the house, then the Amite floods turned it into a mold garden. Now they led a community of like-minded people who had given up on the system.

Chopper and Suzane thought the world was still worth fighting for. It was a source of contention every time he took a flatboat to his parents' compound and asked them to protect a witness.

But he was beginning to agree with his folks. People didn't care about changing a corrupt world, as long as it worked for *them*.

He raised the lift gate.

"Know you ain't gonna kill me, dog. Rosie won't pay." He spat a red loogie on Chopper's jacket.

Chopper took a wide zip tie out of his pocket and looped it around the broken arm, up near the elbow. Tightened it like a belt around the Sailor Jerry-style mermaid on Ora's forearm, then cinched it into a corset.

"You killed that boy. I'm getting my bounty, then they'll nail you for it."

"In that hood? That corner boy'll probably steal my bike and the guns. But I'll tell my warlord you did. Then you'll have the Heimdall Brotherhood on your ass. How you like that, boy?"

The HB was a pissant Outlaw Motorcycle Club that ran meth and trafficked women. They'd been around for decades, tied somehow to rebel hate music that played on jukeboxes across the South. The guns were a new angle. As was a safe house in a mostly Black neighborhood. That did not fit with their white supremacist ethos.

Chop let Clutch finish the long cut of "Electric Worry," then turned back. Ora's right hand had turned purple. "My hand's going numb."

"Tell me what the guns are for, Ralph." He dropped the street accent he'd used to frighten Timmy and switched to the educated flat tone that served him well at his Baton Rouge magnet school. It delighted teachers, but it also really pissed off racist cracker motherfuckers who thought, rightly so, that he thought he was better than they were.

"HB's got sick motherfuckers who like to run trains on you Black boys. How's that for a change?"

His uncle had told him the white men did that on the plantations, to crush the souls of the enslaved. They called it buck breaking. He was not surprised the practice had been revived.

"Cut me loose and they won't know your name."

"My name's Chopper. You're gonna learn how I got that name." He cut the mermaid tattoo's throat with a whisper slash.

Ora gritted his teeth and swore.

"Folks burn trash out here. You toe through the ashes with your boots, you'll find bones. I left a lotta hands here, and there's a lot of you race war crackers with only one hand left to wipe their ass."

"I ain't one of them. I joined up to protect my ass in Nasty-Toe-Cheese. They don't tell me nothing."

"A boy named Keshawn went missing in Jeannetta."

People didn't know what they knew. Get them blubbering, and they often let out words with import they didn't understand, like a holy roller speaking in tongues. "You blew Timmy's brains out before I could talk to him. Tell me more about those buck breakers who like Black boys. And before you answer, let me tell you from experience, Rosie will pay me the same whether I haul you in with two hands or one."

Ralph jerked his cuffs and tried to turn so Chopper couldn't get a good swing at the swollen hand. "I just heard talk! I was trying to scare you."

He ran the blade along Ora's hairy knuckle and shaved it clean.

"Timmy jerked off by the window. But I ain't into chicken."

Chopper cinched a tie around Ralph's pinky finger. "You have Japanese sleeves like a Yakuza. You know what they do when they've dishonored themselves?"

"I swear! I can't get a nut off on a child like that. I like big ol' seventies bush and blondes with big titties! With the veins showing through like blue cheese! I swear on my mother!"

Chopper wiped his blade on the "Mom" heart tattoo on Ralph's deltoid. He had to say he appreciated the man's classic ink. Other than the Heimdall rune, he didn't have the usual cliche skulls, nooses, knives, and iron crosses found on Nazi losers.

He let him breathe for a while.

"You owe me at least one finger. Give me something, Ralph. Did Timmy and the buck breakers take Keshawn? That place stank like a fuck palace."

"Fuck you."

He tossed a handful of zip ties at Ralph's face. "One knuckle at a time. I got tourniquets, tampons, and anticoagulant powders. I'll cut on you as long as it takes. You'll live. You won't want to, but you will. Hobbling around Angola on a life beef, sporting HB ink. You think they'll protect you when you can't work for them?" He nicked the webbing of his thumb.

"I work with my hands! Uh, there was a steel and chrome monster cruising the hood. It was one of those old hoopties you boys like to put dubs on."

Chopper let that go. His phone buzzed in the pattern he used for Suzane. He ignored it.

"I saw it turn the corner, then flashes of it between the houses as it tore ass out of there."

He had pissed his jeans, and the musty smell mixed with the chemicals of the refinery, souring Chopper's childhood reverie. "What kind of car?"

"I dunno, man! I just know bikes."

"Get a color?"

"It was dark. Blue, purple, black."

Chopper answered the phone and gave Ora his back. "Sweetness."

"I told you what I know!" Ora shouted. "I get nerve damage, how'm I gonna ink a good line?"

"Who's that?" Suzane asked.

"I checked Keshawn's neighbors, got a hit. It's a big mess, but I got an HB turd who's talking. Gonna follow where it leads."

"Keshawn went to a charter school for science. He won a scholarship from Calvineau Parish First Evangelical Church."

The Calvineaus bestowed great largesse upon poor Black families so they could deny that the parish that bore their name seceded to avoid integration. "Is there a pattern?"

"Maybe. Tamica was tutored by senior girls also from that church." Tamica was last year's victim. They were both haunted by how close she'd felt at first, and the coldness of her trail. "It's more than we've got. Just be careful."

"I'm gonna lose my hand and you're on a booty call!" Ora shouted.

"I will." He knew to watch his step in Calvineau Parish. "See me tonight."

She made him wait a standing eight count. "Be outside when I turn out the lights." She hung up. She never allowed herself much time. They would have a few hours at most.

He took his frustrations out on Ora's bruised kidney with a snappy jab. When he stopped wheezing, he said, "Tell me about the guns."

"The RaHoWa, dumbass! The racial holy war. It's all the Heimdalls talk about. Banshees called 'em the Hitler Bitches behind their backs."

Chopper snipped the zip tie with a multitool. Cheap guns in Black neighborhoods. An excuse to kill out of fear.

Ralph groaned and kneaded his wrist. "You done ruined my hand for fine work."

"Where you're going, it's all Bic pens and sewing needles."

Ralph pointed his nose at a fine black-and-white rendering of Ozzy Osbourne peeking out the armpit of his black T-shirt. "I did that with an electric toothbrush in Corcoran." It was copied from the album cover of *Diary of a Madman*.

"Ozzy wasn't the same after he left Sabbath."

"Yeah but he's still good. Those first three albums with Randy Rhoads? Don't tell me you've heard better."

Rhoads was a guitar genius. His uncle had introduced him to the man's pealing chords. Chopper remembered how his heart broke when he learned the man making that beautiful music had died the year he was born.

Chopper gave him a bottle of water and closed the lift gate before he started thinking of him as human.

Ralph Ora whined the whole way to Rosie's Bail Bonds. Rosie smiled around his dead cigar when Chop dragged his skip in.

And spat out the stogie when Chopper dropped the yipping wiener dog into his wide lap.

31: EAT THE RICH

The inside of Pastor Eagleton's Cadillac truck was cold as a morgue. Jay counted highway signs to get his bearings. Ardith had brought him a musty black suit jacket from a closet, and he'd polished his prison brogans to a dull sheen.

The pastor remained silent as they joined the snarl of Baton Rouge commuter traffic, which was worthy of New Jersey these days. Lucinda Williams sang out the speakers. Ahead, a police cruiser sat in the greenway.

"You look afraid to meet them. You shouldn't be. They don't choose just any riff-raff to sit at their table."

"Suit just itches."

"Do you know what it means to be chosen, Jay?" The pastor gripped his forearm.

Jay tugged the door handle, but it was child-locked.

"Relax. No need to play your charade anymore, *Jason Demonde.*" He chuckled. "The healer of the world! You are, from the Calvineau perspective. Your grandparents have waited a long time for their little Joshua to return home."

"My name is Jay Desmarteaux." He slowly twisted the pastor's wrist away.

"You were born Joshua Lee Calvineau. The child who was taken."

"What gave me away?"

"You're not as smart as you think. Remember that. Now, let

me give you a taste of the power our blood conveys."

The pastor eased onto the shoulder toward the cruiser. He tapped a button that lowered Jay's window. The trooper looked up from the screen where he read scanned license tags for violations. "Yessir, Pastor Eagleton?"

"Good evening, Officer. I'd like to introduce you to a member of the Calvineau family, Jay Desmarteaux. We're going to dinner at Whiterose. Could you give us an escort through this mess?"

The officer chewed his lip for a moment. "Yessir, just follow me."

"Thank you kindly." He closed the tinted window. The cruiser's lights flashed on, and with a bark of the siren, it rolled onto the shoulder. They followed nearly nose to bumper, kicking up gravel and debris.

He kept silent as the trooper cleared them to the interstate onramp. The Escalade roared away with a honk of thanks, and they took the left lane toward the Atchafalaya.

Jay made note of the way.

"Do you remember your real mother?"

Jay didn't remember killing the Witch. But he remembered enough.

"A little."

"Before you were stolen away by the whore Evangeline?"

Jay rubbed the knuckles of his index fingers with his thumbs, a tactic the prison shrink said helped tame impulses. Such as the one telling him to chop the pastor's throat and dump him over the concrete barrier into the Atchafalaya.

"Mama Evangeline and Papa Andre were good to me." They had found him nearly dead of dehydration and burned the Witch's trailer to hide little Jay's crime.

"Your mother died of grief. She burned herself up with a cigarette in her hand. That's what your grandparents believe, and it would behoove you not to claim otherwise. Mother Hesper will not tolerate it, and you will never see your jailbird stepfather again."

Jay looked at the highway merging to a pinprick, a vanishing future.

"If you want to see Andre Desmarteaux this side of the grave, be on your best behavior at dinner this evening. Your grandmother doesn't take kindly to guff or backtalk. And she's holds a cold place in her heart for the man who stole her baby daughter away."

They cut across the bridge over Bayou Vipère and followed a levee road to into Calvineau Parish, cradled in a tangled offshoot of the Atchafalaya. What was once fields of indigo and sugar cane sowed with enslaved blood had been sold off into parcels of working farms. Tractors kicked up clouds of dirt as they tilled unplanted land. Breaking the flatlands was a double row of towering live oaks, leading two a white two-story plantation that backed onto the shimmering waters of the bayou.

Jay looked up through the sunroof as they rode under the enormous oak boughs. As they neared the plantation, its name became evident. Rose bushes surrounded it, the white blossoms so close together they resembled sea foam, with the big house rising from it like a castle in mist.

They parked in front of a two-story carriage house that had been converted to a garage. The bayou smelled of fish spawning. The pastor whistled as they walked to the servant door at the back of the big house. "I'm afraid we're not front door folk, even if you are a grandson. But there are other rewards beyond belief."

They were met by a tall, older Black woman dressed in gray, her hair tied in a tight bun.

"Good evening, Ella."

"You're late, come quickly, Mister Roy."

"Early is late," Pastor Eagleton said as they quick-stepped to keep pace. "Forget that at your peril."

32: THE HEAVENLY TABLE

The dining room had a stunning view of the bayou through the open shutters on the left and paintings of the Calvineau family on the right. The portraits mimicked the colonial style, a genealogical tableau of pirates and Scots and templars centering around a painting of Calvary, with Jesus stepping down off the cross.

Ella pulled out a hand-carved wooden chair. Jay froze. The snarling face of a wild man was carved on the back.

Papa Andre's work. The Rougarou.

Eleven others circled the sturdy oak table, with the thirteenth empty beneath the painting of the Savior, waiting for his return.

Jay sat. The table was set in silver, and ribbed Wedgwood china plates with gray bands of red and white flowers. A roast seeped red on a platter at the center. At the head of the table, a painting of a stately tall couple in white, a daughter at each side. One was a young, golden-haired Mama Evangeline, the other her dark-haired sister, whose eyes Jay could not meet.

Beneath the painting of their younger selves sat his grandparents.

Time had not been kind.

The painting of Hesper Joy Calvineau glowed fairly with saintly motherhood. The woman smiling at him from the head of the table was a vulturous caricature of her former self.

Pastor Eagleton kissed her cheek, then sat in the chair to her left.

"You're late, Cousin Roy."

"Forgive us, Mother Hesper. The traffic in Baton Rouge is truly devilish."

"Just this once, because you brought our grandchild." She pinned Jay with her hawk eyes. "Give us a prayer."

Samuel Joseph Calvineau gripped a butter knife in his left hand. He was as drawn and lanky as Don Quixote, as if leeches and lampreys had attached themselves beneath his suit and sucked the meat and blood from his frame. His right arm hung limp. A skinny Black teenage boy stood stiff at his side, eyes staring straight ahead.

Pastor Roy folded his hands and bowed his head. In his deep sermon voice he said, "Lord thank you for this meal, and for bringing Joshua back to the family. Thank you for choosing us to serve at your right hand."

"Amen."

The only commandment they give a damn about is Honor Thy Mother and Father, Mama Evangeline had said. *And you'd best not take the goddamned Lord's name in vain.*

Ella made Jay a plate and set it before him. The servant teen at Father Calvin's side began cutting his meat into tiny gray shreds without a word. He'd seen anger, and Jay knew how he felt.

They ate in silence. Jay choked down a few bites, avoiding the eyes of the Witch on the wall above. An ice cold fist closed around his heart and he gripped his silver table knife. In his mind her eyeless sockets swarmed with maggots.

She glared at Jay's plate. "Eat, boy. We don't allow just anyone our table. And we do not suffer disrespect."

Jay cut himself a stub of carrot.

She cut herself a morsel and ground it between little teeth. "If you behave, you may join your birthright. Would you like that?"

"Yes, ma'am," Jay coughed. He sipped water from a hazy crystal glass.

Father Samuel honked.

"He says speak up, boy." Roy grinned, chewing a rare cut.

"Yes, ma'am," Jay nearly shouted.

Father Samuel raised his butter knife like a scepter and bellowed like a baying coonhound. The servant jolted back.

"Father says our doors have always been open to you, Joshua. Our daughter should have come to us when you had your troubles. But no, she has become a spiteful child. Perhaps you can persuade her to come to our table."

"She is not easily persuaded," Jay said.

"She risked it all for you, Joshua," Pastor Roy said. "Don't underestimate yourself. We think you can bring her back into the fold. In fact, we're depending on it. But you didn't come to your family out of the goodness of your heart, did you?"

Jay waited for the pastor to continue. "Sir?"

Hesper perked her painted-on eyebrows. "We know you are not simple, Joshua. Cousin Roy says you came home seeking something. To what do we owe the honor of your presence?"

"I would like to see my father Andre very much."

Father Calvin loosed a bark that echoed off the windows. The serving boy dropped the spoon and his back hit the wall.

"Leave us," Mother Hesper snapped. "Clean up later."

The boy marched to the kitchen without a word.

"That riff-raff is not our blood. We had Evangeline's marriage to him annulled. And his name will not be spoken in this house."

Pastor Roy smiled slyly, eating without a word.

"How would you like me to refer to him, ma'am?" Jay gripped the knife.

She set down her fork. "I'd prefer you not refer to him at all!"

"Then you are unlikely to see Evangeline this side of the grave. We are a family bonded by more than blood. And holding him hostage only turns us against you."

Hesper bared gray little teeth. "How has this lowlife earned your loyalty?"

"I wouldn't be here without him," Jay said. Icy fingers twisted his gut as he spoke. "He and Mama Evangeline saved me."

The table shook and the china rattled under Old Man Calvineau's fist. He bayed once more and choked on his spit. Mother slapped him on the back and Ella held a crystal glass of water to his mouth. "Saved you from what, exactly?"

Jay turned the knife over in his hand. It wasn't weighted for throwing, but he considered it. "Depravity."

Hesper shook with a piercing titter of a laugh. "We do not talk about such things at this table."

"Forgive him, Mother," Pastor Roy said. "He was but a child whose head they filled with falsehoods."

Father Samuel folded his arm. Mother dabbed at her eyes with an embroidered kerchief.

Kill them with kindness, Mama Evangeline had said, when Yankee teachers or affluent parents looked down on him for being country. Jay clenched his jaw to swallow their lies.

"I'm sorry, ma'am. It won't happen again. But don't you think...*he* has earned redemption?"

She tittered again. "Redemption? Is that what you think prison is for? Do you feel... redeemed for axing that little Yankee boy to death?"

He did not. His only remorse was for the time lost.

She tittered her warning birdcall. "You were not imprisoned to be redeemed or rehabilitated. You were there to be *punished*. Foolishly, because you are among the chosen, young man. My thankless daughter could have called upon us, and you would have walked free. Imagine, a Calvineau suffering for taking the life of perverted Yankee trash! It pains my heart." She pointed a wizened dagger of a finger his way. "Do you know what it means to be chosen? Tell him, Cousin Roy."

"Joshua," Roy set down his silverware. "Those chosen to wield the sword of the Almighty are not to be judged for their deeds upon this Earth by man's law. We have our seat at the heavenly table."

Roy stood, "Will you wield the sword with us, Joshua?"

"If I can see my father," Jay said, and raised his table knife, the serrations red with flesh. "I will."

Mother Hesper's eyes glossed with emotion. "It will be done."

33: THE BEAST

Lightning struck purple over the black waters of Bayou Vipère and a crack of thunder thumped in Jay's chest. He was sent to the parlor while Pastor Roy spoke with the elders and had slipped out the rear door.

Ella followed him and stood by the doorway. No sign of the boy servant. The parlor was a museum piece. It exerted a pressure, like being at the bottom of a pool. "Miss Ella? Would you be so kind as you make me a cup of coffee, please?"

"I can make tea, Mister Jay."

"That would be fine. Thank you, Miss Ella."

Her crepe sole shoes walked silently to the kitchen.

Jay padded out in the other direction. The house was dim with old sconce lighting. One room had the door closed and light from under it. He knocked.

No answer.

He opened it after a ten count.

The boy stood by a single bed, holding an old book.

Jay closed the door behind him. "I'm not one of them. If you want to leave, I'll bring you wherever you want. They can't stop me. Do you want to go home?"

The boy shook his head.

"You afraid they'll do something bad?"

The boy nodded.

"To you?"

"To my mom."

Jay nodded back, gritting his teeth. Threats were the monster's language. Guilt over what they might deliver to his mother would make the boy endure their torments. Jay wanted to take the house and its occupants apart joint by joint.

"I'm Jay. What's your name?"

"Keshawn." A croak.

A distant whistle. The tea kettle. Keshawn's eyes darted to the door.

"I'll be back, Keshawn. And I won't let them hurt your mama."

Jay sat in the parlor.

Ella brought the tea on a platter. "Did you find the facilities?"

"Yes, thank you."

He added milk and blew on the cup.

"I knew your Mama Evangeline."

Jay looked up. Her eyes were sharp, the irises ringed in deep brown like old earth.

"She means well, but she doesn't understand what she's up against."

"Keshawn ain't the first, is he?"

"Nor will he be the last." Her eyes were unreadable.

Jay set down his cup. "I'm gonna bring Miss Evangeline home. And we're gonna clean house."

Ella chuckled. "Are you, now?"

Outside, rain pattered on the boughs overhead. Jay dashed into the open garage, breathing in the scent of old engine oil and stale air from cobwebbed corners. He needed air.

Lightning flashed close, illuminating the chrome shark fins and teeth of the grille so brightly that he jumped back into a shelf of old tools. His eyes adjusted.

A gleaming black predator formed in the gloom. He touched the cold fender, slippery with countless coats of wax. He walked its perimeter, one hand on the sleek metal. The roof was brushed stainless steel. The fin points sharp as Bowie knives. Had to be twenty feet long. A big black whale.

The killer variety.

His friend Tony the car nut had told him about the Cadillac Eldorado Brougham. The 1957 was the peer of the Rolls Royce, perhaps even besting it, for the title of greatest hand-built vehicle of the postwar era.

Jay pushed the button on the door handle and it opened silently on oiled hinges. The leather seat cradled him. He slipped off his wet shoes and wriggled his stocking feet deep into the sheepskin carpeting, still soft as a spring lamb. The cabin smelled of leather and polish and something dank and sweet, like the sea creature it resembled.

His hands brushed the keys hanging from the ignition. He gave it a turn and a rumble emanated through the cabin, like he was Jonah in the whale.

He dreamt of sharking the asphalt seas behind the wheel. The highway ahead infinite. The rearview mirror slicked ruby with blood.

He could take a tire iron and end their evil right now. Then close the garage doors, start the motor, and dream forever.

The bleat of a horn brought him back. The rain settled to a whisper. He killed the engine, feeling a static spark as his fingers left the keys.

How long had he been sitting there?

He padded out the way he came and found Pastor Roy in the driver's seat of the white Escalade. The windows were down. "Mother Hesper bade you good night. They retire early. Get in."

As Jay reached for the door handle, the locks clicked shut. "You will get your wish and be reunited with your errant stepfather. But first you must bring your Aunt Evie…the woman you call Mama Evangeline, home."

Jay looked down. Beads of rain dotted the door handle like fat pearls.

"Will you?"

Jay nodded. The doors unlocked. He smoothed the pearls away and climbed in.

"Little Miss Evie has vengeance in her heart, and that makes her weak. Tomorrow, you will see Shooter Boudreaux. And you will bring their wayward daughter home."

As Roy pulled away, Jay looked back at the plantation. In the one lit window, Mother Hesper's silhouette broke the yellow glow, and the long branches of the live oaks reached out like claws, as if to drag him back before the lady of the house.

34: TABASCO ROAD

Andre sawed out the busted glass window of his Mustang with a garrote of baling wire and swept out the shards. It was parked under the boat port behind the house where Leonce Pitou lived with his mama. Mam' Pitou made him a pallet in her parlor and heated up gumbo for him and her boy to eat. Leonce was her youngest.

She watched toothlessly from a wicker chair as he taped a clear plastic tarp where the rear window of his Mustang had been, then filled the dents with red lead and sanded it down before noon, when Evangeline had said to pick her up for ice cream.

The sun came up hard but failed to burn off the insistent rain. He cleaned up the boat port and brought Mrs. Pitou a cup of chicory coffee. Leonce snored on the couch.

"My father used to say when the sun shined in the rain, the Devil was beating his wife."

She drank the coffee scalding hot and gave an empty smile. "She ought to beat him sometime."

"We'd be better off if she did."

"You be safe now. Them Calvineaus been doing evil since Cain killed his brother."

The tarp flapped as he roared the Mustang toward the plantation on Bayou Vipère.

Evangeline ran out from the driveway in clamdigger jeans and a white blouse and threw a purse into the back seat the size of his seabag. She leaned over and planted a kiss hard on his cheek. "I missed you fierce. Let's get the Sam Hill out of here."

"You can say hell, Evie."

She blushed. "Guess I can. Get me the hell out of here, Desmarteaux!"

The tires left twin rooster tails of dirt and pecan shells.

The ice cream shop had lost power in the hard rain and they found the owner pouring tubs of melted treats down the gutter in a white-and-pink swirl, his mutt dog lapping at the stream.

"Well don't that just figure." She unfolded a bus schedule from her purse. "We got an hour. Why don't you take me someplace you like to eat?"

He told her it was no trouble to take her all the way to St. Charles, and she didn't argue.

Andre took her to a house near Pitou's where a woman with beefy bronze arms and her hair tied up in a checkered cloth sold po' boy sandwiches out her kitchen window. He got fried oyster and she had catfish, eating on the hood of the car and wishing they had something cold to wash them down.

Neither of them knew the neighborhood, cruising washed-out streets that had never been paved, while old men sat on their heels and stared as they passed. They came upon a honky tonk and Evangeline lugged her bag with her.

Inside the shack, a rangy, red-bearded man sat at the bar, talking loud. No one but him and the bartender, and a rusty old jukebox playing a nasty Johnny Rebel tune that froze Evangeline at the door. She'd heard her father talk about the sheriff busting up white juke joints that wouldn't play the records.

The man at the bar gave them a smile. "Hello darlin'. Ain't you a couple. I just got out of Natchitoches jail, and my gate money's burning a hole in my pocket. First round's on me."

Evangeline sat on the stool next to him. She didn't want to be the girl from the big house who acted better than the common man. Andre sat next to her, keeping loose.

"Ain't seen a woman so fine in a coon's age. You're a lucky

man." He raised his drink to Andre.

Andre ordered a shot and a beer and Evangeline asked for a sea breeze. She got a shot and a beer.

They shot their shots, and she coughed and her eyes watered, but she kept it down. A sip of beer helped.

"I met a cold-eyed killer in that jail, who said he trained a cockroach to do tricks."

Sure enough, there was a big fat palmetto bug on the edge of the bar chewing on a corn nut. The bartender didn't seem to care, flipping through the racing section of the paper.

"Said he named it Tabasco, 'cause his old man worked for the pepper family out on the salt dome island when they ran it like a company town, and they were low as roaches, how they treated him."

"He teach it to fly? They do that just fine by they self," the bartender said, a barrel of a man with one empty sleeve pinned to his shoulder.

"No, he didn't teach it to play dead, neither. You gonna let me tell my story?"

The bartender spat. "Long as you keep buying drinks."

"So my cellie says he taught this cockroach to jump and roll over," Big Red said. "Took him two years, but he taught little Tabasco to roll over and do backflips like a circus dog."

"Ain't no cockroach live that long."

"Oh, you feed 'em, they'll live forever. When the pigs drop the bomb and blow up this world, only things left'll be roaches. I read that in *Life* magazine. So, he spends two years training this cockroach, gets it to hide in his pocket come freedom day. He's gonna find him a circus, make him a million. But first, he wants a drink."

The storyteller drained his whiskey and signaled for more.

The bartender snatched the wet dollar bill in front of him before he refilled the glass. "Maybe you drink more, talk less. You scarin' away customers."

Andre finished his beer. The hair on his arms prickled, like when he ran point in the jungle. "Let's go, Evie."

Evangeline smiled and sipped her beer. "Oh, come on. I wanna to hear how this ends."

Big Red winked. "Well, sugar tits, he went to a honky tonk much like this one. It was a real shit hole."

She put a hand on her hip and angled away from him. The bartender's piggy eyes turned to slashes. Andre hiked his pant leg over his work boot, where he kept one of Pitou's knives.

"He orders himself a drink to reward himself for his hard work. Then he taps the bar and Little Tabasco crawls out his pocket and sits right next to his hand like a puppy. He ain't got money to pay, but once the bartender sees his roach do tricks, he figures he'll drink for free. He pets the little critter with a finger, and tells the bartender, 'You see this cockroach?'" He pointed to the one crunching on the corn nut. Its antennae wiggled like it was nodding to back to him.

"And the bartender smashes his hand down and says, 'Yeah, we get a lot of 'em in here!'" Big Red smashed a big knotty hand down and shook the bar. The roach buzzed its wings and flitted to the rafters. Evangeline yelped and laughed, and the bartender jumped back, rolling up his newspaper to swat. Then he dropped it, his jaw slack.

The storyteller had a GI .45 cocked on the bar, aimed at the bartender's belly. The papers rustled to the floor.

Andre stepped in front of Evie with his hand on the knife handle. He froze at the click of Red thumbing the hammer back.

"Don't do that, big fella. I'd hate to miss and shoot your girl in those fine titties."

Evangeline splashed his face with the remains of her beer.

He didn't flinch. He licked his wet mustache. "I said let go of that pigsticker, coon-ass. And hands up. All y'all."

They obeyed. The bartender held his one hand up.

The gunman stood slow, turning to cover them. "Cash box."

The bartender made a fist. "You rob a cripple veteran? You cold."

"Colder than your piss-warm beer. I know you run numbers and make the drop tomorrow. Give me the bag, or I'll blast your other arm off."

The bartender deflated and reached under the bar. The bag looked heavy.

Big Red pushed Andre toward the door with one long arm, his pistol held low at his own belt. "Come on, before that old dago finds his balls."

Evangeline backed out the door. She'd taken her daddy's Colt Diamondback in her purse. She held the revolver two-handed, the barrel quivering.

Andre ducked and Big Red booted him in the ass and sent him over the hood of the Mustang.

"What you doing, girl? Don't you wanna go for a ride?"

Evie pulled back the hammer.

"I don't mean the kind I been craving for eleven months and sixteen days. I need wheels and you got 'em. Or I can put a round up your boyfriend's asshole. What you say?"

The hammer clicked on an empty chamber. She jerked the trigger twice more.

He yanked the pistol from her hands and threw her in the back seat of the Mustang like a sack of potatoes. Andre scrabbled up the hood and stopped when Red stuck the muzzle in his eye.

"This bag's got three thousand if it's got a dollar. Drive to Texarkana nice and fast and five hundred of it's yours."

A round cracked from the tin shack.

They piled in the Mustang and roared out of the lot as the bartender chased after them with a Luger, firing all but the last round, in case the bag man didn't believe someone had the stones to rob a Calvineau juke joint.

35: TIGER BAIT

Jay roared the Challenger across the interstate like his ass was on fire. He was later than the White Rabbit in Wonderland, and now he had Calvineau privileges.

Pastor Roy had left him at the curb outside the church with a white, gold-embossed business card that said he was on official Calvineau Parish Church business. It felt like a razor blade in his pocket.

The LSU campus was a small town in itself, centered around Tiger Stadium, a modern Colosseum that seated a hundred thousand Romans screaming for blood on game day. The arena lights rose like a beacon to the sky. He nosed the Challenger beneath willows and oaks, around a black mirror lake and grassy mounds built by the native people who'd been driven from the land of the red stick.

He found Molina's Subaru parked by a bronze tiger statue. She was up against an enclosure, nose to the fence.

There was a barnyard smell in the heavy air.

Jay took the steps three at a time. "Molina. Sorry I'm late."

"I heard you were at the Calvineaus' table." She turned with her thumbs in her pockets. "Was it like heaven itself, like Miss Ardith says?"

"They sure think so." He peered over her shoulder through the fence. There was a pond and a knoll beyond it. "They got a real tiger?"

"Sure do. Mike's not out. Must be feeding time."

"The Calvineaus season their food like Yankees. I'm still hungry if you are."

Steam rose off the hood of the Challenger. "You escape from the *Dukes of Hazzard*?"

"Wanna get some oysters, Daisy?"

"I know a place, but I'll drive."

She took him across the Huey Long Bridge into Port Allen and followed the river until she found a place where they could slurp oysters and watch the barges roll by.

"Reminds me of home a little."

"Where's that?" Jay tipped a fat Gulf oyster he'd blessed with hot sauce.

"Ville Platte." She let her accent come out. *Vee Pla'*. "Grew up with my grand-mère Ambria. Mom had to work, and Daddy was on the road all the time. We raised hogs, grew okra, tomatoes, everything. You get your food from a store, you don't know what you're getting."

"My aunt and uncle had a fishing camp. We ate what we caught. Gar had a lot of bones. Used 'em for toothpicks."

"So, you're a Calvineau?"

"Half, they say."

"Never seen a Calvineau work with his hands. They offer you a job?"

They had. The order to betray Mama Evangeline. "I told them I got one already."

She huffed.

"I'm gonna get to see my *nonc* Andre if I behave. That's all I want from them."

"Then you're gone."

"He ain't going anywhere, and neither am I. They made it clear that I'm the black sheep of the family. I've got to do my penance."

"Feel like prison yet?"

Jay looked down, then smiled. "Not when I'm serving time

with you."

She swatted his hand.

They ate another dozen oysters char-grilled in butter with a sprinkle of cheese and sopped up the liquor with toasted french bread.

On the way back to the Tiger's den, she saw a college bar advertising '80s night, and they caught the tail end. Even danced a Cajun two-step to "Stand by Me" by Ben E. King.

She broke into the lead and twirled him. "Got an early day tomorrow."

When they got back to her car, Mike the Tiger roamed his pen, chuffing from the other side of his pool. A steel beer keg floated in the middle, bashed by his claws. They walked to the iron bars and watched him pace. The enclosure had a double fence to ensure no drunk college students went home an arm short. Mike swiped at the keg and it spun out of reach.

"They say there'll be no more wild tigers by the time we're old," Molina said. "Just in cages."

Jay watched the tiger strut. He had grown old in a cage. "They should be free. Makes me think of my *nonc* Andre. He was a wild boy, but he don't deserve to die in no cage."

"I know a few who do."

Jay did, too.

"The Calvineaus will put you in one, you're not careful. May not be bars on it." She looked across the water, her eyes unfocused. "I like you, Jason. You should get out of here as fast you're able."

"Why's that?"

"Because I think you're a good man."

He wished that was true. He'd felt the red-mist urge to kill as he supped at his grandparents' table. People had no idea what predators slinked among them.

Jay held the tiger's stare.

Mike jumped the pond effortlessly. Five hundred pounds of muscle cleared fifteen feet in half a second. Molina jumped back, and Jay caught her in his arms.

She relaxed against him. It felt good, the kind of good that brought on melancholy for what he knew he could not have.

"I wish I could set you free. I'm sure as hell gonna try."

Keshawn, too.

"Don't make promises you can't keep, Jason."

He thought of swinging Andre's hatchet and keeping his promise. His gut twisted and acid burned his throat.

"You can call me Jay. They know who I am. The Calvineaus need something from me. They're used to getting what they want, but they've never locked horns with me."

The jungle cat huffed a low challenge from his cage.

36: FISHING

Murray Lo had gone in the night. His bed was empty, only the sour sheets remained. Andre stared at the Shroud of Turin imprint in amber sweat staining the scratchy white linen.

"I didn't find him. They said he must've rolled onto his oxygen tube." Salva rolled up the sheets and tossed them in a laundry cart. "They don't want us down here overnight," he said, and scratched at a scaly patch of psoriasis on his hip with thick yellow fingernails.

He smelled of sulfur. Andre knew the smell from robbing factory payrolls west of Lake Charles. It got into your lungs, your hair, your clothes. Somehow it had seeped into Salva's skin. Either that or he'd swallowed a hunk of the burning yellow brimstone and it seethed in his taut belly.

"LeFer likes you. If it means something, put a word in. I could be the night nurse. Might save some lives."

"You ain't fooling everybody," Andre said.

He walked away before he was tempted to swing his elbow beneath Salva's hard nub of a chin. He had not seen the fight that gave the baby-raper his killer rep. Two Cajuns in for killing a Coast Guardsman who found them with an illegal catch had shanked Salva. They wanted the kiddie-diddler's death in their jacket, to cover the soldier-killer stain. One of them survived, in a wheelchair now. Salva had snapped his neck, and stomped his friend's brains in with his brogans.

"You think you better than the rest of us, Desmarteaux?" Salva shouted after him. "Just 'cause you suckin' the warden's crank don't make you a big stripe!"

A few hooted in agreement, others heckled. But no one stood in Salva or Andre's way.

The Fox tipped him to a new delivery at the library. Something had got up writers' asses, and box after box of books had come in from the Liberation Library. He took one about an old surfer named Frankie Machine who ran a bait shop. Not a bad life if you could get it.

Andre missed fishing. He and the boy had taken a rowboat out onto Lake Hopatcong, a big body of water by New Jersey standards, and bottom fished for bullheads. The boy caught one, and Andre another, but he let the boy reel it in. He loved seeing them rise up from the depths.

On Andre's last cast, a foot-long shiner gulped his night-crawler. He swore, horsing it in, when something struck it like a silver-black missile.

The boy nearly tumbled out the boat. Andre one-armed the pole to his hip and pulled the boy in by the seat of his pants. The fish plunged into the weeds, but he reeled it in slow, the boy rowing them patiently into deeper water.

When it was out of fight, the fish gawped its underslung jaw and eyed them like a prehistoric monster that would swallow them whole if only it had time to grow. Had to be four feet long. Andre had seen alligator gar as long as a pirogue, and jackfish that shot like rockets after the perch you wanted to pan-fry, but this was some strange hybrid of both. The shiner's head was sheared clean off, dangling from the hook that pierced the beast's mouth.

He took his needle-nose pliers from his pocket.

"You gonna let him go?" the boy gasped.

"We got a bucket full of catfish to eat, don't we?" He

snipped the hook. The beast thanked him by slashing his hand with its back-bent fangs and lunged away from the boat with a slam of its tail.

They watched the primordial creature disappear into the green murk.

The boy's friend Tony told them it was a muskellunge, the largest predatory freshwater fish in North America. Kid jabbered like a walking encyclopedia with a lisp.

Andre lay on his bunk and flipped through the surfer book, hoping whatever fish they caught got away.

"Doctor Dre, you got mail." He closed the book. That was Skinny-Bo's name for him. Young man had a limp and wore a catheter, trophies from a shootout he'd refused to turn evidence on. He handed Andre a copy of *American Woodworker* and a white church envelope.

No one wrote him. This was from Evie's family's church.

He peeled the corner with excruciating care, as not to tear the contents.

He didn't recognize the hand, but the voice that came off the page made him hunch into himself and shudder quietly.

The boy.

37: YOUR DADDY'S GUN

Jay parked in front of the gun shop. He slipped the knife under his shirt and adjusted the handle for a quick draw. His folks imbued Shooter Boudreaux with supernatural powers in their stories. Yet the Calvineaus had turned him to their side.

At the counter, a young man whose brown biceps stretched his sleeves welcomed him with a smile. The holstered Glock at his hip a mere toy.

"Here to see Mr. Boudreaux."

"Come this way."

The door was marked ARMORY. He rapped on it.

"I heard your father served with Mr. Boudreaux. You should be proud."

"I am, thanks."

"Was he there when they got overran? Said they killed hundreds."

"He never talked about it," Jay said. Which was true. Andre picked shrapnel out of his calf as it wormed its way to the surface, but all he ever spoke to Jay of his time there was when he held up his war hatchet and said never to touch it. *You get dragged off to fight a rich man's war, I'll give this to you. Guns can jam. This you can trust.*

"Send him in." Muffled through the door.

He unlocked the door and let Jay inside.

Clean operating tables where the patients were firearms on

white paper. A TV camera on a rolling rig sat in the corner, its eye aimed at the wall. Shooter Boudreaux sat in a fancy webbed office chair painted in camouflage, a blued revolver before him.

"Well, if it ain't the prodigal son."

Shooter had saddle bags beneath his dead black eyes and an American flag bandanna tied around his forehead. Locks of gray and mouse brown hung over it. A tricked-out Smith & Wesson .44 in a quick draw holster at his right hip.

"We're good, Aldous," Shooter said. "Boy knows how quick I draw."

Aldous let the door swing shut.

He demonstrated, snapping back with the .44 low at his hip. The muzzle drew Jay's eyes like the abyss. The move was rattlesnake quick. "Haven't seen you since you were cradled to your mama's tit."

Shooter flashed tiny gray teeth.

"She was something else. Should've been on magazine covers, not knocking off bank trucks. You were the convincer, you know. They'd pretend to be broken down, and she'd hold you up like the Gerber baby, say she needed to get you home, won't they give her a ride? She could've been holding a cow pie in swaddling clothes, the way those poor boys were blinded by those big ol' titties of hers. We took a couple hundred grand that way. Built my first rifle with my share. Rest is history." He swept a hand over the guns like they were tracts of land.

"Thanks for the story," Jay said. "But I'm looking to find my mama, not relive glory days. Pastor Eagleton said you could help."

"You sure caused a ruckus up north, didn't you?"

Jay studied the man's face for tells.

"Suspect in a terrorist attack on a town monument. Wanted for questioning in the unresolved homicide of a retired police officer. We loved to steal, your folks and me. But you raise hell for sport."

Shooter walked to the other side of the table where the blued revolver lay. "This was Andre's carry piece. Me, I like my odds better at a thousand yards."

"Makes Angola less likely, don't it?"

"Poor Andre. I gave him this wheelgun as a wedding present. They got married by a Black preacher on an isle in Bayou Vipère."

He broke open the table revolver. Six empty chambers like a clock face. He produced a speed-loader from his loose pants pocket, slipped the shells home and spun the cylinder, snapped it closed. He twirled the trigger guard on his finger and held it out by the barrel.

Jay took it by the grip.

"Colt Python .357 Magnum. Won't crack no engine block, that's bullshit. Neither will a .44, but my gun'll blow your spine out your asshole."

He gripped Jay's hand around the Python, left index finger behind the trigger, so the revolver could not fire. He whipped his .44 out the holster, pressed the muzzle to Jay's gut.

Jay stopped his left hook inches from Shooter's jaw. Held it there, trembling.

Shooter met Jay's cobalt eyes with his own. "You almost got yourself killed right there. You been out to Henderson, boy?"

"No, sir." Jay kept his eyes steady to sell the lie.

Shooter stared into his eyes a long time. "Your mama has. She put six rounds into Ti' Boy Garriss. Then she emptied his rifle in my front door. You might have your grandma fooled, but I bet you're just as sly as your mama."

"You know what I did up north. If I wanted you dead, I'd wait in back of that truck of yours. Hack your head off with Andre's hatchet and leave it as a hood ornament."

He kept his eyes steady. One killer to another.

Shooter quick-holstered his .44, then twisted the Python out of Jay's hand. "She'll go for Pitou. He makes knives in the bayou, down from Grosse Tête." He set Andre's Python on a sheepskin-lined case beside a sheet of folded printer paper. A map and directions.

"The po-pos spotted her headed that way. She'll wait, let him feel safe. Then strike while he's got his pecker in his hands. That's her style."

Jay studied the paper. One move was to kill Pitou first. Another was to warn him. "And what's my style?"

"I told Pitou you're coming to talk some sense into her. He's ain't happy, but he knows he ain't got much choice. You're Calvineau, he's little people."

Jay tucked the paper into his pocket.

"Don't wait too long. She got Ti' Boy, but he slowed down. Too much beer and cracklins. Pitou, though? He's still fast as a snake."

"You're all snakes. Backstabbers. Only thing lower is a snitch."

"And you only talking so bold because your Calvineau blood protects you. Just like your crazy mama." Shooter smiled. "You got killer eyes, boy. You want to take your shot, go ahead. See who's left standing."

Jay peered at the cylinder. The Python was loaded with cartridges. He couldn't tell if they were spent or blanks.

"You'll keep."

Shooter huffed. "She's saving me for last. You tell her lots of people put me in their sights." He pulled down the neck of his shirt, revealing the shiny pock of a bullet scar. "They all dead."

Jay zipped the revolver into the case.

"Ain't you gonna say thank you?"

"Not for what was already mine."

When the door shut behind the boy, Shooter Boudreaux took a bottle of Pappy Van Winkle from his desk and drank a glass like water. He'd rigged the Python's timing so it would blow like a frag grenade at the first pull.

Pitou deserved a fighting chance. The Calvineaus might let

him live if he only took their boy's right paw.

Maybe.

He buzzed the counter. Aldous stepped in and shut the door.

"I put the tracker on his car, Mr. Boudreaux."

"Just what I wanted to hear. Mark yourself for eight hours overtime."

"Oh, you didn't have to do that, sir. If you need my help, it would be an honor to serve with you."

"Thank you, Aldous. I'll let you know. Dismissed." He winked.

After the door clicked shut, Shooter poured another glass. Aldous was a good kid, Army. But the color of his skin would enrage the people Shooter was forced to serve with now.

38: BEHIND BLUE EYES

Pastor Roy massaged Molina's shoulders and she made fists and endured it. Jay watched from the Challenger, parked by the shed. He felt the Colt's weight in his hand. Saw the pastor's brains paint the hood of Molina's Subaru. The Calvineaus would mete out punishment upon her if he disappeared. But it felt good to dream.

He put the pistol in the go-bag and locked it under the back seat. Then he sauntered over slow, trying to overhear what the pastor's thin lips whispered. Whatever it was made Molina stare like she'd seen a school bus plummet off a bridge.

"Go on inside, deary. I have to talk to Jay...son." Pastor Roy smiled.

Molina hurried off without a word.

"Do you have your marching orders from Boudreaux?"

"Yeah. He told me where she'll strike next. I'll be waiting."

"Bring your hatchet, Joshua. Leonce Pitou is a sodomite. He'll lust after that tight little ass of yours more than our sweet old ladies do." He laughed. "Or do you miss the brown-eye? That long in prison, I might have been tempted by a girlish darkie with lipstick on."

Jay didn't answer. He bet if he took the pastor's pulse, it would be elevated. His cellie Raina had told him how obsessed with sex and genitals "straights" were, as she called them. Okie called civilians "straights," but she meant something else.

"I'm gonna go. I don't want to miss her."

He frowned, disappointed by Jay's lack of reaction. "You do that. Bring that slut home. We shall abase her and bring her back into the fold." He broke into a smile. "Yes! I saw the way you flexed. You will have plenty of opportunities to do violence with us, Joshua. Take it out on the fornicator, Pitou. Our soldiers are many. They will be watching you. If you don't bring little Evie home? Your Andre and Molina will suffer." He folded his smooth hands.

"I said I would. But you tell that dried-up old crone they're getting a trade. I'll soldier for you when Andre walks free with Mama Evangeline. She'd rather die than sit at their table. I'm bringing her home to be with Andre." Jay drew the knife and held it to the pastor's cleanly shaved neck. The razor edge found a stub of hair and tugged it. "If they play me, I'll kill every one of you, every child with a drop of Calvineau blood, until you shoot me down. You know I can, and you know I will."

Pastor Roy's smile dissolved.

"Now point your filthy pecker out of here and get moving, before I carve a message on your chest to bring to my grandparents." Jay sheathed the knife.

The pastor remained frozen a full count and then burst out laughing, backed away and patted his chest. "Oh, no wonder you like our theatrical maiden, Joshua. You certainly learned the art of the thespian while you rotted in that Yankee jail." He walked away, laughing louder.

In the theater, Molina silently prayed, looking up at the gel lights in the rafters.

Jay knocked on the door frame. "He's gone."

She looked down. "I wished that he'd drive his truck into a wall and burn alive. He brings out the sin in me."

Jay remembered that to some, vengeance was a sin. He stepped closer but gave her space. "I'm supposed to go see my mama tonight. And bring her back to the family. She hates them, and now I know why."

"You're not coming back." Her arms fell to her sides. "Don't. This is hell. If you can get away, never come back."

"I won't leave you here, Molina. I said that." People said things all the time, Jay knew. His habit of following through seemed to surprise people. But it was the only way he knew to be.

She stared at a blank wall, rubbing her Stanley knife like a worry stone. "He made me come to his office, when I started. To talk about expenses, he said. Talks with the back of his chair to me. How he's not sure theater is a good influence for the children, with so many homosexuals in the business. He asked if I've ever been tempted to stray.

"I tell him no, but some of the best Christians I know are gay. They know what it's like to be persecuted, like the Lord. What it feels like to be a Samaritan. To be suspect until proven otherwise."

She flicked the razor open. "Then he spun his chair around, and his pants were open."

Jay knotted his hands to fists.

"He said he should have proof, so I don't sway the children. I backed away and he says if I open that door, he'll tell my PO that I asked the kids if they knew anyone selling heroin.

"He only wanted me to talk. To say the things I've done with men." She ratcheted the razor open and shut. "He says a girl like me must have done lots of nasty things to satisfy her addiction. He's got an imagination, because all I did was hock things at the pawn shop."

No tears. Her eyes burned them off like the noonday sun. "I told him I'm a virgin and his eyes light up like a kid with a birthday present. He wants me kneeling in the pulpit during his sermon. Tells me we can work up to it. He's...touching himself the whole time he says this. And now he thinks you and me are together, and he wants me under there next Sunday. Told me to ask you to let me practice."

Jay felt the red at the corners of his eyes coming and fought it back.

"That's not gonna happen."

"If you hurt him, he'll find my family!" She pointed the knife. "They'll cut up my memaw and go fishing with her parts. That's what your family does!"

Jay spread his hands. "I know. My blood is evil. I'm gonna do what I can to burn all this down, I swear to you."

She looked him in the face. His masks were down, his face scared and young and tired. From behind his blue eyes shone fear and shame and truth.

"You can't do that alone, Jason. Jay. Whatever your name is. No one can."

"I'll have my mama. She's a stone-cold killer."

"Pure Calvineau," she spat.

"I won't leave you, Molina. I don't have many friends. Most of them are dead. But the ones I have, I'll die for. And I'll sure as hell kill for."

She clipped her knife in her pocket. "I know someone who might help." She dug inside her bag. "When I was rock bottom, I thought about doing what the pastor thinks I did. So I went to a church and they brought me to a shelter, and they took me to a sanctuary out in the bayou south of here. And she saved me." She held up a thick business card. "They say she's a witch, but she calls herself a healer. She fed me this root from the rainforest called ibogaine. It knocked me out for two days." The memory clouded her eyes. "The trip was crazy. We were angels in the swamp, freeing souls of the drowned."

Jay wondered if this witch could free him from the shadows of the dead.

She lifted a woven necklace over her head. It was fed through a silver dime with a ragged hole punched through Mercury's face. "She'll show you who you are. Make sure that's what you want, because you can never go back."

Jay knew what he was and hated it. He took the necklace.

"Wear it. The card just gets you there. Getting in, you need that touching your skin."

Jay rolled the stretched necklace down his face. It hung at his throat, the dime lifting as he spoke. "I'll go see her after I get Mama. We won't be a week. We'll come for you before Sunday, Molina. I swear."

She hugged him tightly around his arms. "You don't have to kill or die for me, Jay. Friends don't ask for that. Just let me know when I can run the hell away from here without worrying about my memaw."

She held out the card.

It was black, embossed with silver.

Suzane Gaiter
The Witch Queen of New Orleans

39: ROUGAROU HUNTING

Chopper ran his truck through a gas station car wash before approaching the Calvineau Parish First Evangelical Church in the morning, when parents were driving their kids to school, and his black SUV would fit into the traffic. The parking lot was empty except for a faded Kia with magnets advertising a maid service.

He parked in the lot and followed the sound of a vacuum cleaner. A broad-shouldered woman wore one strapped to her back, hoovering the aisles while her heavyset partner polished the pews. He rapped hard on the door as not to scare them.

They looked pleasantly confused by his presence.

"Ma'am," he said, and took his card from inside his sport jacket. "I'm working a missing kids case. Keshawn Wallace?"

Their suspicion softened into dread. "Another sweet young boy," the older one said.

"He came here to compete for a scholarship." He gave them time.

"Was a girl, I'd know who to point to," the heavy one said. Her friend nodded.

He tilted his head like he was listening in.

The older woman chuckled. "Pastor watches her like a dog at a butcher's window."

He smiled and listened while they polished the wood. The pastor was a pussy hound, with the white sheep of his flock and the staff. The cleaning women made sure to always work in pairs.

He'd have to talk to a parishioner to get more. "Don't come around, even in a suit," they warned. The older one nodded toward a large outbuilding. "Handyman. He's a little rough."

He thanked them and walked the grounds, using the trees for cover. The outbuilding was a theater but had been servants' quarters at one time. There was a rear door.

He heard rushed footsteps, then a sunburned, prison-pale white man in a work shirt and boots burst out the door, carrying a duffel. Chopper ducked around the corner and waited for the boots to crunch away, then followed quietly.

The handyman beelined to a large shed. He had thick arms and shoulders, short legs like a few wrestlers he'd known, and black Cajun hair and features. He disappeared around the back of the shed, and Chopper closed the distance.

Jay pulled the tarp off the Challenger. He folded it, and his eyes set on a black Chevy Tahoe in the parking lot next to the cleaning women's hatchback. The Tahoe had a cop bumper and limo tint.

Recognition sent an icy spear through his bowels. The truck from Henderson.

"Good morning, sir. I'm—"

Jay threw the wadded tarp at the tall Black man in cop jeans and a sport jacket. He was in the Challenger and spewing dirt across the grounds before he formed his next thought, acting on instinct like a three-legged coyote.

Chopper rolled behind the shed and came up on one knee with his compact nine aimed at the purple hot rod.

Black or purple, Ralph Ora had said.

He swore and ran for his truck. He switched the pistol to his off hand and punched at his key fob through his pocket to engage the remote start. The Tahoe rumbled alive.

The Challenger hopped the curb and shrieked up the street,

leaving a white cloud of smoke like James Bond's Aston Martin.

Chopper jumped onto the grass, turned on the police scanner, and flicked on his yellow construction safety flashers. He hit the Bluetooth and told it to dial Junior LeFer. It might be too late to ask permission to take a bounty in Calvineau Parish, but it was better than expecting forgiveness.

The Challenger swerved toward the bridge to Baton Rouge. Chopper smiled and hung up before the call connected. He pushed the pedal down.

Jay shifted and took as much lead as the Challenger would take. The Chevy was an angry black dot in the rearview, coming fast. He roared over the Bayou Vipère bridge and cut around a slow truck. The traffic was already backed up on the highway. He swerved into the greenway and into a subdivision.

On a straightaway the Challenger would be gone, but in the back streets he would spin out in a turn and lose to modern vehicles endowed with the magic of stability and traction control. His heart pounded at the thought of a child running into the street.

Jay cut over a corner of lawn, grateful for the curbless streets without sidewalks. He headed for a cluster of big houses. The Tahoe bounced off the grass and ate up road, flashers strobing from the grille.

Jay shrieked around a corner and dodged a minivan that swerved and blared its horn. He was in a maze of cul-de-sacs, all alike. The houses were all mottled brick ranch dwellings with squat black shingled roofs and carports. The streets all ended in "wood." Torchwood, Goodwood, Sandalwood. A ditch ran behind all the houses to drain floodwaters, so he couldn't cut across to the other subdivision.

The Tahoe's pipes echoed off the houses one block over.

40: BLOWN AWAY

Chopper took the corner at a saner speed than his target had. No one ran like that without a price on their head. He'd planned for hostility, maybe even a sucker punch, but a white man running from him in Calvineau Parish of all places was not expected.

The target was armed with a three-thousand-pound missile, and Chopper knew how violent ex-cons thought. You did not get between them and a stretch without your weapon drawn. He rolled down his windows, listening for the distinctive rumble of the engine. He did not want a minivan full of kids on his conscience, even with a twenty-thousand-dollar payout. Thought about calling a friend in Baton Rouge PD and splitting the take.

An engine roared on the other side of the houses. He rolled in slow, checking garage doors and yards. This boy could swing into a carport, kill the engine, and wait. So he eyeballed each and every one.

He would let him escape rather than chase him toward innocents. The target was stupid enough to drive a banged-up purple Hot Wheels car and leave the scene of two crimes. Maybe he and Ti' Boy were the Rougarou, and he'd tired of sharing victims.

A minivan driver honked.

"Everything good this morning, ma'am?" Chopper put on his friendly cop face.

"Good morning, Officer. I'm sorry I tooted my horn at you, but someone just raced past me toward the cul-de-sac."

"The purple car? We got a call. Did you see him pull into a house, or turn around?"

"No, but he looked like he was late for his own funeral."

"Thank you, ma'am. Drive safely."

There was only one way in and out. He rolled past a landscaper's truck. The men wore masks and ear protection, herding debris with leaf blowers.

He called his BRPD buddy on the Bluetooth and asked for an assist on a fugitive. He blocked the street with his flashers on and listened for the engine. He cursed himself for not spotting the Challenger. If he'd spiked one tire, he'd have the Rougarou, a twenty-grand bounty, or both.

At lunch break, Jay put down his leaf blower and handed two of the old hundreds to the foreman. The cops had combed the subdivision but none of them spoke Spanish, and the landscapers had shrugged to their inquiries. Wearing a respirator mask as he blew the driveway clean, Jay memorized the plates of the tall Black cop's Chevy. A uniform called him *Tewliss*.

The Challenger had just fit into the landscaping trailer. Jay climbed over the trunk and slid in the driver's side window, *Dukes of Hazzard* style. Both mirrors scraped along the walls as he backed out. He rolled quietly toward the interstate and disappeared into lunch-hour traffic.

41: THE KNIFE MAN

Leonce Pitou polished a razor edge on the monster Bowie's leaf blade using a lap belt sander. His tobacco brown forearms were roped with muscle from swinging a blacksmith's hammer, holding blades to the grit-smeared leather of the belt, and scarred from cuts and burns from the forge.

He used a twenty-ton power hammer to shape most of his blades, but a few he hammered by hand. Some he brought to a flaming orange hue in a steel shop forge, and others in coal out in the bayou, left rough to look rustic, objects of science as well as art. This blade was his own replica of a Randall Sasquatch, a huge custom double-edged recurve Bowie done in ripple pattern Damascus steel he'd patterned and etched for a customer with exacting tastes and too much money.

The blade was for a wild boar hunt in Georgia Skunk Ape country, where the feral hogs ran to a thousand pounds or more. Pitou had never hunted them himself, but he'd had to hear the customer expound on how they were tracked by dogs, harried with spears, and finished up close with a knife. The guides had guns of course, but the bragging rights came from ramming a handmade American Bowie into the heart of the beast. Anyone could shoot the damn thing, he'd said.

Pitou had hunted boar on his land with one of Shooter Boudreaux's modified shotguns, and his customer was a fool for thinking they were easy prey. The mothers were wily and protected their children, and the boars were not easily goaded into revealing themselves. Corner them and they could gut a hound with one slash of their tusks.

Or an overconfident rich man with a three-thousand-dollar knife in his hand.

Pitou tested the edge on his horny thumbnail and then swung it at a free hanging six-inch-thick Manila rope he hung over a beam in his workshop for that purpose. The rope barely moved as the water-patterned blade sliced through it. Strands of rope fell to the concrete floor.

The knife had a curly oak handle and a nickel silver guard with two prongs, built to the customer's specifications, to resemble the sword the villain used in the movie *Highlander*. Pitou rarely questioned his customers' tastes, but privately, he thought the richer white people got, the more their tastes resembled that of Times Square pimps they'd seen in the movies.

He'd sat on their toilet seats embedded with Morgan silver dollars, and crafted them pocketknives with glimmering rainbow handles of abalone shell that Huggy Bear would turn his nose up at.

He coated the blade in protective wax and sheathed it in a plain leather scabbard. He was to ship it to a leather worker in Arkansas, where he was told it would be given an ostrich leg scabbard dyed oxblood red, and tried not to think about it.

He was about to set the knife into the prepared shipping crate when he heard the rumble of Detroit iron sputtering over the water. Growing up Black in what became Calvineau Parish, he learned never to be without a blade. He had a dagger in each boot and a slim fighter beneath his leather vest, and he slipped the Sasquatch clone—which he called the Skunk Ape, because he thought the aesthetics he'd been forced to give it stank to high heaven—into his belt for extra measure.

Then he walked to the camp house where he had a nickel-plated Benelli from Shooter Boudreaux loaded with steel buckshot. It held eight rounds and the bandolier held seven more. His eyesight wasn't worth a damn past twenty yards, and he was too vain for spectacles and hated anything touching his eyes, which made contact lenses out of the question, so Shooter had rigged him a semi-auto shotgun that would liquefy anything on two legs that wasn't too blurry for him to see.

What he saw was a purple heap wobble up his road, a pimp hooptie that his tasteless customers might enjoy. He walked out with the shotgun in one hand. He was a loner. When he craved companionship he found it in the bars off Rampart, younger men he rarely saw twice.

Customers only knew about his shop in the Quarter. The forge was a secret, one they talked about on knife nut forums and scanned aerial maps to locate. He made it clear that anyone who visited would be banned from his waiting list, which was five years deep, and anyone who sold to someone banned was also banned. That had kept the creeps at bay.

He fired a round into the trees. Birds scattered and the car buried its nose into the gravel as the driver stomped the brakes.

A hand raised in surrender out the window.

"Go on and back on out of here. This is private land and I'm within my rights to shoot." He used a soft voice for customers, but he spoke this with his gruff Creole patois.

"Shooter Boudreaux sent me," the driver said. "Hear what I got to say."

"He got my mobile." He leveled the barrel at the windshield. The glare hid the driver's face.

"This ain't for phones."

"Speak, then."

"Ti' Boy's dead."

"Ain't nothing to me. You gon' be next, you don't back on out of here."

"It's Evie Calvineau done it. You kill her, you know what happens."

The sweat on Pitou's shoulders turned cold.

"I'm coming out now, boss."

"Slow!" Pitou walked closer, his pointed boots cutting the grass.

"You know me, but I don't know you." The door opened. The driver kept his hands up and visible, like a mime. "I'm the boy."

Pitou stopped with the shotgun aimed at the driver's belly. He knew the kid didn't come from Andre's pecker, but damn if he didn't have the same broad Cajun cheekbones and sad eyes as his old partner. "You best have proof, or your guts gonna be gator bait."

Jay turned around slowly, spread wide, his hands on the roof of the Challenger. "Check the hammer loop of my jeans. You made that hatchet for Andre Desmarteaux."

Pitou dimpled the man's work shirt with the muzzle and gave him a quick frisk for firearms.

"Bet you'll recognize the knife in my belt, too."

Pitou eyed the lady Bowie with the coffin handle. Old and less refined than his latest work. He slung the shotgun. Now that they were close, he had no concerns. He had never met the knifeman who was his match.

Or the axeman.

"That's not a hatchet, boy." He nudged Jay toward the workshop. "That's a war tomahawk."

42: A DUKE OF HAZARD

The back of the workshop was a wall of knives, from daggers that might suit a knight of old to a checkered, rustic blade hammered from a long file.

"See you eyeing my Rezin Bowie. That's close as you can get to what Jim Bowie brought to the sandbar fight that made his knife famous. Made from a farrier's rasp." It was more like a short sword. Impractical to carry.

Pitou drew the Skunk Ape. "I can make 'em pretty, too." Light danced on the Damascus blade and dazzled Jay's eyes, like the Cadillac at Whiterose. Beautiful and deadly.

Pitou set it in the shipping crate.

"Andre said no one could make or use a blade like you. They say they'll let him out of Angola if my mama comes home."

"Your momma ain't going back to her fam. Not alive."

Jay nodded. "She knows my car. We'll talk. You're a fighter. Sometimes you gotta get in the pocket, take a few shots to get inside where they're vulnerable."

Pitou laughed, showing dull teeth. "Sometimes they want you in close so they can eat you. Waiting makes me thirsty. I got a pitcher of sweet tea."

He poured two glasses in his tiny kitchen and nodded toward the back. He leaned the shotgun against the wall.

The tea was so sweet it made Jay's teeth hurt. "I've been on a revenge trip like she is. It eats you up and makes you blood simple. Whatever you did ain't worse than her family. She'll see that. She's got to."

The back porch opened onto the water. The sun had dropped and turned the bayou into a hammered mirror. The knife he'd found in Okie's cache sat on a barrel top.

"I made that as a wedding present. Part of a matched pair. Warden LeFer took Andre's, I hear. He's the one she ought to go after. Not like we had a choice."

A pirogue drifted in the swamp grass. Jay hadn't seen one of the flat-bottomed Cajun canoes since he was a child.

Evangeline sat up in the boat and fired.

The glass in Pitou's left hand exploded and the round punched his shoulder.

"Mama, no!"

Pitou kicked back a leg and threw a dagger from his boot in one motion. Evangeline fired and rolled. The throwing iron sank into the wood of the pirogue.

Jay dropped his tea and kicked the shotgun. "Wait!"

A slender blade appeared in Pitou's hand. He jabbed Jay in the side before disappearing into the workshop.

There was no use talking once blood was drawn.

Jay drew the tomahawk and swung wildly as he charged. Pitou was just inside the doorway and nicked his ear before dancing back. Jay circled, boxing him away from the wall of blades and toward the power press and the sanders.

"You're bleeding bad, boy. How's that feel?"

A patch of red painted Pitou's vest. Jay took a wide stance, giving him a target.

Pitou skipped back and reached for the dagger in his left boot, but his arm didn't obey. The shock showed in his face.

The wolf rose in Jay at the weakness. He hurled the tomahawk underhand.

Pitou skipped and the handle glanced off his knee, and the axe spun across the floor. He closed in.

Jay grabbed at the wall of knives and threw blades wildly.

His killer instinct drained like cold piss down his leg.

Pitou ducked and dodged, timing his steps, taking space, his knife held low for a slash at the thigh or belly that would bleed him out fast. He smiled. "You're gonna die today."

Jay swiped with the long Rezin blade and used boxing footwork to keep distance. His side burned hot and he knew that was bad.

"Get down, son!" A drenched Evangeline stood in the doorway with the shotgun. She fired high and dust snowed from the peppered ceiling.

Pitou ducked and slashed. Jay fell flat and curled into a defensive ball. He flinched at the thunder of the shotgun.

Pitou spun and fell to his knees, mouth gaping like a fish as he stared at the hole in his belly. His fighting knife clattered to the floor, the steel flecked with Jay's blood.

Evangeline stepped closer, shaking her Colt free of swamp water. "You'll die soon enough, you backstabbing son of a bitch." She kicked Pitou over.

She turned to Jay and put a hand on his shoulder, looking him over with one steely eye. "You're bleeding, son."

This chill was warmth from her. The adrenaline kept Jay's tears at bay.

The cut wasn't deep, but it took the fight out of him. She found a bag of shop cloths and pressed one against his side. "Hold that there. I got people who'll fix you up. Just catch your breath before you bleed out on me." She adjusted her eye patch. "Sumbitch nearly stuck me. Didn't think he could throw that far."

Jay winced and held the cloth tight to his side. "What happened to your eye?"

"Long story. You could ask that weaselly prick." She nodded to where Pitou withered like a dying houseplant, his guts strewn out his back.

Jay rested his head on her shoulder. She tolerated it a moment, before patting him like a dog and slipping away.

She collected the tomahawk. "Thanks for bringing your papa's hatchet. He'll want it when we break him out."

"What?" Jay panted like a dog.

"He ain't got much time, son. It's the only way." She retrieved her wedding knife. "You found Okie's grubstake?"

"We gotta go, Mama. Shooter's coming."

She perked like a spooked deer. "I should have killed him, but he needs to die scared. Let's move."

Jay took the big Bowie called the Skunk Ape and shoved it through his belt. The handle held the bloodied shop rag to his side. Pitou stared at the ceiling, dead and unmoving.

She drove the Challenger to where she'd parked her black Dodge Magnum. "Time to ditch this shiny turd. I thought Okie taught you better."

"The Calvineaus want you home," he said, getting his breath. The pain came, and he knew he'd live. "They say they'll let Andre go."

She looked at him like he'd told her deer turds were chocolate-covered raisins. "They say a lot of things, but ain't none of them worth shit. You got to listen to me, now. We're gonna be a family again, for as long as we got."

Jay squinted. Two trucks bounced down the dirt road on the other side of the levee, trying to block them in. "Tell me where to meet you. We got company."

"Son of a bitch." She stepped out the driver's seat and hit the key fob to start the Magnum. "We got to split up, Jay. We'll meet at Andre's old fishing camp. You remember where that is?"

"Mama, I was five!"

"Take the Catahoula levee road to Butte la Rose, I'll find you! Just haul ass out of here and lose them."

She took Pitou's shotgun from the back of the Challenger and took position behind her wagon.

Jay writhed into to the driver's seat. He popped open the

hideaway in the rear seat and grabbed Andre's revolver from it, then dropped the pedal and roared toward the levee. The trucks disappeared under the berm. He shifted gears and launched up the rise over the levee as the trucks came up the other side.

Jay hooted like Luke Duke as his rear tire flattened the left truck's roof and the Challenger's rear bumper tore off its light bar. The suspension blew out on landing, and the trucks met Mama Evangeline's shotgun.

The Challenger's hood bounced up and down like a low-rider as he hit the highway dragging the chrome bumper in a trail of sparks.

43: BURNING BRIDGES

The Challenger roared past a double trailer high above the Atchafalaya, the tops of mangroves and live oaks like green clouds above the heat shimmer on the water. Fishing boats launched from the land between the twin spans of the interstate. One of the trucks had doubled back but he'd lost them in traffic, flying up the shoulder and losing the passenger side mirror and paint in the process.

After Lake Bigeaux, a dual-rear Ram truck groaned past him in the left lane, the windows blacked out. A brown sign announced they were over Henderson Swamp. The big water broke up into coves and patches of cypress knees, the water muddy with a deep slick of dark chocolate down the center, where the bottom had been dredged out.

Jay watched the signs for Catahoula. The engine was deafening; the landing had cracked an exhaust pipe. He was still elated from his *Dukes of Hazzard* jump but felt a deadening in his heart, knowing the car he and his childhood friend Tony had lovingly dubbed The Hammerhead had been finned.

The Ram truck swerved into his lane ten lengths ahead and the tailgate dropped open. The sun illuminated a black shape beneath the truck bed cover and the glass circle of a rifle scope flashed. Jay stomped the brakes and cut into the shoulder.

The first round hit the radiator and blew the Challenger's head gasket. Oil and coolant plumed from under the hood like the stack of coal-fired locomotive. Horns blared behind as the Challenger bounced off the concrete barrier and buried its shark nose into the asphalt.

The second hit the hood latch. The hood flew up and blinded him. Jay slid under the dashboard. The third exploded the windshield into a snowflake. The rear wheels of a box truck hit the rear quarter panel and bounced the Challenger against the concrete wall with a shriek of metal. Cars crashed around him and tires wailed on the pavement.

The engine sputtered dead.

In a black balaclava, the dead eyes of Shooter Boudreaux glared above a rifle in the bed of the pickup truck. Jay grabbed Andre's revolver and aimed. A roar came from behind. A jackknifed tractor trailer filled the rear window. Purple sheet metal and safety glass exploded and he dived out the passenger side toward the muddy water of the Atchafalaya Basin fifty feet below.

44: GATOR SHIT

Shooter put two more rounds into the purple Challenger as it compacted on the nose of the jackknifed tractor cab. They were too close for comfort. He kicked the front bed panel and the biker freak at the wheel lurched the truck forward. The trailer turned over and split open, spilling cardboard crates that exploded and flooded the road with green-and-white cans of Creole Seasoning. Cars swerved and crashed. The cans burst under tires in red clouds like spicy smoke grenades.

The trailer scraped to a stop fifty feet behind them. He kicked the bed twice and the driver slowed to a stop. Green cans rolled past them. Horns honked and distant thumps of cars rear-ending each other echoed over the peaceful water.

Shooter waved for Hambo to follow him. His name for the fat scion of an oil-rich family who bought every Shooter limited edition firearm, took every private class, and flew Shooter around the country on his dad's private jet. He had bought himself a leadership position in the Heimdall Brotherhood, the new foot soldiers of the dying Calvineau clan.

The hefty fella jumped out the truck with a carbine in a sling, fitted with a snail drum magazine and a red dot scope.

"What you doing? Look at the car, he's toast!"

"Soldier, maybes aren't in our dictionary." Hambo and the wannabes ate that shit up. And failing the Calvineau clan was less survivable than getting smeared by a semi.

Shooter jogged toward the concrete with the rifle at port arms. He had never shot off the back of a moving vehicle before, and couldn't predict the shimmy and shake of the old, unregistered truck with an unfamiliar .50-caliber rifle that he'd built to be tossed in the bayou.

He had wanted to wax Desmarteaux when they were over Whiskey Bay, in the pilot channel. A jump from that high, the water would hit you like concrete. But the dumb Nazi driver had taken too long to get in front of the Challenger.

Hambo huffed after him. "He had to break his neck."

The Calvineaus were blood crazy. Thought they came from Jesus. It was no better than working with one of those cults who all wore the same sneakers and tried to bring on the Judgment Day. But he had no choice, and their order was to ice Desmarteaux if he tried to run with Crazy One-Eyed Evangeline.

People began getting out of their cars to survey the damage and help the injured. When they saw the riflemen, they huddled behind their vehicles. Not long before a call went in. Shooter had chosen the kill zone between two exits, over the water, giving them the most time for escape. Nothing but deep gator-infested water, no way to get out alive without a boat.

Ripples in the water below. Almost straight down.

Hambo leaned over the side and sprayed the water with rounds. The carbine was bump-stocked and built off a receiver that would trace to a Virginia dealer who had reported it stolen. Even if the sheriffs fished the rifles out of the water, they'd go nowhere.

"Give me that!" Shooter dumped the .50-cal into the bayou and wrenched the kid's wrist with a compliance hold, took his weapon, and strafed the ripples. The rounds would penetrate a few feet of water. All it would take was one. He emptied the mag and dumped the rifle.

"Kroese said I'm *obergruppenführer*. I think I deserve some respect."

Shooter ignored him and double-timed toward their truck.

Hambo followed, waving a pistol and shouting more Nazi bullshit that Shooter tried not to think about.

By the time the police cleaned up the mess on the highway and remembered that a witness said the dumbass in the purple hot rod had taken a dive into the bayou, Desmarteaux would bleed out and be turned halfway to gator shit.

PART 3: BORN ON THE BAYOU

Lover of swamps
The quagmire overgrown
With hassock tufts of sedge — where fear encamps
Around thy home alone

Freebooters there,
Intent to kill and slay,
Startle with cracking guns the trepid air
And dogs thy haunts betray.

—John Clare, "To the Snipe"

45: BIG SUMBITCH

The swamp was the heart of Louisiana, sickened by man's poisons, but they hadn't killed it yet. It had swallowed their evil without complaint, whether it was chemicals, trash, or the bodies of the slain. It was still loved by people, who had lived in it for ten thousand years or more, plumbing its secrets. Spanish moss bearded the trees, long-legged birds speared fish with their beaks, and flowers perfumed the air. In its deepest hollows, alligator gar stalked prey with needle fangs longer than a guitar man's fingers, and sturgeon the size of Cadillacs swam the bottoms, dodging turtles with shells like kitchen tabletops, amidst the saurians who ruled the water.

The beast had no name, but the people who lived in its neck of the swamp called him Big Sumbitch. Fifteen feet long and half a ton, his back scales were pocked with bullet scars. A rusted hook as thick as a man's little finger protruded from the massive upper jaw, the barb buried deep in the bone. A racket had roused him from his cool, shady den.

A weak, bloody, struggling thing clambered over mangrove knees and dragged itself onto land.

He had feasted not long ago, but not enough to bring on the deep sleep that made the lifelong pain in in its mouth go away. His territory was safe and cool and there was easy meat, but never enough. He tasted the man-thing's blood on the air, fresh.

Big Sumbitch twitched his tail and went on the hunt.

46: PAGAN BABY

After he lost the Challenger in the suburbs, Chopper rode to New Orleans with Rob Halford of Judas Priest wailing on the stereo.

"The Green Manalishi (With the Two-Pronged Crown)." The song was written by Peter Green of Fleetwood Mac about a green hellhound that haunted him in an acid dream. To him it signified money, but the dog was anything that made you do things you didn't want to do.

Like a witch who put a gris-gris on you.

He didn't believe, but she did, and that was enough.

Tchoupitoulas Street followed the water like the belly of a Viking ship. He followed it past the port, where cranes dipped their steel beaks into a container ship, all the way to the Quarter, where he parked in a tourist lot off Canal and walked to Cafe du Monde. Ordered cafe au lait, took a table, and waited.

He felt stung with the loss of the city he knew before the storm. The cafe had not changed, but the city had. The heart was still there but a valve was leaking, not enough oxygen with every beat. Like his old man, it had slowed down, looked the same on the outside, but felt diminished. What was once eternal had found mortality.

"Wesley."

The Amazon mother-goddess towered over him, holding back a silver-slate pit bull on a harness. She wore her hair natural, tied back with a band, a loose sheer dress, and sandals. Her thick arms tattooed with symbols like protective bracers.

Suzane always managed to sneak up on him. She had a witchy way of either clouding his mind, or knowing when he was distracted.

The pup lunged for his face.

"Hope, *desann*."

Chopper held out his hand. Hope snuffled then licked it. Her left eye was a slit of flesh. He kneaded her thick neck. She'd been a bait dog, a rescue. Suzane turned her into a fighter. She'd done the same with victims of predators. They had a compound even Chopper could not enter.

He stood and kissed her cheek, all she would allow in public. Then he ordered fresh coffee and a plate of powdered beignets while she waited.

He licked sugar off his mustache and watched Suzane stir her chicory coffee with one of the fried dough fritters until it was ready to disintegrate.

"Why do we always have to meet here?"

Suzane let Hope lick sugar off her fingers, then dabbed at her lips with a napkin. "I know you can feel the energy of all the people. It recharges me."

People drained him.

Their nights together were more like children playing at fairy tales than lovers. Free of the world's ugly judgment and expectations. Unlike here, where across the open cafe, a thin couple sneered at Suzane's joy at the plate of beignets. He wanted to dump his coffee on them.

He let it bother him. The women whose eyes said *why are you with her when you can be with me?* There was no sacrifice in his love. He had no fetish, no big nana who clutched him to her massive breasts and left him a complex. She was strong but vulnerable, and when she said she would do something she did it and expected no praise, because *that was how it was supposed to be.*

That he could love.

He was not a man who expected medals for decency. He did not think himself a knight, not even a neon one like Sabbath sang about. He was just a man, and when he saw her the first time, leaning over a table at the women's shelter where he'd brought the beat-up girlfriend and child of a bounty, he was taken. And he had remained so.

He told her about the car while they ate. Hope sulked under her chair.

She took a notepad from her bag and flipped through it with sugared fingers until she found the page. "Houma. The Houma girl. Deanna. Her little brother said he saw a 'Hot Wheels car' before she disappeared. But it was black."

"You can paint a car."

He told her about Desmarteaux. The child killer from up north, during the Satanic Panic years. And his theory. "Maybe someone trained him. Or made him. And he's come home to join them. He's not as smart or as knowledgeable. So he showed his ass."

She nodded. They ate. He told her about Timmy Lee Baines, the house full of guns, and Ralph Ora.

"What's Rosie doing taking bounties for the HB?"

"He was Banshee MC, got turned inside. Might be able to flip him. He says they're dumping guns to make an excuse for a race war."

She huffed. "There's already a race war."

"You know what I mean. Nazi Armageddon."

Her eyes turned hard. "Keshawn is my priority. Follow the Hot Wheels car."

He folded his hands. Normally, he would pass the HB data to his fed contacts. Work to take them down. But the FBI had been directed not to focus on white supremacist hate groups. He would need something they could not ignore.

She drained the last of her coffee. "You may drive me home. But you can't stay tonight."

"What about this afternoon?" He stood and offered his hand.

"That's not night, is it?" Her eyes smiled.

47: KISSIN' COUSINS

Andre paid penance at the weight pile. He was old and the knot in his belly had sapped his strength, but he struggled beneath the barbell and traded one pain for another. The forty-five-pound plates were welded to the bars for safety. They wouldn't give convicts giant metal frisbees to throw around, or iron bars to stave someone's head in. No dumbbells, neither. You had 135-, 225-, 315-pound barbells and you liked it. If you wanted to work harder, rep it out.

Andre had hefted the three-plate bar when he first got here. Now two plates got him winded after ten repetitions. He'd once taken third place in a competition to max out reps on two plates held by the Malachi brothers, a religious group at the prison that helped inmates be good fathers to their children.

Now he swallowed his pride and maxed on the little-man bar, one thirty-five, what Evangeline had weighed when he'd last picked her up by her wide hips. She'd snap them long legs around his chest and take him down to the grass and tussle, while Okie would watch and smoke, sometimes join in.

The boy had come along at just the right time, when he sensed Okie had been getting jealous.

Evangeline had said she could handle him, but Andre wasn't sure. Okie's snake-tattooed left arm was quick with a fist and a gun. He was glad he'd never had to learn if Okie had been faster than he was.

"Desmarteaux!"

He racked the bar and sat up. Up on the tower, a CO held a bullhorn.

"You know where to go."

Andre wiped his face on his shirt and waved to the guard, then slow-jogged to the warden's office.

Warden Kane LeFer's desk was clean of papers. Pictures of his family in wooden frames carved by inmates faced out, flanking a brass pen set lathed in the metal shop. Behind him, badges and patches from all over the country. His sheriff's badge embedded in a block of Lucite sat in one corner like a boat anchor. And the wedding Bowie Pitou had forged for Andre. A trophy behind glass.

Two air conditioners pumped from the windows.

"You ought to be resting. Got a doctor appointment coming up." LeFer looked at his computer screen, his bulk overflowing the arms of the office chair. "Don't you?"

Sweat broke down Andre's sides in the chill. "I think so, sir."

LeFer moved his mouse around. "Sure you do. Gotta zap that goiter growing under your tit."

Andre held still. Showing relief could be seen as denying the warden had total power over him, and such hubris before the gods was deadlier here than in a Greek tragedy.

"Just letting your piece cure. It's looking real fine. Been damp these last couple days."

"I know you won't let me down."

"No, sir."

LeFer turned, and his aviators gleamed white beneath the fluorescent lights. "You best see that doctor. You got something to live for now. A son."

Andre looked into the white eyes. LeFer had read the letter. Of course he had.

"Not blood, but a son. Part Yankee, but that can't be helped.

Did his time, and now he's coming home to be with his real family. His blood family."

There were two guards outside with sidearms. He could stick those two brass pens in the warden's throat. Die with a knife in his hand. He wasn't quick as he once was, but his blood was up from the weight pile.

"Don't get stupid. You always thinking with your heart or your pecker, never with your brain, Desmarteaux. He was never your blood. That boy's a Calvineau. You know what that means."

Untouchable. Evangeline had shot a cop once. Nerves, on an early job. The man lived, but would forever hold one arm tucked like a chicken wing. Money made it go away.

They had more money than God.

Which made them holier.

Evangeline had told him the family history. Her mother made trips to Utah to visit the Mormons and their vaults of genealogical documents. The Calvineaus were Acadians who'd intermarried with Border Scots who'd led the Whiskey Rebellion. Then sugar plantations fueled by enslaved blood and backing slave-catcher gangs across the South. After the War Between the States, they built prisons and turned their fugitive slave patrols into constabularies that became the police. LeFer's people had been with them since the beginning, leading the patrols.

They would want the boy.

The boy he knew would rather die than serve them, but prison changed a man. He'd seen trusties turn, with that taste of power. And if the boy wouldn't turn, they would use Andre as leverage.

LeFer smiled. "It means you and I are kissin' cousins."

48: GATOR BAIT

Reggie circled the island with his swamp boat and checked the grow. The patch was remote and the soil rich with a thousand years of rotten vegetation, which quickly turned the plants into massive leafy bushes like something out of the Jurassic. Which was fitting, because the section of the swamp where the Heimdall Brotherhood trained for their racial holy war was home to its very own dinosaur.

The HB gave him a nickel-finish Mossberg Marine 12-gauge pump to patrol with. He kept it slung across his back so he could feel like a pirate on the water instead of a poor boy from Ventress with a broken-down truck and no girl to take riding in it. He couldn't train with them, or sleep in their camp, but he didn't want to be inducted anyway. He just wanted to eat.

Reggie eased the boat to his landing spot and poked at the ground for snakes with a boat hook. He had five supermarket chickens that he'd let rot in plastic bags for a week. Part of his job was to drop them around their island to keep it moated with gators. He never saw them, but the chickens were always gone when he came back.

He stepped gingerly out of the boat and tied it to a mangrove knee, then walked to the edge of the grow with a chicken in one hand, and his Mossberg slung low.

He gagged as he cut open the plastic bag and the smell hit him. It was too damn hot for gloves and pink slime burst all over his hands. He peeled off the wrapper and heaved the carcass underhand. It slapped against a stump. He returned to the boat and went to the next drop. His HB boss, a hatchet-nosed scarecrow named Erdesohn, told him to do it clockwise, and slapped him upside the head when he asked why.

Because I told you, ass face.

Someday he'd blast that fucker's face off with his Mossberg. He loathed their hateful asses, but they were the only job around that paid worth a damn. He'd bagged groceries at the Winn-Dixie, but that wasn't man's work. No matter what his daddy said about any work being man's work. What did his daddy know, sitting on the couch with his legs swole like two hogs, too proud to sue the chemical plant even though three of his coworkers had gotten settlements.

That's not how I was raised.

No, you were raised to die, living on a disability check while his mama worked long nights at the oyster processing plant and your son worked for Nazi bikers.

Reggie sighed and threw another chicken, then washed his hands in the water before motoring to the far side of the island.

49: SUMMER CANNIBALS

Jay Desmarteaux woke to a grinning, freckled face pointing Andre's revolver at him.

The darkness slithered off him like a mass of snakes. Everything hurt, but the kid stood on his ankle, and that hurt more.

"You picked just about the worst place to take a nap."

Reggie wondered what the reward would be for catching a trespasser. Maybe he could fix the truck and stop borrowing his mama's Hyundai.

"Put your hands up."

Jay obeyed, wincing. "I'm 'bout half dead. You get me to town and give me a bottle of water, it's worth five hundred bucks."

Jay squinted, looked the boy over for a bottle of water. It was maddening that breathing damn swamp air felt like drowning, but his kidneys still ached for water. He had hit the swamp water hard after tumbling off the overpass and swam under it to avoid the gunfire. Then police sirens sent him scuttling through tangled islands of mangrove knees, barking every extremity, swatting biting flies, terrified that every hollow might hold an angry water moccasin or a mama gator ready to twist his limbs off like chicken wings.

Reggie wrinkled his pig nose. The man looked like he'd fell out the Ugly-Ass Tree and hit every branch on the way down. "No way you got that kind of money."

"I had that pretty gun, didn't I? I got a stash outside Catahoula." Jay felt Pitou's Skunk Ape Bowie against his spine. He ached just thinking of grabbing it. He had no speed left in his bones. Even if he got Andre's Colt Python back, the kid had a shotgun slung over his shoulder.

Reggie cocked the revolver. It was a damn nice gun, had to be worth at least five hundred by itself.

"Get moving. Keep your hands where I can see."

Jay pulled himself to his feet, gritting his teeth at the pain. "That water in the bag? I'm about to keel over and die of thirst. Then you get nothing."

"The Heimdall Brothers are gonna pay me a big reward for your dumb ass. And I'm keeping this sweet gun either way."

The HB. The Hitler Bitches. They would pay for Jay's head. They'd tried to recruit him in prison, and he and Okie had gotten him out after ripping them off with a rigged boxing match, set up with the Latin Kings. The scar on his shoulder itched where he'd belt-sanded off their initiation rune.

"This is gator bait. Like you." Reggie heaved the bag past the bloody mess of a man. "Turn around."

Jay did. The Bowie's handle stuck out the back of his belt.

Reggie gripped the Colt Python with both hands. "*Don'tyoufuckinmove!*"

Jay didn't.

He waited with his hands up. A green fly landed on his face, but he didn't slap it. Even if the boy was shit scared and stupid. Jay didn't want to chop his head off. He just wanted water and rest.

"Okay," Reggie panted. "Take that pigsticker and cut that chicken bag open. Move slow."

Jay eased the blade out and hobbled toward the ballooned plastic bag of chicken. He dragged the huge leaf blade across and the bag burst with a smell like an ostrich's asshole. He choked back a dry heave and stumbled away.

Reggie began to wonder how he would get the boat back

with this man in it. He looked weak but dangerous. "Put that knife away. You know what, put it on the ground real slow. I'll blow your damn head off."

The muzzle quivered as Reggie held his skinny arms out. He remembered how his daddy said to shoot a sixgun. The memory angered him, now that his father was weak and dying.

"Easy, kid. This is your show."

"Don't call me kid, dammit!"

"What's your name, then? I'm Jay." He sheathed the knife and stuck the scabbard in the ground, handle facing him. Then he stepped back. He pressed his hand to his wound, hunching. He had maybe one burst in him, and could roll and swing the knife. He didn't want the kid's blood and guts all over him. But he didn't want to die, either.

"You think I'm stupid?" Sweat trickled down Reggie's brow. He aimed the gun at the man's head.

"I can tell you ain't killed no one before."

"I will, believe me."

"I believe you. But you don't want to."

"You don't know shit. Maybe I'll just leave you to die out here. How about that?"

Jay was about to beg and fall to his knees, then grab the knife, when the undergrowth exploded.

Big Sumbitch heaved through the swamp grass toward the rotten chicken carcass. Claws like boathooks ripped the ground as the beast launched forward and clamped teeth the size of rifle rounds on its meal.

Jay leapt on instinct and hit the ground like he'd taken a hook to the ribs. The beast was huge and terrifyingly fast. The gators he'd seen growing up had been babies in comparison. It thrashed its tail and cleared the weeds like a scaly, short-legged battle tank.

Reggie screamed and stumbled backward. The beast lumbered between them, holding his prize high. The chicken disappeared down his gullet and he thrust his massive jaw skyward, bellowing a growl that swelled his yellow throat.

Reggie aimed Andre's Python and fired in an explosion of red.

Jay curled up, pelted by shrapnel.

Reggie shrieked, staring at the two bloody lobster claws that remained of his hands. The revolver had detonated in his grip. The twisted barrel smoked on the ground between his legs. Reggie's white Budweiser shirt blossomed red.

Jay crawled back, waving the Bowie like a limp dick before the monster. Had the revolver got wet? No. It had plenty of time to drip dry, and it had gone off like a grenade.

Shooter.

The sneaky bastard had rigged it to explode, then sent him after Pitou.

"Where's your boat? I'll get you home!"

Big Sumbitch had other plans. He slapped Jay aside with a lash of his tail and chomped on Reggie's leg. His screams rose in pitch and went ragged as the beast dragged him away, cut off as the swamp embraced its enormous, rambunctious child.

50: RING AROUND ROSIE'S

When Chopper got to Rosie's there were four bikes in front. Not uncommon for a bail bondsman's lot. One looked familiar. Black gas tank with an 8-ball decal.

Whoever sprung Ralph Ora had juice. Or they'd taken his bike before the police arrived. Either way, it was bad news.

He parked in the rear, backing next to Rosie's silver-and-black Buick Riviera. He loaded the Shorty with slugs and holstered his baby nine, hid it all under his tailored jacket.

He stepped in a fresh spiral of dog shit not ten feet from Rosie's back door.

He had himself to blame. What'd he expect, Rosie to go jogging with a dachshund?

At the far end of the strip mall, the back door of the Chinese place was held open with a brick. Outside it, a man in cook whites smoked a cigarette and watched him as he circled the cinder block building. He hugged the plywood nailed over the closed video store's window and peeked in Rosie's glass front door.

Rosie kept his desk sideways, so his back was to the bricks. His seat hidden by a row of filing cabinets, no target from the street.

Two big men stood on either side of the back door, right hands low at their sides. That left two unaccounted for.

He slim-jimmied the Buick's door and screwdrivered the

ignition. Rosie bragged about how ladies liked to sprawl on the velour bench seat, but there was a downside of driving a vehicle built in '78.

He reversed out of the back lot onto the side street, then jumped the curb and plowed into the bikes, and parked with the fender blocking the front door. Then he ran for the back with the Shooter Shorty held port arms.

Two big white hands with a .45 poked out the back door. A Tyr rune pointed like an arrow on the backs of both. Chopper fired and racked the pistol grip.

The biker fell to his knees staring at his stumps. The steel door thumped against his shoulder.

Chopper hugged the wall in a crouch and stepped closer. Felt a boom like a rifle shot, and cinder block shrapnel cut his cheekbones. An inch-wide hole in the bricks.

Boom.

Another hole, closer to his head. He jumped and landed in a crouch in the doorway, using the handless biker for cover. Inside, a big boy fired a hand cannon that punched through the wall. Chopper pumped two rounds. One rocked the big man's belly, the other erased his face.

A skinny hatchet-faced man with long stringy hair rapid fired a small black pistol. A round crackled past Chopper's ear and two more slapped into the meat of his human shield.

He blasted the last one center mass, and he crumpled. Dropped the shotty and drew the nine. Hammerless double-action German steel. He stepped in with long strides and found Rosie huddled behind his desk, blubbering through swollen lips and jabbing with bloody fingers.

Ralph Ora popped up from behind the filing cabinet firing wildly.

Chopper rolled over the desk and landed on Rosie. The wiener dog yelped and squirmed away, claws skittering on the plastic tiles. He held aim loosely, covering the top and side of the cabinets. Glass shattered and a man swore.

Chopper jumped over the desk in time to catch Ora clambering out the busted window over the roof of the Buick. Aimed to put a round in his ass, then his legs went out from under him.

The straggle-haired biker had him around the knees in a tackle. Chopper's nine bounced out of his hand when his chin hit the floor.

Chopper kicked like a fish and rolled to his side. The biker hugged his leg and pinned them, inchworming his way up with his face down, safe from fists.

The biker punched for his kidneys. Chopper spread his freed legs and clamped them around the biker's middle. The biker reared up for a blow, and Chopper swung his hips to take away his base.

He'd wrestled in school to keep the bullies off his back for being a bookworm, and competed in Brazilian Jiu Jitsu across the southeast when time permitted. He had a solid guard but couldn't crush the man's abdomen to steal his air.

Rigid body armor.

The slug had caved in the armor plate. Chopper swiveled and hiked one leg over the biker's shoulder, then pulled his arm into a triangle choke. Sank it in deep and curled. His opponent's face bloomed purple.

This one would talk. Out in the junkyard. With some persuasion from the cane knife.

The biker's free hand flicked open a blade. He thrust the blade into Chopper's side.

Stopped by his holster. The point jabbed through, a pinprick of fire.

Chopper gripped the man's wrist and clawed at his eyes.

Rosie stuck a little black snub-nose into the biker's mouth and fired twice. The muzzle flash set the man's greasy beard on fire. The gray wisps glowed orange, like steel wool in flames.

The knife wound burned when the blade fell free. The point stuck into the plastic tiles. Chopper kicked the twitching body away.

By the time he got to the front door, Ralph Ora was long gone. Rosie sat in his chair stroking the dachshund, holding a cold bottle of Coke to his face. "It's all right, girl. It's all over."

"The hell were they doing here?"

"I'm fine, thanks for asking." The wiener dog licked his face. "They knew you were coming."

Chopper picked up a leather thong from the floor. Mercury's winged face grinned at him in silver. He planted his shoe on Rosie's desk to retie the charm around his ankle.

He wouldn't tell Suzane. She would say that her gris-gris had saved him.

The small television mounted on the wall barked news he couldn't make out.

"Queenie here took over my house. She sits on the arm of my easy chair. Bites my feet until I feed her by hand, at the table. See what you done to me?" The dog nuzzled under his arm. Its little tail patted his arm as it wagged.

"Probably added five years to your life. They say why they wanted me?" He wiggled a pinky in his ear.

"Just the usual race war shit."

Chopper picked up his weapons and checked the dead. The hefty soldier wore rigid body armor festooned with vintage German WWII insignia. The hand cannon was a Smith & Wesson .500 with Shooter Boudreaux's signature etched into the barrel.

When his ears stopped ringing, he called Junior LeFer's mobile. He didn't want to have to trade the purple Challenger, but he held no other cards. The television showed footage of a crane lifting a car that nearly went over the side of the bridge into the swamp.

The purple Challenger, crumpled like a ball of plum crazy tin foil.

51: HOODOO THERE

Jay paddled past a floating island of water hyacinths, perfume rising from the purple flowers that called for him to sleep. He'd found the dead boy's boat easily enough. An aluminum flatboat with a thirty-five horsepower Evinrude in back.

He didn't want to start the engine and broadcast his location to the Heimdall Brotherhood.

The island was empty of people, but the center had been cleared out and turned into some sort of training camp. Berms with shredded targets at one end, barracks built of tents at the other. Ammunition, but no arms. He took a flat of bottled water and a few MREs and got the hell out of there.

The sun became an ember on the opposite end of the sky. He wanted to get west, so he followed the sun for as long as it gave him light. The water helped, but he needed rest.

As he paddled, his heartbeat slowly became a roar drowning out the sounds of the swamp. The towering trees leered down at him, powdering him with their pollen. Their tiny messengers buzzed in his ears and bit his skin in secret codes that told him where to go.

A face in the water mouthed words to him. Its voice gurgled from the bottom.

Welcome home.

"I'm looking for my Papa Andre's fishing camp. They said it got washed out when the government opened the spillway."

The old water keeps everything. You're born in me and to me you will return.

Jay woke from his sleep-stupor and found himself staring at a dying catfish gulping at the surface, its mouth as round as a basketball. The swamp was still.

He started the engine and headed toward the sunset.

When the sun died and cast a purple twilight over the water, he aimed a lamp and steered with one hand. There was a cove in the distance, a good place to hide.

He swerved to avoid one stump and clipped another. The boat nearly tipped and he threw himself to the other side to right it. The lamp hit the deck and winked out.

Jay cut the engine. The boat drifted in the black. Insects chittered in the gloom.

He scrabbled for the lamp, held it to his chest and flicked the switch.

Nothing.

He gave it a shake and the light blinded him. He aimed it away and clenched his eyes shut until the glare faded. He heard ripples and growls from both sides. He slowly swept the surface with the beam.

A starfield of red eyes twinkled on top of water blacker than the night sky.

A wide set of eyes dunked beneath the surface and he heard scales scrape the bottom as he passed over. The beast rose with a throaty challenge and slapped the water with its tail.

The beasts knew the night was theirs.

Jay released a breath, then took the paddle and slowly backed out of the cove. He made his way toward a big mangrove standing alone, away from the constellations of eyes.

Sleeping in an open craft near land felt too much like he was the meat in a freshly shucked oyster, begging to be slurped by the first brave gator.

He tied off on the mangrove's roots and unrolled a tarp for cover. He found a bottle of motor oil and rubbed it on as bug repellent. He ate from an MRE and chugged water, pissing red over the side. He must have landed on a kidney when he jumped off the highway bridge.

He nodded off every few minutes, jabbed awake by the dull throbbing from his side. Eventually the insects, bullfrog calls, and distant rumble of gators made a demonic symphony that lulled him to an exhausted sleep.

He woke to fat drops of rain crackling on the tarp. A puddle weighed it down in the center. He carefully lifted one side and dumped the water off, letting in drops that soaked his bed of crumpled up trash bags. He sat in the center of the boat, making a peak in the tarp so the rain rolled off. Drops drummed his head like water torture. He turned on the lamp and huddled under a corner of the tarp, then scanned the water to ensure he wasn't surrounded by hungry dinosaurs.

The night was black.

The gators didn't care for rain, either.

Except one.

A set of blue eyes glowed in the distance, fuzzy in the mist that rose off the water. He'd never seen a gator with blue eyeshine before. Dogs, sometimes.

The eyes bobbed and winked behind trees. Whatever owned them circled the cove's edge, low, until they came to the end of a spit thirty yards from his craft.

He stared back.

Will o' the wisps? Wild hog? Papa Andre had told him stories of the Rougarou. The werewolf of the swamp who hunted and devoured incautious children.

Jay gripped the handle of the Skunk Ape Bowie.

The eyes winked out and something heavy hit the water. The mist broke by the cove and his light caught a dying gator writhing with its yellow belly torn open. The boat rocked, and when he tried to aim his light at the beast's prey, it had disappeared.

He settled in the boat, huddled beneath the tarp.

A howl rose in the distance and silenced the insects' chatter.

He got no sleep that night.

52: SALVATOR

Once Andre finished the chifforobe for LeFer, he was put back on outdoor detail. They marched past Red Hat, the infamous brick death chapel that housed Gruesome Gertie, the electric chair. She hadn't sparked since 1991, but the squat, red-capped cell block was a constant reminder that no matter how you acclimated to the regimented life inside, death held its cold blade above your neck and could drop it any day.

The work was rough, digging out busted pipes for patch and replacement. Gun bulls no longer shot you at will from the backs of their steeds while you pulled vegetables from the earth, but you knew they could say you went mad and swung your hoe at them. If you ran, the dogs were set loose, instead of bullets. Rumor was they had been trained vicious, to tear limbs from sockets and crush bones between their jaws.

Digging was punishment from LeFer, for hiding the letter from the boy. Andre had rolled it tight and hidden it in a seam of his mattress that he'd cut with a spring. He hadn't the heart to tear it up and swallow it.

He didn't know why it was so important for them to break a man. It was almost sexual. They didn't want you to do your time standing up; they wanted to take the last shreds of respect you might have for yourself and make you watch them flush it down a dirty toilet. And smile for them as it swirled away.

There was something missing in men like LeFer that riches

and power could not fill. They could not abide the conceit that their fellows should be treated as equals. You could pursue happiness with their boot on your neck all you liked, as long as you admitted they were your betters. If you refused to give them that, the boot ground your face in the muck.

Andre shoveled the slop from around the pipe. The exhaustion felt good, like he was being purified by the dirt. When they found the crack, a Black big stripe named Louie Gaines helped him out of the hole and jumped down with the cutting torch. He whispered sorry as they passed.

Louie had fished out letters Andre had flushed before. Andre held no grudge.

Inmates had died in gas explosions from pipe welds, so Andre got as far away from the hole as the guards would allow. He leaned on his shovel. His ribs felt like they'd served time as the Devil's xylophone.

The river snaked off past Red Hat, a muddy ribbon leading off into the green Elysium of the bayou. The same water that touched the land of the Calvineaus where he'd first met Evangeline, then disappeared into the Gulf, the land breaking apart and dissolving like bread in gravy. He'd read that the state lost a football field a day to the ocean, and couldn't contemplate that someday the land where he'd been born would surrender to the sea.

A hack tapped his shovel with his baton. "How you do it?"

"How I do what, sir?"

"Live with that chi-mo who done your boy walking round in front of God and everybody? Thought you was a man, Desmarteaux."

"What you talking about?"

"Just what everybody knows."

Woody the Fox looked away when he asked. "Salva goes down, they'll fix it so it falls on you. No matter if they find him with a bloody shank in his hand, they'll put his death on your jacket."

Andre twisted his flat pillow in his hands like it was Salva's bull neck. "But it's true?"

The next day in the yard, Woody took him to see Moreau, a dirty cop from Jefferson Parish doing life for murdering his partner.

Moreau looked as tough as a bad cop serving life in a state lockup had to be. Straddling the bench at the weight pile, a massive muscled delta of an upper body heaving the three-plate bar, thighs like hogs. When he finished his set, he stared at Andre over his thick black mustache.

"Been waiting for y'all to come round. You and Okie Kincaid tore through three payroll trucks on my turf and didn't kick up a penny. Why I ought to help you?"

"Boo Boo Ronceveaux just came through processing," Woody said. "He's in Cypress Four." A pretty pimp that Moreau had beaten ugly with a blackjack. He'd want revenge something fierce.

"I should've stomped his head in. He ain't nothing more than a turd on two legs," Moreau said, and toweled off the sweat. "We knew Mary Calvineau was selling her pussy out her trailer but we din't know 'bout the boy. Wouldn't allow that in my parish, even with her name."

Andre doubted that. As long as Calvineau money lined his wallet, Moreau would look the other way at Jack the Ripper skipping into a nursery school.

"Salva worked the plant in Sulphur. We thought he was one of Mary's tricks. After y'all burned her trailer down, we caught him with a boy he grabbed walking home from church. Wanted to shoot him right there, but my partner, he wasn't down with it. I had a drop and everything."

Andre nodded. Mary was Evangeline's sister, the boy's blood mother. They found her dead on the sofa with maggot-filled pits where her eyes had been. The boy near dead of thirst, tied to the leg of the sofa, carrot peeler in his hand. They took the boy home and burned the place to cleanse what they had found.

"You want him done, call your rich bitch and get ten gees to my woman in Lake Charles. I'll make Salva die slow."

Woody guided Andre away before he said anything a snitch might pass along.

Left him with the heavy bag, where Andre punched until he shredded the skin between his knuckles bloody.

53: WOLF CHILD

Jay woke to the smiling maw of a gator climbing into the boat. Teeth clamped down on the steel toe of his mud-yellow work boot. The alligator's claws hooked the edge of the boat and water rushed in. The Bowie's blade rang off its skull between the eyes. The metal cup protecting his toes dimpled as its teeth crushed down.

The gator began to sink into the water. Next came the death roll that popped his leg off at the knee like a drumstick off a roast chicken. *Whack 'em on the snoot*, Papa Andre had said. *And pray*, Mama Evangeline had added.

Jay wasn't much on prayer.

He heaved up and hammered the Bowie's pommel on the gator's nose. It released, and Jay found a *Thank God* escaping his lips against his volition. The reptile clambered up the sinking boat and snapped at him. With both hands, he buried the spade point of the knife behind the beast's head. It hissed then sank, pulling him with it. He wasn't giving up the knife. He hit the muddy swirl of oily cafe-au-lait face-first.

When he was a boy, he'd seen Andre wrestle an eight-foot gator that their Catahoula hound Bebe had cornered by the fishing camp house. On land it was a matter of body slamming the dinosaur on its back and getting your arm beneath the chin. They could clamp down with tons of pressure, but the muscles were weak in the other direction. Get some rope around its snout and you had dinner for a week or more.

In the water was a different story.

Jay hugged his legs around the critter's belly and hooked his left arm around under the jaw. The gator sank toward the bottom where it knew prey would drown and become easy meat. Jay had always been good at holding his breath, but this was the first time with a mad six-foot gator between his legs. Gators hated going upside down, so at least it wouldn't press him down into the muck.

Jay wrenched out the Bowie and plunged the blade into the gator's belly. It went clean through to back armor. The beast writhed and gutted itself. Jay burst to the surface, coughing up primordial soup.

He got one breath before he was pulled into its death throes. He plunged in the knife again and again. The shard of steel glanced off the scutes but sank deep into the gator's heart, spewing dark blood.

The blood and the thrashing would bring more hungry maws.

Jay waded to the nearest spit. Where he'd seen the Rougarou.

Yellow eyes watched from beneath hanging branches of tupelos as he staggered onto shore. The pain in his side flared and he collapsed.

He writhed in the cold mist of the night, biting back his pain. He drifted in and out of darkness, the endless bug-song a cacophonous lullaby. Beneath it, a low huffing breath he could not distinguish from his own.

A pair of cold blue eyes winked in the starlight.

Slowly, a silhouette formed in the darkness, a low-hunkered man-thing.

You are a wolf child.

He woke gasping, to dawn breaking in a bloodred glow through the trees. A bull gator growled challenge from the water. Jay gritted his teeth and got to his knees. Two bigger beasts fought over the fat tail of the dead gator, and more were coming. One spun a clumsy death roll and twisted a slab of prime meat clean off.

The boat was gone.

Jay clutched his side and swung the Bowie like a machete, hacking a path further from the water. He had to find safe shade before the sun got high in the sky. His lips were cracked and soon he would be tempted to drink the tea-stained water.

The trees swallowed him and often exploded with white birds fleeing his advance. The sun was a lamp for the turkey vultures circling him high in the thermals. He stumbled for the last time in a flattened clearing, his vision blurred and fading.

A thick black shape hunkered the center of the circle, like a blasted tree trunk.

Jay swung his blade wildly and fell into the moss. The Bowie bounced out of his hand. The moss was cool and damp and he sucked moisture off it. He closed his eyes and waited for the black creature to bare its fangs and finish him.

Blackness embraced him instead.

54: SALVAGE

Chopper studied the wreck of the purple Challenger in the St. Martin parish impound lot. Deputy Ledoux fooled with his phone in the shade, a hundred dollars richer, looking up occasionally to make sure the skip tracer didn't lift anything.

The rare classic had been accordioned into modern art sculpture. High-caliber rounds had punched through the radiator, the driver's head rest, and the dashboard. A moving vehicle. A professional hit.

He already had one reason to visit Shooter Boudreaux, now he had another.

The trunk had been crowbarred open. A red Craftsman toolbox inside had exploded, spilling socket wrenches and screwdrivers. Chopper rifled through the mess with gloved hands. He made note of a roll of duct tape and a pile of zip ties. He used the same gear on his bounties.

But this car didn't belong to a bounty hunter; it belonged to a convicted child murderer.

"Hacked the boy's head off," Ledoux said. "He was fifteen years old."

Chopper imagined what a young killer might graduate to. Desmarteaux was in prison when the killing began. And the more Suzane talked to old parents whose faces drained as they recalled their vanished children, the earlier the deaths began. They had speculated that their Rougarou was generational, with an elder teaching young acolytes. Maybe the headhunter was the newest.

"Yankee judge gave him life, then some lawyer sprung him. Said it was cruel and unusual to get no parole. And they set him free, you believe that? Beheading people, that's what's cruel and unusual."

"He hurt any girls?"

"Just the one boy. That they know of. Case is thirty years old. They were cagey. Could've been that Satan stuff that went down in the '80s. Maybe these boys were killin' girls and burying them in the end zone in Giants stadium next to Jimmy Hoffa, and he didn't want his partner telling."

Chopper flipped the spare tire and squeezed it, looking for hideaways. He found folded trash bags. Another sign of abduction. He moved to the crumpled interior. The steering wheel had impaled the driver's seat. If he hadn't jumped, this Desmarteaux would be dead. The car was old but immaculate. Not even a dried-up french fry under the seats.

"They say he raised some hell up there. He's got open warrants."

"What for?"

"It don't matter. He shows up, Warden LeFer wants him. Alive."

"What's the bounty?"

Ledoux smirked. "Not having his boot up your ass."

The back seat was crushed, but something shone from the well under the cushions. He gave the cushions a tug and they creaked.

"Your five minutes are near up."

There was a tape in the stereo. Chopper turned the volume knob. A distorted guitar solo warbled out the speakers. He cranked it up. It was "Night Prowler," by AC/DC. The song that had supposedly inspired serial torture-killer Richard Ramirez.

White boy music, but at least the old stuff had some edge to it.

Ledoux shouted over the music.

Chopper pried the back seat with his cane knife until it popped. He pulled out a duffel bag. Ledoux walked over, pissed, making cut-off gestures.

He clicked off the stereo.

"You lose your mind? Sheriff comes back here, it's both our asses."

"Wanted to know what kind of music he liked." He opened the duffel. The shiny object was a Case folding knife, on a sheaf of papers. Ledoux walked around the wreck.

"Y'all missed that." He heaved the bag to Ledoux and used the distraction to slip the papers into his jacket.

Ledoux wrinkled his nose and rifled through the bag. "Told you not to touch anything. Junior LeFer is on his way."

Back in his truck, hidden by the tinted windows, Chopper unfolded the papers he'd taken.

One was a yellowed paper driver's license that read Evangeline Antoinette Calvineau. Another was an arrest sheet from the '80s for a chi-mo named Philo Salva.

A mentor? The timeline was wrong. Desmarteaux was in juvenile prison when Salva was arrested. But maybe they knew each other before.

He committed the details to memory and sent photos of the papers to Suzane. Then he went to talk to Junior LeFer.

"You all right after that shit at Rosie's?"

Chopper waved a hand. "Their team missed these."

Junior gave him a look, then scanned the papers. "Shit."

They traded stares, working over what they knew in their heads, what the other man would hide and what he would share. Chopper respected Junior LeFer as a lawman, he may have got the job through his daddy, but he took it seriously.

"What brought you here? Your Rougarou?" He smirked.

"There's a marshals' warrant for that Desmarteaux."

"Don't try to collect it," Junior said.

That meant Desmarteaux was protected by the Calvineaus.

"What about Salva?"

Junior turned over the yellowed arrest sheet, then held it out. "He's fair game."

"Keep it." Chopper didn't want anything touched by the Calvineaus on his person. That name was a curse.

Curse.

Maybe Suzane and her magic bullshit was rubbing off on him.

"High-powered rifle. Like the one stolen from Ti' Boy Garriss," Chopper said.

"That was recovered. At Shooter Boudreaux's residence." He nodded toward the gaping bullet holes in the Challenger's interior. "Don't know who else could make shots like that from a moving vehicle."

"I know better than to mess with Louisiana's favorite bad boy."

Junior smiled. "You have my permission. I want him uneased."

"How uneased?"

"Witnesses saw men in paramilitary gear on the bridge. Including a big boy wearing German insignia. You know I have no patience for their kind. But there's not much I can do. But I'd look the other way, if someone had a vendetta against them."

The cut in Chopper's side ached. Junior LeFer didn't have the balls to stand up to his father the warden, or his Calvineau bosses. He wanted a cat's paw. An unlucky black cat's paw, to stir shit with the Heimdall Brotherhood.

"And when they strike back at me?"

"They'll be as slippery as your friend Ralph Ora. Best not to get any judges involved." Junior took out a lighter and ignited the corners of the Evie Calvineau's ancient driver's license. He dropped it onto the crushed hood of the Challenger and watched it burn.

55: MOTHER'S FANG

They rose with the sun. Some set out on leaf-shaped pirogues and others on foot, cane knives hanging from calloused hands, long guns or fishing poles over their shoulders.

There were people to be fed and protected.

As they had always done.

The swamp sang with bird chatter blessing the hazy dawn. Drusilla's path was well worn. Her camp was closest, so she always arrived first. Which made it her task to light the pipe and smoke, sprinkle the tobacco offering, and welcome the others. But first, she checked her traps.

One hook was picked clean, another's bait writhed with maggots. The last had a young gator through the jaw. His yellow eyes seared her with hate. She aimed her twenty-gauge at the back of its head and rocked with the recoil. The birds quieted for just a moment, then resumed their conversations.

They would part it out later. She was reed thin and had lost her breasts to cancer two years ago this spring. She had gotten her hair back but not her strength.

The meat would do her good.

She tucked the spent shell in her house dress pocket and replaced it with her last. The Walmart only sold them in packs of five and her grandson wouldn't be by to take her shopping for a few more days.

The path was quiet. She had been coming here since she got

her blood as a girl, holding her memaw's hand, reciting the old stories. From wherever came life, also came death. Those who made life were empowered to protect it.

Some of their ways came from the first people, and others from Africa, passed down on the mother's side in secret. Not all who escaped bondage fled north. They had broken free from its shackles long before there was safe passage. Drusilla's great-great-grandmother had run into the bayou and married into the Chitimacha tribe.

More joined them. Their hidden village lasted through the war and served as a safe haven. Most had forgotten it, but the descendants of those tasked with tending the Mother's Fang passed on their duties. After the big storm, people who'd lost everything, some who'd been caged by their government, returned and revived the lost village.

Drusilla and her women kept a circle cleared around the stone, and baited gators for meat and to keep the sacred place safe. They tended vines of mirliton squash to feed those in need, and lavender gardens among the tupelo gum trees to keep the mosquitoes at bay.

The Mother's Fang was black and pushed up through the bayou like a jagged spike as tall as a cypress trunk. Scarred with strikes from stone blades, the Fang of the Mother was the corpse of a giant snake defeated by Chitimacha warriors, and its writhing coils became the twisty Bayou Teche.

The women kept it secret from the village. They each inducted one acolyte, no more.

Drusilla sat on her favored stump and sparked the bowl of her pipe, said the words to the snake-mother.

A groan made her reach for her shotgun.

She walked the circle and found the place profaned.

A bloody white boy sprawled before the Mother's Fang.

She should have waited for one of the hale women, but she had never been good at doing what others said she should. She kicked the man in the side.

He screamed like a baby squeezed from the womb, then collapsed.

She leveled her gun at his head, ready to blood him for the Mother.

A flash of silver at his throat. She nudged the thong with the muzzle of her gun and lifted a pierced Mercury dime.

The etching marked him as one of Suzane's.

He would live, for now.

If he didn't die on his own.

She took his knife from him, felt his forehead for fever. Drusilla wasn't a healer. She waited for the others, puffing her pipe while the boy writhed in the dirt before the Mother Fang, moaning to himself. Calling for his mama and papa.

Boy was carved like the statue of Jesus dying at his mother's side she'd seen at the Cajuns' church up in Lafayette. And as white. Sickness seeped from a wound at his side.

She held her oilskin of water to his lips.

56: PALACE DEFILED

The dark figure walked slowly across the lot, not avoiding the security camera. Walked right toward it and gave it the finger.

The screen reflected in Shooter's tinted glasses. Who had the balls to hit the palace?

The cellular alarm system was jammed. The backup phone line and the cable had been cut at the box. The nearby streetlamps knocked out with a pellet gun or suppressed pistol. Then the masked man had taken his time popping the cylinders on the rear door locks, pausing to look at his phone, which must've been linked to wireless cameras aimed at the street.

Once inside, the thief ignored the easily sold handguns and went for the artillery.

In the armory, a Browning Automatic Rifle that Shooter had converted to a modern bullpup with a pistol grip. His .44 magnum with the ivory grips, which he'd won his first trick shot championship with. And two .50-caliber rifles worth ten grand apiece.

The thief had also rolled out a hand truck loaded with a hundred pounds of Tannerite explosive rifle targets that Shooter wasn't supposed to have on the premises, but he sure as hell wasn't keeping that shit in his garage. Tannerite wasn't flammable; it required a strike from a high velocity round to explode, but one negligent discharge and you were up in smoke. He should have planted some in the trunk of the Desmarteaux boy's Challenger.

The burglar didn't go for the safe, bother with the cash box, or roll out the cracker barrel full of bargain battle rifles that Shooter kept near the register. The last thing the invader had done was kick over the barrel and arrange four rifles into the arrow rune of the Heimdall Brotherhood.

When the cell jammer was turned off, the alarm company called the local police, and they called Shooter. He watched the BRPD clear the shop and called Junior LeFer. The Calvineau Parish sheriff talked shit about jurisdiction until Shooter asked if he had to wake up his daddy the prison warden.

When LeFer saw the Heimdall rune, he had his men roust the chief of the HB gang from his den. Derro Kroese, a six-four Viking in denim with hair and beard the color of tobacco juice spat in the snow, was not pleased.

Junior LeFer eyed the biker scumbag and the outlaw celebrity like two turd stains on the magic carpet he had inherited. Kane Junior's mother had begged him not to return to the parish after his stint in the Middle East. Go make your own life and be free, she said. But Kane Jr had wanted the comfort of home. His daddy wanted the war hero to have a parade, and the Calvineaus gave it to him. Against Daddy's demands, Junior had worn dress shorts to show off the million-dollar prosthetic in place of his right leg.

Right now he wanted to give both these shitbirds a bionic kick up the butthole.

He knew his daddy was crooked; prison labor built their St. Francisville home. But the whole state was crooked, and if you didn't dip your beak, you were shunned. He'd also learned the state's white supremacist history from his Black professors at LSU. He didn't think much of it until he served with Black soldiers like Wesley "Chopper" Tewliss. They opened his eyes a crack, which was all you needed to see the deep disparities that did not so much linger as remain enforced.

Openly supporting Nazis like the HB was not something he'd expected from the genteel racist Calvineaus. He'd heard that they had let their golden boy Roy Eagleton sing on rebel records under a stage name, racist crap that they forced upon every jukebox in the parish, and much of the state, back in the '60s and '70s, to make bar owners show their true colors or be shunned as race traitors. But arming Nazis seemed a whole another level. Or maybe it was all the same.

"Why would my men steal from their supplier, Sheriff?" Kroese said.

"Because your meth-head crews don't want to pay for 'em?" Shooter said. "Say something, Little LeFer. You're the college boy."

Junior paused to absorb the indignity. "Hitler Bitches aren't good enough to pull this off, but they're stupid enough to try. You lay down with dogs, you get fleas."

"Hey." Kroese frowned at the HB's despised nickname.

"This was a pro. Y'all aren't up to it. You'd back a payloader through the concrete and run off with whatever you could. These cameras show it was one man. None of y'all are shit without numbers."

"And you pigs are?"

Junior LeFer turned on his boot toe and bounced his bionic shin off of Kroese's. The bionic leg had a sharp corner that hit like steel rebar. When the dolled-up biker hunched in pain, Junior uppercut him to the sternum and let him slump to the beige concrete.

"You operate here because you're lackeys for the Calvineaus. Doing shit work, selling guns in neighborhoods where decent people won't tread unless they have no choice. Otherwise I'd kill one half of you and jail the other."

He turned toward the aged sniper. "Same with you, Shitter Boudreaux. Your immunity only goes so far. You want a crotch full of titanium? Call me 'Little LeFer' again."

"There's no need for that. I was out of line."

Kroese groaned around gritted teeth.

"This is that crazy bitch Evangeline, or someone working with her," Shooter said. "You know it, Sheriff. She killed Ti' Boy, she shot my house up with his rifle, and now she's got an arsenal. I'm the victim here. If you'd caught her fine ass, we wouldn't be here."

"I'm not risking my men's lives. Send some of your Nazi pals to tackle her and bring her in unharmed." He stared into Shooter's aviators. "The Cals got every coon-ass on the Vipère looking for her instead of selling shrimp on the side of the road. That shit you pulled on the highway didn't help. Don't play stupid, either."

"That was sanctioned."

"A body at Rosie's bail bonds fits the description of one of the highway hitters. What were they doing there?"

"I don't know anything about that," Shooter said. "Kroese?"

Kroese stood and rubbed his leg. "That coon skip tracer cost us a hundred grand in product and a safe house. His ass is dead."

"Not in my parish," Junior LeFer said. "This war's in the papers. That's got to stop. I suggest you go to the mattresses, put on your thinking caps, and do this quiet like. I'll pass on what I know, but one more public shootout, and the Calvineaus might kick all y'all off the gravy train." Let them kill each other. No humans involved. He headed out.

Shooter kicked the Tyr rune rifles apart. "Tell your boys to arm up, Kroese."

57: SAINT MALO

Jay woke to hot breath in his face. He reached for his blade and his side seized in pain. A blue Catahoula leopard hound jumped back, then nosed in to lick his face.

He raised a hand and let the dog get his scent, then patted its flank. The dog beat him with its tail and kept his body close. Reminded him of Andre's hound Bebe, who had saved him from a cottonmouth as a child.

He was in a small, undecorated room with a screened window. The sun did not reach the bed. The room had a medical smell, and his head was hazy. He was in a hospital-style bed, with an IV hooked to his arm.

Jay checked his side. It had been cleaned and bandaged. He eased to a sitting position. The cord felt taut around his sunburnt neck. He tugged the silver coin.

Molina's luck charm.

He fell off again and woke to a man changing his IV bag.

"Your fever broke. Don't move too much. You've got stitches."

He was in his thirties with close-cut natural hair and rich brown skin. He wore a loose drab shirt and bangle bracelets. Slender hands, like the rest of him, and he moved with slow deliberation.

"Thank you," Jay said. "I'm Jay."

"Name's Zephirin. You can call me Zeph. You want some

water?"

"I could drink a tub full."

Zephirin returned with two plastic Mardi Gras cups. One was worn and illegible, the other read Manny Randazzo's King Cakes. "You get two. Make them last. You're getting fluids in your arm. This is just to quench your thirst."

The cool water down his throat sent him back to sleep.

The next day he could walk. Zephirin switched him to pills and led him outside to a swamp village. A dozen or more sturdy huts on stilts, their roofs gleaming blue with solar panels. A huge satellite dish at one end.

A bowl of gumbo and a plate of greens waited on a handmade table. Jay was too hungry to ask questions.

He shoveled the rich gumbo into his mouth with a wooden spoon. Baby shrimp, chunks of gator meat, shreds of crab and a yellow smear of roe, it tasted like the food of the gods. The heat flushed his chest and drove the weakness from his bones. The Catahoula hound curled up under the table and rested his head on his boot.

"Don't feed him. He ate already."

An older man with gray-dusted hair and burnished brown hands set a gator's head on the table. A pistol at his hip.

Jay winced to stand. "I'm—"

The man set a hand on his shoulder. "Eat. We know who you are."

Jay ate. He didn't know who he was with, but they weren't Heimdall, and that was enough.

The man carved out the head meat with a little rat tail knife, ignoring the dog's whimpering. He packed the skull with salt for curing. "How'd you get here?"

"Swam," Jay said. He picked a strip of shrimp shell from between his teeth. "Waded. Took a boat from some Nazis, but a gator tipped it."

"You met our distant neighbors. We're watching them."

A woman with a freckled bronze complexion and tied-back hair joined them. She also wore a leather gun belt and a pistol at her side.

Jay stood before she could tell him not to. "Ma'am. Thank all y'all for your hospitality."

"I'm Dani and this is my husband, Marlon. This is our camp, Saint Malo. You are welcome here as long as you behave."

"I'm good with my hands. Can fix most anything with a motor."

"If everyone votes that you can stay, we'll keep you busy." Marlon fished two black marbles from a rusted coffee can and pushed them into the gator head's eye sockets from the back, then stuck a broken shingle into the mouth to hold the jaw open, and set it on a bench lined with more gator heads, drying in the sun.

Jay scooped his bowl clean and wished for a hunk of bread.

Dani gave him the tour, walking with a hand-carved stick. People worked: cooking, fixing, performing the daily chores of life. Cajun and Creole, Isleños and Hmong, Black and a few white. Many more women than men. It reminded him of Andre's old fishing camp, which was the first time he'd felt safe as a child.

Dani told him that Saint Malo was named after Juan San Malo, an enslaved man who escaped the Spanish and led raids against slavers with his fellow rebels until he was hanged in Jackson Square in 1784. A settlement bearing his name lasted until the 1915 hurricane wiped it out. She and Marlon started the camp after Katrina, when the troops came and rounded up people trying to survive as looters. They lost their home to another flood and rebuilt here, and were soon joined by like-minded people. The latest were climate refugees from Isle de Jean Charles.

She pointed to various small buildings, mostly wood but some Quonset huts and a few concrete sheds. "Our son's a tech wiz. We have solar and a windmill, and batteries so we're not running generators all the time. This isn't a life of luxury, but when things go bad again, we'll still be here. They'll need an army to take it from us."

"The Calvineaus have one."

"We know all about your family."

"They ain't my family."

"Your blood, then." She stopped and faced him. "That's your house to clean, not ours."

"My Papa Andre's in Angola. I can't let him die in there. I can't." The world grew hazy through his tears. "It's an evil house, I know. They got a boy at Whiterose, a Black boy, kept like a slave. His name's Keshawn. Don't know how much you know about me, but my mom and pop saved me from a hell house when I was five. I was ready to die to get Keshawn out, but he told me they'll hurt his mama."

Her face hardened.

"I ain't afraid to die, Miss Dani. But I can't do this alone."

58: NAZI HUNTING

Robbing a gun shop was high on the list of stupid things Chopper had done, but it felt good to strike at the Calvineaus. Rosie had buyers for the Barrett rifles waiting. The Browning and the Dirty Harry guns, those he'd save for hunting the Heimdalls. Taking out Nazis was no sin.

When his granddaddy shipped off to Europe, it was the national sport. They'd always been in America, under one flag or another.

He told Suzane about the hit, and she sighed at him over the phone. Working with LeFer was dangerous. They'd drop him if things went bad. But they had no lead on Keshawn, and the link to the Calvineaus in the "hot rod" was all they had. He thought it was no coincidence that Hitler Bitches came to kill him once he got close.

Chopper jammed the .44 in the mouth of a Monroe pimp named Wisdom Farallon, after having zip tied him to his bed in his silk boxers. Wiz was a white skip he had picked up a while back for trafficking, who had pled down to a year and a day. The judge was not concerned with the girls Wisdom had beaten and pimped. They were runaways, or kicked out to the streets, and he called their predicament "a lifestyle choice."

Chopper wrote the judge's name in the death book he kept in his mind's dark corner. Cancer ran in his mother's family. If he got the bad news that he had six months to live, there was a list of people who only had five. That judge was one of them.

Wisdom spat blood from the damage the .44's sight did to his throat, then told Chopper about a Heimdall whoremaster named 4-Hondo, who had bragged about running trains on Black girls for degradation videos out of a safe house up in Monroe.

Chopper slipped out the cane knife and scored the zip tie around Wisdom's wrists. "How many girls you run these days? I want to talk to them."

"You chipped my fucking tooth." Wisdom gave him three names and room numbers at a motel off the state highway.

"That means five." He cinched a zip tie high up on Wisdom's left pinky finger. "I'll be kind and charge you for one."

"What you doing!"

The cane knife sank deep into the pressed wood of the headboard. Wisdom howled as the severed digit bounced off his chest, ringed with the zip tie. Chopper wrenched the blade from the wood and cut the zip tie holding the pimp to the bed.

"You're crazy!" Wisdom jumped up and scrabbled for his severed finger on the floor. He grabbed his car keys and ran down the stairs. "They can sew 'em back on. Gotta get ice!"

Chopper gave Suzane's card to Wisdom's girls. Two told him to go fuck himself, but the youngest, a Cajun girl, took a ride with him to Suzane's shelter in the Lower Ninth. On the way, she warned him about 4-Hondo.

"He's got more guns than John Wick. That's where they send us for punishment. You don't come back. They got a camp out in Bayou Vipère. They say they use the burned-out girls for target practice and feed 'em to this big gator they got." She squirmed, restless. "I heard this Witch Suzane got a magic powder that lets you kick fast, is that true?"

Ibogaine. "It doesn't work for everybody, but I've never seen her give up on anyone."

Him, especially.

Suzane folded the girl in her arms and blew Chopper a kiss over her head. He could not enter the sanctuary. There were some boys there, but the grown men went to his folks' place in the swamp. He never stayed there long. He and his dad always ended up in an argument. Or a "spirited debate," as he called it, with Mom waiting for them to settle down before pointing out they were mostly in agreement, and should focus on that.

His uncle had made him and his father both read "Those Who Walk Away from Omelas," by Ursula K. Le Guin. A magic city kept alive by the suffering of one child. His father walked away from Omelas.

Chopper could not leave without the child.

59: RODEO CLOWN

Warden LeFer had been pleased with the chifforobe. Andre thought about his Evangeline and the boy while rasping the ivy vines in the wood, sanding them smooth, staining them so they glowed like the sun was trapped inside. It was a huge piece of work, and when he was done he felt aimless and exhausted. He had been trying to carve a few little animals out of scrap wood—they always sold well—when the guard told him to follow him to the Warden's office.

"Looks like you won't have much to sell next week," LeFer said. "I'm afraid I can't let you take up space in the craft bazaar. Playing favorites puts anger in the hearts of the men. You can put your pieces on the mixed table."

Andre looked through the lenses of the warden's glasses. He didn't like it when you didn't meet his eyes.

"You understand that, don't you? Course you do." He nudged Andre's ribs with his fist. Feeling out the tumor. "After the rodeo, when things settle down, I can put you in for a trip to Our Lady of the Lake. But here's the thing, Desmarteaux. We get a lot of flack from the bleeding hearts up North about our rodeo, because it's almost all Black boys these days. Their reasons are their own. We don't force 'em to do anything. Maybe they want that dollar more than a white boy does. They put on a better show, too. And when a hard-working man brings his family to my show, and gets to see a bad boy convict get thrown by the bull, it makes him feel good."

He kneaded Andre's shoulder. Fat or not, his grip was still iron. "This year, the only damn white man signed up is that baby-raper Philo Salva, bless his rotten heart."

Andre tensed in spite of himself.

"He's strong and fast for his age, and his jacket's clean. Nothing I can do to stop him, without the chardonnay sippers coming down on me. I block him, they might try to get the rodeo shut down for good. The bleeding hearts would love that. So I need a good man to sign up. We need Cowboy Desmarteaux."

He walked around to his chair, which squeaked as his bulk hit the cushions.

"Sir, I haven't had time to train."

"You got natural ability. No training beats that. And no one wants to see Salva win."

Warden LeFer took a sheet of paper out of a folder and set it on his desk.

LeFer turned the arrest report around so Andre could see the face in the mugshot.

"It's blacked out, but that's him saying he frequented Mary Calvineau. And we know what she did with your boy."

Salva was charged with abducting a five-year-old boy from church in 1981. The jagged typing mentioned a trailer outside Sulphur. Where they'd rescued the boy.

"Out in the mud, anything can happen. Salva might take a tumble right in front of the bull's horns. Put him into a bed in the infirmary. Once you get there, you lose hope and waste away, there's nothing they can do. You've seen it. It's the worst way to go. Wouldn't that be what he deserves?"

Andre cracked his knuckles and thought of worse things, and doing them.

60: BAYOU COUNTRY

Zephirin woke with the sun to change Jay's bandages. He carried a laminated bow and a long barbed arrow. Jay followed him to his flatboat.

"You fixing to come along?" Zeph nodded to a rack in the boat house. "Grab a rig."

Jay found a bamboo spear with a three-pronged fork. He took the oars and followed Zeph's direction toward an islet in the bayou's muddy slick. It felt good to get his blood moving. The blue leopard hound yapped from the pier as they pulled away.

Zeph knelt at the prow with his bow. He had tied the fiberglass arrow to the boat with steel leader. The sun's rosy glow lit the water.

Zeph drew his bow and the string twanged. He wound the line around a dock cleat and pulled a fat white carp from the cloudy depths. He slapped it in the middle of the boat. "Razorback."

Jay stuck it through the gills with the Bowie and it flopped no more. They stuffed it in a wet sack filled with water weeds. Zeph oared them around to the shady side and Jay hurled the spear at needle-nose gar with little success.

"You're throwing high. Fish is two foot deeper than it looks."

He had a good arm for it. Like hurling Andre's hatchet, it enlivened some memory deep in his blood, of the Chitimacha paddling canoes among the bayou monsters. He nicked one with a long throw and the spear came out as he reeled back the rope. A gator slid into the water, and with a muddy swirl, his catch was taken.

"Sun's getting high," Zeph said, and slowly turned the boat around. "Razorback's good eating. Gotta watch the bones."

Jay kept his spear ready. They passed a long shadow as the boat house appeared around the bend.

Jay lunged with the throw and caught himself on the gunwale. Zeph righted them with the oars and peered at the spear sticking from the water.

"You done it now."

The water exploded.

Jay looped his arm around the rope. It pulled taut. Zeph ducked under as the rope dragged across him.

"Get it 'round the cleat!"

Jay hit the gunwale with his shoulder and hooked the rope on the cleat. The boat lurched with the throes of the speared creature. Zeph pulled the oars in and took up his bow. The bamboo spear jerked toward deeper water. "Alligator gar," he said. "Lot of fight in them."

A maw broke the surface that earned the fish its name. The teeth were bigger than those on the gator Jay killed. Zeph sank an arrow deep behind the massive head. Jay pulled them in by the rope and snagged the spear, drawing power from its death throes.

"Get it alongside." Zeph paddled them toward the pier. When the fish got close, it clamped down on the oar. "Dang it. Stick that thing!"

They gripped the sides of the boat not to be thrown.

A crack echoed across the water. The gar twitched, a smoking hole where its eye had been.

At the end of the dock, a one-eyed valkyrie lowered the barrel of a long black revolver. Zeph's dog wagged its tail beside her.

"How you been, son?" Evangeline's thin lips broke into a grin. "Y'all can't fish for shit."

61: MOTHER AND CHILD REUNION

Jay picked up Evangeline and spun her around until he got dizzy and they fell to the boards of the dock.

Her boy had always been a puppy. She fought down the fist punching up her throat. How could he still smell like he did when he was five years old? After they dragged him from hell and scrubbed him down, her sister's son had smelled like fresh biscuit dough.

She gripped a hank of his greasy hair to settle him down. "You're gonna crack my ribs, baby."

He helped her to her feet like a gentleman, like she'd raised him. She had half a head on him. He hadn't grown so much up as wide. Strong and rambunctious like a honey brown pit bull. But handsome, still boyish in the face, with a shine of brains behind his blue eyes.

She patted his meaty shoulder like a dog's. "You did good up north, son. I'm proud of you."

He flushed with shame.

"None of that. All those sons of bitches needed killing."

Jay lowered his head. "I don't know how much more of that I can take."

"What you mumbling about? They just tried to murder us on the highway in broad daylight. We ain't done yet."

They would never be done. That was how revenge worked.

His jaw trembled. "What happened to your eye, mama?"

Over coffee, she caught him up on her trail of vengeance. Andre's war tomahawk sat on the table.

"The Calvineaus like old Hammurabi's code. An eye for an eye, a tooth for a tooth. But Shooter wouldn't be much use to them if he couldn't shoot." She swirled the dregs of her coffee in her tin cup.

"Okie sent me to a grubstake up in Gibsland." Jay handed her the Polaroid of her and Andre and Okie.

She looked at it a long time. "We were young fools then. And old fools now." She fanned herself with the photo. "Leroy always was a titty-baby. Most crooks are. My folks let us steal all we wanted, until we took you from that evil bitch sister of mine."

Jay's eyes lost focus.

She touched his cheek. "I'm sorry I couldn't come see you up north. Our blood kin would like nothing more than to lock me away in one of their white mansions until our Andre dies."

"I know I said he was gone. I had no hope, then." He knew that the hard look on her face was the only apology he was going to get. The words weren't in her. "Andre's got the big C."

They both looked out over the water.

"Your folks got a boy at the house. Maybe thirteen years old. Name's Keshawn. I only left him because I had to get to you."

"My evil bitch mama likes to do school outreach. Except when a Black child is smart and knows it, she takes it as an affront. Likes to break them."

Jay sank the war hatchet into the table. "Mama, we got to burn this all down."

She gave him a weary look. "Don't you think I know that? I would have killed them years ago, if it didn't mean sacrificing you and Andre."

Jay looked into his cup. His revenge spree up north had cost friends their lives. Cheetah and Raina burned up in their club when he should have been there to protect them.

He swallowed coffee that had gone bitter and cold. "What

we doing about Papa Andre?"

"We got a man inside who hates the Calvineaus as much as I do. We got to act fast and play smart. In a week, they hold the prison rodeo. Only time we see each other, at the crafts bazaar. Except this year Warden LeFer wants Andre in the rodeo. Means to kill him."

"Well that ain't happening."

She looked across the table with her one steely eye. "They won't lay a hand on me. They know I'll cut 'em from throat to asshole, and if they so much as muss my hair they'll wind up gift-wrapped for the gators. But when my gun's dry, they'll take me."

He told her about Molina, Pastor Roy, and the church. How she had access to the prison through the drama program. And how he had to free her, too.

"She goes in every year with a bunch of kids. Does the scared straight thing, then takes them to the rodeo. I could be the second youth advisor."

Evangeline narrowed her eye. "We don't have time for that. I've got a plan, but you'll have to take one on the chin for your daddy. You can do that, can't you?"

She poured fresh coffee and told him the plan.

Jay held the Skunk Ape Bowie in the sunlight. The Damascus blade rippled alive. His path would remain one of violence and blood.

62: MUSTANG

Jay grinned from the passenger seat of the Dodge Magnum as Evangeline swerved around a truck and rode the ass of a beater coupe. "Look at this shitbird hogging the left lane."

Tony Joe White low-growled from the speakers and rain washed the world gray. When she'd taught him to drive from her lap in her Jeep, she had been just as aggressive and vocal about the shortcomings of other drivers.

They pulled off in St. Francisville, the town nearest to Angola prison. They passed white plantation homes that huddled behind their trees against the heavy rain and took the long road toward the prison. She cut off not long after, taking a twisty back road fast, trampling fallen branches with the muscle wagon's fat tires.

"There's only one road in or out, and on rodeo days it's packed. There'll be a fella selling battle flags and T-shirts on a side road about five miles up, and he'll call law on you for speeding."

Jay huffed. "Some rebel."

The road had washed to gravel, and the Magnum bounced over ruts and humps. They pulled into a small camp of cabins. A forest ranger's Jeep was parked under a carport.

"This here's a Girl Scout camp, closed until spring. They got horses in the stable. You ever ride?"

"Mama, they don't give you pony rides in Rahway."

She laughed. "Silly of me to ask." She weaved along the roads. The road narrowed to where the branches clattered against the wagon's side mirrors.

"You take the trail that peckerwood snitch sells his flags on, you'll come out here."

"How long's that on foot?"

She laughed. "You won't be walking."

Back in Baton Rouge, the rain had broken, but the thunderheads left a chill in their wake as they scudded across the horizon flashing pink with fury. They drove to a storage garage on a spot of higher ground in Zachary, where people parked their RVs. They pulled up to a gate painted beige, and Evangeline dug around in the console and swore for a solid three minutes while Lucinda Williams belted out a tune.

"There it is." She produced a plastic card and touched it to a sensor, and the gate opened for them.

Jay spied the black domes of security cameras at the corner of every building.

"We want them to know," she said, before he could speak. "We ain't stealing. We're taking back what's ours."

She pulled to a large one-story building made of baby-shit-brown bricks, and the familiar pitched roof of ranch homes in the area. It had several rolling garage doors. She parked in front of one and got out, stretched her legs like Elvis showing off his karate on a Vegas stage.

She touched the card to another sensor. The light blinked red.

"Fucker. Shooter changed the code since I stole this baby." She patted the roof of the Magnum. "Got to do it the hard way."

The hard way involved lockpicks. The lock was a heavy cylinder, and she swore as she worked the pins with a set of professional picks.

"I thought you were a jeweler," Jay said, on lookout.

"I'm a lot of things." A motor kicked and the garage door lifted. It was dark inside. Beasts of Detroit iron lurked in the shadows.

She tucked her picks back in their roll-up case and tossed it into the wagon. "Park this hunk of shit halfway in. So the door can't close." She walked into the garage and flipped a light switch.

The fluorescents flickered to life, revealing several loaded F350 trucks in different colors and cab combinations. She pulled a tarp and revealed a bulbous, rocket-nosed fastback, dulled electric blue with a silver hood and cracked white stripes.

A Boss Mustang 351.

Jay recalled arguing cars with Okie, who was a diehard Ford man. *351 is the best small block there is. You can take your Mopar 440, it steers like a boat anchor. Had me a 351 block in a Falcon wagon and outran every law on our tail.*

"This is Andre's. Shooter snatched it up before I could get to it."

Jay ran a hand over the aggressive curves, the silver spoiler. The old paint had been waxed and detailed, but years in the sun had done their damage. The sheet metal had dings, but the wheels sported new tires. He popped the hood and admired the small block. He hadn't seen any of its kind working in the Rahway prison auto shop.

"Let's see how she runs."

"You know cars," she said, and threw him a set of keys.

The battery was dead. He jump-started it off one of the trucks and sat back and listened to the exhaust note. Nothing sang like a Mustang's pipes.

She joined him on the passenger seat and lit a Winston. He found a screwdriver and held the point to different spots on the engine block, putting his ear to the plastic yellow-and-red handle, listening for tics and troubles. The engine ran clean.

Jay picked through tools and gear and loaded the trunk with what he needed. "We're good to go."

She took Andre's war tomahawk and hooked it into a rig under the dashboard. "Lots of memories in this baby."

Jay was ready to make some more.

"You sure you don't want some iron? I got Andre's GI .45 in

my glove box." She climbed out of the Mustang and ground out the butt of her Winston beneath her pointed boot.

Shooter's sabotage of the Colt Python was fresh in his mind. "I ain't practiced since we went hunting squirrels back when I was five."

She pulled him into a hug. "You be careful. There's no evil like old evil. They got the most practice."

"I've been the bait, before. When this is done, I'll tell you all about how me and Okie scammed the Hitler Bitches with a fixed fight in Rahway."

She crushed him close, holding him tight as a bear trap. He inhaled her Winstons-and-violets smell. The one he'd woke to, when she and Andre saved him.

Abruptly, she slapped him on the shoulders and wriggled away. "Stick to the plan and trust me. If it goes sour, let them think they won, and look for the weak spot." Okie's words, coming from her mouth.

She lit a Winston, took a few drags, then let it burn in her off hand while she thumbed a flip phone. Got a few more puffs in while it rang, the defiance melting from her face.

"Good morning, Ella. You know who this is." A pause.

The years hung ragged on Evangeline. The cigarette fell from her trembling fingers.

"Has my daughter finally decided to honor her mother and father?" Hesper Calvineau's voice was loud enough to hear without the speaker.

"Yes, ma'am."

"We are done allowing your little games, Evie. We've permitted this foolishness long enough."

"J-Joshua is hurt. You help him, and I'll come home."

"You are in no position to make demands. A cleansing fire is about to spark. You can come home, or be lost in the conflagration."

She rubbed her nose with her wrist. "I know Andre's gonna die. I made peace with that. Just save my boy, Mama. Please."

Silence.

"Bring him to us and we will see."

"He's coming home. Show me your kindness, and I'll join y'all at Sunday church."

Her eye was the dead gray of a soft-nose hollow point. She snapped the phone in half and tossed it into the weeds. Lit a fresh Winston and peeled away in the Magnum without a word.

Jay stayed a while. The truck depicted on Shooter Boudreaux's Expo postcard sat parked and polished, ready for show. A huge kid's toy, a Ford F-350 long bed with a dual rear, jacked and loaded with chrome stovepipes and rhino bars. Done up in Tiger purple and gold. He worked on it for a good hour. Then he took a piss on the oil stain where the Mustang had been, marking his territory, and distracting from his sabotage.

He slid into the bucket seat and kneaded the Mustang's steering wheel. He opened up the Boss 351 on the highway toward New Orleans.

He felt cocky and unchained from his past. He would see his father again. Whether they would be free or spending the rest of their lives on the Farm, that was open to fate.

63: SALLY JIGGS

Mosca's was a white house with a pitched roof and a sign so small Jay blew past and had to double back, parking the Mustang facing the road. It was early for supper but the lot was nearly full, a raucous song pounding out the open windows.

The plan required him stepping foot in New Orleans, where the Italians still ruled.

He had taken the head of a New Jersey mob boss and left it floating in his Roman bath-style swimming pool. The new boss sanctioned the kill but put a new hit out on Jay to keep up appearances.

Anyone who wanted the New Jersey crew's favor might put a bullet in him. Their consciences went unsullied from whoring out girls barely older than children, or chopping off a working man's hands for not paying street tax, but draw their blood in defense of your life and suddenly they had honor to protect.

This was a peace mission. Mama said Shooter owed the Eye-ties money, and had used his Calvineau protection to stiff them.

Mosca's served food family style, big platters of garlic-spangled seafood, heaping bowls of tangled pasta. Servers bustled between tables, spoons and forks clattered, and Louis Prima and Keely Smith sang a lively duet on the jukebox. Jay liked Italians because they took a bite out of the ass of life. The music and the tang of garlic put speed in his step.

Salvatore Gingerelli, the boss of New Orleans, sat at his table surrounded by men hunkered over plates, eating quietly with napkins tucked into expensive shirts. They had the puffy blood-shot cheeks of heavy drinkers, pale skin rouged from hard living and nose candy.

Jay waited for the hostess, breathing in the ambrosia of olive oil and garlic.

If the mission failed, it would be a good last meal.

Sally Jiggs gestured to Jay with a serving fork.

He wore gold frames and his sparse hair was combed straight over his crown, peppered gray like the hair covering his thick, sun-spotted arms.

His short compatriot, dressed in a plain black suit, stood and pulled out the empty chair. His jacket opened to reveal a shoulder holster. "It's a long way from Jersey."

Jay sat, thanked them, and tucked a napkin into his work shirt, but kept his feet planted, like a tiger ready to pounce.

"You are welcome at my table," the big man said, and tore the heel off a loaf of bread and drowned it in a bowl of shrimp and garlic. "Up New York way, they call me Sally Jiggs. *Mangia*, Jay. Nothing good happens on an empty stomach." He offered the bread basket.

Jay took two pieces, then filled his plate with broiled oysters and chicken cacciatore. The first bite was heaven. A clove of garlic melted on his tongue, followed by a sweet oyster spiked with breadcrumbs, broiled in butter.

"I told you, you never know who's gonna walk in here," a stocky man with a glossy black hairpiece said. "Sophia Loren ate at this table with Harry Connick, back in '88."

"This shit again." The fifth, with his remaining red-gold hair coiffed into a sparse mane, wearing a silk guayabera unbuttoned at the belt. "She had the oysters oreganata, and you ate her *scungilli*."

"To the one who took out Frankie Dee," Sally Jiggs said, and poured Jay a glass of wine.

The table went silent, only the clatter of people eating and the blare of Prima's trumpet. Jay closed his fist around his table knife.

"How'd you walk in here with balls that big?" Hairpiece asked. "Wreckin' balls, you got."

They laughed, and Jay broke half a grin. He twirled linguini on his spoon and enjoyed the tart, heady sauce. The kind that bubbled in a tall pot, like the mouth of a volcano giving forth the earth mother's rich red blood.

"Personally, I thought Frank was a pompous asshole," Big Sal said. "Fuckin' Napolitano, they think their shit don't stink. Look down on us Siciliana and Calabrese. They call us *torreno*, dirt people. The New York crew thinks the same of us here down South, don't they? Frankie sure did."

"He wiped his hands on that silk handkerchief every time he touched something," the red lion said, cutting a veal cutlet.

"All I know is he swung first," Jay said, and sucked a shrimp tail out of the shell, leaving no meat.

"He speaks," Hairpiece said.

"Thank you for supper." Jay dabbed with the napkin. "I ain't had red sauce worth a damn in too long. But I know y'all ain't spilling the wine just to thank me for what I done."

The small man with the gun cracked a grin but remained quiet.

"We're here to talk ancient history," Big Sal said. "I got a whole shelf of history books. It's what makes us, whether we like it or not. You know, these peckerwoods treated us as bad as they did the moolies when we first got here. Lynched eleven Italians in the town square." He gestured with his fork, across the river. "They blamed us for killing the New Orleans police chief and strung us up like animals."

"If my ancestors did the stringing, I'll piss on their graves. But don't pin it on me."

Big Sal smiled like a benevolent grandfather. "If they did, I don't know about it. I had the pleasure of whoring out the great-great-granddaughter of one of the men who led the riot, though. And I love that these inbred fucks have to live knowing they'll never get rid of us. That's why we southern Italians get along with you Cajuns. They've always spit on us. Like we ain't exactly the white man."

"Here he goes," Phil said.

"What? Read your history. We're mixed people. Like this city, in its heart. They use it to shame us, but I embrace it."

Sally's men ate to keep their mouths shut.

"But I wanna talk more recent history. Your mom and pop hit one of our jewelry stores in the Quarters, way back. I don't expect you to remember, you were in your didies. But you were on the job. They used you as cover. The law called you the baby bandits."

Jay had no recollection. His early years were a red haze of horrors in his blood mother's hands, and rare glimpses of sun-bleached joy with Evangeline and Andre. But one was of her scooping him up one-handed as he toddled out of their station wagon and setting him in the driver's seat. *Be right back, sweet pea. No following, now.*

"Your mama used to take you into jewelry stores," the red lion said. "Get all dolled up and eyeball a set of gold watches for her folks on their anniversary, she said. She fed you two of my unset diamonds and a three-carat blue sapphire while I was busy with another customer."

"You were too busy looking at her jugs, Philly," Sal said, and the table laughed.

Jay ate another oyster. "If you want those rocks back, I'm pretty sure I shit them out already."

They laughed.

Blood enemies made brief peace at the watering hole. This generation of *cumpari* played into the friendly silverback image portrayed on movies and cable, but they were just as willing to stuff shrieking children toes-first into a meat grinder in front of their parents as their forebears were.

"We can laugh now, but that's still on the books." Big Sal

sucked the meat out of a shrimp tail.

"Fifteen grand in '73 money," Phil said. "By the time I saw them missing, she had her ass hanging out the door of a blue Mustang, burning rubber up Dauphine."

"Two points a week for forty years," Jay said. "My grandparents have that kind of money, but I know you can't touch them."

No laughter. They kept forking food into their mouths.

"You could do them and us a favor by clearing this off the books. We know what you can do."

Jay wondered why these men of power desired him under their charge. He had a wildness about him, perhaps it gave these men a rise in their drawers to command him around. That, and the fact that the only thing he was good at besides farting up a car seat and fixing every engine made by man, was killing.

The waitress came by with another jug of wine and a pitcher of water. She'd been giving the table a wide berth. It was set by the kitchen door and the juke, noisy and cozy and out of the way. Good for talking when you didn't want others to hear. Jay waited until she left.

"Maybe I can clear two debts at once for you." Jay reached into his pocket.

The little gunman moved without a hint of emotion, drawing his pistol.

Jay launched. The table lurched under his weight. He dimpled Sammy's white dress shirt with the point of his Bowie knife, just beneath the heart. He plucked the little man's gun upside down from the holster with his left hand.

The table froze.

"Easy now," Big Sal said, an oyster speared on the end of his fork.

Jay held the pistol upside down, pinky on the trigger, aimed vaguely at Sally's chest. It was an old convict move, for shooting guards with their own guns.

If the other diners saw anything, they didn't look twice.

Jay dropped the baby Beretta into the water pitcher, then sheathed the knife and sat down.

Sammy sighed and dipped his napkin into the water, then dabbed the red spot on his shirt.

Jay tossed a postcard into the plate of discarded oyster shells. The postcard with Shooter Boudreaux's smug face.

"Friend of your family's," Phil said. "Using their juice to avoid his debts."

Jay worked a lemon seed from the corner of his mouth and spat it onto the stars and bars on Shooter's cap. "Shitbird forgot who lost that war."

"They all did," Big Sal said. "Just like our paisans back home forget they backed Mussolini and got their asses saved by the 'Merigons."

"Let them have it. It's all they got."

"You offering to put him out of our misery?" Sal said. "That won't clear my books."

"I'm not sure I can get Rambo's fluffer to pay what he owes," Jay said, and tossed his soaked napkin on his plate. "Or if he has it. But he owes my mama an eye, and she wants him for one last heist that'll cover her debts and his."

Sally Jiggs looked into Jay's eyes for the lie. "That's a big nut."

"She's Calvineau. She knows where the money is and how to get it. Shooter will be on your territory in two days. You gonna give me sanction, or not?"

Sal took the wine jug and gestured for Jay's glass. He poured, and they drank.

64: SIXTEEN SHELLS FROM A THIRTY-AUGHT SIX

The Boss Hoss trike parked among the Harleys told Chopper that 4-Hondo was present at his base of operations. The bike sported a small block Chevy engine that would propel it and its quarter-ton occupant at speeds nature never intended. The red-and-black ridiculous ride sat behind a weathered cinder block cube with *Leroy's Bar* spray-painted on the side; *Bar* crossed out and replaced with *Lounge*.

Chopper had scouted the place in the dark. He had grabbed an HB soldier taking a piss outside a roadhouse and made him talk in the back of his truck. Took his phone and left him in the water.

Each life taken cut a little piece from his chest, a chunk carved out by a melon baller. Sometimes he counted them and wondered how much of his self was left. But that could wait for the sleepless nights to come.

He watched the building through the scope from across the Ouachita River, crouched behind an upended fifty-five-gallon drum in the brush, barrel resting on a five-pound bag of black-eyed peas stuffed in a tube sock. Finally, two HB soldiers showed up on Harleys, one with a Black girl riding pillion. They dragged the stoned young sister inside.

Chopper's stomach churned at what could happen before he

drove over the bridge to get her once hell broke loose—three minutes was an eternity—but one man versus six required a semblance of a plan.

Suzane had told him that the anger he felt at men abusing women arose from his desire to be needed as a protector. He would not deny its appeal, but in his deepest self he would admit that he saw himself as that young girl. The child he had been, raised by a mother and father who loved his inquisitiveness, his curiosity, his wide-open heart, before the weakness had been tormented out of him by school bullies and coaches who wanted him on the team instead of in the science club.

His mother missed that boy.

That boy missed himself.

He wanted to be that boy with his folks, learning from the old men and women, rediscovering what was lost and what was taken. But the world would not have it.

The world was held in the fists of men who reveled in their power, who would drag a teenage girl by her braids and make her debase herself on video to prove to themselves that they were supreme, against all evidence.

Chopper had planted bricks of Tannerite explosive on the bike's gas tanks. He aimed a Stoner rifle with the scope and suppressor he'd taken from Shooter's arsenal. He sighted on the brick on the trike's gas tank and fired.

The Tannerite exploded with a crack and a puff of smoke. Then the fuel went up in a fireball.

It took a while for the Heimdall Brothers to react, but they came in force. One around either corner of the building, both carrying short M4 rifles with pistol grips and red dot scopes. One hugged the wall and the other knelt, scanning for a target.

They kept good fire discipline, scanning for targets and taking cover behind the motorcycles. When a third and fourth exited the back doors with a pistol and fire extinguisher, Chopper shot the brick of Tannerite he had set by the door. It exploded and knocked them on their asses.

The riflemen returned panic fire, rounds snapping the canebrake around him.

He punched a hole in the heads of both. He had qualified as double expert and kept in practice, firing between heartbeats. The other two men belly-crawled behind the bikes. Chopper hit the Tannerite on a black Softail's tank and it burst in a smaller fireball, tipping over the bikes and trapping the crawling men.

He moved quickly. Tossed his foam ear plugs into the Ouachita and drove his truck over the bridge and into the dusty lot. Left the door open and jogged to the building with the bullpup BAR slung at port arms and the magnum in his hand.

By now the Heimdalls would have phoned reinforcements, and they'd be ready for the hell he brought to breakfast. He called 4-Hondo on the dead biker's phone and told the bellowing voice to shut up.

"Send out the girl or I burn her and all y'all alive." He tossed the phone into the river.

He creeped around the side of the building, the bullpup's three-point sling digging into his shoulders. He held out the magnum revolver in two-armed in isosceles stance, thumbs crossed to absorb the recoil. The bleary-eyed girl stumbled out the back door in purple panties and nothing else. She yelped and was jerked aside by a forearm around her neck. A stubble-faced young man with a crew-cut loomed over her shoulder, holding a tricked-out 1911 gangster style, backing out along the wall.

He shouted a command and crouched with the girl as a shield. Chopper's sights figure-eighted over the girl's head. She whimpered and waved her arms, not holding still.

"Drop, girl!"

She was stunned. Only hearing her own heartbeat.

The biker backed up, not firing.

Trying to lure Chopper past the open door.

Chopper dropped his left hand to the Browning and fired full-auto into the doorway. The recoil tore the webbing of his thumb and the stock bruised his biceps. The blasts were ice picks to the eardrums, and the girl clutched her head and dropped. The biker fired wildly, and two rounds crackled past Chopper's head. One punched him in the chest armor like a palm strike.

He gave the biker back two, one through each lung. The magnum didn't kick hard. Shooter made a fine gun.

And sold quality body armor. Chopper's ribs hurt, but the .45 round was no match for the ceramic plates, which were rated for heavy rifle rounds.

Against shotgun slugs, it was less effective.

Two blasts knocked him to the dirt and sent the magnum spinning away. A hollering human rhino squeezed out the doorway holding a Russian mag-fed shotgun with a wooden stock.

4-Hondo wore nothing but baggy sweat-stained tighty whities and a pair of size nineteen engineer boots that had the backs cut open to accept his massive calves. His right foot had split open the side and a gnarled pinky toenail the size of a walnut protruded from it.

As the euphoria of adrenaline washed in, Chopper thought his beast could club Ti' Boy Garriss and wipe his ass with him. 4-Hondo's body rolled like a pink Kodiak bear loping for its den after gorging on salmon. He kicked the girl aside like a puppy and raised the shotgun.

Pieces of him flew off like confetti and others burst out the side and splattered the cinder blocks as Chopper dumped the twenty-round drum magazine of the bullpup Browning BAR through him.

He didn't hear the rounds so much as feel them. The barrel smoked and seared his skin as it bounced against his forearm. He shrugged off the sling and clawed for the magnum.

No one came out the rear door after 4-Hondo.

The girl was strong enough to be his crutch as they staggered to his truck. "You alone?" he hollered. "Any more girls in there?"

She ignored him and jumped into the truck, pulling him in

after. Ralph Ora bolted out the front door holding a pistol low. Chopper fired twice, blind. Ora ran back inside.

"We gotta go now!" the girl screamed.

A row of bikes slithered down the road like a roaring steel centipede.

One bike clanged off the Rhino bars on the truck's grill as they bounded over the culvert, and two others swerved into the ditch as they roared off road, kicking up dust and breaking through to an empty parking lot, heading toward the two-lane highway.

Chopper remembered his uncle drumming the dashboard as he sang along to Tom Waits:

sixteen shells from a thirty-aught six

He couldn't hear the army over the ringing in his ears, but he knew they were coming.

65: THE PRODIGAL SON

Whiterose Plantation loomed through a veil of live oaks and magnolias. Jay thought about Keshawn in the house, and Molina back at the church. How he'd let them suffer longer because he was tired of killing.

Killing was never the only answer. And he did not like how easy it had become. You left a trail of bloody footprints for vengeance to follow, like the Rougarou hunting you on a bayou trail.

The beast could smell the ghosts of the dead on him.

You are a wolf child.

Mama Evangeline's words, spoken through the Rougarou.

He hid the Skunk Ape Bowie in a hollow beneath the dashboard and rolled the Mustang beneath the boughs into the driveway.

Pastor Roy's white Escalade was parked next to a black Harley Davidson edition Ford F-150 with a rebel flag filling the back window. Jay turned the Mustang around to face out and left the keys in the ignition.

He approached the imposing front door and saw the garage was closed.

A pull in his guts took him to its window to see the black shark inside.

He let himself dream of taking their Cadillac to ride the infinite highway.

Alone. Maybe a dog.

He could not run from his past. It would reach for him with its unclean claws until he faced it.

And that meant walking into prison of his own free will.

He walked to the door and rang the bell.

Ella answered, her eyes showing alarm. "Mister Joshua."

"Good morning, ma'am. I'm here to see my grandparents."

"Mister Samuel is having his nap. You'd best leave a message."

"Thank you, ma'am, but I need to see Mrs. Hesper."

She resigned and led him inside. Pastor Roy and Mrs. Hesper sat in chairs on the back sun porch, sipping tea. Keshawn stood to the side. He blinked at Jay.

"Well, if it isn't the prodigal son," Roy said, not standing.

Mrs. Hesper did not make eye contact.

"Memaw, I have found a way to bring your daughter home."

"You have been disowned, Joshua. They do not tolerate disloyalty." Roy raised his glass.

"I tried to do by my word, but Shooter Boudreaux spooked her, then all hell broke loose. You can't blame me for his blunder. Now she wants his head before she comes home, and I don't blame her. I don't see things her way. I'm ready to hold the whip for a change, under your command. But Shooter has to pay. And I want Molina's hand, if she'll have me."

Roy sipped his tea.

"What do you think, Mrs. Hesper? Miss Molina is of child-bearing age. Good birthing hips." He smiled.

Mrs. Hesper rattled her empty glass until Keshawn filled it.

"I think my grandson needs to be punished. Then I will consider his request."

Roy put two fingers in his mouth and whistled.

A tall Viking jarl rose from a chair outside the sun porch and stepped inside. His long amber beard was streaked with yellow and white. He wore a black leather vest over denim jeans and a clean white shirt. "Well, if it isn't my runaway initiate. Welcome back to the Brotherhood, Desmarteaux."

Jay's shoulder burned where he had sanded off the Tyr rune tattoo the HB gave him in Rahway prison, after he'd learned they'd had him raped to trick him into joining their race gang. He reached for his belt, where the Bowie usually resided.

Kroese raised a beanbag gun and shot Jay in the gut with a round. Mrs. Hesper gasped at the noise, then sipped her tea.

Jay clutched his belly and fell to his knees. The rubber round tore his shirt and left a welt the size of a plum.

Roy extended a loafered foot and pushed Jay so he fell to hand and knee. "Take him to the stocks. He must be scourged."

Kroese and an HB soldier dragged Jay behind the garage.

PART 4: BAD MOON RISING

One eye is taken for an eye.
—Creedence Clearwater Revival, "Bad Moon Rising"

66: MOLINA

Molina had a cell to herself at the Calvineau Parish jail, a dark metal cage with a scratchy wool blanket and a guard outside who whistled the theme to *The A-Team* as he thumbed his phone. She scratched at the rubbery scar on her arm, like a navel, the constant reminder of her past.

Eagleton had her brought in, saying he found a roach behind the work shed. The kids smoked there. She had warned them about it, but there was nothing to do. There were always ones who would seek forbidden fruit. She had, at their age. It had taken a long time to find what she was chasing, but it didn't come in a bottle or a syringe.

The whistling echoed down the hallway, and a shadow loomed over her bunk.

"Hello, Molina." Pastor Eagleton. He tilted his head into the sickly fluorescent light. That tanned sandstone face and that sick little smile.

She folded her arms.

"I wouldn't let a member of my flock rot in jail overnight, even if she is a little cocktease whore."

She had endured overnights in common cells, long ago. Had her shoes stolen, received black eyes and bruises. This was a luxury suite in comparison.

"If you want to sleep in your bed this week, you'll have to do penance, little Catholic girl. Cat lick," he said, his tongue flicked out at a fist held like a cat's paw, and he brushed back his hair with a knuckle. "How many rosaries did you perform on your knees in the heathen confession box?"

He had a deep kink, had probably jerked off to the nuns in *The Sound of Music* as a boy. She didn't care how the sick bastard got his sickness.

"So many, Pastor," she said, and knelt on the cold concrete.

His voice took on a familiar husk as he reached into his pants. He retrieved her memaw's rosary and held it through the bars, the crucifix swinging. She snatched it, but he held it tight, releasing each bead one by one.

She wore the rosary with Christ between her breasts.

"Not here, you slut. You will perform your sacrament in my church, under my pulpit. This Sunday, you will have honored guests. The Calvineaus. Including their wayward grandson, who you rutted with on my church's sacred ground."

They had done no such thing, but she knew better than to contradict him.

"Yes, your friend has joined us. He's bringing his whore mother back to the fold and returning to the flock with full honors. My offer to you stands. But you will perform the sacrament, or your family will suffer the consequences."

She would rather be damned than let him see her cry. She thumbed the first rosary bead and began her Act of Contrition.

"Pray, little Cat-lick. The only God stands before you: Men of Christ who wield power on earth. Your whoremaster Joshua will be waiting for you. Practice on him all you wish, but if you're not kneeling under my pulpit for my Sunday sermon, your father swims with the gators in Bayou Vipère."

His fancy shoes tapped the concrete.

The guard unlocked her cell.

Molina stayed to recite her rosary.

67: DIFFERENT FOXHOLES

Tamica was no more dazed from the war zone than Chopper was. He gave her a Clutch T-shirt from his duffel, and she drove barefoot while he grimaced and unbuckled the dented body armor. His ribs had taken a mule kick from the shotgun slug. He'd broken ribs before and could tell from the sharp pains when he turned or stretched that this was a soft cartilage bruise.

She held the wheel at four and seven. "I haven't driven in a long time. My aunt taught me." Her eyes fluttered at the memory. "You're Chopper. They talked about you. Wish we'd had time to chop a few of their dicks off. Is it true you work with the root witch?"

Chopper took a bottle of Thai boxing liniment from the glove box and rubbed it on his bruises. "Suzane and I have been hunting the men who took you for years. Where you from?"

She wrinkled her nose at the medicine smell. "Thibodaux, but I can't go home now. That's where they'll look first. Let me tell you how they operate. I've been cataloging it for when I could get away. I'm going to need detox."

"Suzane will heal you. We've got four hours to New Orleans. There's water and protein bars. Want some?"

"Water."

He uncapped a bottle for her.

They picked up donuts and tamales at a roadside joint in Natchez, and Tamica told him everything as they ate on the road, the paper boats in their laps orange with grease.

"I was walking home from STEM club. Then this big black car rolled alongside. I feel foolish now for not running, but the man driving, I had seen him at school. Said the Calvineaus saw my promise, and wanted to assist me in my schooling." She dropped a corn husk onto her plate and gave a bitter laugh. "Well, you saw what they consider schooling."

Chopper texted ahead to Suzane.

The sanctuary occupied a chunk of land between the canal and the basin, tucked behind a recycling plant off the Ninth Ward. It had been a storage depot before the storm and was stacked with faded and rusted shipping containers like enormous Lego blocks. How Suzane owned it and kept it powered was beyond him.

Her fees for rich clients let her perform free for those in need. But they always paid her back, somehow. She didn't need spells to keep a hold on you. There was something about being worthy in her eyes, Chopper knew. And Tamica would, too.

He eased down a rutted road, passing mountains of rusted metal getting cut and sorted by payloaders. A ship the size of a city block was moored nearby. He cut around a thick patch of hardy trees grown lush in the flood-enriched soil until he came upon a dull *Tetris* stack of shipping containers that he knew weren't empty.

Tamica stirred in the passenger seat, under his coat.

He rolled forward, pulling around the stack, which shielded a short, corrugated building. Dogs and children ran free in the dirt. A fat calico spied them from its resting spot upon a wooden piling. Women tended a garden, one played guitar in the shade. They came to attention, gathering the children. Two took positions near stacked rail ties.

In an open container high on the stack, a sniper watched him. One of several veteran women who took turns on guard. They knew his truck but would keep him under watch in case he was compromised.

Chopper killed the engine and unlocked the doors, then put his hands on the dash, like he'd been stopped by a trooper. "You have to go alone."

Tamica rubbed her nose and peered out the tinted windows. "I'm jonesing hard."

"She won't care."

Suzane strode out of the building, her lavender sarong floating behind her like streamers. Two guard women flanked her. No weapons showed, but Chopper knew what they had. He'd upgraded their arsenal, courtesy of Shooter Boudreaux.

Suzane came to the passenger side. "Hello, Tamica. Welcome to Medusa's Rest."

68: SANCTUARY

It started as a dog rescue run by one of the women Suzane helped leave an abusive husband. Taking care of dogs was therapeutic, and the land was hidden and easy to protect, so it quickly became a haven. They patched the stacks of containers to power lines, cut open holes for air conditioners, doorways, and ladders in between. Their IT expert Carina cut in to a nearby cell tower and connected a little office to the internet.

They had survived the big storm and the levees breaking. The population averaged a dozen adults, with new women cycling through. Some returned when they needed, to pay back, or to spend time with those they'd come through with, like soldiers at a VFW bar.

Chopper was the only man who knew of its existence. Only because of his mom and pop out in Camp Saint Malo, who took in the older boys and men who needed refuge. He and Suzane had debated the iron rule of Medusa's Rest—no men—and he'd come to see her side. The energy was different here.

Tamica stared in awe of Suzane's mother-goddess majesty.

She was surrounded by women, dogs, and children of all shapes and sizes and colors. Six foot four in flat sandals, haloed by her natural hair, sheer purple fabric flowing over her round, unbound curves. She took Tamica's hand and lifted her from the truck like a child.

Hope the pit bull headbutted Tamica's legs and whimpered. She petted the slate gray dog's massive, scarred head. She crouched and Hope licked her face and she fell back on her butt in the dirt.

The women circled her, hard eyes offering fellowship to her and hatred to those who had done her wrong.

"The past does not own us," Suzane said. "If you join us here, you must own your future. Whether you choose peace or fury, we will be your sisters, always."

She crushed herself into Suzane. The witch queen wrapped her in her arms and let the shuddering tears come.

Chopper rubbed the bridge of his nose. He had seen a lot of ugly in his life. His father had told him to open a record shop, in his uncle's memory. But Chopper had loved more than the music at the shows with his uncle. The outlaw side, the underground. He had felt its lure and had come to understand it. Like a bloodhound smelled a tapestry of trails, he saw a palimpsest of human needs and rages and desires and could follow them with a hound's surety.

It had led him to places no one left unscathed.

Suzane was at heart a healer. Watching her save people was a salve for his deepest wounds and kept them from hardening into scars.

The two guard women gave him nods as Suzane held Tamica and recited her litanies.

Time to go.

He backed down the road, making a three-point turn once he was out of their sight. He kept a room and an alley with a gate for his truck in Marigny and drove there to rest. After he washed up and eased onto his bed, he saw Suzane's text on his phone:

Tonight

69: SINNER MAN

The scent of fish spawning rose from the bayou. The surface dimpled with insects, and their song traveled with the sticky hot breeze. Jay caught his breath in the stocks, facing the big house. The black Cadillac was parked on the grass, with Keshawn at the wheel and Mr. Samuel in the back. Windows down to watch.

"We are the Elect," Pastor Roy said. "God has chosen us to rule his dominion. The Lord has chosen who will rule after Armageddon, and you were born into the fold."

"I was never much for church. Y'all ain't gonna dunk my head in the water, are you?"

Roy laughed. "No, we're not Baptists. Your boon has been granted, Jay. The rules are for little people. You're a soldier of the Lord, now. As a Calvineau, you are forgiven in the eyes of our Lord," he said, and unfurled a bullwhip. The leather scent was salted and coppered with blood. "But our eyes are another matter."

Pastor Roy stroked Jay's burn-scarred lower back with the coil of the whip. "Don't imagine you feel much there. How many lashes, for fornicating on the grounds of my church? We can't have you bleeding through your suit in the pews."

Jay thought about pleading her innocence, but it would do no good. The vile refused to believe that others did not share their appetites.

"And what does the family want from me in return?"

"That's little people thinking, Jay. You are our blood. You can't give us anything more than that, and you can't take it away. As of this day, you are a truly free man. That trouble up north? You're safe from that here. Your blood will protect you."

Roy unbuckled Jay's belt and tugged down his pants. The warm breeze tickled his bare skin and prickled it with gooseflesh. "Molina must have felt pity for a fellow traveler whose life was as rough as her own." He patted Jay's behind with the coiled leather. "You barely look younger than me, and I have twenty years on you."

"You gonna whip me or talk me to death, Preacher?"

"If this punishment does not correct you, I can have Warden LeFer bring the biggest sodomites from his prison to break you."

Jay tensed involuntarily.

Roy chuckled. "Have I touched a nerve? I will soon enough." He lifted Jay's phallus with a loop of the whip. "Cut like a Jew. What was my cousin thinking? We are not bound to the covenant of Abraham."

Roy's boots kicked through the pecan shells. "Bringing in the sheaves, bringing in the sheaves," he sang, with his deep choir baritone. "We shall come rejoicing, bringing in the sheaves."

A gnawed strap of thick bridle leather sat before Jay's mouth, damp and sour from the bites of those whipped before him.

Jay braced as the whip hummed, Roy whirling it above his head. The first crack cut him clear along the trapezius to his shoulder blade. The pain was not the cool bite of a knife slash followed with the sear of air hitting open flesh, but the fire of hot oil from a thrown pot of roux. Like an oil burn, the pain did not fade but dug in deep. A second lash cut an X across the first.

The stocks creaked as his muscles seized. The leather straps held and Jay sprayed spittle through gritted teeth.

"Going forth with weeping, sowing for the Master," Roy twirled the bullwhip like a lariat, dancing to position himself to strike new flesh. "Though the loss sustained our spirit often grieves."

Jay cried out and his knees buckled. He'd taken beatings from fists and clubs and boots, been shanked and bit and clawed and stomped and raped, but the burning agony from the whip's ragged cuts coupled with bare-assed humiliation tore through his every defense.

The pain tore away all artifice and brought a red-misted clarity. He was the Rougarou, the wolf, and could no longer deny himself blood.

Jay's back glistened with blood tracks. He howled and writhed as the lashes rained down.

"When our weeping's over, He will bid us welcome," Roy bellowed, blue eyes alight. "We shall come rejoicing, bringing in the sheaves."

In the window of the master bedroom above Jay's head, Mrs. Hesper looked down upon him, her slender fingers neatly folded.

"That is enough," she called, and walked into the darkness.

70: TAMICA TELLS

Tamica showered and chose clothing from the wardrobe trailer, and played with the children until the withdrawal pains clawed her in earnest.

Suzane gave her iboga bark tea to free her from her need.

"It's not magic," she told her. "Just medicine."

Overnight, she was freed.

Surrounded by armed women in a fortress sanctuary, Tamica opened up. She bore the usual bravado of the war-ravaged survivors unable to sympathize with themselves lest it weaken the armor they had built. Suzane bade her to sit with her alone, in the shade of the container stacks where they could watch the big ships on the river.

"Everyone here went through shit, mine's nothing special."

"There's no hierarchy of pain," Suzane said. "Y'all think I must have had the worst. But it's all the worst. What you survived could kill another. What another took, may have killed you. There's no way to know. There's no rule that you have to talk. But we've been tracking missing school children who have never been found. Young boys and girls who live in a triangle between Baton Rouge, Lafayette, and New Orleans. All thirteen or fourteen years old."

"He drugged me with something. In my Coke. No, it was a slushy. A cherry Coke slushy. It was hot that day."

Not like today. The sun was buried in a white shroud of sky.

Tamica pulled her hoodie around herself as a breeze flicked at the dead weeds.

"Almost gumbo weather, now. That's what my memaw calls it. If she's still alive. She had a stroke and needed a cane." She rubbed at her eyes and leaned into Suzane. "She had a picture of this fancy man in front of a big black car on top of her dresser. He had a smile like he was gonna eat me up. That picture always scared me. I would fall asleep on the couch when we had family dinner, and my daddy put me on her bed with the coats. I'd wake up and see that picture and run back into the kitchen."

Tamica curled into her, and Suzane wrapped her with her arms like the child she still was.

"The one who...he asked to drive me home from school. It was so damn hot that day. The air coming out of his truck was so cold. He said it was okay, we knew each other. And we did, kind of. We saw him after school with his church folks, giving out backpacks full of school supplies. I should've known not to drink that slushy. His eyes ate me up, you know? Just like the man in my memaw's photo."

A tugboat sounded its horn, and a flock of brown pelicans on a rocky outcrop flapped their wings.

"You smell like my mom." She nuzzled in. "They took me to their big house. Said if I served them for a year, they would pay my way through college. It was sick, they made me dress like a servant girl. But the old woman didn't like my attitude, so they gave me to the bikers. They said the boys...they work them too. And when we're used up, they watch the gators eat us. And if we ran and told, they'd do it to our family and make us watch."

They stared out at the water. Suzane kneaded the back of her neck.

"They've been doing this a long time, haven't they?"

"Yes," Suzane said. "You're the first to come out alive, that we know of. They have a boy now, named Keshawn. Tell us what you can, so we can save him, too."

That brought the tears.

"I saw a black car like the one in my memaw's picture, cruising around on Sundays. My memaw said the man in the photo was the man she almost married, a singer who drove an Electra 225. This car I saw was like that car, black and long."

Suzane kneaded her shoulder, milking it out. "Not purple? Like a hot rod?"

"Silver on the bottom, fins like a shark. Everyone knows whose car that is. Mister Calvineau, being driven by his preacher, to see his flock. They have a scholarship at his church. That's how I knew him. I won third place."

The Calvineau clan had the power to do this in plain sight. The parish bearing their name split off to avoid integration, but their church gave out scholarships and donations to Black children in Baton Rouge every year, as if to wash away the sin.

Tamica kneaded Suzane's shoulders like dough as she burrowed in tight. "Why do we have to be so strong?"

Suzane felt quivers of discomfort, to be so close to anyone. She rocked her, calm as a Buddha, as was expected. "If we're tougher than anyone else, it's because they force us to be."

When you cry out and no one listens, you learn to keep that pain to yourself. Suzane had seen it grow like a cancer, weighing women down until their hearts gave out. Together they helped each other carry the stones inside them, tumors of hate no doctor could excise.

A barge rolled past, half shrouded by haze. Its uneven load resembled the head and coils of a sea serpent writhing down the Big Muddy, returning to the mother-waters.

71: IRON LOVE

That night Jay slept on his belly for the first time in his adult life. The salve in his wounds did not touch the pain. A Devil's grin of moon leered through a break in the oak boughs outside his window. The house was old and creaked with every step. Two Heimdall soldiers sat guard, one on each floor.

He was too weak to take them. Freeing Keshawn would have to wait.

Tomorrow morning was church. That narrowed the timeline for the plan.

It meant going back to prison.

He lay awake beating back the fear. If it worked, the rewards would be great.

If it failed…they'd lived through hell before.

In the morning, Ella served him breakfast and the guards were nowhere to be seen. He had free run of the house, except he wasn't running anywhere with his back striped.

Mrs. Hesper had eaten at sun-up, but she came to join him after wheeling her husband to the porch.

"Without punishment, there can be no learning," she said. "Please understand that Cousin Roy did that out of love."

"I understand, ma'am." He ate his eggs and biscuits. "I'm about to go teach Shooter Boudreaux."

She smiled. "It will be good to be rid of his face on every billboard on Airline Highway. He's so tacky. Just remember to stay neat for Sunday church tomorrow morning. And to bring my daughter."

"She swore she'd be there."

"Her word means nothing. If her low-bred lover wasn't dying, she would defy me openly. And I know you would, as well. Don't think I am slow-witted, boy." She sipped her tea. "Like you, I am making sacrifices because my Samuel is sick, and I want him to see his daughter and have his dream fulfilled. In your absence, Derro Kroese became like a son to him. But he is not our blood. It would do you well to work alongside him, for the eventual takeover. His minions will follow the strongest."

"I guess I better learn to ride a hog."

She smirked. "Derro's weakness is his belief in what he says. I know you have no such pretenses. You'll say whatever you need to get what you want, like you do with me."

Jay shrugged.

"That is power. I suggest you use it."

72: MORON LABE

The New Orleans convention center parking lot was packed with expensive trucks with tinted windows and chrome wheels, festooned with flags and decals of skulls and slogans. In the center, two Hummers painted sand camo and olive drab flanked the monster F-350 painted in LSU Tiger purple and gold, with the Shooter Tactical bullseye logo on the hood. A young man in camo cargo shorts and a *Molon Labe* T-shirt sat in a captain's chair, thumbing his phone. Freckles across his face and a chin like a supermodel's ass, he carried a walkie-talkie clipped to his pocket and a black compact pistol strapped to his thigh.

"That is one sweet ride," Jay said, gawking.

"You can buy a ticket for a photo with it inside. Please stay outside the cones."

Jay shovel-hooked him under the ribs. The man hunched and gagged as his liver dumped its toxins and his vagus nerve told his heart that he was dying. Jay stepped aside to avoid the young man's upchucked lunch, removed his pistol from the holster, and fiddled until it dropped the magazine.

He kicked it under the truck, cleared the chamber, then threw the pistol the other direction.

The young guard heaved on his knees. "Empty your pockets." One look at the Skunk Ape Bowie and he obeyed, handing over the keys and the walkie-talkie.

"What's that shit on your shirt mean?"

The guard looked down at his empty holster. "Don't you know your history? The Spartans," he wheezed.

Jay gestured with the Bowie. "Discretion's gonna be the better part of valor today, Socrates." The kid crawled away as Jay carved his message into the paint. Once he was done with the truck, he picked up the walkie-talkie.

"Hello, Boudreaux. This is the sumbitch you tried to kill on the Whiskey Bay bridge. Put your pecker down and come to the parking lot before I take a dump on the hood of your Tonka Toy."

73: LITTLE DITTY 'BOUT CHOP AND SUZANE

Suzane left Wesley sleeping atop the mountain of silk pillows on her wrought iron canopy bed. Hope was curled between his ankles, resting her cheek on one long foot. Suzane had rubbed his contusions with liniment and given him a cup of sleeping tea before their lovemaking. He wouldn't wake until noon. She walked downstairs to work in her office.

She knew Wesley was right this time. They would not hurt the Calvineaus through proper channels. Plenty would believe Tamica over Pastor Roy Eagleton, and her story of enslavement at Whiterose Plantation, but there would be seeds of doubt, the slaughter of her family's reputation—if they didn't make her disappear outright and call her a runaway prostitute with a grudge—and surely, if Keshawn was their new victim, he would be killed.

It had to be done Wesley's way, and he needed to rest before doing it.

He would not care for his wounds properly and could make mistakes when brought low by his pain. Men were weak, that way.

They didn't know pain the same way women did. And the pain they did know, they were shamed from talking about. Wesley had told her some once, after they took medicine together.

The pain he endured as a boy had been hammered into the mask that he wore as a man. He had compared it to the tool a mahout uses to train an elephant, a vicious hook for tender places, that only seems gentle because the elephant is big and strong and its tears look like sweat.

His parents were good people but worked hard, unlike his uncle, a musician and addict who took him places he was too young to process. Like houses where women injected his uncle with heroin, or to the Angola Rodeo, where young Wesley watched a white audience cheer for pain to be delivered unto the untrained inmates by wild bulls, or to the Ringling Brothers circus, where his uncle knew a clown who gave them a tour of the elephant tent.

Wesley remembered the puffy cheeks of the red-faced white man who trained the elephants, his loving words as he twisted the hook.

Don't worry kid, it don't hurt him none. Look how big he is.
But why is he crying?
It's just a reaction to the dust. They don't feel pain like we do.

On the streetcar ride home Wesley cried and his uncle told him if he cried again, he would never take him anywhere.

That was the last time he cried, until his uncle's funeral.

She knew the cases they worked on made Wesley want to cry, and that he would twist it into anger, the permissible male outlet for pain. He thought she didn't know why they called him Chopper, the things he did to pimps and slavers in the back of his truck. Like she wouldn't hear from working girls about why their man had a stub where his coke nail used to be?

She let him have the lie.

She had her own lies to mind.

Wesley limped downstairs before noon, washed and dressed. Respecting her and her place of work. He strapped on his weapons and adjusted his coat in her mirror. Drew the cane knife from which he took his ridiculous street name.

"Tamica said they take the car to church Sunday. I loathe to admit it, but I think Keshawn's only hope is Chopper Tewliss."

Boys and their puns.

Wesley ducked to kiss her, stroked her broad back.

He did look fine, though. She shivered, remembering him lifting her from the bed as she straddled him, his whole body flexing to gather strength, beads of sweat on his forehead as he ignored his wounds. Not wanting her to think he had to strain.

"Sunday, then. I'll tell my folks in Saint Malo that we have two more families coming."

Hope licked his hand before he left.

She felt she was sending him to his doom. And if he was willingly calling his father, she knew Wesley thought so too.

74: A STREETCAR NAMED GODDAMN

Shooter Boudreaux clicked the key fob that unlocked his truck. No guard collecting photo tickets, just a chair and a splatter of vomit.

And carved into the custom paint, two words.

BACK STABBER.

First a whistle, then a muttering from the group who had followed him outside in solidarity, weekend warrior wannabes carrying new hardware they had purchased.

"Coward," Shooter said, hand on his quick-draw magnum.

A roar of engine and squeal of tires drowned him out. Shooter recognized the exhaust note as the lightning blue fastback fishtailed into view, trailing a smoke plume of burning rubber. The khaki-and-polyester polo posse aimed black rifles the Mustang's way, muttering half-hearted threats. Shooter took cover behind the fender of his truck, amazed that none of the assholes fired a negligent discharge.

"Trigger discipline," he barked.

When the smoke cleared, Desmarteaux grinned like he'd just left Shooter's wife rode hard and put away wet. "How you doin', Shitter?" Red dots from three laser sights hovered on his chest.

The boy talked like his stainless-steel balls would protect him. "I liberated the Mustang you stole from my Papa Andre, back when y'all were robbin' armored trucks together. Before you ratted him and my mama out for immunity, you backstabbing, yellow piece of shit."

Shooter strutted closer, hand on his piece. "You know what we do to horse thieves around here?"

"You tried to kill me once. That's right piss-ants, I'm living proof this sumbitch can't shoot for shit. He tried to wax me over Whiskey Bay, and here I am." He waved a Bowie knife. "I'll give you one more shot. I'll even bring a knife to a gunfight. That's if you can catch me in that little-boy truck of yours."

Desmarteaux spun the tires and burned rubber out of the parking lot.

"Hold your fire, he's mine." Shooter clambered into the truck.

The Mustang couldn't jump curbs like his Super-Duty could. Desmarteaux left a trail of smoke, driving like a damn fool. Shooter plowed over a neutral ground planted with bushes, pounding the horn as cars honked in indignation and his posse hooted in admiration, filming with their phones. Some ran for trucks of their own and gave chase.

The Mustang swerved up Tchoupitoulas and cut left up Canal, right for the Quarter where its speed was useless. The Desmarteaux boy was committing suicide.

Which was fine with Shooter. It was too late to save his position with the Calvineaus; Kroese had openly bragged that they had their own source for military weapons for their crazy racial holy war and showed off a grenade launcher. Not the old M-79 so many had smuggled home from Vietnam, which you could find rusting in National Guard armories, but an M32A1 with a six-round rotating cylinder, fresh from the Marine Corps quartermasters. Shooter couldn't compete with that.

Which meant he was worth less than gator shit.

Tourists scattered as the Boss Mustang shrieked through an intersection, cutting around a red-and-yellow streetcar. Boy couldn't drive worth a damn. Smoked the tires in every gear, fishtailing all over. The truck matched the Mustang in horsepower but was double the weight. The Mustang's bumper disappeared under the truck's hood. All it would take was for a taxi or a dumb shit tourist to cut Desmarteaux off and he'd plow into the Mustang and crush it, then he could goad the kid into swinging that Bowie around and wax him in front of a crowd of cheering fans.

No Louisiana jury would convict him.

Losing the Calvineau money would hurt, but executing a convicted murderer in public would be ratings gold. Boost him into the big cable TV leagues. He wouldn't have to grow out his beard and pretend to be a backwoods shaman like that duck call salesman.

The Mustang cut across the streetcar lines and roared the wrong way up Canal, swerving around an airport jitney. Too much traffic. The seat belt warning bell chimed.

Now Shooter had him. A streetcar clanged one block ahead. He jumped the neutral ground, fans pumping their fists and hollering as they recognized the truck. He floored the pedal and the diesel heaved ahead, tire pressure sensor blaring.

He swore. The tires for this thing cost nearly a grand each. He could run them over potholes big as shell craters without a problem. What the hell was wrong?

The Mustang veered sideways as the kid palmed the wheel and shot across the tracks in front of the streetcar. With a wall of oncoming traffic ahead, Shooter had no choice. He cut the wheel hard and dropped the hammer. The truck lugged and stalled like he was dragging a boat anchor.

Shooter clipped the Mustang's rear bumper, and the red-and-yellow face of a streetcar filled his passenger side window. The glass exploded, the air bag punched him in the face, and Canal Street turned upside down.

75: WITCH TO BURN

Derro Kroese drove a van loaded with weapons to the old hangar outside Port Hudson where he trained with his crew when he didn't feel like taking an air boat out into the swamp. He had a couple squads training out there, cycling in and out, led by active military.

They had a stash of military ordnance in an abandoned nuclear silo in Texas, ready for the race war. The country had to blow, like that rig out in the Gulf. They would deliver military weapons to militias across the country in trucks purchased by the Calvineaus and allow them to operate independently like the *Werwolf* insurgency the Nazis planned after losing World War II.

First, he had house cleaning to do. The bounty hunter who'd taken Ralph Ora was hitting back.

He worked mobile and was hard to strike, but they knew who he worked for.

Kroese hailed from Jena, Louisiana. His parents had the cheapest house on the nicest street. They gave him whatever he wanted, but what he wanted was to be everything they didn't want him to be.

They sent him to prep school and promised him a Camaro Berlinetta if he graduated, so he punched out the principal and got kicked out. His father wanted to send him to military school, but his mother talked him into sending Derro to stay with his grandfather up in Monroe.

His grandfather drank at the American Legion, where he played Johnny Rebel hate records on the jukebox while he talked about the Japanese he killed and how he hated seeing their cars on the road. He taught his grandson that the Nazis got their ideas of racial purity from America, from the laws of the South and the scientists of eugenics in the North. He gave him a book written by a man with a Viking pseudonym that said Jesus was a weakling meant to keep white men from taking their birthright, and from there, Derro found the Nordic sagas and misread his own beliefs into them.

Tyr, the god of war. And Heimdall, the whitest of gods.

His grandfather left him everything when he died.

He grew his hair long and rode a hog bought with the inheritance money and used the rest to seed the Heimdall Brotherhood. He sold copies of hate books at gun shows, dealing in military memorabilia that was exclusively mementos from the losing side of World War II and the Confederacy. He advertised in the backs of mercenary-wannabe and outlaw biker mags and sent his photocopied screeds with every package.

VIKINGS ARE THE PARAGON OF WHITE MANHOOD
JOIN THE HEIMDALL BROTHERS

He wrote to men convicted of hate crimes in prison and filled their commissary accounts. He talked new recruits into vandalizing Black churches and assaulting mixed race couples and civil rights protestors, then used them to recruit inside prisons.

He never served time himself. As the Calvineaus would say, that was for little people.

Now he was fifty-five years old and had followers in every state and a dozen countries. The real rush came when Timmy Lee Baines built him a website with a forum for brewing hate, which he began by celebrating mass shooters. He trolled reporters and celebrities online and they thought by pointing to his hatred, the sunlight would disinfect it. Instead, it pointed thousands of eager followers to his door.

He spent the money on weapons and bikes to build cells across the country.

His grandfather told him about how Samuel Calvineau brazenly drove his shiny black Cadillac to lynch Black men of his parish that he considered uppity, and schoolchildren who sassed their white teachers.

He tied them in barbed wire and fed them to the gators.

So when he learned that a Calvineau boy was in prison up North, he told his men to recruit him.

Jay Desmarteaux had been tattooed with the Tyr rune of the Heimdall Brotherhood at Rahway prison, after they had paid five Black gangbangers to rape him.

Then that old con Okie Kincaid tipped Desmarteaux to their scam. Worked with the kid to set up a grudge boxing match with a Black inmate, not only to rake in winnings when fixing the fight, but to give cover for a riot where the Latin Kings took out their enemies and stole the hooch business from the HB.

The kid sanded off his Tyr rune tattoo in the wood shop to erase his allegiance.

When the Calvineaus found out Kroese had hurt their last blood son, Junior LeFer picked him up and brought him to Angola, where the warden introduced him to the hunting dogs they used to catch escaped inmates.

Kroese would have allied with them willingly, but he respected the show of power. They needed servants. He would serve, for now.

The Calvineaus saw death coming for them. They wanted their legacy to be the RaHoWa, the racial holy war that would cleanse the United States, then the world. Shooter Boudreaux bought the weapons. The HB distributed them to allies and sold cheap handguns in Black neighborhoods. To keep the white sheep scared, so they would side with their new leaders when the war came.

Kroese rolled past their storage hangar and the guard jerked awake in his captain's chair, sweeping the back forty with his rifle. The kid couldn't count his balls and get the same number twice, but he was Calvineau.

The alliance had its downsides, but every war needed fodder. "Arm up. We got a witch to burn."

76: SCOUT'S HONOR

Jay rolled the Mustang into the closed Girl Scout camp. He took the trail slow and parked behind the furthest cabins. Mama Evangeline's Dodge was already there.

He found her cleaning her pistol on a picnic table, a thick Stephen King book open beside it. He set a greasy bag from Popeyes Chicken on the table. "There's a two piece and a biscuit in there with some fries."

"I'll eat later." She held the muzzle over a white page, squinting down the barrel, looking for fouling. "We're gonna prevail, but not without trials and tribulations."

Jay was not a worrier. He focused on one thing. It made him terrible at chess but difficult to feint in the ring.

She tapped her eye patch. "I got the sight."

The things he'd seen in the swamp made him unsure if she was joking. He wasn't sure if he should tell her—or anyone—about the Rougarou.

"You ready to do your part?"

"Yeah." Jay smoothed back the longish hair over his ears and weaved his fingers behind his head, winced. The stripes on his back burned. The idea of prison terrified him. But if it meant freeing Papa Andre, he would trade places with him. "Now, I got an idea. A little more hell-raising might get us all out of there. The goombahs you liked to rob back when I was a baby. I'm giving them my cut of the take, to clear your debts. That'll give you free passage through New Orleans. It also takes the price off my head, at least outside of New York's reach."

She thumbed six tall magnum loads into the cylinder, closed it, and aligned the first round.

"Keep talking."

"First, let me show you something." He took her to the Mustang. She slipped the Colt Diamondback into a holster canted over her rear jeans pocket.

She poked the banged-up quarter panel with her boot. She whistled at the twisted chrome of the rear bumper. "You're hell on a car, son."

"I've been driving six months. I'm no getaway man," he said, and walked to the trunk. "But I'm getting pretty good at fixing shit when it's fucked beyond recognition." He keyed the trunk and raised the lid.

Shooter Boudreaux squinted as the cloudy afternoon light shone on his gagged and airbag-bludgeoned face.

Evangeline drew and sighted on Shooter's left eye, her wrinkled smoker's lips pinched together white.

"Go get a shovel from the work shed and get to digging," she said. "You forgot to wrap this present."

"Your folks"—she glared with her eye—"I mean, the Calvineaus—they wanted me to ice him. They got this Nazi shitbird named Kroese, head of the Heimdall Brotherhood, to take his place."

"So? He's got debts to pay. He owes me an eye."

"He probably can't shoot too good, you do that. But he can cover our retreat. He's got no one else to go to."

She bit her lower lip and traced the muzzle along the dark pouch beneath Shooter's left eye. "You trust this piece of shit?"

"No, but he'll do what it takes to survive. And unless we take down the Calvineaus, he's as good as dead anyhow."

Jay pulled the blood-mottled handkerchief from Shooter's mouth. "Why don't you tell her how much you want to live, Shitter? I got to get to church. I'm getting my first communion today."

"The Head Nazi in Charge told me they got a new source. Military," Chopper spat. "What would Okie do, Evie? He'd fuck the fuckers where they breathe."

"Don't you say his name, you backstabbing shit."

"This gets the goombahs off his back and ours, this goes right," Jay said. "So work something out."

Evangeline thumped Shooter's crotch with the barrel of her magnum. "Think on that, first."

He groaned and curled in the trunk. "You always were a cast iron bitch."

She sighed to Jay. "You always got to complicate things, son."

He grinned and strutted to the Mustang. He could barely feel the lashes on his back. "See you at church. Don't skip out on me. Without you there, they might send me to the cemetery instead of Angola, after what I'm fixing to do."

77: SUZIE NEEDS A SHOOTER

Suzane sat in her office with Big Freedia thumping from the hidden speakers, surrounded by books and art that made her happy, while she worked her cases. Undocumented women came in droves, now that even the courtrooms were not safe. The abusers were brazen, and a phone call could send their victim and her children to separate prison camps. Immigration lawyers were overwhelmed. And the sanctuary could only house so many.

She looked up at a replica statue of Queen Scota, the African princess whom Scotland was named after. She offered no guidance.

A creak came from the massive front door. Wesley had reinforced it for her beyond her own improvements, after the levees failed. The bottom floor had been gutted, but the door was original, made from ship wood that had survived many storms. Once a skinny white man in a summer suit had tried to buy it from her, as if she did not know its value or history. When she refused, they came to steal it in the night, and were met with Hope's teeth.

Now that door creaked as if under great pressure. She put two fingers in her mouth and whistled.

A thump from above as Hope left the bed. In three bounds, she was down the stairs and at her side. She gripped Hope's nape. "*Gad.*"

She sent a 911 to her warrior women, then swept her phones

into a steel safe mounted in the floor, slammed the lid, and spun the dull brass dial.

The door groaned like a ship at sea, and Hope growled to answer its challenge. The door would not give, but the steel frame was anchored to less sturdy wood. They had reinforced it, but she couldn't afford a house made of stone.

She fired off a script on her computer which locked her system down. One of many countermeasures Wesley took great joy in demonstrating for her after he installed them.

The door frame splintered with a crack like a gunshot, and they burst in through the blackout curtains.

They were in her home.

The Witch Bitch's place stank like a hippie's asshole. The room was dimly lit by antique lamps and the walls were covered in bookshelves and art of jungle people.

"You are one big ugly bitch." Kroese lighted a long Cuban cigar and puffed the cherry alive.

He'd made the connection between the bounty hunter and the Witch Bitch long ago. She had sheltered some of their featherwood women after they were brainwashed into betraying their race, but one had come crawling back, and told him about the huge woman and her network.

At first he took the loss of their whores as the cost of business; there were always more dumb bunnies to put to work. But when the featherwood described the big Black bitch they called the Queen, he took it personal. She was young and had built more than he had in half the years. She had women in the DA's offices, she had cuck police, and she had street whores and fags working for her all across the state.

She filled a recliner behind a huge wooden desk, one hand on a book, the other out of sight. The soldier to his right held a Benelli shotgun, and the other closed the door to the street, then twirled his crowbar like a majorette's baton.

"Bet you're wondering how we found you." Kroese exhaled blue smoke.

"I am not hard to find." She didn't look scared. She would be, soon enough.

"Your buck hit our film house. We came to get back our property."

"She is not property, and you will be leaving without her." She opened the book to a drawing surrounded by symbols. "I would advise you to leave my house. Now." She leaned back in her chair.

Kroese and his men couldn't help but look at the pages of the book. The runes surrounded a woodcut of a naked woman with enormous tits and a bush the size of the Amazon rainforest. From it, rays of light struck out and set fire to little crumpled skeletons at her feet.

"I call upon Ashtoreth to strike you down," she said, and slapped her hand on the furious goddess.

The room went black.

Kroese's men shouted and fumbled for their tactical flashlights. He drew his 1911 and its night sights glowed, but he could see nothing. The windows were covered in double blackout curtains. All the light had been artificial.

There was a snarl and a scream, then the shotgun blasted the ceiling, blinding them with its muzzle flash and slapping their eardrums with its report.

Suzane toed the kill switch and snapped a command. Hope bolted for the nearest man and clamped her teeth on a leg. Darkness was nothing to her. Hope had been trained to bite low, never to jump. One man shrieked with what was surely a mangled calf.

The men swore and fumbled in the blackness. She shuffled for the dim blue glow of the brazier, clutching a vial in her hand. She knew the room by heart, crammed as it was with magical ephemera and antiques from the island of her ancestors. She whistled twice for Hope to release and follow.

A gunshot sucked the air from the room. Her heart clenched. Hope would die for her, as would Wesley. She had done much to keep them both from committing such foolishness. She found the brazier and crouched on a settee.

Hope butted her leg. She gasped in thanks.

A white beam of light cut through her office, sweeping her desk. The shotgun blast had torn a hole through the leather of her chair.

"My leg!"

A pistol cracked and something shattered.

She emptied the vial into the coals of the brazier, then spread the sweet smoke with a hand-fan woven from hemp. She covered her mouth and shuffled behind the staircase, where a bookshelf swung open to reveal a tiny panic room that two of the sanctuary's expert carpenter women had built to her specifications. She squeezed in after Hope, then barred it shut.

It was not airtight, nor was it fully bulletproof, but it was just big enough so she could hide women and children on the run. She found the lockbox and fingered the combination. In it, she kept a burner phone, a powerful tiny flashlight, and a gas mask, among other things. She had weapons on the walls, and a hatchet in the attic in case of floods, but nothing she would use on another living creature.

She took the phone from its charging cord and thumbed away. An app controlled the sound system. The speakers fired up with low frequency drones like the death song of a demon whale. It was an album by a bunch of silly bearded white men in monk's robes that Wesley had given her, which he said he used to clear his head. It did not soothe her, quite the opposite, but it served well to sow confusion.

Hope whined quietly at her feet as the men outside stumbled in the smoke, their swears and shouts muffled by the bookcases. They were angry.

Soon they would be very, very frightened.

In her experience, men of violence found the effects of the soul-revealing psychoactives she had poured into the brazier incredibly unpleasant, especially without a friendly guide.

78: SACRAMENT

Pastor Roy Eagleton smiled at his flock. Young boys sat in seersucker, girls in Sunday dresses, their proud white parents leading them through the doors and into his pews. The old mammies had polished the wood to a gleam. Sometimes Samuel and Hesper would come with him to watch them do the work. The old man could sometimes even speak a word or two, while his wife kneaded his gnarled hand.

Molina's students served as ushers and choir girls, and the throats of the organ pipes hummed "Bringing in the Sheaves" under Ardith's practiced fingers.

Outside, the wind whipped at the tree branches, threatening to storm. It had been teasing all week, between the sun showers. An early depression had made it to the Gulf and hunkered down over the hot water gathering steam. The prediction was that it would break apart on the coast into rain and thunder, but you never could tell in the cone of uncertainty.

Roy always felt energized by a storm. When the power was out, he could imagine the purple dream of the past, of what would have been, had the South prevailed. Before his stroke, Samuel Calvineau would bring out an old hand-cranked ice cream maker and cut fresh peaches from Ruston into the mixer as a servant turned the handle. They would eat from Wedgwood china bowls and watch the sun set golden-green over the bayou, then take a ride in the 1957 Cadillac Eldorado Brougham—the finest handmade metal carriage produced by this nation.

Pastor Roy shook the hands of his parishioners as the black shark rolled in, a young Calvineau at the wheel, wearing a chauffeur's cap. The parishioners parted on the church's wide steps and greeted the white-suited father and primly dressed mother of the church. Roy kissed Hesper on the cheek and shook Samuel's good strong hand, then led them to their seats at the frontmost pew, nearest to his pulpit.

Where Molina would be waiting, her lips freshly rouged with the lipstick he had given her.

As a pastor, he could marry, and he had after Evangeline had spurned him. A good Calvineau girl who believed in their mission and worked in the school until cancer took her. Molina did not know it, but she was being tested for her replacement. He knew women loathed this duty, but he judged their future obeisance by how eagerly they submitted to it, how well they feigned carnal worship on their knees.

He told her she should gargle with Cat-Lick holy water before accepting him into her mouth, and that his seed would purify her.

The look on her face was precious.

The Calvineaus sat in their pews, a hand-embroidered pillow under Mister Samuel's bony ass. Roy stepped behind the pulpit. A purple curtain was draped over where Molina knelt. He had chosen her well. She was well-learned in suffering for others and would translate that into his pleasure.

He reached between his robes, released his erection from its prison, and parted the velvet curtains with it. He gripped the fine polished mahogany of the pulpit and felt the warm grip of a hand around his member.

Mrs. Hesper smiled up at him as Ardith began keying "A Mighty Fortress is Our God" on the pipe organ. This was Molina's cue. She was not to release him until the organ pealed its final tones.

His hymnal sat closed, bookmarked by the pages of his sermon. He cleared his throat for her to begin. Her grip tightened.

Her fear would make it sweeter. He savored the clench of a terrified throat.

A mutter passed over the crowd. In the back of the church, a woman in a short blue dress walked the aisle, sporting a black eye patch.

Evangeline Calvineau had come home.

"Welcome home, wayward daughter," Roy said. "A seat has been kept for you at your parents' pew, all these years."

Her heels clicked on the hardwood and she took the empty seat at the end of the pew beside her father, on his paralyzed side. Purse clutched in her lap. "Guess I won't burst into flames, Mama."

Mother Hesper leaned out to give a chilly grin of triumph.

"And now, a special sermon about the prodigal son." Pastor Roy opened his hymnal and frowned at the page.

On the page of his sermon, a page had been inserted. *Preach mother fucker* had been scrawled in a clumsy hand, above a neatly written block of words.

A voice rose from the pulpit curtains. "You best read what Molina wrote, unless you want your dick in the collection plate."

Desmarteaux.

Roy stood straight and snarled under his breath. "I can't kill you, but I can make you wish you were dead."

A harsh, calloused hand squeezed his balls, and a zip tie hissed closed around the base of his penis. Cold steel pressed against its root.

"So can I, Pastor." Jay spat the last word. He scraped the blade up Roy's root and shaved the finely curled hairs.

"That whore will burn in hell!"

The organ faltered and stopped, Ardith peeking from her perch in the balcony. The worshipers gasped, and Mrs. Hesper's eyes turned cold.

Jay let the blade bite in. Blood seeped on the steel.

Roy had not known fear like this since the day Andre

Desmarteaux handed Evangeline his war hatchet. There was a Satanic light in her eyes as she swung the blade at his Corvette and cracked the fiberglass. He saw the same light in her eye now, as she sat in the front row. She wanted flesh, and her adopted son had come to claim it.

"I have sinned," Roy wailed.

The parishioners muttered to themselves, looked at their folded hands. Some cried and took tissues from their purses.

"I am a predator who rapes the women of our flock," he cried. "And I help the Calvineaus prey upon the children of the poor."

Jay drew the blade.

Roy's scream rattled the speakers. He stumbled back from the pulpit, robes stained red. Shrieks and gasps echoed through the nave.

Pastor Roy collapsed against the altar, surrounded by his shocked assistants, and howled.

79: SMOKE ON THE WATER

Kroese kicked over the brazier and it released a cloud of stinking fog, like a damn dry ice machine at a concert. The coals smoldered and gave the floor a dull blue glow. The whole place vibrated, and the floor felt spongy.

One soldier whimpered on the floor, clutching his leg. The pit bull had hit him hard and then bolted, a trained war dog. Moved so fast he couldn't lead it to take a shot.

"Bandage him, dammit!" Kroese snapped at the other soldier, who held a small flashlight in his mouth. He set down his crowbar and pulled a bandanna from his pocket.

"The fuck is that sound? Feels like we're in a C130 going down!"

Kroese took the flashlight and stomped around the staircase.

"We know you're in here!" Where the hell could a three-hundred-pound woman go so fast? He hadn't even heard footsteps. She moved like a ghost.

You have failed me, boy.

His grandfather's face formed in the dark, like a mask made from a rotting shroud. Kroese shined his light and a tooth-filled Black face leered from a shelf. He roared and drew down on it.

It was a black African statue, like from a horror movie. He kicked it over.

"You okay boss? Can't breathe in here."

His heart pounded, and his breath was short. The smoke.

The bitch had dosed them with something. He holstered his weapon and swept the room with the flashlight.

She couldn't have run up those stairs; she was too big. There had to be secret stairs going down. He shoved a chair aside and pulled up the corner of a rug. The floorboards mocked him with their lack of a trap door or secret tunnel. Who was he fooling? This was New Orleans. Dig two inches and you find water.

He punched the wall and a painting fell.

"Gimme your crowbar, she's under the floor!" He took his Ka-Bar and stabbed at the wood, prying at the boards.

No answer.

"Get your ass over here."

A wail. "The floor is lava!"

He kicked at a planter of herbs and went to get the crowbar himself. The floor wasn't lava; it was smoke. A sea of white faces, crying up to him to be saved.

The unwounded man was curled on the divan clutching his knees, staring at the burning blue coals.

The dog-bit soldier tightened the bandanna around his calf. "They're gonna eat my legs! The orcs are gonna eat my legs!"

Faces leered from dark corners of the room. Glowing eyes from statues and crystals. Mocking him. He was weak, naked, and short-dicked in a jungle of muscular and sensual Black men with porn star cocks, all laughing at his little chicken skin balls.

Kroese was a boy again, fishing in the creek in Jena, kicking over crawfish towers and using them for bait, when he came upon three Black boys swimming in the shade of waist-deep water. They were naked but he couldn't stop staring. The water glistened on their skin like diamonds scattered on polished hardwood, but what struck him was their ease with themselves. It jeered at his loneliness and disgust of himself, his acne-puckered face and the blue veins that showed through his sunburned, mole-studded skin.

That image followed him through his mediocre life at school. He always took the easy path. Why bother trying, if you got by when not trying at all?

You were born better than these kids, and you let them do better than you? The look of disgust on his father's face. *We let them in our schools, but that doesn't mean we let them do better than us.* The look on his mother's face felt like he'd stuck an icicle down his pee hole.

Kroese felt that again now and gripped his crotch to not piss his pants.

"You have desecrated this place!" The Witch Bitch's voice echoed from the walls. She was here, mocking them in the dark. "Leave or you will be consumed."

The walls writhed with blackness. Kroese lashed out with the Ka-Bar and screamed.

Then they were blinded by whiteness and deafened by explosions.

Two women, one with a shotgun and the other with a laser-sighted pistol, had burst through the curtains. The pistoleer held them open. Sunlight beckoned.

"Do not soil this place with more blood!" The Witch's voice echoed from the walls. "Leave and you will be spared."

Kroese and his soldier hoisted their wounded comrade and tumbled out the open door into the street, covered by the warriors.

Suzane shuffled from the panic room, her freckled cheeks glowing from the excitement. Hope slammed into the shotgun-toting woman's thigh with a love-whimper.

"Thank you, Lauren." Suzane slumped against her, then sank onto the divan.

"We gotta ready for war, Suze," the warrior said, after she and Amina cleared the room.

80: REAPER'S RIDE

Jay crawled from under the pulpit in a blood-spattered choir robe, wearing the Devil mask from Molina's production of *Faust*. The congregants gawked.

For a moment, Jay stared back at the abyss. "I'm ringing Hell's bells!"

Samuel Calvineau sputtered imprecations in the front row, raising his cane like a cavalry saber. Evangeline patted his cheek. "This was for you, Daddy. We know you steal children, you evil son of a bitch. And you will be judged."

His eyes rolled back white. He collapsed in his cushioned pew and people surged to help him.

Hesper pointed at her daughter. "Drag her back to Whiterose!"

A hefty bearded man in an uncomfortable suit grabbed for her. Evangeline fired through her purse, and he fell, clutching his gut. The crowd screamed and the doors crammed in panic.

Jay shucked the robe and strode toward the rear door, leaving the hell he'd raised. Roy plowed through the terrified choir and staggered after him, gripping his crotch. "I will not be unmanned!"

Jay loped over the grass to the work shed, where an engine putted and drowned out Roy's agony. They turned the corner, where Molina waited.

Roy's eyes bulged as Jay held his severed penis over the chute of the wood chipper.

"I made him swear not to kill you," Molina said over the engine's sputter. "So get to the hospital before you make a liar out of me."

Jay dropped it in and a spray of blood and giblets misted out the chipper. Roy fell to his knees and gaped.

Jay tossed in his latex gloves and the Devil mask, then nudged Molina toward her Subaru. "You best get to Saint Malo. Your folks are waiting."

She nodded, looking dazed. "Talk to Woody, when you get to Angola. He's the biggest of big stripes." She hugged him, then jogged to her car.

The black Cadillac was parked in a spot marked off by cones. Jay was drawn to it and followed the urge. The polished fin reflected his face, like it had swallowed his soul. The keys dangled from the ignition. It pulled at him like a black hole, its invisible fist gripping his insides below his navel.

The plan was to surrender here, where they were unlikely to kill him, but he couldn't leave Keshawn. He opened the door and sank into the plush sheepskin seats, turned the key and felt its engine thrum like the heartbeat of the universe.

The cool blade of a cane knife scraped the stubble of his throat.

A placid, dark face with bright eyes filled the rearview mirror, eyes that would watch him die and lose no luster. "Drive me to the boy, or you're gonna learn why they call me Chopper."

Jay's hand drifted down the wheel and the cane knife bit in. He swallowed. "Easy. You mean Keshawn?"

The man's breath blew hot on his neck.

"He's alive as of two days ago."

"He'd best be, or you're dying hard."

"Keshawn was taken by Pastor Roy Eagleton. I just tossed Roy's pecker into the wood chipper."

Out the windshield, the pastor stumbled into his white truck, leaving a bloody smear.

The knife didn't loosen on his throat, but Jay felt the man's gaze diffuse as it took in the scene. "Keshawn is at Whiterose Plantation. They got Hitler Bitches guarding the place, prepping for their racial holy war."

"Heimdall Brotherhood?" The knife gave him an inch to breathe.

Roy's truck wobbled out on four flat tires, sending people scattering. The parking lot was too jammed to escape now, not without plowing over people. Calvineau Parish police blocked the road.

"I was going back to get Keshawn," Jay said, rubbing the line of blood into his neck. "But it looks like I got a date with my daddy in Angola. Beat this car back to Whiterose, and you'll find the boy. Do me a favor and kill as many Hitler Bitches as you like. Burn the damn place down while you're at it. That's what I'm fixing to do."

Chopper eyed the police, then climbed out the suicide door and jogged toward the fence. Phone to his ear.

Jay stroked the sheepskin seat as he stepped out of the Cadillac. He fell to his knees as the parish police came running. Mama Evangeline waited by her Dodge, her pistol cocked.

"You shoot my boy, you die next."

She covered them as they cuffed Jay and shoved him into the back of the cruiser.

Roy stared out the window of his truck, his drained face flattened against the window glass. An intrepid parishioner plucked at the door handle in a gambit to kill the engine, but it was locked.

Jay truly hadn't wanted to kill the man.
Death was too kind.

81: HOME TO HELL

Junior LeFer drove Desmarteaux to his daddy's prison himself.

Mrs. Hesper wanted her grandson's head, but she would change her mind. Junior didn't want one of his men killing the knife-wielding psychotic and paying the price.

"You'll like my daddy's place. He'll keep you busy to the end of your days."

The Desmarteaux kid was silent in the back of the Explorer. He'd been inside most of his life, and once he'd heard he was headed to Angola, he calmed like a spooked horse with its eyes covered.

"You cons always find a way to get back home," Junior said. "I think y'all like it. Somewhere deep inside, you know you don't belong with good people."

"Good people, like Pastor Roy. That's who you think good people are. People with money." Desmarteaux laughed.

LeFer Junior's father had never raised a hand to him, nor had he shamed him in front of others. Junior knew from his early days that power was his father's only love, and after years of decrying it in private, he was beginning to see the light.

The old man wouldn't live forever. His enormous appetite would be his downfall, and then his son would rule Angola prison. Junior dreamt of the reforms he could implement.

"I hear you got a thing for the theater director. Don't act like you maimed the pastor for anyone but yourself."

Junior's father had tapped into the American desire to punish those deemed morally wanting and ran with it, building an industry of prison labor that required the people tolerate the longest prison sentences of any state. The other parishes were getting wise, selling their jail beds to companies who profited from keeping them full. It kept taxes low, and that was enough for the majority to buy in. People who built their identities around being landowners, mortgaged to the bone, who feared that losing the revenue from enslaving the incarcerated might raise their bills to the brink.

"I helped a friend who couldn't help herself. I didn't do it for a paycheck." Desmarteaux looked out the window as they took the winding road through the woods to the prison.

If Junior had done anything of consequence to deter the Calvineaus from their predations, he would have lost his job as parish sheriff, and someone worse would be in his place. So he did what little he could and considered it heroic.

Sometimes he and Tewliss had a chat about all the good Junior could do. It was a drug that muted the pain of making the amoral decisions required to get to the level of power where change could be effected.

He had kept a few Black men from dying in the swamp. Once he knew they were targets, he told them they had to flee with their families. Their land was reclaimed by the bank or the parish, but they would be alive. He'd put away a few rapists, too. Mostly men who preyed in bars. But girls who'd reported athletes for assault, how could he tell them the truth? That the community would rush to defend the man who had raped them?

He had a woman officer who'd been raped in the Army sit with the victims and explain that at most, the rapist would be shamed a while. Then the people would turn on her and come to his defense. Was that worth it? Or you could be strong, and tell your friends to stay away from him, and take it as a lesson learned.

It was a shit world. A sheriff has power in a parish, but it was like steering a train. The tracks were laid long ago, and unless you dug them up and made new paths, there were only so many places the conductor could go.

Like the road to Angola, which had no turn-offs.

Jay watched the woods fly past. Inside, he felt terror. On his first day of release, he'd been hit by a kind of agoraphobia after so many years inside. He'd slept in a bathtub to be in a room like a cell the first night. But he had no desire to return to the manmade Hell of incarceration.

They passed the man selling Confederate flags and Blue Lives Matter T-shirts from a table. Then the woods opened up, and he saw the Farm.

Jay stared at the enormous compound. They drove past men tilling a field supervised by an armed man on horseback, then hugged the levee. Okie had told Jay that the inmates who'd built the levee were worked worse than the enslaved, because they were not considered valuable property. If they collapsed, they were buried in the levee. A wall of corpses to divert the river from washing the plantation away.

It didn't hit him until they rolled toward the main camp with the fences topped with razor wire and the guard towers. His fingers dug into the seat between his legs.

"You think you're smart, but you're gonna learn why we don't cross the Calvineaus."

Junior LeFer led him to the first sally port in a daze. They took his work clothes and traded them for denim. The clothes he'd had on could have passed for prison blues. He'd never realized or thought about it, but it weighed on him now, with Junior's words.

Maybe this was where he belonged.

With his Daddy.

82: RAID ON WHITEROSE

The Cadillac had been easy to follow. The driver followed a private ambulance the whole way to Whiterose. The old man had been stretchered in by EMTs. His wife rode in the back of the Caddy.

Chopper hung back and shadowed them, but once they got off the interstate, he looked up the plantation on his phone and took a different way, riding atop a levee and cutting through muddy farm roads to approach from another angle. Suzane's phone wasn't answering. He could use backup. No time, now.

He switched to four-wheel drive and followed tractor ruts along their property. As he neared the big house, a row of cotton and indigo capped the end.

Nostalgia for the age of sharecropping.

He parked behind a large magnolia blocking the view from the house, armed up, and reconnoitered. The sat-view had not shown much detail thanks to the treetops.

Suzane wanted the parents of the stolen children to surround the Rougarou as they brought him to justice. Not dead body in the swamp justice, but the public kind.

She repeated Audre Lorde's words, "You can't dismantle the master's house with the master's tools," but didn't want the tool to be the guillotine.

Chopper believed that would never happen with the Calvineaus. Rich white folks only got taken down by other rich white folks.

Anyone else tried, and they became an example.

But other examples could be made.

The Heimdall Brothers were on red alert thanks to his aggressions. He had the Shorty shotgun holstered, and a suppressed rifle slung and held at port arms. He leaned on a trunk of the magnolia and used the scope to sweep the grounds.

Attacking a plantation owned by a powerful family was unheard of. Not since the 1811 uprising that began in what became LaPlace. Only two slavers were killed, and a hundred enslaved lost their lives as punishment.

A garage sat on the other side of the rose garden, a sea of white. The doors were closed. The upper windows of the big house had a view of the garden, so he took a loop around two pecan trees, hackles tingling as the pecan shells crunched under his boots. He snipped the phone line to the house with his multitool.

Around the corner, three men sat at a picnic table playing with their phones and puffing smokes, out of view of the house. Two in khakis and white polo shirts, polyester armpits darkened. Another gray-bearded biker type in jeans and a black T-shirt with Gothic lettering, sidearm tucked in his pants, next to a sunburned plumber's crack. Battle rifles sat on the picnic table next to a pitcher of tea and glasses on a tray.

Hitler Bitches.

He pulled back and planted a cell jammer in the branches of the magnolia to give it the best range. The battery would last hours. He checked the remote and watched the signal on his burner wink out. Then flicked it back on. A blip would go unnoticed, but when they all went out, the alarm would go up.

He waited and studied the lay of the land. A typical plantation; the servant quarters had been converted into a garage. The cooking would have been done here, to keep the big house cool and undirtied.

And with no one home, that's where the hostage would be.

He took achingly slow steps to get to the back of the garage.

He kept the building between him and the men and slipped into the open front doors. He slung the rifle and drew the Shorty. Loaded with slugs. He looped a lanyard to his wrist and creaked up the stairs. Three doors at the top. Lock plates on the outside, padlocks hung from them, unlocked.

All but one.

Chopper let the sawed-off dangle from the lanyard and made short work of it with his cane knife.

He heard a scrambling beyond the door. When he opened it, a boy of thirteen stood in the dim light, looking down. He wore slacks and a white shirt buttoned to the collar, polished but untied shoes on his feet. On a single bed sat a stack of old hardback books.

"Keshawn?"

The boy's expression of fear melted into confusion.

"I'm Wesley. But people call me Chopper. You're going home."

"But—"

"Your mom and sister are safe. Get anything you care about and tie those shoes. We're gonna have to run like hell."

83: DADDY KANE

Walking the halls in prison blues turned Jay's skin to Jell-O. Guards led him out of Camp E and down the chain-link fenced paths to the next dormitory, and the late summer heat barely touched him. Riflemen in towers silhouetted by the sun into black spiders looking down, throwing long morning shadows. The chill broke into a cold sweat across Jay's shoulders.

The guards waved them through another sally port to one long hallway that connected all the dorms. They didn't have dorms in Rahway, but it was the same. All men, mostly dark-skinned and hollow-eyed like shelter dogs.

One older Black man waited in prison blues and brogans, his eyes deep and his posture unbroken.

"This here's the Cal boy, Woody. He's in dorm two." The guards handed him off.

"I'm Jay."

"I know your name," the old man said, walking. "Everyone will. That's why you're with me."

Jay followed.

"I'm Woody, but they call me the Fox." He spoke in a low con whisper. "Your mama told me the plan. It's a good one, but Andre's sick, and the rodeo might kill him."

"If it does, he ain't going alone."

"Don't go thinking like that. There's always a way out."

"How long you been inside?"

Woody stopped ten paces from a door. "Fifty-three years."

"How come you still here, this is so easy?" Jay low-talked, mouth slack, out of habit. No one was close enough to hear or read lips.

"They had me in solitary longer than your whole stretch. I got out of the hole. There's hope for me but not while LeFer's in charge. My mama's ninety-five and still comes to pray with me. I'll outlive Kane, if I'm able." He gave a sly smile. "Especially if he keeps eating crawfish pies like Nilla wafers." He unlocked the door.

Jay stepped tentatively.

"Just remember, whatever they do, you need to be in the rodeo." He held up a fist and Jay gave him dap.

The door jerked inward and a nightstick hooked Jay back by the throat, pulling him inside. He sank at the knees to get out of the choke, and another stick thumped against his calves.

The guards shoved him to his knees and dragged him into a chair. The office walls were covered in photos of a large white-haired man, always in a checkered shirt, posing with lawmen in suits and decorated men in uniform. A bathroom door opened, releasing a rank scent, and the man from the photographs stepped out.

Warden LeFer smiled, his steel-rimmed spectacles gleaming beneath the fluorescent light. "This little pissant's the one causing so much trouble?" He clucked a thick white tongue. "My son's losing his touch."

The guards knew better than to chuckle.

"Foxton, you forgot my tea," LeFer called out the door. "And go out to the tents and bring me some meat pies. One of each. They best be hot when they get here."

"Yessir, Warden," Woody the Fox said, patting his shirt pocket like a little boy. "I'll bring 'em hot, sir." His brogans tapped down the hall double time.

Warden LeFer bent over Jay and drew up his jowls in a fearsome smile. "Joshua Calvineau. I hear you go by Desmarteaux, like our resident craftsman Andre. I've had him since 1985, when he and your mama tried to rob an armored car with that year's prison rodeo money. They were gonna use it to fund breaking you out, up North. So any silly plans you got now? I'm always two steps ahead. I'll let you play yours out for my amusement, nothing more."

He gripped Jay's shoulders and leaned down.

"I'm your daddy now."

84: RAKED OVER THE COALS

The ambulance rumbled up the front road to Whiterose, the Cadillac right behind. Tires crunched on the old pecan shells and the soft huff of the big V8 engine reverberated off the walls. The Cadillac huffed its last, and Keshawn waited, standing at attention, as heavy feet creaked up the steps.

The ones he'd first mistaken Chopper's for.

A key reopened the padlock and a woman's polished crepe-soled shoes entered.

Chopper watched from under the cot.

"Go serve the lady her tea. And be quick about it." The voice was weary and without compassion. Keshawn stepped past, took a cuff upside the head without even trying to duck, and double-timed down the stairs.

The woman paused a moment, then followed.

Chopper gave her time to exit the garage, then crept after them. Keshawn was right. She would have screamed, and the Nazis would be on them. Smart kid. Chopper had told him where he'd parked the truck, and that the keys were in it. Keshawn said he could drive a little.

Outside, the HB boot boys talked among themselves. Chopper circled the garage, rifle at his shoulder, and peeked around the corner. The three armed men posed before a pillory built for punishing the enslaved.

Chopper had seen such a thing at the Whitney Plantation

Museum. This one was crusted with dried blood. He could see the flies lighting on the stains through his scope.

One had his arms in the stocks, while the biker held up a bullwhip darkened from use. The last stretched his arm out with his phone to get all three of them in the frame.

Chopper shot him first.

Pop pop pop. Pop pop pop. Two center mass then a head shot, as he'd been trained. Shooter's suppressor turned the shots into hammer blows. Soldiers would know the sound. Civilians would be confused and come looking.

Chopper jogged up the Whistle Walk, the old well-trod path from the servant quarters to the big house. The kitchen was in the house now, and that's where he found Keshawn, frozen with a pitcher of tea in his hands. The woman in the gray servant dress stood behind him. She had straightened hair tied back in a bun and looked at Chopper like she'd seen the Devil.

"Keshawn comes with me. You can, too."

"No, she's—"

Ella stepped behind Keshawn and brought an arm around his throat. She reached for the knife block.

He couldn't shoot an old man. He shot the knife block instead. She screamed.

Keshawn elbowed her in the belly and squirmed away. "Let's go!"

Chopper heard shouts from in and outside the house. He followed Keshawn out the door and released two bursts of covering fire, then went to disable the vehicles and lead them away from the kid.

He found two pickup trucks parked out of sight of the house and popped the front tires with single shots. Now for the ambulance and the Caddy.

He rounded the corner of the garage at a full clip, then his legs got cut from under him. He hit the pecan shells face-first. The old woman swung a painted green rake and pinned Chopper's forearm to the ground with the thick metal tines.

Chopper snarled and reached for the shotgun with his other hand. He got a boot in his face.

Ralph Ora snapped up the Shorty shotgun and aimed as Keshawn disappeared around the magnolia. He pumped and fired until it clicked dry.

"Good job, Ella." A Viking jarl smiled down at Chopper. "Boy, they're gonna build memorials for the shit we're gonna do to you."

Ora cracked Chopper across the face with his own shotgun.

Chopper wished it had all gone black. Instead, things went red and muddy, and he heard his own muffled screams as they dragged him through the dirt.

PART 5: RUN THROUGH THE JUNGLE

WELCOME TO THE ANGOLA PRISON RODEO!!!!

NOTICE

- You are about to enter a penal institution. By entering this institution, you have consented to a search of your person, property and vehicle.
- All weapons, ammunition, alcohol and drugs must be deposited at the Front Gate before entering the institution. Any of the above items found on your person or property could result in your arrest and/or removal from institutional grounds.
- All purses, diaper bags, belt pouches, etc., will be searched before you enter the rodeo grounds. No food items or ice chests will be allowed. Ice chests must be locked inside the vehicle.
- All pocket knives should be locked inside your vehicle; along with any prescription medication not needed during the institutional activity.
- All vehicles are to be locked. All tools must be locked in a toolbox or inside the vehicle. Please lock your vehicle.
- No cameras or video equipment are allowed. Please leave these items in your locked vehicle.
- No umbrellas or stadium seats are allowed inside of the rodeo arena.

ALL UNLOCKED VEHICLES WILL BE SEARCHED

85: FATHER AND SON

The warden's office was cramped and smelled of fried dough and sweaty feet. Jay sat facing the warden, hands cuffed in his lap. In a photo on the warden's desk, he recognized the cop who drove him to the prison, wearing desert fatigues and sunglasses.

"Why'd you have to go and cut off Roy's pecker?" LeFer asked, around a mouthful of meat pie. Flaky crumbs fell like hail on his desktop. "Now your grandfolks think you're a mad dog, fit for a cage."

"They know why." Jay reached with cuffed hands and took a crawfish pie off a paper plate translucent with grease. He managed to stuff most of it in his mouth before LeFer overcame the shock at his boldness and slapped the rest from his hands.

"That's how you think it's gonna be?" he roared, face red. "I can't kill you, but your daddy's another matter. Get Desmarteaux in here."

The guard shut the door behind him.

Jay looked sadly at the remainder of the meat pie's ejecta on the thin carpet, as he swallowed down the rest. "They make a good meat pie. Good as Natchitoches."

"We ain't here to get friendly." LeFer moved his plate out of Jay's reach.

"The pastor got what he deserved. I should've stuck it down his throat and let him choke to death. But I'm trying to refrain from killing. Like y'all here in prison, I want him to rehabilitate himself."

"Roy survived, but what's killing to you? I know what you did up North. How'd you like me to give you to the U.S. Marshals?"

"I haven't had a good slice of pizza in months, so that'll suit me fine. But you won't do that. Mama told me all about you LeFers. Suckin' my family's ass since the beginning of time. You want a taste of mine, it'll cost you."

LeFer smiled and picked up another pie. "Your ass still for sale? Your *real* mama used to sell it out of her trailer. I got her number one customer here. Philo Salva. Maybe you'd like to have a conjugal visit?"

The meat pie turned to stone in Jay's belly.

"But if you're a good boy, I might let you sic a couple of our dogs on him. Put him in hospice and let him die slow, basting in his own juices. You got all the time in the world. Because Salva ain't going nowhere. And neither are you."

LeFer sat back with the last meat pie. "You ruined the last crawfish pie. Gonna pay you back for that. All your grandfolks care about is whether you can deliver another son. You can soak up a whole lot of pain and still manage that." He took a bite and savored it.

Jay was acquainted with pain. The warden needed an introduction.

When the guard brought Andre to the office, they found Jay behind the warden's chair, one arm around LeFer's throat and Andre's wedding Bowie held to his eye socket. The guard drew his pistol.

Andre chopped his wrist, sending the weapon to the floor. He kidney punched him until he fell to his knees, then shut the door behind them. "Don't pick up your piece. We're gonna work this out."

The guard clutched his wrist.

"Talk to him, Desmarteaux!" LeFer barked, his pink face sheened with sweat. The chair wobbled side to side, and a blot of blood spread beneath his eye like a gangbanger's teardrop tattoo.

"This ain't a good play, son. Let him go."

"It true he got Salva? Know who he is?"

"It's true," Andre said. "Baited me to kill him. Wanted an excuse for me to die here."

"You dying anyway!" LeFer cried. "Tell him. Your daddy's got cancer, I'm gonna get him treated."

Jay drew a line to the warden's throat. "Should bleed you out right now, you son of a bitch."

Andre stepped closer, slowly. "That's how they work. Like the Devil. They dangle what you want right in front of you. You do this, we both die in here. They'll keep us apart. Think, son. You've done time. There's good time and bad time."

Tears trickled from Jay's eyes.

"They got me in the rodeo," Andre said, his eyes crinkled. "I need my li'l podna."

Jay stabbed the knife into the desktop and let LeFer drop. He took nervous steps.

"I missed you, Pop." Jay threw his arms around him. He was strong.

Andre flinched at the unfamiliarity of touch and the pain in his ribs, but held close.

"It's all right, son."

The guard crawled out the door. The warden hit a button on his desk phone and wiped at the blood on his face with a tongue-wetted handkerchief. "You touch me again, you'll die in the sweatbox."

The Desmarteaux boys were still clutched together tight when the guards came and broke them up and dragged them to adjoining cells.

86: STRANGE BEDFELLOWS

Evangeline didn't trust Shooter further than he could piss, but the boy was right: they needed him.

She would not rope in anyone from Saint Malo to clean up her family mess. She was grateful to be allowed there at all, with the evil her family had done.

In her heart, the misery of thirty years with Andre and Jay in prison was her punishment for fleeing Whiterose when she should have burned it to the ground with her family in it.

She'd been raised on harvests sown in soil made rich with blood. And while she'd dedicated her life to fighting her family, she was merely a contrary child, a nuisance to them, nothing more.

They drove in silence, north of Lafayette to equip from Shooter's personal armory. His compound was on a big piece of land with a barred gate and a berm built around it as a defense against both water and attack. A prepper's paradise. The house was brick with steel shutters, built on a rise with a view of the cleared land in all directions. No trees near enough to fall in a storm, a satellite dish fit for NASA, a propane tank shielded by steel walls, a windmill and a water tower.

"You invested your last haul well, dincha?"

Boudreaux sighed. "LeFer took most of it. This is from the

TV shows and running guns to the Nazis for your family."

She spat on the ground. "My blood, not my family."

He disabled the security and unlocked the vault-like door. Inside, he punched buttons that fired up a generator. A ventilation system started moving the stale air. LED lights flicked on as they walked the hallway. "Too bad they didn't stick to rebel music. You remember that shit?"

"Don't chum up to me. I got reason to kill you every time I see my face."

He smacked his dry lips. "That's fair. They wanted me to ice Andre, but I threw my shot. Had to make it look good, or LeFer would nail my balls to the wall. I'm sorry about the eye. It was collateral damage."

"I don't feel it growing back."

He led her down a hallway. She kept back, hand on her Colt.

"You think I like working with Nazis? None of us knew what tangling with you entailed."

"Entail. Big words, TV boy." But he was right. She'd been a rich girl playing revolutionary.

"You had the money to go where the Calvineaus can't touch you."

"I left Louisiana for Vietnam, and I swore I'd never leave again. Not even for that big Hollywood money."

She understood. She'd gone north for the boy, but his love had been like a piece of home they could carry.

He punched keys on a wall unit and the garage door opened, revealing another jacked diesel F-350. This one was relatively low profile, tiger-stripe camo. Her Dodge was parked outside. She clicked the fob that lifted the hatch.

"If you got to pee, there's a chem toilet by the laundry room."

She followed him to the gun vault. He punched the code and the door seal popped with a whiff of air. Lights glowed on.

"This looks like Rambo's romper room."

She folded her arms, hand on her magnum, while he filled the back of her wagon with gear. She tucked a box each of .45

hardball and .357 hollow points into her bag, then plucked a few M-84 stun grenades from a box. "You mind?"

"Mi casa es su casa."

He carried a .50-caliber rifle and a few ARs to the Dodge, then the ammo. Then buckets of Tannerite.

"You don't think we'll need the grenade launcher? Or are you saving that for the End Times?" she said. "We're all gonna be free, or die trying."

"Hell, your folks want me dead anyways." He picked up the rotating cylinder M32A1 Milkor. He loaded it and a belt of ammo into the car, then locked up. "Can I have my piece?"

She handed him the .44 barrel first. When he reached for the muzzle, she cocked the hammer quick. "The boy gets the mercy from Andre. Remember that."

Shooter looked into her steely eye. "We get them out, I consider all debts paid."

She nodded, eased the hammer down, and spun the gun on her finger to hold the barrel. "And we never cross paths again."

87: CELL MATES

Jay and Andre studied each other's faces through the bars. They were both creased heavy around the eyes and beneath their eyebrows, two thick slashes from brow to temple, giving them the look of perpetual worry. Jay's nose was thicker, flattened by boxing gloves, his chin strong and shaved clean. Andre's was painted pepper gray with his beard, his nose unbroken and sharp. They weren't blood, but Jay had somehow aged into a broader-shouldered version, six inches of height taken and sculpted into hard-working muscle.

"Sure good to see you, Pop, but this ain't the way I wanted it."

Andre hiccupped a silent laugh. The boy always had a way of brightening the worst of times. He guessed that was how he'd survived the hell they'd saved him from, and then twenty-five years of prison.

Andre leaned from his bench and pressed his forehead through the bars. Jay followed suit. You could just about touch. Fingers weaved through the bars, clutching as if in prayer.

There was little permissible contact inside. You slapped hands, shoulders. Embraced when celebrating rare good news, but only brief, lost-in-the-moment touches. It killed a man slow. Made him frightened and mean.

They had a silent moment, passing energy between them. The incessant noise of prison faded away, the chatter, clangs, and music.

Everything they had wanted to say to one another over the years had been spoken silently in their heads, as they enacted this reunion, never thinking it would come.

The guards had to hit the bars with their batons to bring them back. "Got a visitor."

Philo Salva was lean and shaved bald and his strength rippled beneath his lean old runner's frame. He shaved his body clean in the showers, clogging drains and using up hot water, but none would challenge him.

Jay stared through the bars at Salva. Trembling, hands at his sides knotted into fists.

Somehow, Salva still smelled of rotten onions and the sulfur from the town of the same name.

Andre fell to his bunk in shame for not having killed the man who had violated his child.

"Say it," the guard said, and prodded Salva with his baton.

"He knows who I am," Salva muttered. "Kid, you want to kill me, you can try. Many have, and I'm still here."

"Say it." The baton slapped the back of his thigh.

"My cell door's open, you want what you been missing since you were a boy."

Jay didn't hear the words. He was back in the Witch's trailer.

After the guards took Salva away, Andre talked him back to the world. It took hours.

89: THE WILDEST SHOW IN THE SOUTH

The morning of the rodeo was like any other at the Farm. Mess bell rang early, and men climbed out of their bunks, dressed and made small talk, before lining up for the count. Under LeFer, the prison fed itself, and that took labor. They needed the nearly six thousand lifers, and there were not enough guards to follow everyone.

Woody the Fox had been transferred from his private cell with the big stripes to a dorm so they could deep search his quarters. He woke early with the morning crew of cooks, and gave dap to men as he passed, bumping fists, and went to deliver LeFer his breakfast.

He had passed messages and contraband over the course of a month, and as he headed for his morning jog around the yard, he signaled with nods, or small changes in behavior—in prison you live by routine, and something as small as not returning a wave spoke volumes—to set things in motion.

Woody had been given a life term by a Calvineau judge, when twenty years and parole had been the norm for his crime. He would never get back the thirty years they stole but watching their empire crumble from his gray-bar castle would have to suffice.

* * *

Andre Desmarteaux woke with a storm of acid in his belly.

The boy related the plan to him in whispers.

It would've been smarter to smuggle in citizen clothes and fake papers and drive him out the front gates. Angola wasn't Alcatraz. Men escaped, usually without violence. They were found eating out of dumpsters behind a Sonic Drive-In, or holed up with their families, and sent right back to the Farm.

Thirty years hadn't killed the outlaw in him. The plan gave him a rise. That night, he had dreamed of rolling with Evangeline in the back of his Boss Mustang, when they were young and reckless instead of old fools.

If it went to hell, it was a good way to die. As long as the boy made it.

Andre knew better than to hope.

Hope killed you in here. They could take hope from you, like they took everything else.

It broke his heart to see the boy fall right into prison life. Lining up for inspection, keeping space in line for the mess hall, looking strong but not making eye contact.

They ate grits and eggs and coffee for breakfast and then loosened up with a jog around the yard together.

"Got twenty riding on you, Desmarteaux!" the rifleman in the guard tower called.

Then Andre took the boy to the dog pens. He worked there when he could. Dogs were good for the heart, even if he was training them to attack inmates who took a run for it. The dog handler sicced a wolf mix on a Black inmate dressed in enormous padding. The inmate ran and the dog took him down easily, clamping jaws on the back of his arm.

"Hey, boss."

The trainer called back the dog and gave him treats. The inmate crawled to his feet and stretched out the pain of the tumble.

"Hell you doing here, Desmarteaux? LeFer'll have my ass, you get hurt today."

Andre shrugged. "Rodeo ain't for a couple hours. Wanted to show the new fish the dogs."

"You ain't fooling nobody. You want to pull a muscle and give it to the Fox. I don't blame you, you're in a lose-lose situation."

The white guards had suggested there would be retaliation against him if he beat the Fox, and he let them think it. Nothing scared men in power more than people working across the color line.

Distant horns sounded.

The rodeo had begun.

Two young blonde women rode chestnut mares hard through the mud, American flag vests and shorts flapping as they dangled from the stirrups, stood on the saddles, and waved their Stetsons to Tim McGraw drawling out the speakers.

"Welcome to the wildest show in the South!" Warden Kane LeFer announced, standing like Caesar in the box above the gates where the bulls and broncos would emerge. The stands erupted into cheers. They had a good crowd today. The threatening storm had kept some folks home, but the gate was juicy.

"Let's hear it for the Liberty Riders! I want to thank y'all for coming today. To come see what we are doing, putting these boys to work paying their debts to society, and making the state of Louisiana great!" He waited for the cheers to die down. "I want y'all to know how your tax money gets spent, and today these boys are giving some back. The state penitentiary feeds itself, and the surplus feeds the parish jails. All the money made here at the rodeo goes to put dollars back in your pocket."

He always scheduled the armored car pickups when the taxpayers could see them. Sometimes it held up the security line, but it was just for show anyway. They didn't open trunks or check IDs. Rolling past beefy Louisiana troopers in sunglasses was all part of the spectacle.

We are the law. We keep you safe. Your money is well spent.

Seeing that made people feel like the seven hundred million in taxes they paid to run the state corrections facilities was worth it. Louisiana had the highest murder rate in the nation, but what else you gonna do but lock up them bad boys? At least now they were hoeing their rows, making things, getting thrown by wild animals for your entertainment.

LeFer beamed at the crowd. His stomach gurgled. Something had not sat right with it since his morning tea and meat pies.

"Y'all ready to see some real action?"

Below, Jay and Andre and waited with the rest of the inmates who'd signed up for the rodeo. The smell was close, manure and nervous sweat. They felt the stomping of the crowd, the rumble of the speakers.

Two rodeo clowns up front each wore a baggy shirt with black-and-white prison stripes and filed out to take position. If a bull went wild, they were your lifeline.

"Git on, Salva. You're up with the first crew." A guard shouted, louder than necessary. Jay bolted stiff, and Andre gripped the back of his neck like a pup's.

"I'll give the warden what he wants," Andre said. "I'm dying whether it's in here or outside. You listen to your father."

He knew from his rodeo days that you don't taunt the bull by having the clowns run at it right away. You torment it so it can't think, then you can dodge its rage, or in Spain, stab it right through the shoulder into the heart, killing it before it even knows it's dead.

90: SISTER OUTLAWS

Evangeline strode through the camo and cargo shorts crowd. Her disguise wasn't much: bug-eye sunglasses in lieu of her eyepatch, frosted blonde hair tied back, and one of Jay's AC/DC T-shirts with the sleeves and neck cut out, over a sports bra working double-time. Enough room for the Colt Diamondback to ride low in her jeans. She hated imprisoning her feet in tennis shoes, but she would have to run today, and run hard.

She sucked Diet Coke through a straw and walked the perimeter of the chain-link fence that kept the crowd separated from the muddy gladiator pit. Her boys weren't on the dirt yet.

The crowd was riled. A bronco had tossed a tall Black inmate like a rag doll and he'd landed hard, pulled away by rodeo clowns, clutching his hip. There was no alcohol served, but they were drunk on righteousness. The cowgirl show had fired their blood, the pair trick riding to a rocked-up remix of *Proud to be an American* while waving white Stetsons, sheathed in star-spangled swimsuits that showed off fine specimens of American thigh.

Evangeline bet that had made the men in the crowd sprout a crop of patriotic bone-ons. And the women would imagine themselves as gun-toting Miss Americas on horseback, Wonder Women lassoing bad boys and dragging their asses to justice. She felt a flush across her chest herself.

Such was the power of ceremony.

She squeezed into her row to the only empty seat, next to the raven-haired church girl. She wore a baseball T-shirt that read Louisiana Music Factory, black sleeves covering strong arms.

Evangeline hip-bumped her skinny ass as she sat down.

"My son needs you to be strong."

Molina swallowed and watched the show. She had taken her folks in their RV to Saint Malo. They weren't happy about it, but her dad would do what he did best: fix things.

"I don't bite unless provoked. You on board? Things are about to get a little wild." Evangeline patted her arm.

"I'm all in, Miss Evangeline." Her voice was shaky, but she had steel.

"Mind me asking why? My boy's a charmer, but this ain't no high school play."

"Pastor Roy had me in a bind. Jay cut me loose." She shivered at her unintended play on words.

"My cousin Roy. I should've gelded that little shit a long time ago." She slapped Molina's thigh.

Molina flinched. Girl was still shell-shocked from the bloody mass.

The rodeo clowns led Jay out with three other inmates. Molina sucked in a breath.

"It's all copacetic, girl. Warden's onto us. We gotta play fast and loose." She poked Molina's hand with a car key. "Drop the bag of clothes under your seat when the crowd's distracted. And keep your seat until they make you leave."

The crowd whistled and laughed as the inmates, decked out in convict stripes, sat in flimsy chairs around a poker card table, playing it cool while the rodeo clowns teased and tormented the steer.

"When it's done, hole up at Saint Malo."

In the mud, the steer barreled through the table. Andre shoved his chair back and dodged like a matador, but Jay was hooked and tossed high. Evangeline's fingernails left crescents in Molina's arm.

"My boys come alive when things turn to shit."

Evangeline left her drink on her seat and squeezed out of the row, heading toward the armored truck. It plucked at her heart to leave her boys. There was always that moment on a job when you had to have godless foxhole faith in your partners, that they would do what they were supposed to do when they were supposed to do it.

She kept a couple backup plans like pocket aces but trust always made Evangeline feel right jittery.

92: GLADIATORS

Jay watched Salva and his five-man crew try to rope a bronco from the gate. They competed for time, green city-boys, with a handful who had competed in the rodeo before.

"You watch the bull, not him," Andre said. The world was an impressionist painting to Jay, his blood pumping hot.

"Stay with me, son," Andre said. He bumped foreheads.

Some people just need killing. There had never been one who needed it more than Salva. But Jay's righteousness was tainted with shame.

"You leave him to me." He kneaded Jay's shoulders.

The hacks handed out flak jackets. Andre took one and strapped it onto Jay, dressing him as a child. He rapped on the front. "The hacks give us their junkers, but they still work."

It stank like old boxing gloves.

"Why ain't you wearing one?"

"Slows you down," Woody the Fox said. "You ready? We need you frosty."

Jay slapped himself across the face, both cheeks, hard enough to raise welts. "I'm all right! I'm all right." His boxing ring face came to life, dead-eyed, a scarred Cajun sand shark out for blood.

"Convict poker! You boys are up."

The roar of the crowd was the snarl of a jungle beast.

Andre tugged Jay by the flak vest and they stumbled into the churned mud and manure of the rodeo pit. A card table and chairs were set for them. A rodeo clown handed them cards as they sat down, playing cool for the crowd. Andre tried to give Jay the seat with a view of the bull gates but Jay took the one with his back to it.

A fourth inmate shivered, dropping half his cards in the mud. "Don't you old cons gimme your poker face," he said, and they laughed.

"Watch my eyes. And don't think you're gonna win this," Woody said.

The gate slammed open. The crowd cheered, drowning out the calls of the rodeo clowns and the stomps of a ton of prime American beef on the hoof as they led it around, let it build up speed, and taunted it to charge the poker table.

"Stay cool!" Woody eyed his cards, held them up high to jive the crowd.

The charging bull was a freight train on four legs and the air seemed to flee before it, followed by the hot plume of its breath. The inmate's cards went confetti as he dived into the mud. Andre launched himself back off his chair and rolled to his feet like a gymnast, his face a rictus from the pain.

Woody smiled. As the bull hit the table, a lightning bolt hit Jay in the ass and made him move. Not since facing the bull gator had he felt nature reach down from his brain stem and drag him by the balls to where survival might lay. He leapt aside and the bull whipped its horns like a boxer in a one-two, hooking his arm and flinging him like a plastic monkey in a barrel, high in the air. The crowd rose to follow his trajectory. He twirled and rolled as he hit the muck. A rodeo clown heaved him up and away as the bull circled and stomped the card table to flinders.

Woody smiled from his chair, holding out his cards. "Full house!"

Andre high-stepped through the mud to where the boy landed. Jay scrambled to his feet, gritting his teeth.

"You break a rib, son?"

Jay smiled through the pain. "I'm good, just landed where Roy gave me a whipping."

"That son of a bitch. He's your half uncle. His daddy's in the bayou."

Jay began to ponder Roy's lineage and his desire to continue the family line with Mama Evangeline, but then the bull bucked around again, kicking divots of mud in the air.

Warden Kane LeFer smiled down at his colosseum. He thought of all inmates and employees as his charges in his private fiefdom, under his protection. But he also knew where his biscuits were buttered, and the Calvineaus wanted Andre Desmarteaux dead. He had killed bad men before but took great care to keep his conscience clean. Working for lynchers like the Calvineaus was one thing. Knotting the rope was another.

The Gospels were unclear on the fate of Pontius Pilate's soul, but even Cassius, who rolled dice at the Lord's feet as he died was welcomed past the gates of Heaven. A soldier doing his duty. The Bible was clear on following the law, and it was not murder to put the Desmarteaux boys and Salva in the pen together. What they did was on their own souls. LeFer led them into temptation, and he never liked blaming the temptress. Plenty of his fellow lawmen would blame a man with a fat wallet for getting robbed and giving them the paperwork, but he always blamed the thief.

If Desmarteaux took Salva's life out there, it would be murder, and killing a murderer was justice.

A chill ran through his guts. Then a temblor shuddered through his bowels. He was familiar with guilt, and this was something else.

He heaved himself up and shoved a hangdog guard aside. "Where's the damn shithouse?"

93: BULL SHIT

When it came time for bull-dogging the bronco, the inmates spread out wide. Salva kept far from Jay and Andre. He knew he was LeFer's sacrificial lamb.

The white bronco bucked and kicked, goaded by a flank strap pulled tight to torment it. The rodeo stock were well trained, but the inmates weren't. And the chance of cash to give to their family drove the men to take chances a seasoned rodeo performer never would.

They had mere seconds. Woody flipped his wrist and sent the lasso true, but the horse juked at the last second. Salva scooped up the noose and flung it high. Jay knew nothing of livestock. He took a running jump and shouldered the beast, which surprised the bronco as much as everyone watching. He bounced off like a toy, to the crowd's laughter. Woody jerked the rope and caught the beast high on the neck.

Salva passed close, rank of sulfur.

Jay gagged. Andre shoved him as the horse spun to kick. "Get on the rope!"

They got hands on the rope and pulled the horse's head down so it planted its hooves. The referee called it.

Woody laughed and slapped Jay and Andre on the back. Salva clapped his hands and stayed away.

Andre Desmarteaux ran like a young man, partnered with his boy.

***

LeFer had told Salva that what happened on the dirt didn't go on your jacket. The kid was off limits, but Andre had to die.

LeFer strutted through the crowd with butt cheeks squeezed tight, forearming his way toward the blue portable toilet by the front gate. A straight-tail crawfish must've got into one of his pies. Dead before it was boiled.

A tow-headed kid did the pee-pee dance in front of the shithouse, tugging a curled balloon ribbon. "Lady's been in there *forever*."

LeFer rapped on the door. "Official business," he said, using his cop voice. "Hurry it up in there." He leaned back, hands on his hips, surveying his domain. Men nodded and women smiled, not knowing he was doing all he could to hold back the sluice gates.

The door rattled and a wrinkled dishwater blonde woman teetered out, sheepish. "I'm sorry, maybe you need more bathrooms."

LeFer bumped her aside without a word. A flaming hot turd was piercing his ass like Torquemada extracting confessions.

"Mister! I was here first!" the kid whined.

LeFer backed in and dropped trou before the door closed. "Tie your pecker in a knot!" he snarled, and twisted the lock.

A river of fire exploded out of him and blue chemical splashed his cheeks. The relief was immediate. The odor was effluvious. The sound and rush of heat in the hot enclosed box positively volcanic.

LeFer wondered if this is what inmates he confined to the sweatbox felt.

"Now for the roughest and toughest part of the show!" the announcer bellowed over the PA. "It's time for Guts and Glory, where a convict tries to grab a hundred-dollar poker chip from between the horns of our meanest Brahma bull, Ferdinand!"

LeFer had given the bull its ironic moniker. The beast looked like one mean son of a bitch but was no wilder than any of the other stock. It had gored an inmate who'd been dumb enough to try to get it in a headlock once, and no one tried that again. He wanted to see who died first, Andre or Salva. Whoever walked out of the rodeo on two legs was going into the sweatbox to die for his sins.

LeFer rose, but felt an aftershock before he could reach for the paper roll.

A crash from outside echoed through the plastic walls.

Woody and Andre called out commands and suggestions, but Jay heard nothing. It was difficult to concentrate while you circled and juked around a ton of rampaging muscle. The bull's hooves—and this was a bull, with balls like two cannon shot in a tow sack—cut divots of mud and churned the earth. Its wild eyes stalked them, and it swung its horns in a figure eight like a swordsman keeping them at guard. The poker chip glinted between its horns.

"Wish I brought your damn hatchet," Jay said, and dived aside.

"Me too!" Andre slapped the bull's ass and ran. The rodeo clowns waved red cloths to keep it from busting through them.

Salva made a run for the chip. He was fast and lean, and his palm struck the bull's muzzle as he slid alongside, out of hooves' way. He skidded into the mud. Jay wanted those hooves to stomp him. A clown scooped him up to the crowd's cheers. Salva's hand was empty.

Woody the Fox tugged a horn and got the bull's ire, then ran serpentine for the fence. The clowns scattered as the bull charged him. He hunkered and jumped, going for a fake-out that Jay recalled from a Bugs Bunny cartoon.

Except this bull was smart. It ducked low and tore a gash in the fence where the Fox's head had been. It stamped and he rolled away. A rodeo clown whipped his cloth on the bull's face and distracted it.

"I'm going for it," Andre said. He had the angle; the bull was on the clown. He gritted his teeth against the pain and jumped in with a high sweep, the move he used when he nabbed Guts and Glory the first time.

Salva went at the same time. His boot came down on Andre's calf, dropping him at the bull's feet.

The bull reared and stomped. A hoof caught Andre in the ribs and his face wrenched with agony. The bull ducked its head to gore.

"Papa!" Jay was at the bull's flank as Andre bent in two. He looped an arm over the bull's massive horns and dropped his full weight, twisting its head away. He'd seen rodeo riders bring a bull down, but they dropped from horseback and knew what the hell they were doing.

In the seconds Jay was airborne, time stretched. He thought how bad it would have been if the bull fell on him or Andre. Then he hit the mud and the air was out of him and he scrambled as the clowns and Woody lured the bull away. Andre curled up, red-faced as a boiled crawfish.

94: BABY DRIVER

Keshawn had only driven his mother's Kia, taking lessons in the parking lot of the closed chemical factory. Chopper's truck was huge and fast and bounced all over the rutted road. He had no idea where he was going, and he bled from the shoulder, butt, and thigh. He had fallen face-first into the pecan mulch and felt two more blasts go over his head. Shredded leaves fell like confetti.

The truck was far and his leg burned but he got to it while the men were kicking through the trees looking for him. He had rolled out slow, wincing with each jab of the gas pedal.

Two men ran to a blue pickup after he flew past them on the farm road, bouncing across a field and busting through a cow fence to evade them. Keshawn looked in the rearview, but the dust trail clouded their pursuit.

He dragged a post and twenty feet of barbed wire onto the paved road. Heard it scraping back there but didn't dare look back. The truck had a GPS screen and he jabbed at the buttons until a map showed up, but he didn't recognize the names.

The post snapped off and the wire scraped and sparked on the pavement. He swerved wide around a slow-moving car, and they honked and swore as he passed. He felt sick to his stomach. His bloody leg stuck to the seat. He squeezed a hand under his thigh and it came back red.

The road behind was empty. He slowed down but was afraid to stop. Found a black T-shirt to tie around his leg. His mom had taught him how to dress a wound when he skinned his knee white once while playing. This didn't hurt half as much. It was like a shot at the doctor that didn't go away. But he felt weak and knew that was bad.

A hornet buzzed at his side and he jumped. A phone vibrated in the center console. Old heavy metal music ringtone. He tugged the lid of the console but it was locked.

His fingers left red smudges as he poked at the GPS screen. What had Chopper said? He went through the recent choices. His mom bought him a tablet young, and he fixed the phones and even clunky old computers for people in his neighborhood. This was a junk interface, but he poked through it.

These things were a privacy nightmare. He found Chopper's path through the state, a bowl of spaghetti with a big empty meatball in the middle, in the waters of the Atchafalaya. All were labeled as trips but one wasn't. A place he'd driven by heart and not used directions.

Keshawn tapped that waypoint.

A horn blared. In the mirror, the blue pickup truck came fast.

95: GUTS AND GLORY

Why'd that boy have to go and do that? Woody thought, stealing a red flag from a clown and whipping it wild. The bulls hated when you headlocked them. Bulls liked being king of the show, stomping all around like a row of cows they would get to stud were watching.

Woody hadn't rode in years but he always watched the show. Ferdinand was fast but predictable, unless you pissed him off.

And headlocks pissed him right the hell off.

It was too soon, but they only had the one shot. Woody whipped the flag at Ferdinand's horns and ran for the spot in the fence.

Andre gritted his teeth as Jay pulled him to his feet. Something had torn loose inside, wet and sloshy like an udder of milk.

"You all right, Pop?"

He waved the boy off. The bull had kicked him right in the tumor and squashed it like a ripe melon. It burned like poison but lit a fire under his ass.

The bull was confused by Woody and the clowns, charging one, then juking for the other. Salva was creeping up, going for the chip.

He punched the boy's meaty shoulder. "Let's get that sumbitch. Just like Woody told you!"

Jay took the left, going straight for the bull's ass.

Salva hopped closer, judging the bull's dance, ready to reach, grab, and dive past the clowns.

Desmarteaux hobbled alongside, clutching his side. Using the bull as cover, he threw a jab to Salva's kidney that stopped him head.

Then Jay grabbed the bull by its literal balls.

It kicked straight back without warning. Salva's teeth flew out like a cup of dice with a bloody spray behind. The bull turned fast, looping a horn toward Jay's gut, a frothing white devil. Jay staggered, legs caught in the mud. A clown tugged his arm but his boots were stuck.

Andre shoulder-checked Salva headlong into the bull's horns.

The bull's horn pierced through Salva's pelvis and out his ass, and the beast bucked with him flailing atop its crown. The crowd screamed.

The bull slammed Salva and used him like a boxing glove, throwing Jay, the rodeo clown, and Andre into the mud with the force of a car crash.

Rodeo men burst out of the gates with ropes. A rope looped over Ferdinand's horns, with one man on it. He was yanked off his feet. Woody whipped Ferdinand on the nose then ran for the fence.

Salva's rag-doll limp body hit the mud face down.

The bull hit the fence and tore through it like toilet paper. That morning, a friendly white lifer named Darrell had snipped the wires and zip tied them back, at Woody's request.

It was not the first time a bull had gotten loose at the Angola Rodeo, but it was the first time a pissed-off blood simple beast had burst through the fence chasing its most infamous lifer. The crowd cleared ahead of them. Woody dodged under Ferdinand's horns and snatched up the rope. The audience stood in their seats, and guards barked into radios. Ropers jumped through the fence, giving chase.

Woody ran ahead, pulling the bull away from the crowd.

Andre helped Jay up from the mud. "That was plumb crazy, boy."

Jay kicked a clod of dirt over Salva's wrecked body, and they limped together into the chaos.

96: PURE OUTLAW

LeBlanc loved the armored truck job. It was prestige, mostly. You wore your shades and looked tough while guards brought money bags with actual dollar signs painted on them for show.

Women loved the uniform, and while they couldn't drink at the rodeo, many stopped at a drive-thru daiquiri stand before the show. Some came up to squeeze his arm. Like this top-heavy blonde in the sunglasses.

Perk of the job. He'd had his work shirts tailored so the sleeves were snug to his biceps.

"Ooh," she said. "That's some muscle." Her freckled cleavage dazzled him.

She had mileage on her, like a classic muscle car. Tight jeans and a loose blouse, to give those puppies room.

"Ma'am," he smiled, "please step away from the vehicle."

"Aw, I wanna show you something." She lifted her shirt.

Drunk tourists on Bourbon Street did this, but not here. He pushed her shirt down.

He felt a revolver jab his trim stomach. She squeezed the barrel under his belt.

"Can't miss from here," Evangeline whispered, keeping close to hide the piece. "If you want to go home with your balls attached, get your partner to take us a selfie."

His partner Broussard stood in the back of the truck, hands on his gun belt. The doors were open, showing off the moneybags.

"He's not supposed to leave the back."

"We'll go to him." She wriggled the Colt Diamondback until the sights hooked the guard's scrotum. He tiptoed alongside her to the back.

Broussard saw her gun and reached for his holster.

"You want your partner to have babies, don't you? Why don't y'all get in back and lose the gun belts?"

When LeFer heard pistol shots, he didn't care that his boudin was dangling. He kicked open the shithouse door mid-squirt to see what in the hell was going on.

Hell was right. Ferdinand was loose, and a cowgirl had climbed on top of the armored truck, firing into the air and hollering. LeBlanc and Broussard hopped away below her, handcuffed wrist to ankle.

Not just any cowgirl. Evangeline Calvineau.

The crowd gawped at the warden and his shit-splattered thighs.

Woody the Fox ran toward him grinning like a tomcat, holding the poker chip and a rope connected to Ferdinand the bull, who charged with blood in his eyes.

Real blood.

Kane LeFer shrieked and crossed his arms over his face.

Woody cut left and the bull cut right, clotheslining the portable toilet, toppling it and LeFer balls over ass. A diarrhea daiquiri of sewage and electric chemical blue deluged the warden to the nostrils, hot as bathwater. It plugged his ears to the screams of the crowd.

Under the bleachers, Jay and Andre changed out of their muddy prison denim into the civilian clothes dropped by Molina. She reached down with a set of keys. "Your mama said the car's in 5-H."

Jay squeezed her hand in thanks. "Maybe I'll see you in Saint Malo."

Their eyes locked in a moment of regret—longing for some way they could make time together that wasn't a pipe dream—before they both came up blank.

"Catch you on the flip side," Molina said. She squeezed his hand, then joined the panicked crowd.

Andre winced and pulled on a pair of clean jeans. He felt pummeled, but his adrenaline hadn't run out. They left their muddy clothes and wiped off their boots on them.

Andre struggled with the T-shirt. Jay helped him pull it on.

He spat on the corner of the shirt and wiped the mud off Jay's face. "Thank you, son."

Pistol shots cracked the air.

"That's the signal," Andre said, grimacing as he hunched beneath the seats toward the outside. "Your momma was hell bent on hitting the cash box since LeFer stole our share." The waxiness had gone out of his face. He looked right devilish. "You feeling old, boy?"

"I got thrown three times, Pop!"

"You didn't get kicked like I did."

They limped through the crowd. Rodeo men had three ropes on Ferdinand the bull and guards directed the crowds into the midway for safety, away from the exits.

Andre squeezed his hand and limped toward the armored truck. Jay strolled in the opposite direction, following the crowd, peering back with them at the spectacle.

"Do not attempt to leave," the announcer sputtered over the PA system. "We have the situation under control." Two black-and-whites blocked the gate exit, barking their sirens.

Andre hoofed it to the armored truck. Evangeline slid down the hood and opened the driver's side. Guards drew down on the truck as she plowed backward through the gates, but none fired. Too many people. The squad cars crunched in impact and spun in the armored car's wake.

The remaining police Chargers kicked up rooster tails of dirt and grass as they gave pursuit. Once the bull was tuckered, men from the crowd joined inmates in holding the ropes until a seasoned rodeo man ran up and unbuckled Ferdinand's flank strap. True to his name, once the tormenting strap was removed, the bull sat on his beefy ass and peacefully pondered the humans and their strange ways.

The tow-headed boy, now in piss-stained shorts, flipped open the door of the portable toilet. Warden LeFer was there under a pool of blue-swirled turds and toilet paper somewhere, but all that was visible was his Confederate battle flag belt buckle of silver and gold, and the pointed toes of his alligator boots.

97: THE ESCAPE

Jay jogged in mock panic with the crowd, then cut toward Dodge Magnum. A blanket covered the back seat. He unlocked the hatch and peeled it back.

Shooter Boudreaux winked, curled atop a small arsenal like some kind of mercenary dragon. "You're late. We best get moving." He lifted a scoped rifle with a muzzle brake like a shovel. "You're gonna want to roll all the windows down."

The Magnum had a hemi engine but handled like the wagon it was. It hauled its prodigious ass with a lot of sound and fury, but the wheel had no feedback, like messing with a sex doll. Jay roared off the grass after the police Chargers.

Ahead of them all, the armored car swerved to keep the squad cars from passing. The road was flanked by shallow ditches, no chance to pass.

Jay drove straight up their asses and jerked the wheel right, clipping a rear fender.

They weren't expecting an attack from the rear. The Charger squealed and spun and crunched against its partner before launching over the ditch and into the trees with an explosion of air bags.

The other car overcorrected and skimmed the ditch, spewing branches and debris. Jay punched the pedal and scraped past, stomping the brake to ride the armored truck's tail.

"Pop the damn hatch!"

Jay popped the lid and drafted the truck, matching its swerves. An explosion jolted the car and rang his ears as Shooter fired. In the rearview, the Charger planted its nose with smoking tires. Shooter had blasted the hood open and cracked the engine with his .50-cal.

"You had to show off, didn't you?" He could barely hear his own voice. Shooter either wore earplugs or had deafened himself as well.

A Crown Vic blew past the Charger, lights flashing. Shooter picked up a cut-down AK47 loaded with twin ammo drums and jackhammered the asphalt, angling low to ricochet into the trees.

The Vic squealed to a sideways stop.

Shooter shoved out a gray brick of Tannerite that tumbled end over end behind them. He gave it a burst and it exploded in smoke and flames.

No pursuit cars exited the smoke.

"We lost 'em!" Shooter hollered. He kicked the seatback when Jay didn't hear.

Jay tried to pass the truck, and it swerved to keep him back. He honked, and the brake lights flared red. The Magnum's grill crunched against the rear deck and both vehicles lurched to a stop.

The rear doors of the truck opened, and Evangeline heaved a burlap sack of cash onto the Magnum's hood. She held up a radio. "They got the road blocked ahead. Get moving!"

Shooter rolled out the back and Jay followed. Andre climbed out of the front of the truck.

Shooter rested his hand on his quick-draw rig. "We good, Andre?"

"What you think, Shoot? Let's get through this." Andre held his hands high.

"We ain't got time for this!" Evangeline tossed Jay a bag of cash. It was light. A ringer.

She heaved one to the Shooter next, filled with coins. He snagged it one-handed, and the weight jerked him down, ruining his draw.

Andre whipped the war hatchet overhand.

The spike gouged Shooter in the right eye, sticking in deep. His .44 magnum boomed in the dirt. With his other hand, he gripped the haft of the ax. Jay clubbed his gun arm down and kicked the weapon away, leaving him howling on all fours like a gutshot wildcat.

Andre limped closer, left hand under his shirt, clutching his burst tumor. He stomped Shooter's face to the dirt and wrenched out the axe with a crunch. "An eye for an eye, you son of a bitch."

Junior LeFer waited at the roadblock with four men armed with M4s. He held only a radio and leaned on his metal leg. He hadn't heard from his daddy.

That wasn't like him at all. The only time the old man hadn't looked over his shoulder was when he was overseas, and then he Monday-morning quarterbacked him after he read the reports of the attack that cost Junior the leg.

Why didn't you send someone else?

His father didn't know how to lead. He only knew power. The world wasn't a prison. Or maybe it was. Junior would disagree with his father's orders, but he'd follow them just the same.

Far up the road, the armored truck rolled around a corner out of the trees. It jerked to a stop and his men aimed their rifles.

"Shoot for the radiator and the tires. They're run-flats, but it'll slow them down."

The truck weaved slowly, then heaved forward.

"Here they come! Make your shots count!"

Rounds pinged off the metal and reports crackled off the trees. Chunks of rubber flew off the tires, but the truck kept coming. The radiator was likely armor plated. The driver's door was shielded from sight, but Junior caught a flash like the sun glinting off a side mirror as it opened and closed.

He squinted to see through the wavy, armored windscreen. Empty.

"Cease fire! Get in the ditches now!" He swatted shoulders and kicked with his metal leg. The truck came fast.

Junior LeFer was the last to hit the ditch, and the stacked squad cars crunched together with the impact.

The Desmarteauxs had swapped the cash bags for Shooter's explosives, and dumped him on top, pinned under his .50-cal rifle. A gas can wobbled between his legs with a brick of Tannerite mashed to it.

Evangeline knelt in the trees with a grenade launcher and fired.

The armored truck disappeared in a black plume of smoke, as yellow, pink, and blue scraps of paper fluttered down, butterflies ahead of a storm.

98: THE SPLIT

Jay stared as his parents stuffed the money beneath the Boss 351 Mustang's spare tire, back at the Girl Scout camp. Andre cleared and checked weapons. "You sure you don't want any heat?"

"No, Pop. I'll miss your hatchet, though."

"I thought you'd want this." Evangeline handed Jay the Skunk Ape Bowie handle first. "Ditch my Dodge. I put five thousand in her glove box."

"I got to clean house first," Jay said. "The Calvineaus got a kid up at Whiterose."

Evangeline tossed an empty money bag into a burning trash barrel. "I've been fighting them my whole life, Jay. They had Andre. There was nothing I could do."

Jay turned the key. The engine growled to life. "Now they don't."

"You said you told the bounty hunter. Andre, talk some sense into this boy." She sighed and loaded the Mustang.

"This is on us," Jay said. "No one else can stop them, or will. I am sick of killing, but I can't drive away from that. You did it for me."

"Don't do this for us," Andre said. "We did what we did 'cause it was right. Only right thing we ever did."

"I got to." Jay rumbled down the rutted road, not looking back to see if they followed.

99: BURN IT ALL DOWN

Jay drove the Magnum to the front gates of Whiterose Plantation. He turned the car around and left the keys in it. The house was dark and the voodoo Cadillac was parked in front, raindrops sparkling like black diamonds across its lacquer in the purpling sunset.

It pulled at him like a dark star. He fought to stay on target. Crew cab trucks were parked in back with men huddled around, faces lit by cigarette cherries or aglow from phone screens. The only light in the house was his grandmother's window, her silhouette rocking.

There was a party on the boat dock.

A Black body stood against a piling.

Not Keshawn.

The bounty hunter.

Bloody but alive, fighting his bonds. Surrounded by too many armed men. A distraction was in order. Jay took a can of gasoline from the garage and crept back to the house along the whistle walk. The kitchen door was unlocked. The room was dark and filled with an intoxicating smell.

Ella stood at the stove, warming up gumbo. The old stove roared with bright blue flame.

"Where's Keshawn?" Jay asked, and set the can down.

"Locked upstairs," Ella said. She took a key off her chain and handed it to him. "Third door. I've got to bring Mister

Samuel his gumbo."

Her eyes were unreadable in the dim kitchen light. "Any guards?"

"They're all at the hanging tree."

Jay squeezed her hand and walked quick to the stairs.

He unlocked the door.

A spidery-thin woman's silhouette stood at the bedroom window. A king bed carved by Papa Andre loomed in the corner like a dark throne.

"Where's Keshawn, Miss Hesper?"

She tittered and turned. The torches from outside lit her face. "Beyond your help, Joshua."

"He's all that was keeping you alive." Jay unsheathed the Bowie. The blade glimmered like a jewel.

"Death does not frighten me. Have you come to inherit your birthright?"

"You think money cures everything, don't you? Your kind are all the same. I'm not here to inherit this evil place. I'm here to burn it down."

"We all have our crosses to bear, Joshua. A boy belongs with his mother."

"Just 'cause a kitten's born in the oven don't make it a biscuit," Jay said. "I'm Evangeline's son. And we both reject you. Your line dies with us."

She giggled through clenched teeth. "Our legacy is in place. The family name will never be forgotten, after we cleanse this land."

Fire seared Jay's thigh. He fell to the floor with a pair of knitting needles stuck in his hamstring. Ella stepped past him.

"You all right, Miss Hesper?" The two women hugged by the window.

Jay pulled out the needles with a snarl. He gripped the Bowie and growled from all fours, the Rougarou alive in him. He bit back the pain, scuttled back out the door, and locked it behind him.

Keshawn was not in the house or the garage. It was like the Calvineaus to make him watch his savior die. If he was alive, he'd be on the dock.

Jay poured gasoline down the dining room under the paintings of Calvineau forebears, and in the carpet of the parlor around the library of red-bound books with the family history. Then he tossed the can at the pot of gumbo on the stove and the fumes burst into hellfire, lighting the ceiling aflame and shooting past him along the trail he'd made. He crawled out the door, the burn scars on his back throbbing with memory.

He limped toward the dock, the house aglow behind him.

Torches flickered over the swamp in the twilight, will o' wisps among the moss beards hanging from the boughs. Jay thumbed the handle of his Bowie knife like worry beads and walked to hide his limp. Chopper looked beaten but alive.

"Today the savage has more rights than the master," Pastor Roy preached. Samuel Calvineau nodded along, strapped into his wooden wheelchair.

Kroese looked bored. His flunkies, soft men in polos and khaki shorts, drank beer from clear bottles and cheered along. Some wore pistols.

The torches lit the eyes of gators in the water, waiting for their meal. Chopper stood bloody before the empty boat launch, breathing hard, barbed wire thorns wrapped around his naked body. A rope bound his wrists and held his arms high, strung over a bough with a well-worn notch.

"We are no match for this beast, but the Lord gave us dominion over all the animals. The lords of the bayou will take him apart tonight for our pleasure."

"Like hell you will," Jay said, walking past them onto the dock. "I'm the heir to this dynasty, not you."

Roy ducked behind Chopper. The elder Calvineau sputtered and raised a gnarled hand.

The polo boys looked to their boss. Kroese smiled through his yellowed beard. "Your grandson is a race traitor. In Rahway he sided with the mud people. We should feed him to the gators next."

Jay took a bottle from the cooler and popped the cap on the wooden railing. "I think you might want to form a bucket brigade." He took a slug to ice the pain and hiked a thumb over his shoulder to the plantation house, the bottom floor in flames.

"A fitting conflagration, to purge the old and welcome the new," Kroese said to Sam Calvineau. "Thank you for the arms to fight this war, but your leadership is no longer required. You feasted in this mansion while we suffered the indignity of rule under the mud people, because you needed our labor. I say, let it burn."

Samuel Calvineau howled. The Heimdall Brotherhood laughed and drank their beers, cheering the fire.

"Let's feed the gators so we can hit the road," Kroese said. "Desmarteaux first."

Roy said, "Give me his knife. I will be avenged!"

Headlights cut through the dusk with a rumble of engine. The doors of the Boss Mustang opened, and Andre knelt with a rifle.

Jay whipped his beer at Kroese's face and drew the Bowie. Kroese fell back in a spray of beer and blood. His men shouted and went for their weapons. Jay shoulder-checked the nearest into his comrades. One shot a hole through the dock and the others shouted and aimed over their buddies' shoulders.

Evangeline sauntered up with her Colt cocked. "Weapons in the water!"

Andre popped two rounds over their heads.

Glocks hit the water and the men put their hands up. Evangeline swept her barrel over them, a pirate in wedge heels. "Get your asses off my land."

They huddled off the dock. Andre covered them, scanning through the night scope.

Jay kicked Kroese in the ass. "Run, little Nazi."

Samuel Calvineau seethed, pounding his leg with his fist.

"Oh, Daddy," Evangeline said. "You been trying to get me here for nigh on thirty years, why you look so mad?" Behind her, the upper windows of the plantation glowed with flames.

His lower lip trembled.

"Because you, Mama, and Roy got to pay for what you done. I thought I was brave, leaving all this behind, but I was a coward for letting y'all live your evil lives. But no more." She screwed up her lips and raised her gun.

Roy shoved Chopper off the dock and ran. The rope creaked under his weight as he swung out over the bayou, his bloody feet dragging through the water.

The glowing eyes winked out as the gators went for him.

Jay dropped his blade and grabbed the rope high. Chopper screamed and curled up, lifting his bare feet as he swung back and forth. Blood drops dimpled the water.

Evangeline aimed and put a bullet between Roy's shoulder blades. He dropped in the dirt.

A bull gator's maw scissored open beneath Chopper and snapped shut. Jay tugged on the rope, but Chopper outweighed him.

A rifle cracked and a chunk flew off the gator's prehistoric head. The water thrashed beneath and it did not rise again.

The plantation in flames cast a glow over the bayou, illuminating a small navy of pirogues and flatboats. At the head, Dani from Saint Malo paddled a boat where Suzane sat draped in purple silk, with Keshawn under one thick arm. In another, a short-haired white woman racked the bolt of her rifle and the shell plunked in the water.

They paddled beneath Chopper. Jay lowered him, then cut the rope with one swing of the blade. The woman with the rifle produced a multitool and began snipping the barbed wire. Suzane rested her palm on Chopper's head.

Chopper whispered to Keshawn. "I was supposed to save you, not the other way 'round."

Women captains formed a line of battle with Suzane at the center. The crews held hunting rifles and break-open shotguns. Zephirin drew his bow.

"The Calvineaus will no longer prey on our children," Suzane said.

The women wore strength on their faces, but their eyes betrayed a deep weariness at having had to be strong for so long.

Samuel Calvineau stared back with silent hatred. Behind him, the plantation burned bright. Two shadows thrashed against the bedroom window, ghosts in the flames.

Evangeline spat in his haggard face. "Y'all can have your justice," she told the Saint Malo Navy. "Take as long as you like."

Suzane was unmoved. "This is not our foulness to clean."

Evangeline walked to her father without a word. She planted a boot on his chair and sent him rolling backward off the dock into the bayou. He bobbed up, goggle-eyed with terror. Something large shoved him, then dragged him under before he could scream. The water roiled, and there was nothing more.

The women looked away.

Some blinked away tears. Others glared at Evangeline for subjecting them to the horror that her family had inflicted upon their families for generations.

She could not meet their eyes.

Chopper squeezed Suzane's hand, and she stroked his fool head. "It wasn't worth this, Wesley."

"Yeah, it was."

Red-and-blue lights flashed through the dark.

Men with rifles poked through the trees. Kroese at the head, nose bloodied, holding out a pistol. Andre and Evangeline drew on them.

"You're outgunned," Kroese honked through his busted nose. "We'll put every one of you in the swamp."

They were answered with a domino clatter of cocked weapons from the Saint Malo navy.

"Hey! All y'all take it easy. This is the law!"

Junior LeFer stepped through with a personal cadre, who took cover behind their squad cars and put laser sights on Kroese's men. Junior looked from the Heimdall Brotherhood to the women on the boats.

"You boys get the hell out of my parish."

Kroese smirked. "Your daddy's, you mean."

"Not anymore." His face was blank except for regret twitching at the corners of his eyes. "So take your asses out of here and don't come back. Your colors are going up as bullseyes at our target range."

"You cannot simply let them go," Suzane said. "We are all watching!"

"I'm letting you both go," LeFer said. "If you don't like it, you can get in the back of a squad with them."

Kroese and his men retreated, weapons up. "We'll find you, Desmarteaux."

"I reckon you will," Jay said.

"You ladies go home, now." Junior LeFer waved them on. "This is all over."

"You own this," Suzane called to LeFer. They began paddling into the dark, their flashlights and lamps bobbing over the water like the spirits of the dead trying to find their ways home.

The heat from the house burning brought sweat to all their faces.

Evangeline shook her head at Junior LeFer, pistol down, but cocked and ready. "We ain't going back."

"I best not hear any of y'all set foot in Louisiana ever again." LeFer set his jaw. "You killed my daddy."

"Your daddy killed his own self," Andre said.

Junior LeFer did not retort.

* * *

Jay and Evangeline helped Andre to the Mustang.

"Where we going to go?" Jay asked.

"You go wherever you please," Evangeline said, an arm around her man's neck. "But we're gone to Texas."

"How'm I going to find you?"

"Get to Nacogdoches," she said. "There's a fella there with a dojo, who they call Kung Fu Bill. He'll tell you where we hole up."

They hugged again. Andre shuddered.

"Aw, Pop."

"I don't feel a thing except free. Thank you, boy." He kissed Jay on the forehead, like he had when he was a boy.

Evangeline ruffled his hair. "Find you a good outlaw woman. One that's smarter than you."

Andre grinned. They climbed into the pony car and rumbled away.

The roof of the big house was in flames, and LeFer barked into his radio. Sirens on the highway, as the fire engines came running.

Jay limped to where the Voodoo Cadillac waited beneath the rain-soaked boughs of the live oaks, and embers danced like fireflies. The black road beast was an icon of human desire and hatred, carved into to an obsidian razor. A vampire made steel, built for marauding on the asphalt veins of a blood-soaked country.

The door shut like a coffin, and flames dappled the windshield as Jay Desmarteaux left the ashes of his heritage in the rearview mirror, and aimed the death machine's chrome maw toward whatever fresh hell the future might bring.

100: DIRTY EVIE AND CRAZY ANDRE

As they hurtled toward the two-mile-long Georgia Pacific train that chugged down the Arkansas, Louisiana & Mississippi line outside Monroe, Evangeline crushed Andre's hand over the Boss 351 Mustang's gearshift.

They had spent the heist money in casinos and hotel room with hot tubs and drank the minibars dry, laughing like children, waking cocooned together in the soft sheets. They ate their fill and left a pile of cash for housekeeping.

At Our Lady of the Lake, the oncologist had sputtered that she couldn't believe Andre could still walk. They bought all the oxy she had, and buzzed on it until the money ran out.

The train horn lowed as it blocked the crossing.

Andre downshifted and took the curve hard, crushing them closer together. He turned and buried his face into Evangeline's sweet nest of hair. She closed her eyes and pressed her face to his neck, breathing in his welcome scent.

He put the pedal to the floor.

The Mustang took air on the rise and impacted on a double-stacked container car, crumpling in on itself like a can of Bud before it exploded in a sunburst of flames to the mourning wail of the locomotive horn.

The train kept rolling, devouring everything that crossed its path.

ACKNOWLEDGMENTS

I would like to thank Don Winslow, Shane Salerno, Paul J. Garth, Lynn Beighley, Todd Robins, Christa Faust, Lawrence Block, Rusty Barnes, David Cranmer, Ethan Grossman, Andrew D'Apice, Sparkle Hayter, Joseph Brosnan, Molly Odintz, Josh Stallings, Bill Loehfelm, Hoss Milani, Joe Donia, Neliza Drew, and all my Patreon subscribers for helping me through the last year of hell. And thanks to James Lee Burke for the inspiration, big mon.

THOMAS PLUCK has slung hash, worked on the docks, trained in martial arts in Japan and even swept the Guggenheim museum (but not as part of a clever heist). He hails from Nutley, New Jersey, home to criminal masterminds Martha Stewart and Richard Blake, but has so far evaded capture. He is the author of *Bad Boy Boogie*, his first Jay Desmarteaux crime thriller, and *Blade of Dishonor*, an action adventure which BookPeople called "*The Raiders of the Lost Ark* of pulp paperbacks."

DOWN & OUT BOOKS

On the following pages are a few
more great titles from the
Down & Out Books publishing family.

For a complete list of books and to
sign up for our newsletter,
go to DownAndOutBooks.com.

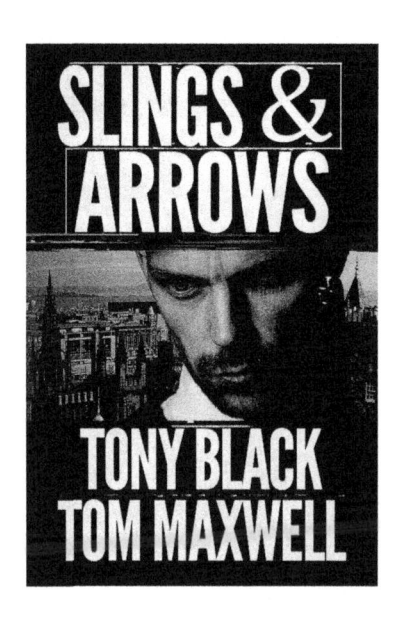

Slings & Arrow
Tony Black and Tom Maxwell

Down & Out Books
September 2021
978-1-64396-233-7

A strangled prostitute found on a prize-winning fairway. A stabbed pensioner, wasting away in a rubbish-strewn house. And a brutally murdered banker, his car sabotaged en route to a plush home.

All have suffered the slings and arrows of outrageous fortune, something Edinburgh DCI Kenny Gillespie knows all about.

Slings & Arrows is a fast-paced psychological thriller that pulls at the edges of a fraying society.

This Time For Sure
Bouchercon Anthology 2021
Hank Phillippi Ryan, editor

Down & Out Books
September 2021
978-1-64396-211-5

Introduction by Hank Phillippi Ryan with stories by Sharon Bader, Damyanti Biswas, Clark Boyd, Lucy Burdette, Karen Dionne, Elisabeth Elo, Elizabeth Elwood, Alexia Gordon, Heather Graham, G. Miki Hayden, Edwin Hill, Craig Johnson, Ellen Clair Lamb, Kristen Lepionka, Alan Orloff, Martha Reed, Alex Segura, Steve Shrott, Charles Todd, Gabriel Valjan, David Heska Wanbli Weiden, and Andrew Welsh-Huggins.

100% of net revenues received benefit the New Orleans Public Library.

Person Unknown
Michael Penncavage

All Due Respect, an imprint of
Down & Out Books
October 2021
978-1-64396-223-8

Life is going great for Steve Harrison. Only thirty-five years old, he's already a Senior Vice President for a major financial firm. He's admired by his co-workers, his friends, his wife—and his mistress. There's nothing he can't handle. The world, as they say, is his oyster.

And all of that is about to change…

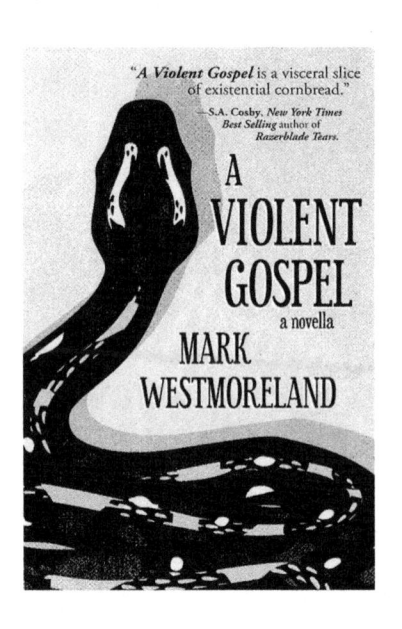

A Violent Gospel
Mark Westmoreland

Shotgun Honey, an imprint of
Down & Out Books
September 2021
978-1-64396-194-1

If there's a bad idea in Tugalo County, chances are that Mack and Marshall Dooley are behind it. When the brothers heist a snake-handling church's money-laundering operation, things go south in a hurry.

When Mack goes missing, Marshall cuts a deal with a local crime boss to rescue his brother. Navigating a storm of wild women and a literal nest of vipers, the Dooleys can't trust anyone other than themselves to get out of the mess they've made.

Printed in Great Britain
by Amazon